STAR WARS™

EMPIRE AND REBELLION
RAZOR'S EDGE

STAR WARS™

EMPIRE AND REBELLION

RAZOR'S EDGE

MARTHA WELLS

arrow books

Published by Arrow 2014

2 4 6 8 10 9 7 5 3 1

First published in Great Britain in 2013 by
Century
Random House, 20 Vauxhall Bridge Road,
London SW1V 2SA

www.starwars.com
www.randomhouse.co.uk

Addresses for companies within The Random House Group Limited can be
found at: www.randomhouse.co.uk

The Random House Group Limited Reg. No. 954009

A CIP catalogue record for this book is available from the British Library

ISBN 9780099594253

The Random House Group Limited supports the Forest Stewardship
Council® (FSC®), the leading international forest-certification organisation.
Our books carrying the FSC label are printed on FSC®-certified paper.
FSC is the only forest-certification scheme supported by the
leading environmental organisations, including Greenpeace.
Our paper procurement policy can be found at:
www.randomhouse.co.uk/environment

Printed and bound by Clays Ltd, St Ives, PLC

To all the friends I met through Star Wars *fandom all those years ago. Especially Z. P. Florian—wish you were here.*

ACKNOWLEDGMENTS

I'd like to thank Jennifer Jackson, Shelly Shapiro, and Jennifer Heddle for giving me the opportunity to do this book.

When *Star Wars* came out in 1977, I was thirteen years old. I had always had a lot of trouble trying to convince my parents to take me to movies, so I read the novelization first. I ended up being able to see the movie nine times while it was still in the theater. That doesn't sound like a lot compared with the numbers that some people managed, but for where I was in my life at that time, it was an achievement.

I was already a big science fiction and fantasy reader and had been since I'd discovered that section in the public library at a very young age. This was long before the Internet, and I'd never met any other SF/F fans; I'd been told, despite all the books in the library and bookstore, that I was the only one. When you're a kid, you believe it when authority figures tell you things like that, or at least I did.

So *Star Wars* was a huge revelation. I wasn't alone, I wasn't a freak, there were tons of people who liked SF/F and this movie, and here was the proof. I bought as many of the toys and books as I could. I found *Starlog* magazine, and I discovered fanzines and fanfiction, which led me to finding other fans and SF conventions, and made me a lifelong fan. Over the years, other movies and TV shows took *Star Wars'* place to a certain extent, but you never forget your first fandom love.

THE STAR WARS LEGENDS NOVELS TIMELINE

 BEFORE THE REPUBLIC
37,000–25,000 YEARS BEFORE
STAR WARS: A New Hope

c. 25,793 YEARS BEFORE *STAR WARS: A New Hope*

Dawn of the Jedi: Into the Void

 OLD REPUBLIC
5000–67 YEARS BEFORE
STAR WARS: A New Hope

Lost Tribe of the Sith: The Collected
Stories

3954 YEARS BEFORE *STAR WARS: A New Hope*

The Old Republic: Revan

3650 YEARS BEFORE *STAR WARS: A New Hope*

The Old Republic: Deceived
Red Harvest
The Old Republic: Fatal Alliance
The Old Republic: Annihilation

1032 YEARS BEFORE *STAR WARS: A New Hope*

Knight Errant
Darth Bane: Path of Destruction
Darth Bane: Rule of Two
Darth Bane: Dynasty of Evil

 RISE OF THE EMPIRE
67–0 YEARS BEFORE
STAR WARS: A New Hope

67 YEARS BEFORE *STAR WARS: A New Hope*

Darth Plagueis

33 YEARS BEFORE *STAR WARS: A New Hope*

Cloak of Deception
Darth Maul: Shadow Hunter
Maul: Lockdown

32 YEARS BEFORE *STAR WARS: A New Hope*

> **STAR WARS: EPISODE I**
> **THE PHANTOM MENACE**

Rogue Planet
Outbound Flight
The Approaching Storm

---

22 YEARS BEFORE *STAR WARS: A New Hope*

> **STAR WARS: EPISODE II**
> **ATTACK OF THE CLONES**

22–19 YEARS BEFORE *STAR WARS: A New Hope*

> **STAR WARS: THE CLONE**
> **WARS**

The Clone Wars: Wild Space
The Clone Wars: No Prisoners

Clone Wars Gambit
  Stealth
  Siege

Republic Commando
  Hard Contact
  Triple Zero
  True Colors
  Order 66

Shatterpoint
The Cestus Deception
MedStar I: Battle Surgeons
MedStar II: Jedi Healer
Jedi Trial
Yoda: Dark Rendezvous
Labyrinth of Evil

19 YEARS BEFORE *STAR WARS: A New Hope*

> **STAR WARS: EPISODE III**
> **REVENGE OF THE SITH**

Kenobi
Dark Lord: The Rise of Darth Vader
Imperial Commando 501st

Coruscant Nights
  Jedi Twilight
  Street of Shadows
  Patterns of Force

The Last Jedi

10 YEARS BEFORE *STAR WARS: A New Hope*

The Han Solo Trilogy
  The Paradise Snare
  The Hutt Gambit
  Rebel Dawn

The Adventures of Lando Calrissian
The Force Unleashed
The Han Solo Adventures
Death Troopers
The Force Unleashed II

REBELLION
0–5 YEARS AFTER
STAR WARS: A New Hope

Death Star
Shadow Games

0

> ***STAR WARS: EPISODE IV***
> ***A NEW HOPE***

Tales from the Mos Eisley Cantina
Tales from the Empire
Tales from the New Republic
Scoundrels
Allegiance
Choices of One
Honor Among Thieves
Galaxies: The Ruins of Dantooine
Splinter of the Mind's Eye
Razor's Edge

3 YEARS AFTER STAR WARS: A New Hope

> ***STAR WARS: EPISODE V***
> ***THE EMPIRE STRIKES BACK***

Tales of the Bounty Hunters
Shadows of the Empire

4 YEARS AFTER STAR WARS: A New Hope

> ***STAR WARS: EPISODE VI***
> ***THE RETURN OF THE JEDI***

Tales from Jabba's Palace

The Bounty Hunter Wars
The Mandalorian Armor
Slave Ship
Hard Merchandise

The Truce at Bakura
Luke Skywalker and the Shadows of Mindor

 NEW REPUBLIC
5–25 YEARS AFTER
STAR WARS: A New Hope

X-Wing
Rogue Squadron
Wedge's Gamble
The Krytos Trap
The Bacta War
Wraith Squadron
Iron Fist
Solo Command

The Courtship of Princess Leia
Tatooine Ghost

The Thrawn Trilogy
Heir to the Empire
Dark Force Rising
The Last Command

X-Wing: Isard's Revenge

The Jedi Academy Trilogy
Jedi Search
Dark Apprentice
Champions of the Force

I, Jedi
Children of the Jedi
Darksaber
Planet of Twilight
X-Wing: Starfighters of Adumar
The Crystal Star

The Black Fleet Crisis Trilogy
Before the Storm
Shield of Lies
Tyrant's Test

The New Rebellion

The Corellian Trilogy
Ambush at Corellia
Assault at Selonia
Showdown at Centerpoint

The Hand of Thrawn Duology
Specter of the Past
Vision of the Future

Scourge
Survivor's Quest

THE STAR WARS LEGENDS NOVELS TIMELINE

NEW JEDI ORDER
25–40 YEARS AFTER
STAR WARS: A New Hope

LEGACY
40+ YEARS AFTER
STAR WARS: A New Hope

DRAMATIS PERSONAE

Alia Terae; pirate (human female)
Anakaret; smuggler (Twi'lek female)
Andevid; pirate (Aqualish male)
Aral tukor Viest; pirate flightmaster (Lorrdian female)
C-3PO; masculine protocol droid
Caline Metara; captain, *Aegis* (human female)
Chewbacca; copilot, *Millennium Falcon* (Wookiee male)
Dannan Kelvan; second in command, *Aegis* (human male)
Degoren; Imperial commander (human male)
Han Solo; captain, *Millennium Falcon* (human male)
Jerell; aide to General Willard (human male)
Kearn-sa'Davit; rebel (Videllan male)
Kifar Itran; rebel (human male)
Leia Organa; rebel (human female)
Luke Skywalker; rebel (human male)
R2-D2; masculine astromech droid
Sian Tesar; rebel (human female)
Vanden Willard; rebel general (human male)

A long time ago in a galaxy far, far away. . . .

CHAPTER ONE

LEIA ORGANA HAD A BAD FEELING ABOUT THIS.

"At least their timing is spot-on," she said, watching the transmission download on the comm screen. She and General Willard were on the *Gamble*'s small bridge, where Captain Denlan and Lieutenant Esrai occupied the pilot's and copilot's seats. They had just exited hyperspace, the starfield steadying in the viewport as the ship slowed to sublight speed.

Captain Denlan said, "If we'd been a little later taking off, or if our hyperdrive hadn't been tuned just right, we would have missed it."

"Well, we didn't," Leia said, more sharply than she had intended. If only the Rebel Alliance could have afforded to equip all its ships with the comm equipment necessary to receive hyperwave transmissions, this vulnerable moment could have been avoided. Still, so far the mission had gone as planned. There was no reason she should be on edge like this . . . but she was. At least, she told herself, they wouldn't have to wait around for long.

"I'm just glad fleet command got the time conversion right," Esrai said, her hands making quick adjustments to the control board. "That would have been embarrassing."

"*Embarrassing* is one word for it," General Willard commented. He was standing next to Leia's comm station, his attention on the percentage-complete bar on the download screen. He was a tall, spare human with short graying hair, and Leia knew him well enough to see that he was uneasy as well. "Princess?"

"We have it." Leia turned her chair around to face the computer console and checked the log to make certain the entire message had been recorded. It had. Now they just needed to decode the transmitted coordinates and program the jump to the meeting where they were to negotiate the purchase of raw materials for the construction of Echo Base, the new secret headquarters of the Rebel Alliance.

With the base so near to completion, the last couple of months hadn't been easy. So many things had gone wrong, and the Alliance was dangerously short on resources. Leia would allow herself to breathe a little easier only when this mission was over and the materials secured.

"We're done here," she said. "Captain—"

"Wait." Esrai's voice was sharp. "I've got a sensor contact. It's pretty far out but—"

So much for breathing easier. Every nerve in Leia's body told her something had just gone terribly wrong. They were in the Mid Rim, at the farthest edge of an uninhabited system called Eschaton. With nothing more than a scatter of cold barren planets and one glowing ball of a striped blue gas giant, the system should have drawn little to no traffic; there was no reason for any other ships to be here. She snapped, "Take us into hyperspace—*now!*"

She started to turn her seat forward. Then something hit her from behind and slammed her into the console. The safety straps ground painfully into her chest. Her ears rang and her eyes watered; heat washed against her neck. A heartbeat later she realized it had been a blast impact.

She twisted around to see Denlan and Esrai slumped over their consoles. The controls sparked with stray energy, the metal blackened with the force of the blast, and smoke streamed into the air. Leia fumbled for the straps with numb fingers, opened the buckles, and pushed to her feet. She took a step forward and fell to her knees. She landed next to General Willard, who had been thrown into the base of the comp-console.

She said his name aloud but couldn't hear her own voice. Her ears still rang with the ship's alarm klaxons, strangely distant. The general's face was bloody and his eyes were closed, but as she put her hand on his chest she felt him breathe. She gasped in relief, then grabbed her chair and pulled herself upright again.

Through the viewport, all she saw was a wheeling starfield; the ship was in an uncontrolled tumble. Every readout on the bridge was either redlined, blinking in an emergency setting, or blank. She stumbled to the pilot's seat and gripped Denlan's shoulder. She started to pull him up off the sparking console and then froze, her stomach twisting. The control panel directly in front of him had exploded and blown a hole in his chest. Gritting her teeth, she let him go and turned to Esrai, who was slumped over sideways. Leia felt for a pulse at the lieutenant's throat, and her hand came away slick with blood. Dreading what she would see, she lifted Esrai's hair aside. There was shrapnel embedded in her temple. Esrai's dark eyes were open but fixed, dead.

Leia squeezed her own eyes shut, willing her stomach not to turn. Then the deck thumped and shuddered under her, and she grabbed the back of the copilot's seat. They were still taking fire. She looked for the sensor screen to get some idea of where their attacker was.

One of her ears popped, and the din of klaxons grew louder. But one alarm was close at hand and particularly insistent. It came from one of the few functioning readouts on the command panel and showed a rapidly dropping percentage. BRIDGE CONTAINMENT SHIELD FAILING, Leia read, and her gaze went to the viewport. There was a deep, ragged crack in the lower quarter.

Leia swore and lunged across the bridge. She hit the release on the hatch and leaned down to grab Willard. The only reason she wasn't breathing vacuum right now was that the containment shield had automatically covered the port when it detected the breach; she didn't know how long until it failed, but the alarm suggested that could happen at any moment.

She pulled Willard into a sitting position and then realized the hatch wasn't open. She stood and hit the release again. No response.

"Oh, you have to be joking," Leia snarled, and popped open the plate for the manual release. The containment-shield warning screamed in her ears as she pulled the lever for the manual override. She felt the hatch's locking mechanism click, but it still didn't slide open. She dug her fingers between the seals, braced a boot against the comp-console, and put all her strength into dragging the doors open.

Slowly the hatch moved until she had just enough clearance to force her shoulders through. From the increasingly frantic shrieks of the containment alarm, she didn't have time for any more. She leaned down, clutched the back of the general's jacket, and started to pull his unconscious body through the opening.

Right at the point where she thought she was going to get both of them stuck and they were going to not only die, but die in an extremely undignified position, she heard boot steps pound toward her from the corridor.

"Here!" Leia yelled, her voice sounding harsh and desperate to her own ears.

A crew member appeared in the compartment door, took in the situation, and lunged forward. She grabbed General Willard under the arms and threw her weight backward. Leia lifted his legs and squeezed through and out of the bridge, then pointed toward the compartment blast door. "Hurry, the hatch won't seal, no time—"

She knew her words were coming out incoherent, but the woman understood her. Together they dragged the general across the compartment and out into the corridor. As soon as they were clear, Leia dropped his legs and flung herself on the door control to hit the emergency seal. It slid shut just as the containment alarm shrieked one last time, then abruptly went silent. Leia felt a rumble and a thump through the metal as the bridge's port gave way.

Breathing hard, the woman asked, "The captain and Esrai are dead?" She was a tall human, with dark brown skin and braided dark hair pulled tightly back. She would have been lovely except for the haggard worry in her expression. Her nose was bleeding and the skin around her eyes was bruised, as if she'd had a face-first encounter with a console or a bulkhead.

Leia nodded. "When the first blast hit." The deck rumbled under her feet, a vibration from a near-miss blast impact. They needed to get the ship away. There was a comm panel near the hatch, and she pushed the all-ship alert. "Han Solo! Han, can you hear me?"

At first the only reply was the rumble of the fire-fight. Then another comm answered. She heard yelling in the background and a voice said, "He's operating the guns with Barani, Your Highness. Are you all right? The bulkhead doors to the upper deck are down, we can't get to you—"

That was all Leia needed, the pilot most experienced at this sort of desperate situation locked out of the control deck. "The bridge is depressurized," she said. "I'm going to engage auxiliary control and take the ship into hyperspace. Just try to hold them off a little longer." She had no idea who "they" even were, though it was safe to assume it was an Imperial ship. She didn't want to admit over the open comm that she hadn't even gotten a glimpse of their attacker yet.

"Yes, Your Highness," the voice said, and Leia heard him yell, "She said to keep shooting!" before the comm switched into standby.

"We need to get to auxiliary control." Leia hesitated, looking down at Willard's inert body; he was breathing, and there was nothing she could do for him until the ship was out of danger. She started down the corridor, the other woman following. Leia wanted to run, but the deck rolled underfoot, a sign that the grav controls were beginning to fail.

She looked at her companion. "You—" The woman wasn't wearing any insignia; because of the mission, no one aboard was wearing anything that might identify them as Rebel Alliance, and most were dressed in plain fatigues or as civilian spacers. But Leia vaguely remembered seeing her in the *Independence*'s fighter bay. "You're a pilot? Can you fly this ship?"

"I'm an X-wing pilot. I've flown slow cargo transports, airspeeders, but—I'll try."

That was all Leia could ask for at the moment. The *Gamble* was a small converted freighter with a crew of twenty, no fighters, but far more quad lasers than its size and cargo space warranted. The conversion and installation of the extra armament had left the ship's corridors narrow and the layout a maze. Esrai had said the controls were as jury-rigged and altered as the rest of the ship, and Leia's vision was starting to blur. "I'm sorry, I don't remember your name—"

The deck pitched and threw them both into the bulkhead. The other woman took hold of Leia's arm and, pushing off with her free hand against the wall, towed her down the corridor. "I'm Sian Tesar. I was down in engineering when you came aboard."

"Oh, good. I always try to meet the entire crew, so I don't have to ask someone if she's a pilot while we're in the middle of a firefight." Leia was dizzy, and her head was pounding.

They reached the shaft that led to the auxiliary control, and the gravity held on just long enough for them to climb down and into the little cabin. There was no viewport, just a screen for the sensor data. It was blank, hopefully only because the controls were powered down.

Punching in the command override to transfer control from what was left of the bridge, Leia held her breath. If this didn't work, they were dead. Everything seemed to hesitate; then readouts started to light up, and she breathed in relief.

Sian dragged herself into the pilot's seat and hit the master to power up the boards. She winced as the screens came to life. "Our deflector shields are down, and we've got turbolaser fire incoming. I can't see what's shooting at us."

Leia wrestled herself into the second chair and fastened the straps. "If it was anything close to the size of a cruiser, this would be over by now." She powered up the navicomputer and was relieved to see that the hyperdrive was still there, at least for the moment. But capacity was down nearly 50 percent, she realized, checking the diagnostics screen. *That's a problem.* The blast that had sent such deadly energy through the bridge controls must have gone through the engine systems, too, meaning the *Gamble* couldn't jump directly back to the fleet. She also couldn't program a jump to the conference location, because the coordinates hadn't been decoded yet.

As Sian coaxed the sublight engines back online, Leia had the nav system check for valid coordinates nearby. They could look for a port later—right now, they just needed to get away. She glanced at the screen just as the sensors caught an image of their attacker. "It's a light corvette," she told Sian. Which meant the Imperials hadn't known about this mission for long. If they had had the time, they would have sent something much bigger.

Sian swore and pushed the control yoke forward. "If they get us in their tractor beam, they could board us."

"Then don't let them get us in their tractor beam," Leia said, making her voice cool despite the pounding of her heart.

Sian flashed her a sudden grin, proving Leia's estimation of her correct. "Can do."

As Sian turned their uncontrolled tumble into a deliberate spiral, Leia adjusted what was left of the shields to compensate for the failed sections and directed more sensor data to the screen. She had to fumble for controls that weren't where she expected them to be; fortunately Sian was a quicker study and seemed to adjust rapidly to the layout of the console. The ship shuddered again at a near miss; on the weapons screen Leia could see the *Gamble*'s turbolasers still returning fire.

Sian put the ship through an evasive maneuver that made all the failing systems redline. She flew the converted heavy freighter like an X-wing, a strategy that Leia highly approved of, even though it was probably the only way Sian knew to fly. Then suddenly the ship swung out of the corvette's kill zone and into a clear starfield.

"Come on, come on," Leia muttered, glancing at the navicomputer. The alert pinged as it finally fixed on a set of coordinates. She confirmed them and configured the jump, narrowing her eyes in concentration, trying to think past the aching pain in her head and make sure she didn't tell the computer to drop them into a star. "We're going into hyperspace," she said, and slid the control levers down.

Leia felt the engines stutter; then sudden power surged through the ship and the starfield blurred into streaks of light.

The readouts jumped between redline and normal, then finally settled on a range Leia interpreted as "not great but not likely to explode anytime soon." She slumped back and put her pounding skull gently against the worn headrest. That was the kind of excitement she could have lived without.

Sian let out a long breath. "We made it." She glanced at Leia. "Sort of."

"Yes, sort of," Leia agreed grimly.

While Sian went to see if she could get the blocked blast doors open to the lower decks, Leia took a moment to find a data card in the supply case in the auxiliary control locker. She checked the navicomputer and saw it had the transmission, copied over from the main console in the bridge when she had transferred control here. She saved the transmission to the data card and then deleted the original from the system.

The comm was starting to buzz with reports of wounded. The *Gamble* had a small medical unit and a medic, whom Leia hoped could handle the injuries until they could get to a safe facility with a medical droid.

And she needed to find out who had told the Imperials where the *Gamble* would be coming out of hyperspace. It was tempting to think that the intel could have come from somewhere in Kearn-sa'Davit's organization. He was the Alliance agent who had arranged the meeting with the traders with whom she was to negotiate. But Leia knew the leak was far more likely to have come from someone in the Rebel Alliance's chain of communication. She rubbed her eyes wearily. This could be a terrible setback to their plans for Echo Base.

The screen signaled that the transmission had been transferred to the data card and deleted from the nav system. She popped the card out of the slot and slipped it into her vest pocket. She would still need to decode it, but at least the transmission was safe. Even if the Imperial corvette had intercepted it, only Leia and General Willard had the decoding key. *So it's just as safe as we are,* Leia thought, appreciating the irony. With a groan, she unstrapped herself and started to climb back up the shaft to the bridge deck.

The gravity returned when she was in mid-climb, slamming her against the wall before the compensators in the shaft adjusted. "That's great," she told the compensators and the universe in general. "Thank you so much."

She climbed out of the shaft just as Han bolted around the corner. Sian must have gotten the blast doors open to the lower part of the ship. "Good," Leia said. "I need help with General Willard. He's hurt—"

"Leia—" Han caught her shoulders. He didn't look injured, except for a developing bruise on his forehead and some smudges and burn marks on the sleeve of his white shirt that must have come from proximity to an explosion. "Can you hear me?"

Leia glared up at him. "Yes, obviously."

Han touched the right side of her face and held up his hand. It was covered with blood. "You're bleeding."

"Oh. No, it's—" She stepped back and pressed a hand to her ear. No wonder Han thought she was hurt. The blood was all down her cheek, in her braids—it must have been sprayed across the bridge cabin when Denlan and Esrai had been hit. "That's from Captain Denlan. Or Lieutenant Esrai. They were both—they're both dead." Leia turned away and started down the corridor, almost swaying into the bulkhead. She couldn't stop moving now; if she did, she was afraid she wouldn't be able to start again.

General Willard still lay in the corridor where she and Sian had left him. Leia knelt beside him, overbalanced when her head swam at just the wrong moment, but managed not to fall on him. He was still breathing, and when she carefully felt his skull she found blood and a lump but nothing more alarming. She looked around, realizing she had misplaced Han at some point, but he arrived a moment later with a medkit.

He knelt on Willard's other side, tearing the kit open. "You look like hell, Princess."

"I know that, thank you." Leia reached for the diagnostics scanner, and Han handed her a coldpack instead. Maybe that was best. The small readout on the scanner just looked like a green blur to her at the moment. She put the pack against the lump on the general's temple and was relieved when he stirred a little and murmured something. She said, "That's a good sign."

"Here." Han was trying to hand her another cold-pack.

"I don't know where else he's hurt yet," Leia said, exasperated.

"It's for you." When she stared at him, Han said, slowly and clearly, "Put it on your head."

"Oh." Leia pressed it against the side of her face and winced in relief. The chill revived her a little, the darkness that hovered at the edges of her vision receding as the vertigo faded. Which was a good thing, because Sian and Jerell, General Willard's aide, were hurrying down the corridor toward her.

"Your Highness!" Jerell said, sounding horrified. "The general—"

"He's alive," Leia told him. "He was knocked out when the first blast hit. Who is the ranking officer on board?"

Jerell was a slim, pale human, another Alderaan survivor, and he looked very young at the moment. Uneasily, as if all too conscious of giving bad news, he said, "You are, Your Highness."

"Right." *That's what I was afraid of,* Leia thought grimly. Han aimed the diagnostics scanner at her, then frowned at the results. Leia pretended to ignore him. She was fairly certain she had a concussion, but she didn't have time for it just now. "I need a status report on the damage and the wounded. Are all the crew accounted for?"

Still watching her worriedly, Jerell said, "Yes, Your Highness. There's seven wounded, including General Willard. Mostly burns from when a panel in the engineering compartment and a laser cannon operating console exploded." He glanced at the sealed door to the bridge compartment again and swallowed hard. "Captain Denlan and Lieutenant Esrai are the only dead."

That was almost half the crew injured. Leia needed to see the medic and find out exactly how bad it was. Minor burns and breaks could be dealt with on board, but if they needed to get to a medical facility, finding one that wasn't under Imperial control could be . . .

"Should I prepare a transmission to the *Independence*?" Jerell said.

"I'll do that." Leia made herself focus on the here and now. She hoped it hadn't looked as if she had zoned out for a moment there. "Someone told the Imperials where we were coming out of hyperspace. I'm not convinced it wasn't someone in the fleet."

"An Imperial agent?" Sian asked.

Jerell frowned, startled and apparently offended. "There can't be. Our security is too thorough."

"Yeah, I've heard that before," Han put in. Leia would have rolled her eyes, but her head hurt too much. Jerell was one of the officers in charge of secure communications, and Han knew it.

"It's far more likely to be someone involved with this merchant Davit." Jerell glared at Han. "Maybe you're more used to civilian traders and criminals who don't have any loyalty—"

Han started to reply, but Leia interrupted with, "Jerell, if you have to make that kind of slight, don't do it in front of me. Han, you know exactly what you're doing, please stop. Sian—"

"I didn't say anything. Your Highness," Sian said.

Leia extended her hand. "You can help me up."

As Sian hauled her to her feet, Leia added, "You're on watch in auxiliary control until I can find someone to help you. And be sure you take care of your nose."

"Take care of my—" Sian touched her nose and winced. "Right."

Commander Degoren leaned back in his seat, his jaw so tight with suppressed anger it made his teeth ache. The rebel ship had vanished into hyperspace, a dissipating ion trail the only trace left behind. He had never cared for commanders who raged or threw ranting fits, so he just made himself say flatly, "That's unfortunate."

The crew at the bridge consoles didn't cringe outwardly, but he could read the tension in the set of their shoulders. They knew as well as he did that if Degoren had to report to his superiors that he had lost this chance, a quick execution was the best they could hope for. The worst was a long, slow execution in the form of a transfer to a post on whatever hellhole the Empire currently sent its disposable personnel to.

Sorvir, his second in command, said, "If we'd had more time to prepare—"

Degoren cut him off. "Yes, because excuses always impress Lord Vader." Even when the excuses were true. The Imperial agent hadn't been able to get a transmission out until it was almost too late, and theirs had been the only ship within range. They hadn't even had time to summon the surveillance ship they worked with in this sector. It was several systems away at this point, acting as a decoy for a smuggling operation they had been on the point of breaking up before they had received these emergency orders. He shook his head. "All we can do is wait for another contact."

From what Degoren understood, the agent had been in deep cover for a long time, waiting for the right opportunity. The fact that Degoren's customs corvette had been the closest Imperial ship able to respond was both a blessing and a curse. If Degoren succeeded, the reward would be unimaginable. Advancement in the Empire had been something he had always wanted but that had always seemed just out of reach. But if he failed to capture Princess Leia Organa, the punishment would also be unimaginable.

He didn't intend to fail.

CHAPTER TWO

WITH A FRESH COLDPACK pressed to her head, Leia tried to sort out the disaster that was currently the *Gamble*. After calling Sorel, the chief engineer, on the comm and getting a status report that amounted to "It's really bad, but I don't think the ship is going to blow up," she asked Han to go down to engineering to help out.

According to Sorel, an energy pulse from one of the first blast impacts had traveled through the ship's drive train, causing two consoles to explode in engineering and damaging one of the laser cannons. It sounded like the uninjured personnel needed all the help they could get to keep the hyperdrive online long enough for the ship to get where it was going, and to make what repairs they could to the sublight engines and other systems.

Once the medic, Sarit, appeared with a portable stretcher on a repulsor unit, Leia went with him to take General Willard below.

They settled the general in a cabin near the medical cubby, where the crew member who had been pressed into service as Sarit's assistant was handing out bacta patches for burns and medication for minor concussions. Willard was still too groggy to really seem to know what was happening, though he woke enough to squeeze Leia's hand when she spoke to him.

The general taken care of, Sarit told her, "All the other injuries reported so far are treatable with what I have here, mostly burns and some contusions." He was an Andulian, with gray skin, long white hair, white furry brows, and atrophied gills in his cheeks that gave him what on a human would have been drooping jowls. To Leia, the "jowls" made him look old and reassuringly knowledgeable, but after talking to him for a short time she realized he was young, maybe even younger than she was, and unnerved by the whole situation. He peered at her uncertainly. "Ah, your head?"

Leia lowered the coldpack and saw that it was bloodstained. "It's someone else's blood," she said.

To his credit, Sarit just made a sympathetic noise and handed her a packet of antiseptic cleaning pads. Leia went to the tiny refresher attached to the cabin and scrubbed until the blood was out of her hair. It didn't do her headache any good, but it was a relief to get the blood off.

Then she found a command console in a small compartment that had once been an office for a cargo agent. She put the data card into the slot, displayed the recording on the screen, and entered the decoding algorithms. After a moment, she could read the transmission. There were the coordinates, and a short note explaining that the destination was a commercial space platform called Arnot Station; Kearn-sa'Davit would be waiting for them there.

The message also included a warning that the station was deep in pirate territory, which was annoying but hardly surprising. Pirates weren't uncommon in sectors where the Empire's attempts to consolidate its power or root out rebels had left local governments in disarray.

Davit, the Alliance agent, was a distant acquaintance of Han's, apparently met years earlier during a stint of work in the Corporate Sector Authority. Leia assumed that by "work," Han meant smuggling and other criminal activity, but she hadn't tried to find out; one thing she had learned in the two years since the Battle of Yavin was that knowing too much about Han and Chewbacca's non-Alliance-related business, past and present, just made her left eyelid twitch.

Frowning thoughtfully, Leia accessed the nav data. Once they came out of hyperspace, Arnot Station would be only another short jump away. She was pleased to see there were other commercial stations within reach, and at least two fairly large trading ports. The existence of other nearby ports would make their destination less obvious, if the light corvette was still out there searching for them. And she had no reason to think it wasn't.

Leia tapped her nails on the console. If she was right that the intel that had brought the Imperial light corvette down on them had come from the Alliance fleet or its communication chain . . . It didn't matter. She still had to see Davit. They couldn't give up this chance to get the materials for Echo Base.

*   *   *

The next thing Leia needed to do was find help for Sian up in auxiliary control. Looking over the crew roster, Leia noticed they had a young combat transport pilot by the name of Ilen aboard who had logged shifts flying the *Gamble* in the past. She flushed him out from under a console in the engineering bay and sent him up to take over for Sian.

"That's all right," Chief Engineer Sorel told her when she informed him of the change in assignment. "He's good with weapons systems, but he doesn't know much about working on hyperdrives. There's also Barani, the young Mon Calamari. He's got freighter piloting experience. I'll send him up, too."

"Good." Distracted, Leia looked down the bay, where every access hatch seemed to be open and every console half taken apart. The whole place still smelled like it was on fire, and smoke drifted in the air. Not far away, an older woman with a torn tunic and pressure bandages wrapped around her shoulder and collarbone carefully adjusted the settings on a console, then shouted down into the open access hatch at her feet, "How about now?" Fluctuating light reflected up from the hatch, and the answer was an incomprehensible grumble.

Cautiously, Leia asked, "What exactly is our situation?" She found herself wincing in anticipation of the answer.

"Uh." Sorel wiped at the sweat on his forehead. "It's . . . Did we find a safe port yet? I think we've got one more short jump in us."

"That's my priority right now. Do you think we can manage this?" She showed him the relative position of Arnot Station.

Sorel's expression cleared. "We could do that."

Leia made her way through the bay until she found Han; he was on the floor and hanging halfway down into an access hatch, using a sensor to check various components in the coolant systems and swearing a lot at the results. She crouched beside him.

"How is it going?"

Han rolled over and propped himself up on a cross brace. "How does it look?"

"Terrible," Leia admitted, keeping her voice low.

"Good guess, Your Worship."

Oh, good, he's calling me that again, Leia thought sourly. She knew better than to react to it by now. Her friendship with Han had been somewhat more fraught than the easy camaraderie she had with Luke Skywalker. Leia knew Han still had mixed feelings about working with the Rebel Alliance, and while he often expressed those feelings in the most aggravating way possible, she wasn't unsympathetic. Han was as reticent about his past as it was possible to be and still communicate with other beings, but it was obvious that he had had a hard scrabble to survive at times and was fairly bristling with trust issues. Leia had grown up with the Rebel Alliance and bent most of her life and will toward it, but she wasn't so narrow that she couldn't see Han's perspective. She just felt compelled to argue with it a lot.

She held up the datapad so he could see the screen. "Have you ever heard of Arnot Station?"

"No." Han frowned at the readout. "What is it?"

"It's the location your friend Davit sent us for the meeting. Fortunately, it's close enough to reach, even with our damaged hyperdrive."

"He's not my friend." Han considered the limited information on the station. "That's pirate territory."

Leia had been thinking about that. "It's odd, though. The shipping in this area is mostly agricultural, or mineral, or supplies for subsistence settlements. Not much in the way of luxury goods or shipments of currency. What's attracting the pirates here?"

"Could be a lot of things," Han said. Before Leia could make a frustrated comment, or give in to the urge to smack him with the datapad, he added more helpfully, "But this Arnot Station looks legit. Lots of small and medium freighter traffic, a couple of bigger local shipping lines, no Imperials. Davit's merchants must have picked it. It's probably where they do most of their business."

"Good." Leia sat back. "Maybe we're due a safe port."

Han's expression was highly skeptical. "Yeah, the universe doesn't work like that."

That, Leia already knew. "I'm going to send a secure transmission directly to General Madine to report our situation. I'd like to ask Chewbacca to meet us at this station so we can use the *Falcon* as our escort ship on the way back to the fleet."

Han eyed her suspiciously. "Why the *Falcon*?"

"It's the only ship we might have immediate access to that has the armament to act as an escort. And I don't want to take a chance on anyone else finding out where we are, and repeating it to the wrong person." Leia had already drawn her own conclusion; she wanted to see if Han agreed. "Someone told the Imperials where we were coming out of hyperspace.

Presumably it wasn't Davit, since he already knew our final destination, and if he was setting a trap for us he could have done it at the meeting."

"I was wondering if you'd noticed that." Han absently tapped the sensor against his palm.

"Yes, sometimes a lifetime of training in concealing things from the Empire does actually come in handy." She pushed to her feet with a groan. Now that the effects of adrenaline had had a chance to fade, she was starting to feel every bruise and strain. "I hope Chewbacca can get here quickly. I need backup I can trust." She looked down in time to catch an expression flit across Han's face. It was self-conscious and oddly vulnerable, and hard to define. Then she realized he had been a little taken aback by her casual remark about trust.

He caught her looking at him and retreated down into the access hatch, muttering, "Yeah, well, just remember Chewie and I don't come cheap."

"I know you don't come cheap; do you have any idea how much a brand-new Isolator costs?" For setting up the meeting with Davit and coming along on the trip, Leia had arranged payment for Han in the form of a Vintredi Apex Isolator. The Apex Isolators were sensor jammers, newly upgraded models, and a shipping contractor who had family members in the Alliance had managed to send them an entire cargo hold full. Chewbacca was now back on the *Independence,* installing the Isolator in the *Millennium Falcon.* The devices were meant for Alliance transports, but the *Falcon* went on enough missions to justify receiving one. Leia would never forget the downright misty look Han had gotten when the packing cases had been unloaded from the Sullustan supply transport.

"I'll run a tab for you!" Han said to her retreating back.

Leia went back to her command terminal in the compartment near the crew cabins to record her coded message to Madine. Then she called auxiliary control to send Ilen the coordinates for Arnot Station and to tell him to make the next jump as soon as the *Gamble* was able.

Leia hit the comm for engineering to warn Sorel that the ship would be making another hyperspace jump soon. "This is Leia Organa—"

She heard arguing voices. Someone said, "Sorel, Captain Solo says we should take the dampers offline. That's going to reduce the safety factor—"

Han's voice cut through the others. "You're worried about the safety factor? What's the safety factor for being blown to hell by an Imperial light corvette? How does that figure in?"

Sorel answered, "Kifar, yes, it's a problem but Solo's right, I don't see how we can keep the drive online without cutting the dampers—"

"Taking the dampers offline is too dangerous," Kifar objected. "We can get the extra boost from—"

Han interrupted, "That's not going to—"

Leia rubbed her aching forehead and said, "Engineer Sorel, do I need to come down there?"

All the voices went silent. Leia had meant the question seriously, honestly wanting to know if they needed her down there to arbitrate. But with the last shreds of her patience giving way, perhaps her voice had been a little clipped, or she might have spoken a little too loudly. It wouldn't be the first time. Whatever, it was getting results. Sorel cleared his throat and said, "Um, no, ma'am. Your Highness."

"I've ordered Ilen to make the jump to Arnot Station once the ship comes out of hyperspace," Leia told him. "Do you concur with Captain Solo that it's necessary to take the dampers offline to reach our destination?"

"Yes, Your Highness."

"Then do it." Leia cut the connection. Just to check, she pulled up some of the readings from the auxiliary control and engineering consoles. All she could see was a summary of the vital systems activity, but it was enough to make her bite her lip in consternation. Han hadn't been exaggerating. With so many systems operating in the red, she wasn't sure how the ship had managed to jump to hyperspace, how it was staying in that state without exploding, and why anyone seemed confident that it could actually make a second jump. Maybe they would need the *Falcon* not as an escort but to evacuate the *Gamble*'s crew.

When Han knocked on the open hatchway and stepped into the compartment, Leia handed him the data card. "Here's the message for Madine. Would you send it for me from auxiliary control?"

"Right." Han took the data card and handed her a packet of meds. "Sarit wants you to take this. It's for your concussion."

Leia frowned at him. "He didn't think I needed anything before."

"Yeah, well, you were on the all-ship comm when

you broke up that fight in engineering, and Sarit reconsidered."

Leia grimaced. She hadn't realized she had hit the all-ship comm. She couldn't afford mistakes at the moment, especially foolish mistakes like that. She tore open the packet and dry-swallowed the two capsules.

"And you need to get some sleep if it's going to do any good," Han added.

"Is that your opinion or Sarit's?" Leia snapped, knowing she was being unfair. She wasn't pleased with the idea that someone had apparently decided that an intervention was needed and that Han was the best one to approach the monster in its lair.

"The whole crew took a vote." Han tossed and caught the data card. "I'll get this sent as soon as we come out of hyperspace."

"Thank the crew for me," Leia said, trying to be cool but knowing she just sounded grumpy. "And Han, don't mention to anyone else that Arnot Station is where we're meeting Davit. Not yet. Just that it's the nearest port we can reach."

Han frowned. "All right. Got a reason for that, or just paranoia?"

"Paranoia," Leia admitted. She couldn't shake the feeling that the less said about the meeting with Davit, the better. And restricting as much information as possible might help her isolate the intel leak once they got back to the fleet.

Han said, "Welcome to the club, Your Worship," and sauntered away.

Leia wanted to call a cutting remark after him, but her head hurt too much at the moment to let her think of a good one. She was even too disgruntled to watch the movement of Han's hips as he walked away down the corridor. Not that she should be watching that at all, she reminded herself.

She took a deep breath, composed her thoughts, and then, deliberately using the all-ship comm this time, gave the crew the update on the hyperdrive's status and their intention to head for Arnot Station.

"Solo."

"What?" Han was sitting on his heels on the floor of the main engineering bay, checking the sensor diagnostics for the alluvial dampers. He glanced up to see Kifar Itran looming over him.

Han swore wearily under his breath and pushed to his feet.

Itran was a big man with a strong build, so much so that he might have had ancestors from a world with higher-than-normal gravity. His facial features and heavy brow were equally strong, and his skin had a faint orange tint to it, echoed in streaks in his short shock of brown hair. "Was this your idea?" he asked belligerently.

That kind of attitude was about all Han needed right now. He was tired, and he had gotten lightly singed when the energy pulse had lit up the laser cannon controls. He also didn't like being cornered against the panel behind him. He took a step forward, making Itran fall back. Han stepped past him and leaned his hip against the workbench. "You want to argue about the dampers again? It's working."

"Not about that. I know you went up to talk to Her Highness."

Han eyed him suspiciously for a moment, then said, "So?"

"Was it your idea to go on to this station? We should be staying put, calling for help from the fleet."

Han gestured pointedly around at the panels, some of which were still smoking. "Nice that you think we should stay put and give the Imperials a chance to find us, but the rest of us want to live."

Itran persisted, "Was it your idea?"

"The Princess doesn't need me to get ideas. She knows what she's doing." Han had run into this kind of trouble off and on. He knew he had never matched the Alliance's profile of a new recruit and that to them he looked an awful lot like somebody who would sell them all to the Empire for a quick credit. Telling them that it was just another job to him didn't help. Telling himself it was just another job didn't help, either.

"From what I've heard, this whole mission was your idea."

"You heard wrong." Han wasn't going to clarify that. He didn't want to be in this conversation, and he sure as hell wasn't going to go into detail about what was said and decided in Alliance meetings to which Itran had clearly not been invited. He made his expression deliberately bored. "Either say what you want to say, or go find something else to do."

"I just think it's suspicious. You're involved in this mission and we get hit by Imperials. I've heard you've got a lot of influence with the Princess. Maybe you're using it for your own purposes."

Such as getting myself blown up or captured by Im-

perials? Han wondered. Itran was angry, and looked like he wanted somebody to blame for it.

"You think I'm the one giving orders on this ship?" Han responded. "Why don't you go ask her about that?" He hoped Itran would be just that dumb. He wasn't sure how many of the rebels who worked with Leia knew the calm façade concealed an impressive temper, but Han enjoyed watching it in action. It was on his list of things he found the most attractive about Leia Organa.

Itran's eyes narrowed, but before he could respond, Sorel emerged from behind the tall set of sensor connections a few meters away and said, "Kifar, you're off duty. Why don't you go get some rest?"

Itran hesitated self-consciously. He'd obviously had no idea that the engineering chief had been within earshot. He said, "Sure," and turned to go.

As Itran vanished into the back of the bay, Sorel joined Han. "What was that about? Is he that mad about the dampers?"

"No. Something else."

Sorel sighed. "He's new. He's been working on the supply transports, mostly in the Outer Rim. I don't know that he's ever been in a firefight. The first time is never easy."

The engineer was right about that, at least, Han reflected. And maybe that was all it was.

Leia had no problem staying awake for the next hour or so, while the *Gamble* came out of hyperspace, the transmission was sent to Madine on the Alliance fleet, and the nail-biting worry began as the ship rumbled, hesitated, then finally made the next jump that would hopefully leave them within easy sublight distance to Arnot Station. Only when they were back in hyperspace did she drift off.

"Princess."

Leia bolted upright to see Sarit standing in the hatchway. She had been having a nightmare in which she was on the terrace of the summer palace on Alderaan, talking to Lieutenant Esrai, when the whole scene dissolved in an energy blast that Leia was somehow unaffected by. The dream had ended in a vivid image of her looking down to find Esrai's blood on her hands. Reality gradually reasserted itself, and she realized she had slumped over in the chair, her cheek feeling tight and scratchy where it had pressed against the old cracked simulated leather of the headrest.

"I'm sorry to disturb you," Sarit said, "but General Willard is awake and asking for you."

"Yes, thank you." Leia checked the time on the console. They should be coming up on Arnot Station soon, the ship hadn't exploded, and her headache, while still present, no longer felt as though some giant riding animal was stomping on her brain. She pushed to her feet, yawned so hard her jaw cracked, and tried to push her raveled braids back into order. After a moment, she gave up. There was no one on the ship who was going to be scandalized by the fact that Princess Leia's hair looked like a small creature had been living in it.

Leia went to the next cabin and found Sarit checking over General Willard with a diagnostics scanner. The general was sitting up on the bunk, propped against pillows; his forehead and temple showed the ugly purple of bruises, and he looked as if he had aged a decade. But he focused on Leia as she stepped into the cabin, and said, "Good to see you, Princess." His voice sounded raspy and weak.

"I'm glad you're awake." Leia smiled. She was sure he needed more sleep, but it was a relief to see him coherent and well enough to sit up.

"He isn't to get up or agitate himself until I can get him to a medical facility with a full scanner setup," Sarit told her.

"I won't let him get agitated," Leia promised. Sarit sounded a little shaky himself, and she wondered if he had had a chance to sit down since the attack. "But I do need to talk to him in private. Why don't you take a break and get some rest before we reach the station?"

The medic blinked, as if the idea had never occurred to him. "Oh. Oh, yes, I suppose I could."

Sarit wandered out into the corridor, and Leia pushed the release to close the hatch behind him. She sat down on the stool next to the general's bunk. "How do you really feel?"

"Terrible," he admitted. "Denlan and Esrai?"

Leia squeezed his hand. "I'm sorry."

Willard took a deep, shuddering breath, then winced and half lifted a hand to his head. "Blast it. I was afraid of that, when Sarit wouldn't tell me how they were." He looked up at Leia. "What's our situation?"

"It's not terrible, but it's not good, either," she said, and gave him a quick rundown on the condition of the crew and the ship, and of what they were doing to remedy it. She told him about her decision to head on to the station once they finished the emergency jump, and to send the message to Madine to ask for the *Millennium Falcon.*

"Sorel thinks we have at least three to four standard days of repairs ahead of us, so I knew we needed a backup ship in case we have to leave the station in a hurry." Then she leaned forward. "Vanden, someone knew where the *Gamble* would be, when we would be at our most vulnerable, while receiving that HoloNet transmission. That light corvette knew exactly when to come out of hyperspace to hit us."

Willard frowned, absorbing her words. "It's more likely it's someone in our communications, isn't it? If Davit wanted to betray us, he could have done it at the meeting."

"That was my thought," Leia said. "Whoever betrayed us had to do so almost at the last moment, as if they didn't find out what the coordinates were until right after we did. Otherwise, the Empire would have sent more than one ship. I think the corvette was sent after us because it was the closest available ship, the only one that could get there in time." She grimaced. "I know I don't have much to go on, except the timing." And her instincts.

Leia didn't need the reassurance, but it was still gratifying when Willard said, "Yes, the intel more likely came from the fleet." He tried to sit up straighter, and sank back with a groan. "We're going to have to figure out how to isolate this leak, find out who it is."

"That will have to come later. At the moment we've done all we can." If a traitor had managed to infiltrate the Alliance's chain of communication to and from the fleet, there was no telling what damage had already been done. But Leia didn't see anything she could do about it, at least at the moment. For now she had to concentrate on making certain the *Gamble* didn't come to harm or become yet another Alliance ship that vanished into space, its fate unknown. She glanced at the time again. "I should go and let you get some more rest. We'll be at the station soon."

She started to stand, but the general caught her hand. His expression weary and rueful, he said, "I'm sorry I can't be more help."

"You *have* been helpful," Leia told him, and meant it. When your decisions affected people's lives, it was important to have the advice of someone who didn't always think you were right just because of who you were. Or who your father was.

Luke Skywalker was deep into the engine compartment of his favorite X-wing when he felt a large hand grip his ankle. *It's a good thing I know who that is,* he thought, resigned. "Chewie, I've got both hands in the proton torpedo launcher!" he protested. R2-D2, down on the deck beside the X-wing's cradle, beeped in annoyance at being interrupted. The little droid was connected by various cables to the astromech socket and had been running diagnostics.

Chewbacca rumbled a long comment. C-3PO, whom the Wookiee must have brought along to translate for him, said, "Master Luke, he says that it's important and you should get your little—uh, you should get down here right now." The golden droid added, presumably to Chewie, "That was rude, you know."

With a sigh, Luke slid out of the engine hatch and dropped to the deck. Pulling his protective goggles off, he asked, "What is it? I thought you were trying to get that Isolator installed." Turning around, he saw who was standing there and stopped short. "Oh, General Madine."

Madine didn't answer immediately, his cool glance taking in snubfighter cradles and tech stations nearby, as if checking to see how many were occupied. The fighter repair bay for the *Independence* was normally crowded with pilots, techs, droids, and other support personnel, repairing damaged fighters, keeping up their maintenance schedules, or practicing in the simulators kept at the far end of the bay. But it was near the shift change, and few voices echoed around the big space. Wedge and the other members of Red Squadron were off on a mission; Luke should have been with them, but his X-wing's targeting computer had started to throw error codes at the last minute and his part in the mission had been scrubbed for now. Keeping his voice low, Madine asked, "Can you be ready to leave with Chewbacca immediately?"

"Yes, sir." Luke glanced at Chewie. Wookiees didn't show concern the same way humans did, but his posture conveyed tension and impatience. "Do you want me to put together a squad?"

"No, just you," Madine said. "Come aboard the *Falcon* where we can speak privately, and I'll give you the coordinates and explain."

Luke didn't miss the significance of "aboard the *Falcon* where we can speak privately." If Madine was worried about being overheard on one of the flight decks of the *Independence* . . .

This can't be good.

As the *Gamble* exited hyperspace, there was a clunk that left Leia's hands white-knuckled on the arms of the comm chair in auxiliary control. Han was piloting, with Ilen as backup, and both men hurriedly worked over the consoles, shutting down the hyperdrive. Something deep inside the ship made the deck vibrate. An alarm started to shriek, and Han absently slapped a control to shut it down. Leia could see various readouts creeping up into the red again.

Then the vibration sputtered to a halt and the stars streaked back into reality.

"The hyperdrive is offline," Ilen said with relief.

"Nice job," Han commented absently, and Leia saw the back of Ilen's neck flush with self-consciousness. Han tended to be sparing with compliments to other pilots.

"Do we still have sublights?" Leia asked. She looked at the sensor screen just as a recognition code for Arnot Station popped up. She allowed herself a silent, relieved breath. They had made it. The station was only a short distance away, within easy reach of a distress call if the *Gamble* failed now.

"We have one engine. It's holding stable," Ilen said.

"So far," Han said, confirming Leia's long-held belief that he was the most pessimistic person she had ever met.

Ilen asked, "Should I take us in, Your Highness?"

"Yes, let's get into dock as quickly as possible."

A check of the sensors confirmed that the station was on the outskirts of a system that included several inhabited planets, all of them listing small agricultural settlements. There was no sign of Imperial presence. As they drew closer to the station, the bright blob on the sensor screen resolved into an image of a large torus with a docking ring all along its center. It was clearly ancient and battered, with hatches marred by old burns from docking accidents, and hull plates that were pitted and blast-scarred.

And then the sensor alarms went off.

CHAPTER THREE

HAN SAID, "WHAT NOW?"

Leia gripped the arms of her seat. *Not again!* "Imperials?" The comm came to life with a gabble of conflicting transmissions.

Han shook his head. "Somebody else is having a lousy day, too."

Leia frowned at the screen, not understanding, as Ilen hit the ship's alert to warn engineering and gunnery. Then the sensor screen resolved into a blurry image.

Between the *Gamble* and the space station, two ships were locked in combat. At first, all Leia could make out was that one seemed to have the advantage over the other, and that neither was broadcasting an Imperial ID. The current winner was larger than the *Gamble,* sleek, and well armed, but the sensors couldn't get a clear image of it.

Ilen said, "The one under attack is a freighter . . ."

"Yeah, a real freighter, unlike us," Han said, hands moving over the controls to coax more data out of the sensors. "No extra weapons."

Leia tensed as a distress call sounded from the

comm. At least one other frequency was open, and it was broadcasting shouts of alarm, sobbing, frantic commands, and the rumble of blast impacts. Han said, "The ID is for some agricultural mercantile from what sounds like a local system. The attacking ship . . . Yeah, that's a faked ID." He looked up at the screen. "We're looking at a pirate."

Ilen threw a worried glance back at Leia. "We can't help the freighter . . . can we?"

Leia set her jaw. The comm transmissions were making more sense now, as the system sorted them and upped the gain on the urgent ones. One was a desperate plea to the station, the voice tripping and slurring through the words in Basic. There were twenty-three beings on board, the speaker was saying, all civilian traders. The comm controller on the station returned a reassuring litany that help was coming soon. Leia could see on the screen that the station was too far away for its defensive weapons to drive off the pirates. It didn't look to her as if a rescue ship would even arrive in time.

And the *Gamble* was just too damaged to help.

"We can't afford to intervene," Leia said, hardening her voice, trying to keep the emotion out of it. She saw Ilen's shoulders slump in resignation.

"We've got compromised deflector shields, the hyperdrive is out, and the sublights are hanging on by pure luck," Han elaborated. "We've got no choice here."

"I know," Leia muttered. But it didn't matter how good their excuse was: they were still leaving the crew of the merchant ship to die or be taken prisoner.

The sensor view wheeled and compensated as Han changed course. Readouts redlined and beeped in alarm as the *Gamble*'s strained systems protested. He took the ship above the battle, out of range of the other ships' guns, then jerked his chin at Ilen. "Hail the station, tell them we're coming in with sublight damage, and we can't assist the freighter." He added, "At least now we won't need a fancy cover story to explain how we got shot up."

Leia agreed. As Ilen contacted the station, she watched the sensor view. She couldn't take her eyes off it, much as she wanted to. The merchant ship still fought back, firing a quad laser at the pirates, but, as Han had pointed out, it didn't have the *Gamble*'s augmented systems, and its weapons were woefully inadequate. She told herself they were lucky the pirates had trapped the freighter, and not the *Gamble*, on station approach, but she didn't feel lucky. *I'm so tired of watching and not being able to do anything to*—Then the sensors beeped to signal a fix on the pirate ship, and a clear schematic of it popped up on the screen.

"*What?*" Leia sat up straight as a bolt of cold shock went through her. "That's an Alderaanian gunship!"

Han stared at the screen, brow furrowed. "What, the pirate?"

"Yes!" Leia snapped, cold shock turning to hot fury. She tore at the buckles of her straps, fuming. "I know where all the gunships are." After Alderaan's destruction, the surviving gunships had all managed to contact the Alliance, some of them badly damaged, their crews injured. "Display the ID!"

Han put the string of ID information up on the screen. "It's a fake, Your Worship," he said pointedly. "The planet of origin—"

"That doesn't matter, the ship is Alderaanian. The name—" The name was the *Aegis*. She knew that ship, or at least knew of it. She didn't think she had met the officers or crew personally. All the other information in the ID string was false, but whoever had altered it hadn't bothered to change the name. "I know that ship. It was on the system defense patrol."

The gunships had been a deterrent, meant to protect Alderaan's system, trade routes, and commercial shipping from just this kind of attack. They gave assistance to ships in trouble, protected and assisted civilian traffic. Not all of them had been officially accounted for, but that was to be expected: when the planet was destroyed, some must have been grounded on Alderaan, and some must have been close enough to the planet that they had been caught in the blast wave. She had been certain all the surviving Alderaanian naval ships had been found. This one must have been attacked at some vulnerable moment before it could make contact with the Alliance, taken by the pirates, and the crew . . . She had to know where the crew was.

It was like having an old wound ripped open, except this wound had never closed. She had just learned to pretend it didn't exist, most of the time.

She shoved to her feet and stepped up behind Ilen to reach the comm board. She put one of the spare headsets on and silenced the other frequencies, then opened a new one to call the gunship. She made it a closed connection, so the station wouldn't be able to monitor the transmission. Ilen stared at her, wide-eyed, and Han said, "Leia, damn it, stop! You're just gonna get their attention—"

Leia ignored him, too blind with fury to care. "*Aegis,* I know you were an Alderaanian gunship. If you tell me where you obtained the ship and where the original crew is, I won't fire on you."

Leia heard Han swear. She just hoped her bluff would work. Her pulse was pounding so hard she couldn't hear herself think. She wasn't sure what response she wanted from the pirates. They would have killed the crew, or sold them into slavery somewhere across the galaxy. Even in the latter case, it must be far too late to save them. Unless she could find out what system they had been sold in . . .

She said into the comm, "I just want to know what you did with the crew."

"They've stopped firing on the freighter," Ilen said, his voice low and tense.

Han said, "That's because they're about to start firing on us."

He probably isn't wrong. Leia watched the sensors. The merchant freighter hung helpless in space. It had stopped returning fire and was apparently no longer able to use this opportunity to flee. The *Aegis* hadn't changed its position. Leia could tell from the gunship's outline that it had been augmented, though she wasn't sure exactly how. Most pirates had special equipment for locking onto captive ships and drilling through hatches, as well as other methods of subduing their prey.

The comm was silent. The *Aegis* would be reading the *Gamble*'s ID by this point; it was legitimate, listing the ship's original commissioning on Sullust. She hit the pickup's mute to tell Han, "Keep heading toward the station."

"Yeah, Your Worship, I thought we'd do that."
He checked the sensors again. "You could've waited
until we were a little closer to the station's defense
perimeter."

Yes, she probably could have. *If I was in my right
mind,* Leia thought, *I would have.* She stared at the
comm, willing it to respond.

Then the comm beeped, and a voice from the *Aegis*
said, "Who are you? How did you know this ship
was Alderaanian?"

The voice spoke Basic, and Leia thought it might be
human, might be female, but through the faint but
persistent static it was hard to tell. She hesitated. Despite her hopes, she had been expecting to be told to
go to hell, or to be told that the crew had been spaced,
or that it was none of her business, or most likely to
get no answer at all. This sounded as if someone on
the ship was willing to talk. She turned the pickup on
again and replied, "I recognized it. I'm a survivor of
Alderaan."

Urgent now, the voice said, "Tell me . . . Tell me
who you are. Tell me how you survived."

Han leaned past Ilen and hit the mute on the comm
board again. He said to Leia, "They want you to keep
talking."

"I know that." Leia bit her lip, tried to push aside
her anger and fear for the fate of the *Aegis*'s former
crew, to think this out logically. "If they're trying to
stall us . . ."

Earnest and worried, Ilen said, "If we stall them,
the station might be able to send ships out here to
help the merchant freighter."

"That's the point I'm trying to make here," Han

said, exasperated. "We're the ones who should be stalling them—"

"—so why do they want me to keep talking?" Leia finished. She glanced at the sensor screens again but the *Aegis* still hadn't moved, and the *Gamble* was too far away now to get a weapons lock on the gunship unless it changed position. *Tell me how you survived,* she thought. Why that question, phrased that way?

She pushed Han's hand off the mute and said into the comm, "I was offplanet. Why do you want to know? Tell me who you are." She hesitated, her heart pounding, and spoke on a hunch. "Tell me how *you* survived."

There was a silence that seemed to go on forever. At last the voice said, "I was offplanet."

Leia nodded to herself. Han shook his head, mouthed the words, *She's just repeating what you said.*

But the voice continued talking. "We were on the far end of our patrol circuit, at the outer rim of the system. The sensors picked up the blast wave. We tried to go back, to see for ourselves . . . but there were Star Destroyers in the system. We fled."

Leia wet her lips. The *Aegis* must have been boarded at some point after that by pirates, before it could reach an Alliance base, or meet up with other surviving Alderaanian ships. But if there was one survivor of the crew aboard, there might be more. "Who has control of the ship now?"

There was another hesitation. Then: "I do. I'm Captain Caline Metara."

Leia's throat went dry. "Of the House of Metara?"

"Yes." The word was almost breathless.

Leia couldn't believe it. The Metara family had served for generations as councilors and ambassadors in Alderaan's government. The ones who hadn't gone into planetary service had been teachers, researchers, physicians. This had to be a trick. "How do I know you're not lying?" she demanded, her voice coming out harsh and strained.

"My mother was Gerane Metara; our family seat was in Crevasse City." Metara's voice rose in frustration. "Tell me who *you* are! I almost . . . I think I recognize your voice, but it can't be . . ."

Leia had to be sure. "What was your father's name? What was his last post?"

"His name was Stavin and he was an artist. It was my mother who was an administrator in the education council." Metara's voice hardened. "I've answered all your questions. Tell me who you are!"

Han shook his head frantically at her. But Leia said, "I'm Princess Leia Organa."

The comm went silent. Ignoring Han's swearing, Leia said, "Why did you attack that merchant ship?" She couldn't believe the *Aegis*'s crew had chosen this course voluntarily. There had to be some reason for it. Maybe they believed the merchant ship was working for the Empire . . .

"We attacked it." Metara's words were clipped, harsh. "We attacked it because that's what we do to survive now."

An Alderaanian crew, members of the planetary protection and defense force, had turned pirate? A sick sensation grew in Leia's chest.

"We intend to sell the cargo," Metara continued. "We won't hurt the crew."

Won't hurt the crew. Leia's vision almost whited out from pure anger. Only years of training and iron self-control kept her voice even. "You've already harmed the crew. You know that, unless you muted their distress calls."

Metara didn't answer.

Leia grimaced. The silence meant Metara knew that her ship had already killed or injured some of the merchant's personnel. She took a deep breath, forcing her anger down. She didn't want to back Metara into a corner. Not just yet. She tried again. "Let the merchant ship go, and we can talk about your situation. I can help you."

This time there was no hesitation. "I can't let the ship go."

"You can." Leia made herself sound calm rather than urgent. She shifted to put her back to Han, whose increasing agitation was interfering with her concentration. "You're a free agent; you don't have to do anything. Let the ship go and we can—"

"Come to us."

"What?" Leia was taken aback. "What do you mean?"

"Get in an escape pod. We'll guide you into the bay. We can talk on board."

Han moved so he could glare at her. Leia set her mouth in a grim line. She didn't need anyone to tell her what this sounded like. If the *Aegis*'s crew had so abandoned the principles of Alderaan as to steal and kill nearly helpless civilians, then it was all too possible that they wouldn't shrink from kidnapping and ransoming an Alderaanian Princess. "I can't do that. You know why."

The comm went silent again. Leia waited a long moment, torn among disgust, despair, and a final stubborn thread of hope that Metara would change her mind. *After one brief conversation with you?* she asked herself. *You're good but not that good, Leia.*

Then the deck jolted underfoot and she grabbed the back of Ilen's seat to steady herself. "What—"

Han twisted back around to the pilot's board and hit the controls for their remaining sublight engine. The *Gamble* shuddered, more of the readouts red-lined, but there was no surge forward. "Blast it!"

"Did the engine go offline?" Leia demanded.

Confused, watching the sensors, Ilen said, "We're caught in a tractor beam!"

"Yeah, we are." Han quickly adjusted the controls, then eased back on the overstressed engine. With an ironic grimace, he said, "Looks like they decided they really want to see you, Princess."

"Alderaanian gunships don't have tractor beams," Leia said, baffled. *But pirates do,* she realized, and swore under her breath. She felt the sublight engine drop out as Han shut it down to keep the already damaged systems from overloading. "I saw that they'd had the ship altered. I'm sorry, I didn't consider that they might have added a tractor beam."

"I did," Han said. "But we still should have been out of range. They've got an augmented tractor; those're rare for a ship that size." He threw her a grim look. "They must be really good at what they do. It's not easy to buy a toy like that."

Leia stared at the control board, thinking hard. "We still have weapons. I don't suppose our shielding miraculously healed itself while we've been talking."

"Yeah, no." Han flicked through several status screens, wincing. "They take one shot at us and we're in pieces."

"They haven't fired yet." Leia tapped her fingers on the console. "If we wait until they pull us in for boarding, then fire all our cannons—"

"If we're lucky." Han shook his head. "We'd go down fighting, that's all. We might take them with us."

Ilen touched his headset. He had been monitoring the station's comm frequency. "The merchant's sublight engines are dead, and someone on board says they can't get them restarted. The station launched a rescue ship."

The comm frequency clicked back on and Metara said, "Princess Leia—"

Leia said, "My crew tells me you must be excellent pirates to afford this sort of tractor beam. Congratulations on your new career path, Metara. I'm sure your mother would have been very proud."

The words came out with all the sarcasm Leia had been holding back, but there didn't seem much point in suppressing it. The *Aegis* had made its intentions clear.

Metara said, "I—I understand what this looks like. But we just want to talk."

Metara had the upper hand, and Leia wasn't sure why she hadn't used it. "I'd prefer to talk without my ship trapped in a tractor beam."

"We want to talk here, face-to-face. Use an escape pod, and we'll bring you on board. We have no intention of holding you prisoner, or harming you in any way. You don't have to come alone."

Leia shook her head, mostly at herself. This was a terrible idea. "If I do that, will you let both my ship and the merchant ship go?"

Ilen twisted around to stare incredulously. Han was trying to mouth something at her that was extremely critical of her mental faculties. She turned her back on both of them, listening intently.

She heard Metara's sharp intake of breath over the static. Then Metara said, "Yes, Your Highness, I swear it. On my word as a Metara."

Leia had to roll her eyes at that. *On your word as a Metara turned pirate*, she thought. But she said, "Then I'll come to you."

"I know what you're thinking," Han said, and Leia's first impulse was to snap, *Of course you don't.* Before she could react, he continued, "But the fact that they used to be Alderaanian doesn't mean anything now. When they decided to take this ship and go pirate, they knew what they were doing. That's not a step an entire crew takes lightly. They knew they'd be welcomed by the Alliance, knew they could get help, get repairs, supplies, whatever they needed, just like all the others did, just for the asking. And they didn't ask. They didn't turn pirate by accident or 'cause they had to. Just because you're here, just because they're sentimental enough to want to see you, doesn't mean anything."

So he *did* know what she was thinking. Leia pulled the headset off and hung it on its hook. She had just made an all-ship announcement to inform the rest of the crew of the identity of the *Aegis* and of the *Gam-*

ble's situation, and what she intended to do about it. She could imagine General Willard's reaction and only hoped he didn't injure himself further trying to get out of bed.

"I understand that," she said to Han. "But we don't seem to have a choice anymore. I can at least get the *Gamble* away and save the people on the merchant ship. I have to do this."

"Uh, Your Highness . . ." Ilen was still monitoring the other frequencies through the headset. "The pirate—the *Aegis* just told the station controller that they'll blow up the merchant ship if the station's rescue ship doesn't stand down."

Leia's gaze went to the sensor screen again as Han climbed out of the pilot's seat. The station's rescue ship, a converted freighter fairly bristling with quad laser cannons, had been on a direct course for the merchant. It must have received the threat, because the sensors showed it breaking off its approach. It slowed and circled back while it was still out of weapons range of the *Aegis*.

"The station must think they're serious," Ilen added.

"That's because they *are* serious," Han said.

Leia turned away. She had to hurry before the merchant's situation got any worse, before Metara decided to fire on the *Gamble* to emphasize her demands. She climbed the access shaft with Han right behind her, and stepped out into the corridor to find herself facing Jerell, Sian, Kifar, Barani, and several other crew members who should all probably have been doing something else. They scattered out of her way as she strode past.

Still moving down the corridor, Leia took rapid stock. Anticipating disembarking on the station, she had changed into a clean dark shirt and put on her jacket, as well as her blaster belt and sidearm. Metara hadn't said anything about coming aboard unarmed.

Jerell followed her, his expression confused and almost hurt. He was an Alderaanian, too, though his family had not been a prominent one and he had spent most of his youth offplanet. "Your Highness, you can't—"

"You didn't know any Metaras, did you?" she asked him. "Perhaps when you were in school?"

"No, Your Highness." He held out a comlink. "But General Willard wants to speak to you—"

Behind her, she heard a scuffle in the corridor, which she suspected was Han conscripting Barani to take over as Ilen's copilot. "Is that a secure comlink?" she asked Jerell.

"Yes. We thought you'd need one. It's set to connect to two others; I have one, and General Willard has the other."

Leia accepted the proffered comlink and heard the general asking, "Leia, are you certain—"

"Yes, I'm certain I want to do this." Jerell followed her, listening to her end of the conversation. She told the general, "I don't have a choice, Vanden. Just because they know I'm on board doesn't mean they won't destroy this ship." She took a deep breath. "And maybe I can talk them into giving this up and joining the Alliance."

"Leia, they are traitors." General Willard's voice was harsh. "If they weren't, they would be with us already."

"They aren't traitors. We don't know that they've ever worked with the Empire—" Leia caught herself. If the *Aegis* had gone so far as to prey on civilian ships, they might have done anything. She finished, "We don't know what they went through."

"We know what *we* went through," the general said.

She took the small side corridor around to the ship's first array of escape pods. "Yes, I know that. Believe me, I know that. And if you have another way out of this, I'd like to hear it."

Willard was silent for a moment. "I can't lose you, too. Be careful, Leia."

Leia didn't want to be lost, but she felt she didn't have a choice at the moment. She would just have to see what options arose when she reached the *Aegis*. "Whatever happens, I can't let them keep using one of our ships this way." She cut the connection and told Jerell, "General Willard will be in command while I'm gone, of course, but he'll need your help. Go to auxiliary control so you can relay his orders to Ilen."

"Yes, Your Highness," Jerell said, and turned to obey. But he called after her, "Be careful!"

Han took two long strides to catch up with her, shouldered past Jerell, and said, "I know what you're doing."

"I know what I'm doing, too," Leia said, and congratulated herself on her even tone. She stopped at the first pod hatch and opened the control pad to initiate the automatic systems check. The pods were meant for the larger crew complement of the *Gam-*

ble's pre-conversion state; each one had room for five large passengers.

"Yeah, you'll either talk them out of this, or die trying." Han leaned against the bulkhead beside her, his voice low and grim. "Or make sure they die trying."

Leia's hand froze on the control pad. It was odd that, in this moment, it was Han of all people who seemed to understand what this meant to her.

Keeping her voice low, too, she said, "I can't let them keep doing this, in Alderaan's name. I can't." If she couldn't talk Metara into at least reconsidering her course, she would have to find out as much about the *Aegis* as she could, whether it meant to stay in this area and where it might go if it didn't, so it could be tracked down later.

Han gazed down at her for so long that she started to feel uncomfortable. At last he said, his voice cool and calm, "Then it's a good thing I'm going with you."

Before Leia could tell him he absolutely was not, Sian said, "What, they didn't say she had to go alone? I'm going, too."

"No," Leia began, "you are not—"

"And me," Kifar added. "I know how to jury-rig an escape pod to reattach in its berth. Might need me on the way back."

Exasperated, Leia said, "We have no idea what these people truly want. It's too dangerous."

"Princess," Sian said, "it's probably more dangerous here. Besides, it won't look good if we let you go alone."

The diagnostics finished and the round hatchway slid open. Inside, the pod's systems were powering on, the readouts on its control board lighting up. Leia had run out of time to argue. "All right. We'll go together." She just hoped they didn't regret it.

CHAPTER FOUR

THE POD'S INNER HATCH cycled with a whoosh, the air that had just been pumped into it mixing with the corridor's atmosphere. Han stepped inside, and Sian followed him. Kifar politely gestured for Leia to precede him.

Leia stepped into the pod. It had five seats and a simplified control station that could pilot the occupants out of danger while they waited to be picked up by a rescue ship; it could even be set to make an emergency landing, if necessary. The storage containers built into the walls would hold rations, medical gear, and other supplies. The upholstery smelled a little musty, but the pod didn't look as if it had ever been used.

Han took the seat nearest the control station, and Leia sat across from him. As Sian strapped herself in and Kifar sealed the hatch, Leia tapped the small comm board and hailed the *Aegis*. She said, "Captain Metara, I'm about to launch the pod. I have three crew members with me."

"Copy that," Metara replied. "We're waiting for you."

Leia acknowledged that and signed off. Sian said, "Ah . . . did that sound a little creepy to anyone?"

Checking the controls, Han said, "Yes." Kifar nodded.

Leia admitted, "Just a little." She had no idea what was going on in Metara's head—not an ideal position to be in when preparing for what would surely be a tense negotiation. She nodded to Han, who hit the launch sequence.

There was a thump as the pod ejected from the cradle. Leia leaned back against the seat as the brief burst of acceleration pushed them away from the *Gamble*. Once clear of the shelter of the ship, the pod fell into the tractor beam. Watching their approach through the small viewport, Leia saw that they were heading toward the *Aegis*'s shuttle bay. Alderaanian gunships had all been equipped with two shuttles, for use in rescue operations. Her jaw set. Now the pirates probably used them to board captive ships, she thought.

Han had brought up the pod's limited sensor suite. "The tractor beam let the *Gamble* go when it picked us up."

"Good." Leia took the secure comlink out of her pocket to test it.

"Careful," Han said. "If they've had their systems juiced up, they might be able to break the lock and listen in."

"I won't say anything they don't already know."

Leia called the *Gamble* and reached Jerell immediately. "Tell Ilen to take the ship into the station's defensive perimeter."

There was a pause, and Leia knew he was relaying

the command to General Willard. Then Jerell replied, "Uh, we were going to wait here for you, Your Highness."

"You can wait inside the defensive perimeter. That way you can't be used against me." She was giving the *Aegis* what it had asked for; she didn't want Metara to get the idea to ask for more and threaten the *Gamble* again if Leia didn't comply.

There was another pause, then, "Yes, Your Highness."

Leia breathed out in relief.

The pod approached the shuttle bay, and the doors cycled open. A landing tractor caught the pod, drew it forward into the bay, then eased it into a docking cradle. Leia felt the rumble as the bay doors slid closed, and a few moments later the pod signaled that the bay had repressurized.

Leia nodded toward the hatch. "Open it." Kifar hesitated, and she added, "If they wanted to kill us, they would have done it before now." At least, she hoped so.

Kifar gave her a resigned nod and hit the open sequence for the hatch. As they climbed out, Han caught Leia's arm to steady her. She didn't need it, but she appreciated the gesture.

The bay wasn't large, but there was space for more pods on this level. Overhead, two sleek shuttles hung in launch cradles.

"How many crew?" Han asked in a low voice.

"The standard was thirty-two crew and officers, but the ships were designed to hold more in case they had to transport evacuees off damaged ships," Leia whispered back.

"So they could've taken on more once they turned pirate," Han said.

The inner bay doors opened and five humans strode in, a woman in the lead. They weren't wearing Alderaanian uniforms, which was something of a relief to Leia. They wore the utilitarian clothing spacers usually favored: pants, shirts, and vests or jackets in grays or dark colors. If Leia had been planning a pirate career, she would have approved; their outfits wouldn't get them a second look at any commercial port or station. They were also all wearing sidearms, and they all looked a little nervous.

The woman in the lead was slim and elegant, with pale skin and short dark hair, and only a little taller than Leia. She stopped a few paces away and said, "Your Highness. I'm Captain Caline Metara."

"I'm sorry we have to meet under these circumstances, Captain Metara." Leia was aware her voice was dry. She was finding it hard to maintain a calm, neutral demeanor in the face of Metara's confident, professional appearance. Piracy apparently agreed with her. "Now that I'm aboard, I'd like you to allow the station's rescue ship to tow the damaged merchant vessel into dock."

Metara answered so quickly that Leia knew she had anticipated the request. "I'm afraid I can't do that. We haven't had time to remove the merchant's cargo yet. And while you can vouch for your own ship's conduct, you can't control the station's picket ship. If I let it come close enough to take the merchant in tow, it will fire on us."

She was probably right about that, and Leia hadn't really expected a different answer, but it was a further test of her already stretched-to-the-limit temper. "Very well, then." She wanted to add, *And I hope not too many more of the people aboard the merchant ship die while we're having our lovely little chat,* but just managed to suppress it.

Metara seemed to realize she was perhaps not Leia's favorite person at the moment. She gave her a grave nod and said, "Please come this way. We can talk more comfortably in the ship's lounge."

"Let's do that," Leia said. Her jaw was starting to ache from the tension of trying to keep her expression under control. She caught a wary look from Han.

As Metara led them through the bay blast doors and into the corridor, she said, "We had heard rumors that you survived the destruction, but we weren't sure how much to believe of what was reported on the Imperial-controlled news services." Her voice trembled a little, the first indication that she was aware of the awkwardness of the situation. "I assume your ship is a rebel vessel."

"It has an Alliance affiliation," Leia said, glad to see the hint of vulnerability. Vulnerability meant doubt, and if Leia was going to talk Metara out of this, she needed a way past that polished demeanor.

The last Alderaanian gunship Leia had been aboard was one of the survivors that had joined the Alliance. She knew they were all much the same, but it was still something of a shock to walk down the familiar corridors, to see how little had changed aboard this ship. The crew was obviously being careful with the maintenance, though there were a few signs of normal wear like small tears and stains on the concussion padding around the blast doors, or mismatched metal finishes where the consoles had been repaired with different materials. She noticed that Metara was taking them through the crew quarters, and not past any of the engineering or weapons sections, and she wondered exactly what augmentations the ship had been given.

At last Metara stopped before a doorway. Leaving her entourage in the corridor, she led her guests into what was obviously a crew lounge. Furnished with couches built back against the bulkheads and cabinets where games, readers, holo sets, and other entertainment items would typically have been stored, the room was clean, kept as well as it would have been had the *Aegis* still been under the control of the Alderaanian planetary security forces. Leia saw the ship's original commission plaque with the Alderaan planetary seal proudly displayed above the forward doorway and had to grit her teeth. How could they live as pirates and keep that plaque on display, as if they still had any right to it?

Two crew members waited for them in the lounge. "This is my second in command, Dannan Kelvan," Metara said, gesturing, "and our engineer and weapons officer, Alia Terae."

Leia realized again that she had been expecting people who looked more desperate, more affected by their decision to turn pirate. Terae and Kelvan were both younger than Metara, Terae with very pale skin and blond hair pulled severely back from her sharp features, and Kelvan slender and tall and dark-skinned, with an earnest expression. Terae's attitude made Leia think of a rebellious adolescent who had been caught in some act of disobedience, and Kelvan looked grave and uncomfortable. Leia saw the discomfort as a good sign. If Kelvan or any other members of the crew weren't as committed to this course as Metara was, she might just have a chance to talk them around.

Metara invited them to sit down. Leia took a seat on one of the couches, and Han flopped down beside her, seemingly unconcerned. Terae's gaze flicked over them suspiciously, and Leia tried to see her group through the other woman's eyes: Han dangerous, Sian cool and calm, and Kifar stoic. Leia had no idea what she looked like. She suspected she just looked angry.

She watched Metara silently. She wasn't interested in exchanging pleasantries, especially as there was no telling how much this delay might already be hurting the injured aboard the merchant ship. She waited to hear what Metara wanted to say.

Metara broke the silence abruptly. "We didn't watch Alderaan be destroyed and then suddenly decide to become pirates. That isn't what happened."

Leia inclined her head slightly. "What did happen?"

Metara took a deep breath. "We were in the outer perimeter of the system. We intercepted some Imperial transmissions and realized that an attack was taking place. We set a course for Alderaan but didn't arrive in time. We never actually saw the Death Star." Her expression tightened at the name, as if it still cost her something to say it aloud. Leia knew how that felt. "Our sensors and communications were taken out by the blast wave, and we had to stop and make repairs. We had no idea what had happened, at first. Then we were finally able to make our way back and

picked up the edge of the debris field. It was . . . a
terrible moment."

Watching Metara intently, Leia realized that the
captain had thought a lot about how she would explain what had happened, though it was doubtful
that she had ever cast Leia in the role of the person
she would be explaining it to. Perhaps she had rehearsed the speech in her thoughts, imagining herself
justifying her actions to her commanding officer, or
one of her parents, or a mentor. That didn't bode
well. It meant that Metara had been shoring up her
defenses for a long time.

When Leia didn't respond, Kelvan said, "Everyone
on the crew had lost . . . everyone, everything. Our
families came from Chianar, Aldera . . ." At the
mention of the Alderaanian capital, he shifted in embarrassment and looked away, as if suddenly remembering who Leia was. That she had lost everyone, too.

Her voice a challenge, Terae said, "Where were
you, Your Highness? When it happened."

"I was aboard the Death Star," Leia said, keeping
her tone cool, hoping she was betraying nothing. She
had rehearsed this, too, and performed it so often she
could do it as evenly as if she were speaking of some
minor diplomatic incident.

Terae stared, and Metara's brow knit. Aghast, Kelvan said, "I thought that was a rumor."

"There are many rumors about what happened,
but that one is true. I . . . escaped," she said, not looking at Han, "not long after. I was on Yavin Four
when the Death Star was destroyed." But Leia wanted
them to keep talking about themselves, not her.
"What did you do then?"

Metara rubbed her palms on her pants. "We detected some other surviving ships, on the outer edges of the system. They told us they knew where to make contact with the Alliance, that they were going to join it, to fight the Empire. My crew discussed it, and . . ." Her expression hardened. "We felt it was Alderaan's association with the Alliance that led to its destruction."

She spoke the words as if she expected an argument. Leia said, "That is certainly true. Is that why you decided not to join the Alliance?"

"Yes." Metara lifted her chin. Leia's failure to argue the point had clearly thrown her off her prepared speech, and her tone turned defensive. "We wanted to fight the Empire on our own terms."

Leia wanted to ask how attacking traders with no Imperial affiliations qualified as fighting the Empire, but she managed to refrain. "This was a decision you all agreed with?"

She wanted to find out if there had been any dissent among the crew at that point. From the way Terae and Kelvan both looked at Metara to see what their response should be, she felt the answer was probably no.

Terae said, "If Alderaan had kept to its principles of peace and neutrality, the Empire would not have attacked."

And if the Empire had not been corrupt, venal, and determined to destroy any hint of resistance, the Empire would not have presented a threat to Alderaan's peace in the first place, Leia thought. This was not an argument she wanted to have again, but she seemed perpetually doomed to repeat it. Her punishment for surviving, perhaps. "Alderaan was too powerful, too influential. Sooner or later, the Empire would have found a reason to attack us, no matter how peaceful and neutral we claimed to be."

She met Metara's gaze. "And becoming a pirate is an odd way to embrace the principles of peace and neutrality." She added deliberately, "Pirates are one of the chief suppliers of the slave trade currently flourishing under the Empire." She had been trying to halt the trade in sentient species since she had first become a Senator, and she probably knew more about it than the soulless bastards who profited from it. If Metara thought she could operate as a pirate and somehow keep her hands clean of the slave trade, she was a fool.

Terae bristled. "We would never stoop to that! That's not what we're—"

Metara stopped her with a glance. She told Leia, "We have never sold crews into slavery. We do not take captives."

"Then what do you do with the people left alive on the ships you target?"

The question hung in the air a moment. Then Metara said, "We leave them aboard. After we've gone, they can call for assistance if their systems are too damaged to repair. All we're interested in are the cargoes."

It was naïve at best, and Leia was sure Metara must be aware of that on some level. There were bound to be casualties; the crews of the targeted ships would believe they were fighting for their lives and freedom, and they wouldn't hold back. And there had to be ships too damaged to repair, for whom help didn't arrive in time. Not to mention the loss of property that could send small shipping concerns and merchant companies into financial ruin. "It's a hard way to make a living," Leia said, an edge of irony in her tone.

Leia meant that it was hard on the victims, but Metara said, "Believe me, we're all too aware of that. At first all we were concerned with was survival."

Han said suddenly, "There are a lot of jobs you could take on with a ship like this. Hauling freight or guarding merchant trade routes in backwater systems is boring, but you can live on it."

Leia didn't glance at him. She knew that pirates often preyed on smugglers the same way they preyed on legal shipping, and that it was likely that Han had had personal experience with their depredations. And Han had had to scramble to make a living in the murkier margins of the galactic trade routes; that Metara professed not to be able to survive with this ship and her loyal well-trained crew must be like a slap in the face. But Leia would have preferred him to stay out of the conversation, mostly because she was worried enough about her own penchant for sarcasm and didn't have the time at the moment to worry about Han's.

"That's what we did at first," Kelvan told him. "We also hired out as a picket ship for small trading posts, but . . ." He glanced at Metara again. "We encountered Imperials."

Leia suspected that "encountered Imperials" was a diplomatic way to describe whatever had happened. She had dealt with her own overwhelming moments of rage after Alderaan, though watching the Death

Star be destroyed had helped. She suspected that what Kelvan meant was that Captain Metara had let her rage come before the good of her crew and ship.

"We wanted peace, but it turned out we wanted revenge more," Metara said.

Yes, there's that "we" again. "So you were recognized and attacked as an Alderaanian ship?" Leia asked. "Or you fired on Imperial ships?" She was certain now that she knew what had happened. Metara had stepped up as a strong leader, a source of security and stability at a time when everything familiar and safe had been wrenched away in the most painful way possible. The crew would have drawn closer together, formed even tighter bonds and more intimate relationships than before. Metara wasn't the captain of this ship—she was the head of a family. She might listen to the others' opinions, but the final decision was hers, and they wouldn't go against her. This was going to be even more difficult than Leia had anticipated. And it wasn't as if she had ever thought it would be easy.

Metara ignored Leia's questions. "We discovered the local Imperial governor had trading concerns, and we attacked the freighters he owned. After that, we had to leave the area. We came here . . . because we had heard there were opportunities to strike at Imperial shipping."

Leia hadn't heard of much Imperial shipping in this part of the Mid Rim. If there had been, the Empire would have a larger presence here and the local traders wouldn't be such easy prey for pirates. Before she could reply, Kifar said, "That merchant you hit is from an agricultural trader. How is that striking at Imperial shipping?"

He was right, but Leia didn't need any help, and she didn't want anyone changing the subject but her. She caught his eye, and he leaned back, his mouth grim.

Metara frowned, but not at Kifar. It was clear the merchant ship was a sore point, but Leia couldn't tell why. She didn't think it was the moral failure that concerned Metara. Metara said, "That is in the nature of an obligation."

Leia lifted her brows. "Attacking the ship was an obligation?" She didn't like the sound of that. "How?"

A ship's alarm rang out over the comm system, and everyone flinched. Metara pushed to her feet and moved a few steps away to take a comlink out of her jacket pocket. Leia watched Metara speak quietly and then listen to the answer. Terae and Kelvan watched their captain worriedly. Han leaned over and whispered to Leia, "If it's that Imperial corvette, we could be in trouble."

Sian and Kifar leaned in to listen, Kifar frowning. If it *was* the corvette, that meant someone who knew their movements was reporting to the Imperials. There was no other way the Imperial ship could have found them again so quickly. Leia started to say, "If it is—"

Metara turned around and said, "Please excuse me a moment, Your Highness." She jerked her chin at Terae and Kelvan, who both stood and hurriedly followed Metara as she strode out through the forward door.

The door sealed behind her, and Han, Kifar, and

Sian all drew breath to speak. Leia held up a hand to
stop them and glanced at the door into the corridor.
Two of the crew members who had escorted them up
from the hangar bay still waited out there, facing
away from the lounge. She took out her comlink and,
keeping her voice very low, said, "*Gamble*, come in.
What's happening out there?"

"Princess, another ship just entered the system and
is heading for us at attack speed." Jerell sounded agitated. "It's not Imperial, but we can't read the ID and
the sensors say it's heavily armed."

"It's another pirate," Han said.

Sian was startled. "How do you know?"

Han shrugged. "This sector is lousy with pirates. It
might be a heavily armed root crop freighter coming
to the other trader's rescue, but the odds are against
it."

Leia told Jerell, "Get the *Gamble* out of there. Head
toward the station and dock."

"But no, Your Highness, what about—"

Leia cut across the protest. "You can come back for
us later. We can't risk the ship."

There was a hesitation at the other end, and Leia
knew Jerell was checking with General Willard.
"Blast it," she muttered.

"You think this pirate is working with the *Aegis*?"
Kifar asked. "I know that out in the Tingel Arm, they
say pirates work in big groups, almost fleets."

"It's possible," Han said, most of his attention on
Leia and the comlink.

Jerell replied, "Yes, Your Highness, we'll take the
ship into the station now."

Han sat back, visibly relieved, and Sian muttered, "Finally."

Leia agreed. She slipped the comlink back into her pocket as the forward blast door slid open. Kelvan stepped out and said, "Your Highness, Captain Metara has asked if you would please join her on the bridge."

Leia stood, and Han, Sian, and Kifar stood with her. Kelvan added, "Just you, please. For security reasons only."

Leia hesitated a beat, but Metara had still left them with their weapons. She turned to Han, whose expression suggested he thought they should perhaps use those weapons. She said, firmly, "Wait here, and don't do anything rash."

Han lifted a brow. "Define rash."

Leia defined rash as just about everything Han did. "Just wait."

She followed Kelvan through some short corridors and onto a raised observation area above the *Aegis*'s bridge. Terae stood at the railing, watching the activity below with her brow furrowed in worry. Leia spotted Metara seated at the comm station, wearing a headset and having what was obviously a tense conversation with whoever was on the frequency.

Some of the consoles, including the weapons console, Leia noted, had been replaced with units and boards that didn't match standard issue. She didn't think they were repairs; she assumed they were tied into the ship's augmented systems. They would have had to install controls for the tractor beam and whatever weapons systems had been added.

From where she stood, she had a good view of the

image on one of the sensor holoscreens. The approaching ship had the outline of a large cargo hauler, but gunports had been added both above and below the bridge, and there was extra bulk built up around the module where the cargo doors should have been.

Leia looked at Kelvan. "What ship is that?"

Kelvan was distinctly uncomfortable. "It was sent by . . . our benefactor in this area."

"Your benefactor?" Leia repeated. "The benefactor who paid for all this extra equipment, the tractor beam, augmented weapons?"

Kelvan seemed to be trying not to wince. "Yes, Your Highness."

Leia had the impression that Kelvan didn't approve of the arrangement, at least not entirely. She wondered if, despite his misgivings, he hadn't protested, or if he had and Metara just hadn't listened to him. Prodding for information, she said, "Not an Imperial, I presume."

It was Terae who answered. "No! Of course not." She hesitated, then added, "The ship is from a pirate fleet. They have a base near here."

Leia swore in realization, drawing a startled look from Kelvan. "An organization of pirates supplied you with these altered systems and now you owe them service." Suddenly Metara's attitude toward the merchant ship's cargo made a lot more sense.

Terae shook her head, reminding Leia of a sulky teenager. "It's not like that. It's a business arrangement."

Business arrangement, for the love of—"Do these other pirates operate by your principles, or do they sell captured crews into slavery?" Leia managed not to put too much sarcastic emphasis on the word *principles*. "Or did you not bother to ask?"

She saw Terae's expression turn bleak for an instant and thought, *So the answer is yes*. That was hardly a surprise. Terae said, "We don't have to act as they do. Once we've fulfilled our obligations, we can leave."

"Yes, a great many people have said that when accepting 'arrangements' with the Empire," Leia said drily.

Terae's whole body stiffened in offense, and even the more level-tempered Kelvan looked away, his hands tightening on the railing. Before either could reply, Metara pulled her headset off and stood so abruptly that the bridge crew stared at her. Leia saw the captain take a deep breath for self-control, saw the tension leave her shoulders and her posture return to confident and calm. Metara was good at this. But then, if she hadn't been good at it, this crew wouldn't be here right now.

Metara crossed the bridge to climb the few steps to the observation area. Though her face was still cool and neutral, Leia could read in the slight tightening at the corners of her eyes that what she had to report wasn't good news.

"They told me what that ship is," Leia said. "What does it want from you?"

"They want us to come with them, as we said we would." Metara projected calm, but the underlying strain was just barely evident. "I told them we hadn't had time to take the merchant ship's cargo, and they said they were taking the entire ship. If we don't comply, I know they'll fire on us, and we're outgunned."

She turned to Leia. "I'm sorry, I didn't—I meant to keep my word to you, but I can't now. And if we let you leave in the pod, or even give you one of our shuttles, they'll have you before you can reach the station's perimeter."

Leia pressed her lips together to keep from saying the first thing that came to mind. Or the second. Her secure comlink would be out of range as soon as the *Aegis* left the vicinity of Arnot Station, so she and the others were on their own. She couldn't afford to alienate Metara now. She settled on, "That merchant ship has injured crew members. And you know what pirates will do with them."

For a moment, real anguish flashed across Metara's face. "I know, and I didn't mean for this to happen! Believe me, I never intended—" She shook off her distress and an instant later was the calm professional again. She turned back to the railing and ordered, "Thomen, the *Wastrel* will be tractoring the merchant in and locking onto it. Prepare to follow them into hyperspace."

Despite the coolness with which Metara gave the order, she was clearly conflicted, and that gave Leia her first real hope that the *Aegis* could be saved.

She pressed the advantage. "Did you tell the pirates that I'm aboard?" If Metara thought there was some sort of "honor among thieves" code among pirates, that they wouldn't sell Leia and the others out to the Empire at the first opportunity . . .

Metara looked honestly startled, as if the thought had never occurred to her. "No, of course not. I can't avoid going with them now, but once we can leave, I'll bring you and your people back here, or wherever you can rendezvous with your ship." She added, "If you don't trust us, and believe me, I understand why you wouldn't, I can drop you off at a safe commercial port, where your ship can meet you."

"I see. Thank you." Leia felt the tightness in her chest ease. Metara's words had the ring of truth; someone who wasn't planning to release them wouldn't worry about the details of how to get Leia back to her ship. Metara had felt she had to see Leia in person because, whether she realized it or not, she wanted to justify her behavior to someone who represented the Alderaanian planetary security forces and civil authority that she had once served. Leia didn't think Metara had gotten what she needed out of their meeting, but it was clear Metara didn't want her hurt or captured, either.

She thought Metara had gotten in over her head, and that Metara knew it, but saying so now would be a terrible mistake. Leia had been looking for a common ground with the *Aegis*'s crew, a way to put them all on the same side so further negotiation would be possible. This could be her best chance. "Do you trust these pirates?"

Metara glanced at Terae and Kelvan. Terae's shoulders hunched uncomfortably; Kelvan's expression was grave. He said, "We didn't have much of a choice. They claimed we were poaching on their territory, that we had to join them or leave. And we needed repairs we couldn't pay for. If we didn't accept their help, we would have had to sell the ship for scrap." He shrugged helplessly. "I don't know what we would have done then."

Leia knew. The crew would have had to break up,

drift off, look for other ways to survive. People who had lost everything would lose one another, too.

Metara admitted, "I trust them to hunt us down and destroy us if we don't fulfill our end of this bargain."

Leia lifted a brow. "Perhaps I can help you with that."

Metara stared at her. "What do you mean?"

"I'm not sure yet. I need to know more about your situation. But I have a great deal of experience in talking my way out of tough corners." Leia added deliberately, "You may not be as trapped as you think."

CHAPTER FIVE

AFTER THE *AEGIS* WENT into hyperspace, Kelvan led Leia back to the lounge. As she stepped in, the others were already on their feet, giving the impression that the door sliding open had just interrupted a particularly intense conversation. From their expressions, especially Han's, the fact that the ship had gone into hyperspace had not escaped anyone's attention.

Kelvan hesitated, as if he felt all the awkwardness of the situation but had no idea what to do about it. He just nodded to Leia and left, letting the door slide shut behind him.

"What happened?" Han demanded.

Leia explained briefly, keeping her voice quiet. When she finished, Han said, "You know how much trouble we could be in, here."

"Yes, I know, Han, but thank you very much for pointing out the obvious," Leia said with some asperity. "I think we could also have an excellent opportunity."

Han clapped a hand over his eyes.

"You mean an opportunity to recruit this crew?" Sian asked dubiously.

"It's certainly a possibility." Leia knew she sounded more confident about that than the situation warranted, but if she didn't believe in the *Aegis*'s crew, no one would. "This is going to give me time to talk with them, and if I can help them get out of this situation—"

"The situation of being in debt to some pirate lord, and headed to his base with us aboard their ship?" Han said, annoyingly accurate. "That situation?"

"Surely they won't betray the Princess," Kifar said. "I mean, they're pirates, but they're still Alderaanians."

Han gave Kifar a withering look. "It's hilarious that you believe that."

Sian didn't look happy, but said, "We're stuck here with them; we might as well make the best of it."

Before Han could respond, Metara walked into the lounge, accompanied by Terae and Kelvan. Leia asked her, "Where exactly are we going, Captain?"

"To a meeting place for the pirates in this area," Metara told her. "They call it a clearinghouse."

"A what?" Sian asked, but Leia had heard the term before.

She explained, "Pirates come from other sectors, places with richer trade routes. They bring their stolen cargoes and trade or sell them at the clearinghouse to fences and dealers or other pirates." They would also bring captive crew and passengers here, to sell them far away from wherever they had originally been taken prisoner. Leia kept her voice cool by habit, but she was thinking that this explained a great deal about the level of pirate activity in this sector.

"That's correct." Metara rubbed her palms together, distracted and clearly still uneasy. "We haven't been there before, and I haven't met their leader. Our arrangement was made through intermediaries, who gave me access to the funds to have the modifications made. They also gave us the location of a shipyard that wouldn't ask questions."

"But why do they have a clearinghouse here?" Kifar asked. "What's the attraction?"

"The attraction is that this place is too backwater for the Empire to do anything but collect taxes," Han answered. "And there's no local patrols or militia to worry about, just a few armed merchants and farmers."

Metara remained focused on Leia. "You said you could help us. How? Were you suggesting that you pay our debt?" She looked troubled by the thought.

"And what would you want in return?" Terae put in, clearly skeptical.

Leia ignored her. She knew the Alliance had no spare funds to pay off the *Aegis*'s debt, and she wanted to avoid handing over money to pirates and slavers. "That wasn't what I had in mind. But if I can convince the pirates that we have something to offer them worth more than your service, and if we can get them to release the merchant crew and then let us leave . . . I don't know if it's possible, but it's worth a try."

Han stared incredulously at her, but Metara was nodding slowly.

"You're going to lie to them, in other words?" Terae asked. "Break our agreement with them?"

Metara gave the younger woman a cold look that suggested she had heard about all she needed to from Terae. But Leia said, "When it comes to trying to stop a crew of innocent bystanders from being sold into slavery, yes, I'm happy to lie with the best of them."

* * *

Leia had hoped for an opportunity to speak to the other *Aegis* crew members, so she was pleased when she and the others were invited to eat with Metara and the rest of the off-duty crew in the ship's galley. The table in the compartment was only large enough for one shift, but it seemed as if everyone who didn't fit had crammed into the two corridors and the doorways that accessed the galley, listening intently to the conversation. Leia suspected that Metara was fairly expert at gauging her crew's mood, and knew that denying them the opportunity to see and speak to Leia would only foster dissent.

Also, Leia didn't want Metara to think she was trying to sway the loyalty of her crew. *Well, I am, but I'm not planning a mutiny.* Leia had seen enough as the crew assembled for dinner to know that they weren't afraid of Metara. They obviously liked her and trusted her; trying to drive a wedge between them and their captain would be as ineffective as it would be cruel.

The situation was a tricky one. Leia felt she had made some progress with Metara, getting her to admit that making the deal with the pirate clearinghouse had been a mistake. It gave them a goal in common, and Leia wanted Metara to keep thinking of her as an ally and not an enemy. She didn't want to lose that ground. It might not be possible to convince Metara to join the Alliance, but maybe Leia could convince her to abandon piracy and find a more legitimate occupation somewhere far from here. She had conducted some negotiations in the Senate under her father's tutelage that were almost as personal and delicate, and she was going to have to use every trick he had showed her.

The food was only the usual uncreative shipboard rations, and Leia ate without paying much attention to it. She spent her time answering questions from the crew and listening as they spoke, tentatively at first and then with more confidence, about Alderaan.

Then one of the crew asked her, "But what were you doing out here, Your Highness?"

"I'm afraid I can't tell you that," Leia said, with a slight smile to soften her reply.

"You mean, you're here on Alliance business?" Someone nudged him, and he said hastily, "I'm sorry. I just didn't think—I assumed—"

"That I was a figurehead? A symbol?" Leia said. She got that a lot, and it wasn't as if Mon Mothma and other members of the Alliance High Command hadn't tried to make it clear that that was how they preferred it. Leia knew that being a symbol was part of her duty to the Alliance, but she wasn't sure Mothma and the others really understood what they were asking of her. Unlike living, breathing people, figureheads were made of stone and incapable of mistakes; Leia wasn't certain how long she could bear that weight. Failure at some point seemed inevitable, and she hated to fail.

"I didn't think they let you do anything dangerous," the young man persisted, then winced in embarrassment when someone—probably Kelvan, judging from the angle—kicked him under the table.

Leia heard Sian make a quiet snort of derision, obviously remembering their moment of near-explosive decompression on the *Gamble*'s bridge. She glanced

up at Han, who was giving her a look that was so
sardonic she almost snorted herself. "Well," she said
drily, "the Imperial Senate was always fairly dangerous," and used the moment to segue into a funny
story about a junior senator's aide who had climbed
down a maintenance shaft to avoid Senator Palpa-
tine.

At the end of the meal, with the tension eased and
the crew talking more naturally among themselves,
Leia caught Metara watching her with an expression
she couldn't quite read. She wondered if the captain
regretted bringing her aboard, if she thought Leia
might already be gaining too much influence over the
crew.

Leia decided she was going to have to keep her efforts subtle, at least until she had more of a chance to
work on Metara herself.

Leia and Han were on the bridge observation platform when the *Aegis* came out of hyperspace.

Sian and Kifar were back in the lounge, but Han
had insisted he accompany Leia when Kelvan came to
take her to the bridge. Leia hadn't objected. She
wanted his opinion, and she wanted to encourage any
situation that allowed them to move more freely
around the gunship. Metara still seemed to be easing
into the idea of seeing them as allies, and Leia wanted
to keep pushing that envelope.

Kelvan hesitated, then asked Han, "Are you the
Princess's bodyguard?"

Leia watched Han fight a short battle with himself,
while she stared archly at him, braced for whatever

innuendo-laden response he would come up with. He
finally said, "I'm her pilot."

Kelvan glanced at Leia, but just then an alert ping
sounded over the comm system, telling them that the
ship was only a few moments from exiting hyperspace, and Kelvan clearly decided he didn't have time
to argue about Han coming along. As he led them
through to the bridge, Leia noted that he hadn't
needed to contact Metara for permission, either. He
and Terae might have more authority on the ship
than Leia had originally thought.

When they reached the bridge, Han and Leia remained in the observation area with Kelvan. Metara
and Terae were below, standing behind the four crew
members who were operating the bridge stations. The
Aegis came out of hyperspace smoothly, the stars
streaking back into coherence. The main sensor
screen was clearly visible from the observation area;
it showed empty space, except for the *Wastrel,* the
pirate ship that had led them here. They must have
emerged from hyperspace a good distance away from
their destination. Leia assumed that was the local etiquette, designed to give any picket ships time to identify the newcomers.

Leia watched Metara conduct a brief conversation
on the comm headset, probably with the *Wastrel,* as
the two ships traveled farther into the system on their
sublights. Then Han said, "There it is."

There was nothing to see in the viewport yet, so
Leia watched the sensor screen. A scatter of dots and
numbers showed sensor contacts with five other
ships. *That's not too bad,* she thought. Then the
screen blossomed with dots as the other contacts

came within range. That small scatter of ships had just been the outliers.

There were ships all over the screen, some locked together in clusters, some orbiting separately. All were gathered around something that the sensors interpreted as a large dark mass, bristling with spikes of energy.

Kelvan looked almost as horrified as Leia felt. He murmured, "There's more than fifty of them." Below, Terae stared at the sensor screen. Leia couldn't see Metara's expression, but her shoulders were tense. More confirmation, Leia thought, that Metara hadn't known what she was getting her crew into.

Han glanced over at Leia. "Enough pirates for you, Your Worship?"

"I'm thrilled," Leia muttered. This many pirates could totally destroy Arnot Station and all the small planetary settlements that were supplied by the local trade routes.

The mass at the center of all the ship contacts grew larger. Leia was afraid for an instant that it was a massive ship, something even larger than a Star Destroyer, but the sensors seemed confused as to just what it actually was. It emitted comm signals and power, but large sections of it were inert. Many of the other ships orbited it, but it was far too small for a moon, let alone a planet.

"What is that thing?" Kelvan asked.

"That's what I was wondering," Han said. "I thought it was a dead station they had towed out here, but it looks like there's lots of raw minerals . . ."

The crew member at the sensor station must have been working on the problem. Metara stepped up behind him as the sensor view formed into an image of an irregularly shaped mass, with glowing spots that showed power sources emanating from all over it. Dark spots marked hatches and bays large enough for huge cargo transports to enter; the sensors seemed to be indicating that it was hollow, riddled with meandering shafts, but also with the shapes of pressurized areas that looked constructed—"It's an asteroid mine," Leia said, startled.

Han agreed. "Must be an old, played-out one. It might be a leftover from the Republic, or before."

Asteroid fields with valuable minerals often drew rushes of prospectors and mining corporations, which then left once the most accessible veins had been played out. Some of the original planetary populations in this area might have come from miners and support personnel who had stayed in the sector after the mines shut down. Leia said, "And it's one more reason why the pirates chose this area for their clearinghouse. It's huge, there must be plenty of room to repair ships, store cargoes, meet with dealers, whatever else they need." She looked at Kelvan. "And hold prisoners until they can be sold to slavers. Like the merchant crew."

Kelvan's expression was conflicted. "We didn't have any idea this was such a big operation. I think we convinced ourselves it was just a business deal."

Metara had called it that, too. "Would it have made a difference?" Leia asked.

He shook his head. "Maybe. I don't know. We were desperate." He lifted one hand helplessly. "We've been desperate for so long."

Leia nodded understanding. Desperate, and he,

Terae, and Metara were responsible for the safety of the other crew members.

Han still watched the sensor screen, obviously troubled. "Clearinghouses aren't meant to stay in one place. They have to move pretty frequently, depending on how much business they do and how much attention they attract. But this setup looks permanent."

"I wonder if this is more than just a clearinghouse," Leia said. If some Imperial official was connected to this place, that might be a reason why the Imperial authorities were so uninterested in the pirate traffic in this sector.

Han shrugged. "We'll know more once we get inside."

The images on the sensor screen were getting larger and clearer every moment. It wouldn't be long now.

The *Aegis* was given coordinates for a docking port, and it approached the asteroid mine under the shadow of what felt like every pirate gun from the Outer Rim to the Core Worlds. Leia reminded herself that it wasn't really that bad. Of course, if all the ships started shooting at once, it might as well be.

The asteroid had probably once been a spheroid, but extensive mining had hollowed out one whole hemisphere, and malformed one of the poles, so the shape from this angle resembled a half-moon wearing a floppy cap. They were close enough now to see that the surface was covered by pits, holes, and craters that bore the marks of drilling and digging until it was hard to tell if they had been caused by natural impacts or had been carved out by the abandoned mining apparatus that lay everywhere. Leia saw a large blast scar surrounded by the remnants of a crashed ship—no, two crashed ships—scattered across the dusty surface. It was impossible to tell the age of the crash, or whether the wrecks were pirate ships destroyed in some conflict or an old mining accident.

The docking port to which they had been directed was built into a ridge protruding from what was roughly the middle of the asteroid. It was an open port, without an air lock, protected only by a containment field. It looked as if it had been originally meant for droid-operated loading transports.

"Not exactly a warm welcome," Leia commented to Han. They stood alone on the observation platform. Terae had left the bridge to return to engineering while the ship docked, and Kelvan had joined Metara below. "It's not a very secure berth."

Han shrugged. "Maybe, maybe not. As far as we know, they don't have any reason to kill us. Yet."

True, Leia thought. Though the *Aegis* might be worth more without a crew than with one, if the pirates had any inkling that Metara meant to refuse to supply captive crews to slavers.

Han jerked his chin toward the screen that was tracking the *Wastrel* and the captured merchant ship. "They're going to another berth on this side. I bet it's that big one right there."

Leia watched, noting the position carefully. "That's good to know."

Han eyed her and she eyed him back. She said, "We're not leaving without them."

Keeping his voice low, though still managing to convey just how exasperated he was, he said, "It's not your fault they're here."

Glaring at Metara's back, Leia whispered, "Believe me, I know exactly whose fault this is."

The pilot carefully took the *Aegis* through the opening into the berth. It was a big space, suited to a much larger ship, with a metal superstructure built onto the arch of the rock ceiling that might be meant for transporting ore containers. Leia felt the shudder through the deck as the *Aegis* touched down on the scarred stone landing surface. The young pilot had positioned it right in the middle of the bay, ignoring the faded lines and circles meant to tell the long-ago droid transports where to land.

"The bay is repressurizing," Kelvan reported, checking his console.

Metara put down her headset and crossed the bridge to the observation area. "Their leader wants to see me," she told Leia. "Or at least I assume it's their leader. The title is 'flightmaster,' and I'm not sure if he actually controls the ships docked here or just their right to use the station itself."

"Is he the one who paid for your repairs and new systems?" Leia asked.

Metara nodded. "Yes. Though we only spoke through intermediaries. I was never even told his name."

"Let me go with you," Leia said. She purposely did not look at Han, but felt him stiffen next to her.

Metara shook her head. "I'll report to you what we say, and you can advise me—"

Leia interrupted, "That won't work. I can't help you if I don't know exactly what you're up against."

Metara sighed. "Your Highness, I have a great deal on my conscience already. I have no intention of adding to that. If anything happens to you—"

"If this flightmaster gets the idea that there's someone on this ship you're reporting to and consulting with, it's going to do nothing but make him suspicious. We can tell him that I represent another pirate ship, another group of pirate ships, that has made you an offer. Working with my group, you'll be able to pay your debt quickly with interest. If he's a businessman, that should be all he cares about." Leia bit her lip, thinking about the merchant crew. "I'm not sure how we're going to get your prisoners back."

"Our deal was for the cargo, not the ship itself or the crew," Metara reminded her. "But obviously the flightmaster changed his mind."

"We might be able to work with that, argue that the crew still belongs to you because they weren't specifically mentioned." But Leia doubted she could get the pirates to simply hand over the prisoners. "We might have to offer to buy them." The thought of giving money to slavers grated on her, but she just didn't think it would be possible to take the prisoners by force. "If I can get the pirates to agree to that, and we can return to the station, I can get the funds from my ship. If they ask for more than we have, I can send for it." Hopefully, the *Millennium Falcon* would reach Arnot Station before they returned. "I don't know if this will work," she told Metara. "But we have to try."

Metara watched her a moment, her expression unreadable. "I won't go to the Alliance, no matter what you do for us."

Leia was willing to give up on that point, or pretend to give up on it, at least for now. "I understand. Do you want to use this ship for piracy and slavery?"

Metara's answer was reassuringly immediate. "No. Not slavery. I won't promise never to attack another ship, but it was never my intention to capture this crew."

"Then we have the same goal." *For now,* Leia thought. *Later, we'll see.*

Han stopped Leia in the corridor outside the bridge, where they had a moment of temporary privacy. It had been hard enough keeping his mouth shut in front of Metara and the others. He said, "If you're going to ask me if I think this is a good idea—"

"I'm not asking you." Leia appeared amused by the idea that she might. "I need you to look out for Sian and Kifar while I'm gone. Make sure they don't get into any trouble, with the *Aegis*'s crew or the pirates."

Which meant she was entertaining the idea that she and Metara wouldn't be back soon, that this might not be just a quick chat with the flightmaster. "We're supposed to be looking out for you. That's why we came. Remember, I'm your 'bodyguard.'" With hooked fingers, Han supplied the air quotes to make the double meaning obvious.

"I thought you said you were my 'pilot,'" Leia air-quoted back at him. "Han, I don't have time for this." She looked at him with steely determination. "I have to help these people and I need you to . . . not try to stop me."

Yeah, yeah, he knew she needed to help these people. She needed to help *all* the people. "Then let me go help them with you."

"They only asked for Metara. It's going to be awkward enough when she brings *me* along. More people would just make it worse."

"Awkward?" Han lifted his brows at the choice of word. She was right, but he hated to send her out with no backup except Metara. The captain was a fanatic, and he would sooner trust a Hutt gang lord than a fanatic. "It'll be *awkward* if they shoot you."

"It'll be just as awkward if they shoot all of us." Leia folded her arms and gave him the I'm-the-Princess-and-you're-not look. "I'm not going to argue about this."

Han still wanted to argue, just out of principle, but it wasn't like he had a better idea. It was a little late to try seizing control of the bridge and taking over the ship by holding Metara hostage, which was his favorite of the bad ideas he had come up with while they were in hyperspace. He hadn't brought it up at the time, because even then he could see that Leia was making subtle inroads to accomplish exactly the same end without needing to draw a blaster. She had somehow managed to make herself Metara's partner in this whole disaster, and by going along to negotiate with the flightmaster, she was moving to become Metara's boss. Watching her operate like this would have been daunting if he weren't finding it quite so attractive.

He threw his hands in the air, making up for giving

in by doing it with as little grace as possible. "All right, fine!"

"Good." Leia handed him the comlink she had brought from the *Gamble*. "Hold on to this for me. If we're searched or have to give up our weapons, I don't want to have to answer questions about it. Metara is going to have one secured to the ship's comm; the pirates should expect that. Please go update Sian and Kifar on the situation. And don't sulk about it."

Han put the comlink in his pocket. "You're the boss, Your Holiness." He knew she really hated it when he called her that. Leia gave him her death glare in return and stomped away, heading back to the bridge. Han wondered again what strange turn his life had taken that he had ended up as friend and verbal sparring partner for the last Princess of Alderaan. He just didn't want to be the guy who got her killed.

On her own, Leia was pretty good at not getting herself killed, no matter how hard the Empire had tried. At least he was here with her this time to keep her out of trouble. What worried him more was how far she might have to go to save these idiot Alderaanians from themselves. The kids who thought they could play pirate without getting their hands dirty were bad enough; Metara, who had talked them into this and ran the ship like a cult leader in a religious colony, worried the hell out of him.

Han told Sian and Itran what the situation was, and predictably, Itran said, as if this were somehow all Han's doing, "Are you out of your mind? The Princess shouldn't be here in the first place!"

"You think?" Han said, pretending to be genuinely interested in the answer, just to see what Itran
would do.

Itran railed about it and Han continued to prod
him while thinking—just a little—about shooting
him, until Sian finally said, "Will you two calm down
and be quiet? The only thing we can do right now to
help the Princess is present a united front, so let's just
do that, all right?"

Han thought Sian didn't care so much about pre-
senting a united front as long as he and Itran both
shut up. Which they did. The silence gave Han time
to worry more about Leia's plans. The fact that everyone from the *Aegis* and the *Gamble* who accompanied Metara and Leia down to the bay floor was
armed didn't reassure him all that much.

The bay was big, carved out of the rock by the same
massive digging tools that had chopped up the rest of
the asteroid. The air had just been pumped in, so it
wasn't stale, but it was cool and too damp and had a
metallic taint, probably from faulty recycling units
somewhere in the system. The moisture had combined with the rock dust in the air to coat the metal
panels and stone surfaces with a dirty muck. Stretching across the rocky ceiling was a heavy metal superstructure, a loading mechanism for the ore transports
that had once docked here.

Two big blast doors in the far wall opened to a
corridor, where a few armed pirates waited, probably
assigned to keep an eye on the newly recruited ship.
Taking a quick look around, Han immediately noticed the second, unguarded way out of the bay. A
moment later Sian nudged his arm and pointed up at

the superstructure overhead. He gave her a quick nod.

Three of the guards came forward into the bay, two humans and one Aqualish. The Aqualish was short, with green-gray skin, bulbous dark eyes, and two short tusks covering the lower part of his face. The two humans were both male, both big, dressed in dirty leather and carrying blasters. The Aqualish said, "The flightmaster wants to see the captain. Who's the captain?"

Metara stepped forward. "I am." She indicated Leia with a jerk of her head. "She's coming with me."

The Aqualish grunted but didn't object. "The rest of your crew stays here, till the flightmaster says otherwise. We don't want strangers wandering around."

Metara glanced at Kelvan and got a reluctant nod from him. She told the Aqualish, "We understand."

He turned away. "Then follow me."

Han watched Metara and Leia follow the Aqualish away, his misgivings growing. Leia didn't even look back. The Aqualish hadn't told them to hand over their weapons, but maybe that would come later, when they were away from the ship and any help. Most of the guards had been left behind, loitering just outside the blast doors.

One of the Alderaanians said to Kelvan, "I don't like this, sir."

Kelvan looked like he hated it. "No one does."

The Princess wasn't going to budge from this place until she could take that captured merchant crew with her, and Han wasn't exactly keen on leaving them here, either. He had seen too many slave pens for that. To test Kelvan's resolve, he said, "We need to find out where they're keeping their prisoners."

Kelvan's reaction was to look toward the bay door, clearly considering how difficult it might be to get through it. "The Aqualish said we're not to leave the bay, and trying to come up with some excuse might make them suspicious. I don't want to risk that while the captain and Her Highness are away from the ship."

Unexpectedly, Terae said, "Maybe we could ask to see the merchants, pretend we consider them our property."

Han hadn't thought Terae was on board with the idea of rescuing the merchants and escaping the pirates, but maybe he'd been wrong.

"Maybe." Kelvan's expression was doubtful. "Our deal was for the cargo of the ship, there was never anything said about the crew, which was why we didn't think these pirates were slavers. But Captain Metara is not going to want us to act without her here. For one thing, it might contradict something she's about to tell them."

Kelvan was right, but he clearly wasn't averse to hearing more suggestions. Han decided to take a chance on him. "Yeah, we're going to have to do it without anybody noticing."

Terae gave him an impatient glare. "That's the point: we can't."

Han jerked his chin up. "There's another way out of this place."

Everybody looked up. The superstructure overhead formed a track for guiding large repulsor carts of ore through the loading bays so they could be lowered to

droid-controlled transports. High in the carved rock
of the inside bay wall, the track curved, then stopped
at a large hatchway that probably hadn't been opened
since the last mining company had left. Next to it was
a smaller maintenance hatch that Han thought should
be easier to open. "They've been using these bays so
long, they've forgotten those hatches are up there."

Han saw Kelvan's expression go from reluctant and
skeptical to intrigued, and knew he had him. Kelvan
said, "That might work."

"I'll go," Han said. "We know they took the merchant ship to a dock down that way; we find it, we
might be able to figure out where they took the crew."

"I'll go with you," Sian said.

Itran nodded. "Me, too."

"No," Terae said, before Han could. She nodded to
Han and Sian. "You two, and me. More than three
and it will be too difficult to move around quietly."

"Two can move around more quietly than three,"
Han said. He didn't want Terae at his back any more
than he wanted Itran.

Terae didn't like that. "If you two leave here alone,
we have no guarantee you'll come back."

Sian laughed. "Really? And then what would we
do?"

Han folded his arms. "Well, there goes my plan to
live forever in the droid-access tunnels of a half-dead
asteroid mine."

"He was really looking forward to that," Itran
added, surprising Han. He hadn't thought the guy
had a sense of humor.

Terae bristled, and Kelvan said, "Lieutenant Terae
goes with you, or no one goes. And it's a scouting

mission, only. Don't do anything until we can report to Captain Metara."

Itran drew breath for what was clearly going to be an objection, but Han had a lot of experience in pushing people over lines, and knew Kelvan had been pushed as far as he was willing to go. He said, "It's a deal."

The *Aegis* carried standard survival gear, which included a fibercord grappling hook. Han also picked up a small satchel of tools, since it looked like they would be dealing with access hatches and other equipment that had been old when the Republic fell.

Once they had climbed out the ship's topside access hatch, Han threw the grappling hook up to catch on the lowest girder of the ore track. He climbed up quickly, Sian and Terae after him. They managed to do it quietly, and the crew member Kelvan had stationed near the ship's ramp didn't signal a warning that the guards stationed by the bay doors had been alerted by any noise or movement above.

The ore track was an open tube made of metal girders, with relays embedded in it to send instructions to the repulsor ore carts. Judging by the width of the track, the carts must have been at least ten meters across; the girders were wide enough to stand on, but the gap between each pair was about two meters— more than enough to fall through and plummet all the way to the stone floor of the docking bay. But running along one girder was a half-meter-wide ledge that had probably been designed for small maintenance droids to perch on while they repaired relays and dislodged the occasionally wonky cart. And there must have been a lot of wonky carts, Han decided, because as he made his way carefully along the ledge he found giant dents in the girder he was using to steady himself.

They reached the side of the bay, a wall of deeply scarred rock. The small maintenance hatch was to one side of the giant ore-cart hatch, and only about a meter high. The rock around the seals of both was crumbling, which didn't give Han warm fuzzy feelings about this place's pressure integrity.

"Does it have power?" Sian asked from behind him.

Han tapped the control panel and heard the click as the hatch responded, but nothing happened. "Yeah, but it's stuck." He worked his fingers in around the panel and popped it off the wall. A little flurry of crystalline insects scurried out and away across the rock, and Han managed not to yelp in surprise or jerk back and knock Sian or himself off the ledge.

From the back, Terae said, "Hurry it up."

Oh, she's going to be fun, Han thought, and hit the manual release for the smaller hatch. Although heavy, it slid upward easily enough once he got his hands under it.

Han had expected a dark maintenance tunnel, but this was only a short passageway, the width of the inner bay wall. The recycled air released wasn't any staler than the air in the bay, and at the end of the tube there was a dim glow of light from below. He motioned for Sian and Terae to stay quiet, and crouched down to step through.

The meter-high passage had been meant for meter-

high droids, and moving along it was awkward. At
the end, it opened back onto the ore-cart track, which
crossed above a wide corridor and terminated in another set of hatches on the far side. Han held on to a
girder to steady himself and leaned out to look down.
He could see the floor of the corridor and, several
meters along it, the bay doors and the guards waiting
there. A few of them sat on the floor, talking and
playing what looked like death dice.

They were distracted, but not so distracted that
they wouldn't hear three humans climbing across the
girders overhead and prying open the hatch on the far
wall. Fortunately, Han wasn't sure they wanted to go
that way—it was likely to just lead into the droid and
ore-cart access tunnels. Leaning out a little farther,
he could see another, wider ledge running under the
girders, parallel to the wall, following the wall of the
corridor about five meters above the floor.

That's more like it, Han thought. The walkway ran
the other way, too, passing above the bay doors and
continuing in the direction the Aqualish had led Leia
and Metara. Han struggled with temptation for a moment, but trying to walk directly over the guards'
heads would be stupid. He had to trust the Princess
not to get herself killed.

Motioning to Sian and Terae to follow, he held on
to the girder and, keeping one eye on the guards, put
one foot down on the parallel ledge, then carefully
shifted his weight onto it. It creaked, but softly, and
the guards didn't notice. He took a step along it to
make room and steadied Sian as she stepped down.
She, in turn, steadied Terae, and then Han led the
way slowly down the ledge and away from the guards.

CHAPTER SIX

THE AQUALISH LED LEIA and Metara through the wide bay blast doors and past the other guards, who stared at them with wary curiosity. The fact that the bay was being guarded at all was worrisome; Leia wondered if it was a standard precaution, or if the *Aegis* was already under suspicion for some reason.

The docking ring corridor was carved out of the raw rock, long and curving with a high uneven ceiling mostly lost in the shadows, with only floating lumas providing wan light. As they left the bay behind, they passed a round doorway into the asteroid's interior that was big enough to fly a small landspeeder through, but it was dark, and the draft coming up from it smelled of mold and rot. Something about it made Leia's skin creep.

"So what's your business here?" the Aqualish asked.

Leia drew breath to answer, but Metara beat her to it. "Our business is none of yours."

The Aqualish snorted. "Your business is the flight-master's. You think any different, you're a fool."

Metara didn't reply, but her expression grew even stonier.

Leia sighed mentally. Alienating the Aqualish, a potential source of information, was just shortsighted.
"Oh, I know you're right about the flightmaster," she
said. "I'm just wondering why there are guards on
our bay, and why we're getting a personal escort. Is it
like that for every new ship here?"

The Aqualish glanced back at her, assessing her before he spoke. "The escort's because otherwise you'd
never find your way around. The guards on the bay
are just for the ships the flightmaster has a special
interest in."

Special interest—that wasn't encouraging. Leia
hoped it further impressed on Metara that she had
gotten herself and her crew in over their heads.

They passed more sets of bay doors in the docking
ring, all sealed, and a few large, interior tunnel entrances. Ahead of them, the next set of bay doors slid
open and a group tumbled out, mostly human and
near human, dressed in flashy clothing and with very
well-cared-for blasters in evidence. All were intoxi-
cated. The one in the lead was a dark-blue-skinned
Twi'lek woman. She leaned casually against the wall,
waiting for her drunken companions to sort themselves out. This was the toughest and meanest-looking
Twi'lek Leia had ever seen. One of her head-tails was
badly scarred, as if someone had tried to cut it off.
Leia suspected whoever it was had paid dearly for the
attempt.

She found herself meeting the Twi'lek's gaze, and
gave her a nod. The Twi'lek nodded back, then hissed
appreciatively at Metara as she passed by.

They took the next interior corridor. Leia breathed
more easily: either the air was better down here, or

she was getting used to the stench. Heading down a ramp that spiraled through the roughly cut rock, Leia almost stumbled and had to catch herself; the gravity had just lightened. The bottom of the ramp led into another corridor, where the gravity abruptly shifted back to standard. Dusty power panels and conduits were mounted on the rock walls, and the floors were littered with scraps and broken components clearly left by scavengers.

At last they reached a room filled with old couches and what looked like a dead holodisplay. The far end was lost in shadows. The Aqualish stopped and gestured toward a walkway that led into the darkness. "Go on," he said. "She's waiting for you."

As the human guards draped themselves over the couches, clearly settling in for a boring wait, Leia and Metara exchanged a wary glance and started across the room to the walkway.

They found themselves in a shadowy cavern where there was just enough light to see that the walkway was above a shaft that dropped a couple of levels down, with scaffolds that must have once supported platforms and stairways. Leia stopped Metara with a hand on her arm. Keeping her voice low, she said, "You brought me here to do the talking, so when we begin the negotiation, let me do my job." They had had this conversation back on the ship, but Leia wanted to emphasize it.

"I will." Metara gave her a sharp nod. *Right,* Leia thought, and hoped that the grim atmosphere of this place would have a dampening effect on Metara's ego.

A short set of steps led down into a large chamber

that must have once been the control center for the mine. It was full of pirates, male and female, some human and many of other species. As they stepped down into the room, most of the sentients inside turned to stare with various degrees of curiosity and hostility. Fortunately, Leia was used to being stared at, usually with less curiosity and more hostility.

A big, curved viewport, almost covering the far wall, looked out on a huge, dark space hollowed out of the center of the asteroid. From where she stood, all Leia could see through it were lights, reflecting off pitted metal beams, and the enormous, half-hidden shapes of what must be old mining apparatus, like giants hiding in the shadows.

The other walls were lined with old consoles, all of them cannibalized for parts in some distant past; a few powered-down droids lay in heaps in the corners. Couches and chairs were scattered around, all uniformly lush and comfortable, draped with rich fabrics, but the styles differed widely, making clear they had been looted from other places. The main seating area was on a raised platform in the center of the room, with a big half circle of chairs and a low, chased-metal table supporting a decanter and glasses. A human woman stood near it, facing out toward the dark space beyond the viewport; she was clearly the leader.

Slender and tall, she wore her dark hair slicked back into a compact style of waves that was both elaborate and practical, designed not to get in her way. A scar marred the pale skin of her face, starting at her right cheek, stretching across her nose, just missing her eye, and arrowing up her forehead to her hairline. Small metal disks etched with elaborate patterns studded her temples and cheekbones, placed to call attention to the scar rather than to hide it. Over dark clothes, she wore a very fine, brown leather coat that fell to her knees, the inside lined with red fabric with the gleam of shimmersilk.

Turning to face Leia and Metara, she gave them the polite, bland smile of a good hostess and gestured for them to come up. "I am Captain Aral tukor Viest. Welcome."

Metara walked up onto the dais. "I'm Captain Caline Metara, and this is Leia Durane." Durane was the false name they had agreed on earlier.

Leia nodded to Viest. Metara continued, "I understand I have you to thank for the funds to augment my ship."

Viest lifted a brow. "Did you want to thank me? That's not the impression I have." She regarded Leia. "And you? You aren't one of Captain Metara's crew, and you certainly aren't subordinate to her. Who are you, exactly?"

And then Leia put together the name, the faint accent in Viest's voice, and her highly accurate evaluation of both of them, and thought, *Oh, no, she's Lorrdian.* Leia's simple plan for how Metara would introduce her as a new partner in her ship and how Leia would offer to take on the *Aegis*'s debt was suddenly much trickier. Perhaps too tricky.

Lorrdians had been enslaved for several centuries back in the time of the ancient Republic. Forbidden by their captors to speak, they had managed to develop an extremely subtle sign language of facial expressions and slight gestures. Over time it had evolved into a sophisticated kinetic language, but it had also allowed many Lorrdians to interpret the body language of other species and human cultures, to read their intentions and to tell if what they said was the truth, or not.

Metara looked at Leia in confusion. Leia knew Viest wouldn't have missed the captain's involuntary start of surprise and dismay. She was going to have to make her cover story skirt a lot closer to the truth to convince Viest and make their plan work. She smiled tightly.

"You're right. I have my own ship. Metara and I met recently and discussed an alternative arrangement."

Viest tilted her head. Her expression was difficult to read, but Leia doubted she was pleased. "Alternative to my arrangement with Metara?"

"Yes. We wanted to discuss our options with you." Leia had learned the hard way in the Senate that the key to fooling a Lorrdian reader was not to let the conversation turn toward anything you didn't want to discuss. Of course, the problem was that a good Lorrdian reader would be well aware of that tactic.

After a moment, Viest sank into one of the wide chairs and gestured to the couch across from her. "Have a seat, and we'll discuss these options." She was as elegant as a high-caste Viridian matron inviting Leia to tea, except for the gleaming, pointed ring-sheaths on her fingers meant to resemble claws. Leia sat down with Metara, reminding herself to move like a spacer, to keep her posture loose and easy. Viest was the real thing and could act however she wanted; Leia had a façade to maintain. She said

to Viest, "I like your setup here." "Like" wasn't anywhere close to the truth, but she thought Viest would
accept it as the polite fiction that it was.

"I'm happy with it." Viest leaned forward, picked
up the decanter that had been sitting on the small
table, and poured two more glasses of liquor. Most of
the other pirates had moved away from the dais, with
only a few lounging on cushions near the central seating area. They could be anything from bodyguards to
Viest's harem; it was hard to tell from their dress
and demeanor. The recycled air smelled of ryll and
other spices, and a tart, almost caustic scent that Leia
assumed came from the liquor. Despite the casual
atmosphere, everyone was armed to the teeth. *Hal-
lucinogens, intoxicants, and energy weapons,* Leia
thought grimly. *Who doesn't like that combination?*
It probably said something positive about the pirates'
self-control that the place wasn't littered with dead
bodies.

As Viest passed them the glasses, she said, "And
what sort of ship do you have, Captain Leia Durane?"

Accepting the drink, Leia answered, "It's a converted freighter, with a crew of twenty. But I work
with a large group of ships. We find it safer, and more
profitable, that way." That wasn't a lie; it was just a
very vague description of the Alliance fleet. She obscured her face by raising her glass and downing the
liquor. From the smell, she had known it was a strong
spice liquor; she hoped it would slow her involuntary
facial movements and her body language, both of
which Viest was using to read her. "We kept hearing
rumors about this place, and I came to see if any of it

was true. There's nothing like it in the Tingel Arm."
Her voice came out a little raw from the liquor.

Viest considered her thoughtfully. "You don't have
a clearinghouse? Seems inefficient."

They had chosen the Tingel Arm because Han's
knowledge of the pirate activity there was suspiciously extensive, and he had filled Leia in while the
Aegis was in hyperspace. Leia was able to reply confidently, "Nothing on this scale. The clearinghouses
there don't have a permanent site—they have to keep
moving around. There was a station platform that
operated for a while, but it was raided by the CorpSec.
Very inconvenient." She added, "Do you have much
trouble with the Empire?"

Viest's eyes hooded, just a touch. Leia wouldn't
have noticed if she hadn't been looking for it. Viest
said, "Not out here, that's why we picked this spot.
But many of the ships that bring their cargoes here
travel the Corellian Run and the Hydian Way, and
they've had a number of close calls. We're careful, if
that's what you're asking." Leia bet there were plenty
of ships here that would flee at the first hint of an
Imperial presence, but she wondered just what Viest's
personal relationship with the Empire was. The
woman was too opaque for her to tell if that minute
reaction to her question had been fear or hate or
something else.

Viest changed the subject smoothly. "How did you
meet up with Captain Metara, here?"

She kept directing her questions toward Leia, ignoring Metara, and Leia knew that wasn't a good
sign. Metara was supposed to be Viest's new business

associate, yet Viest was treating her almost like an underling.

"Our families were acquainted, back on Alderaan," Leia replied. "When I came to this area, we ran into each other by accident."

Viest's gaze went from Leia to Metara and back, and her smooth brow furrowed ever so slightly. Viest asked Metara, "So you want to work with her people instead of mine?"

As Leia had expected, Viest hadn't pried any further into the connection between them. She had read the truth off the faint movements of their eyes and expressions and didn't know enough about Alderaan to ask any revealing questions. That was a moment of relief, though Leia tried not to show it.

The relief was short-lived. Metara hesitated for a bare instant and then said, "Yes," and glanced at Leia.

You didn't need to be a Lorrdian to read that one. But all Viest would get out of it was that Metara was conflicted about working with Leia, which wouldn't hurt their story.

"And how do you plan to get out of your arrangement with me?" Viest asked.

It was a deceptively easygoing question, and Leia tensed. Metara said, "We thought you could tell us what payment, or arrangement, you would be willing to accept, to release my ship from its debt."

Viest sipped her liquor. Then she turned back to Leia. "You looking to bring your cargoes through here?"

"I hadn't thought about it," Leia told her, again truthfully. "Are you offering a deal?"

Viest gave her an edged smile. "Well, we're awfully particular."

Leia matched her smile. "So am I." She decided to take a chance, turn the conversation back toward Viest. "There was a crew and passengers on that merchant ship that Metara captured. Do you run sentients through here, then?" This could be a difficult moment, if Leia hadn't accurately judged the situation. Lorrdians as a culture had a history of being virulently opposed to slavery, but that didn't mean the flightmaster shared that belief.

Viest frowned, but it was in thought rather than disgust. "When we can. Not much market around here, so we have to rely on the slaving guilds as subcontractors. You?"

"No. But we might be looking to get into it. I wanted to take a look at a working operation, see if something similar would be feasible for us." This was an even more tenuous combination of a little truth and a lot of lie, and Leia hoped Viest would interpret any faint signs of agitation on her part as normal criminal caginess.

Instead of answering, Viest poured herself another drink and lifted the bottle inquiringly. Keeping her expression neutral, Leia held out her glass for a refill, while silently cursing her own impatience. *I think I made a mistake.*

After a short time Han, Sian, and Terae rounded a curve in the docking ring corridor and found themselves out of sight and earshot of the guards at the bay doors. There seemed no benefit to staying up here, so Han hung the grappling hook over the edge of the droid track and they climbed the three meters to the corridor floor. Once they were down, as he was storing the hook and fibercord in the satchel, Terae whispered, "What are we supposed to do if someone sees us?"

"Act like we belong here," Han told her. It seemed pretty obvious. With so many ships berthed here or in orbit, there was no way anyone could keep track of who might be wandering around, and it wasn't as if the pirates wore uniforms. "That should be easy for you."

Terae stiffened in offense, but she couldn't manage to find a reply before Han and Sian started down the corridor.

The place was quiet, shadowy, and daunting, and stank of rot and bad recycled air. Though Han had seen worse. The closed bay doors they passed seemed weirdly menacing, as if they concealed something other than empty docking chambers. He was reminded of old stories of dead ports and space stations, abandoned due to plagues or strange catastrophes, and what happened to the idiot crews who landed on them anyway. He could tell Terae was a little unnerved and trying unsuccessfully to hide it. Sian walked with one hand hooked on her blaster like a sensible person, her expression giving nothing away.

Han heard voices and dissonant music echoing from somewhere and then the docking ring split, one section ending in a wall of rock while the second turned into a ramp that curved down to a junction of three corridors. Spot-lumas floated around, lighting the area. And in there, a party was going on.

In the middle of the junction a large piece of machinery lay on its side, so gutted that Han almost couldn't tell what it was from this angle. Then he spotted the arms with mounted tool extensions and thought it must be an old-style mining droid. A bar had been set up inside the gutted machine, and two pale yellow Bith, whose height and large heads made them stand out above the crowd, were serving liquor out of pressure containers. The customers sat on makeshift chairs and tables that had clearly been fashioned from leftover pieces of the dead droid. Off to the side, under an awning made from the domes that had once covered the droid's repulsors, a group of musicians played.

Han swore under his breath. There was no way around this spot without backtracking past the guards at the *Aegis*'s bay doors. Keeping her voice low, Sian asked, "We're going to have to go through that?"

"Yeah." Han wasn't thrilled about it. He only hoped that he was right about this place getting so much traffic that there was no way to tell who should be here and who shouldn't. And that this wasn't a private, invitation-only party.

Terae stepped forward to look down on the bar. "Since we have to go down there anyway, you think we could ask someone where they keep the prisoners?"

Sian said, "*You* could ask them."

Terae glared at her and started to make an angry reply, but Sian continued, "No, I'm serious. You're supposed to be working with these people. Ask them what you do with a captured merchant crew."

Terae hesitated, then pasted a tough expression on her face. "All right, I will."

"Just watch what you say," Han told her.

Terae's demeanor clearly conveyed that she didn't want or need his advice. As she started down the ramp, Han found himself exchanging an exasperated look with Sian. *These kids really have no clue what kind of game they've bought into.* He wondered if Metara did.

As they walked down the ramp, some of the drinkers paused to eye them, but nobody objected to their arrival. There were a variety of beings scattered around the seating area, a few Han recognized as being from the Mid Rim, like the reptilian Trandoshan, but most others were from farther afield. Near the band, lounging around or dancing languidly, were a number of sentients—some human—wearing slave collars. They were also wearing a lot fewer clothes than any of the patrons at the tables, so it was pretty easy to guess what kind of entertainment they were there to provide.

Han led the way up to the makeshift serving area, mostly to have something to do while scoping out the crowd. The mix of strong, acrid scents from the pressure containers made his throat itch, but it was actually a relief from the rot and mold in the air. The Bith who was serving handed them metal cups without asking what they wanted. Han sniffed his and found it was some kind of alcohol laced with ryll, and strong enough that the fumes almost made his eyeballs melt. The Bith didn't ask for payment, and no money was exchanging hands anywhere in the bar, leading Han to believe this must be a service provided free for the crews who docked here.

Terae downed half her drink in one shot, then split off to approach a group of aliens whom Han recognized as Letaki: bulbous heads, four eyes, beaked mouths that looked like they'd make drinking uncomfortable but not—judging from the drunken way they were waving their tentacles around—impossible. Good choice, he thought: they would likely be too unfamiliar with human expressions to find Terae's behavior suspicious. Han made a mental note not to file Terae away as too ignorant to be dangerous, despite her naïveté about the *Aegis*'s current activities.

Han left the bar to look for a spot away from the band area and out of earshot of others, where he and Sian could blend in with the scenery. Near the edge of the crowd, he found a bench made out of one of the dead droid's armatures, and he and Sian took seats on it.

Sian tasted her drink and grimaced. Han didn't know her well. He had seen her on the *Independence* a few times, when he was killing time with Luke and the other pilots. Watching Terae and keeping her voice low, she said, "Solo, do you think the Princess has a chance of pulling this off?"

"Of getting the flightmaster to let us leave? Maybe." Han figured it was far more likely that they would have to blast their way out at some point. He just hoped they could find a way to do it that wouldn't involve being blown to pieces by all the heavily armed and probably twitchy trigger-fingered ships in orbit.

"No, I mean, does she have a chance of recruiting these Alderaanians into the Alliance?"

Han thought there wasn't much chance of that. He thought Leia more than capable of convincing some of the individual crew members to give up piracy, but as a group they were too stubborn and too attached to Metara. Since saying so felt like he would be undermining Leia without her being there to defend herself, he said, "I don't know. And as long as we get out of here, I don't care."

"I don't think Metara is going to change her mind. And I talked to some of the crew." Sian shook her head. "It's just . . . Maybe I don't understand where they're coming from. My family didn't want me to join the Alliance. They aren't Imperials, but they're comfortable on Commenor and they don't believe in rocking the ship. But I saw and heard enough about the Empire that I knew I had to do something. I don't know how I would have felt if . . . Well, if my home had been destroyed, much less the whole planet, nothing could have stopped me from joining the Alliance to kill as many Imperials as I could. I can't imagine just sitting on the sidelines."

Han figured that if there was anything that could get someone to risk it all and join the Rebel Alliance, it would be having their home planet shot out from under them by the Empire. But just because Sian couldn't imagine something didn't mean there weren't people who would do it. He had seen the Alderaanians on Yavin and with the fleet go through shock and survivor guilt, breaking down, burying themselves in their work, or dedicating themselves to revenge.

Leia, though, was a special case. She was the only one who had watched it happen from the front-row seat of the Death Star, and she was the only one who felt personally responsible for it. It was too much for one person, even Leia, and there were times when he had seen the pain of it tearing at her. It frustrated him that she felt it was somehow all her fault, but he knew there was nothing he could say about it that wouldn't make it worse, or just lead to a shouting match.

She was also the only one who might have a chance of cracking Metara's defenses, but Han couldn't shake the feeling that it was all going to end in disaster. Sian was still waiting for a reply, so he just said, "She might break Metara down—there's no telling yet."

Sian sighed. "I know the Princess is tough, tougher than most people realize. But I don't know if thinking she can talk sense to Metara is irrational or . . . inspired."

"I wonder that a lot myself," Han admitted. Some days things did fall more on the irrational end of the scale. Though he was pretty certain Leia felt the same way about him, probably with more reason.

They watched Terae work the Letaki crew. Han tossed his drink back just to get rid of it. Sian managed to unobtrusively pour the rest of hers into the armature's innards.

Terae returned, her face flushed from the liquor, and said, "They told me how it works. We need to go down this way, and then cut back toward the docking ring."

They left the junction and the party behind and started down the ramp. It was darker through this section, the floating lumas less frequent, and there was more debris in the corridor. Smaller doorways led to corridors that were shrouded in darkness or blocked by rubble and metal debris. This place was like a large and unappealing shadowport, only you *knew* that everybody was a pirate, instead of just suspecting it. Han felt his nerves itch even worse than they had before and wished he had brought Chewie. It had seemed more important at the time to get the sensor jammer installed immediately, mostly because he was afraid someone would change their mind and pull it for a more important ship. There were people in the Alliance who didn't like the fact that Princess Leia Organa kept company with a Corellian smuggler, and none of them would be happy that the *Falcon* had gotten one of the coveted jammers, even though it had been in payment for services rendered.

And maybe spending so much time with the Alliance fleet had gotten him out of the habit of places like this. Han was getting too used to being able to walk around without worrying about getting shot in the back or worse. *You're losing your edge, Solo,* he told himself. *You've got to do something about that.*

Once they were well out of earshot of the bar, Terae said, "We were on the right track—the holding area is near where the *Wastrel* docked. They bring the people they capture here, mostly crews and passengers off ships, but some of the bigger pirates will raid small backwater settlements. They hold them here until one of the slaving guild ships comes to collect them. The slavers pick who they want and bargain with the flightmaster, who takes the payment and parcels it out to the individual crews. No one is happy with the system, from what I could tell. They all think the flightmaster is cheating them."

"Of course the flightmaster's cheating them," Han said. "That's the only reason you set up a system like that—so you can cheat everybody dumb enough to use it."

Sian said, "What do they do with the people the slavers don't want?"

Terae shook her head. "I didn't ask."

Han had no intention of letting her get away with that. "They get spaced. Or if they're lucky, they get shot and then spaced," he said. "What did you think?"

Terae pressed her lips together, then drew breath to answer.

That was when the first figure dropped out of the ceiling. Han ducked sideways and drew his blaster; he fired at the two nearest and hit one. Their attackers were dressed in filthy dark clothing, their heads covered, so ragged Han couldn't tell if they were human or not. They were armed only with old tools, which would have been almost laughable except for the fact that one of those tools was a hand rock drill. One landed on Sian, but she had her hand on her blaster and fired it through the holster as she went down. Wounded in the leg, her assailant jerked backward off her, and she scrambled to her feet.

Terae wrestled with one while another danced around, trying to hit her with an arc wrench. Han shot the dancer, then something hit him from behind hard enough to knock him flat, though pure survival instinct made him keep his grip on his blaster. He twisted and rolled and managed to grab the pry bar with his free hand before it hit his skull. The guy was panting in his face, growling, but Han was mad, too.

He jerked his blaster down and fired point-blank. The guy went limp with a cry, and Han wrenched the pry bar away and tossed the body off him. Another landed on him before he could get up, but Sian kicked that attacker in the head. Han shoved him off and rolled to his feet.

Four of their attackers sprawled unmoving on the floor, two limped rapidly off into the shadows, and one had a blaster burn in his leg and struggled to stand. Someone yelled an incomprehensible order and the others broke off, bolting for the nearest openings. Two paused to grab the wounded one and haul him away. Han watched them disappear down the shadowy tunnels and then pivoted, making sure no others were nearby. He remembered to look up this time, too.

Terae eased up out of a crouch and demanded, "What was that?"

Breathing hard, Sian looked at Han. "Dock thieves?"

"Yeah." Han nodded. He leaned down to pick up his satchel. "That's what happens when a pirate ship maroons crew here and they can't find another berth." He tried not to care about the way they had dragged their wounded friend off. He doubted things were bad enough that they meant to eat the guy, so they had probably been together long enough to bond. He shook off the uncomfortable thought. It just meant that they would be all the more desperate. It was a pointed little reminder of the times he and Chewie had come close to losing the *Falcon* in a port where their options would have been just as limited.

Sian nodded grimly, carefully watching the grids

overhead. Terae started to speak, her face set as if she wanted to argue, then she shook her head.

Han hoped Terae was enjoying the tour she was getting here of the less thrilling aspects of pirate life. But all he said was, "We need to keep moving."

Viest savored her drink, and Leia worked on calming thoughts to keep her face and her body language under control. From Viest's lack of reaction, she must not have betrayed herself too badly. But something in her face or voice must have indicated too high a degree of interest in the merchant captives. Finally Viest asked, "So do you want stock from us? Or you want to buy into our operation?"

She calls them "stock," as if they were bales of plant fiber. Leia hoped the involuntary curl of her upper lip would be interpreted as a superior smile. "Just testing the waters."

"But we aren't talking about the proposition on the table, are we?" Viest said. She focused on Metara. "So why do you want to work with her and not me?"

Metara shrugged and took a sip of her drink. Leia clearly read that as stalling for time to formulate an answer and had no doubt Viest did, too. Finally Metara said, "Leia and I have a connection, that's all." She hadn't stumbled over Leia's first name, as far as Leia could tell. Viest would sense any hesitation. Metara added, "I pay my debts, and I'm sure we can come to an arrangement. With the augmentations you purchased for my ship, I can easily make enough to pay you back with whatever interest you ask for."

Watching Viest's expression, Leia didn't think that

was going to go over well. This was why she had
asked Metara to let her handle the negotiation. At
least she had the consolation of knowing her annoyance would be correctly interpreted by Viest.

"So it's just that simple, is it?" Viest said. "I invite
you into my business, trust you with my personal
funds to repair and upgrade your ship, and you want
to cut me off without a second thought when an old
friend comes along."

Metara stared. "I'm sorry. But our arrangement is
just business. It's not a matter of personal loyalty."

Viest lifted a brow. "It is to me."

Leia let go of her last hope of still pulling off her
original plan. Viest was clearly exaggerating her
pique but also clearly had no intention of letting Metara out of her agreement, at least not in this conversation.

"If a buyout isn't to your liking," Leia said, "we
can still all three do business together. I'm open to
suggestions." And she really was open to suggestions,
because unless she thought of something else, they
were going to lose the merchant crew to slavers and
be stuck on this rock for a long time.

Viest considered them both for a moment, then set
her glass aside. "If we're going to do business, then
we'll need to get to know you better."

Leia didn't like the sound of that. There was just a
little too much anticipation in Viest's voice. "I thought
that's what we've been doing here."

"That we have," Viest said, and smiled in a predatory way that she made no attempt to conceal. "But I
like to have my new partners show all of us their mettle."

Mettle, really? Yes, this wasn't going to be good. Leia kept her voice only mildly interested. "And how do you do that?"

"We play a game," Viest said. "Or, they—you—play a game."

On the surface, a game didn't sound nearly as bad as the other array of horrible things that had paraded through Leia's imagination in the past moment. But something in Viest's expression told Leia that it might just be worse. "What sort of game?"

"A test of skill and reflexes." Viest nodded toward the port that overlooked the dark space beyond the control center. "The arena is in the center of the mine. The grav generators are turned off there, so it makes a good zero-g playing field." Her eyes narrowed. "Makes a good way to tell the serious players from the ones who just like to talk."

Leia decided there was no reason for her persona to go along with this, especially since it had trap written all over it. Viest knew they were lying, but she wasn't quite sure just what they were lying about. If they were lucky, Viest thought this was only an attempt to cheat her out of her investment in the *Aegis*. Not that the consequences of that would be any less danger-ous, but at least Viest wouldn't suspect Alliance in-volvement. Leia said, "We don't go in for the frivolous much, where I'm from." Also a strictly true state-ment.

"Let me sweeten the deal for you," Viest said. She looked as if she had no intention of being talked out of this but would find it amusing if they tried. "If both of you play and win, I'll give you my interest in Metara and her ship, free and clear."

That deal was a little too sweet, Leia thought. Best to decline and try to offer a payment again. But before she could reply, Metara said, "If you throw in the merchant ship we captured for you and its crew, you have a deal." She glanced at Leia. "And I'll play alone, or with one of my crew."

Leia found herself meeting Viest's complacent gaze. She let herself smile faintly, though she was thinking, *I hate working with amateurs.* Viest knew everything that Metara really wanted now, and would make her pay dearly for it. And she knew, too, that Metara had a stake in protecting Leia. That Leia was not just another prospective business partner or former acquaintance willing to help fund Metara's piracy; that Metara cared about her safety.

Viest's smile was now considerably more satisfied. "It's a deal—if Leia here plays our game, too."

There was no choice. Leia lifted her glass in salute, then downed its contents. The drink burned her throat and sat heavily in her stomach. Her voice grated as she said, "I'm happy to oblige."

Viest raised her glass to Leia. "Good."

Han had been hearing voices and movement ahead for a while; then the tunnel opened into a huge docking and cargo area. "This is just dandy," he muttered under his breath.

The ramp they were on branched off into a gallery along a row of bay doors, and the main branch led down to a loading area where there were several openings to huge tunnels. Several of the derelict repulsor guide tracks stretched across the loading area, and the floor held stacks of pressure crates and barrels of all sizes. A number of aging, slow-moving droids wandered among them, sorting them and rearranging the piles. A group of pirates stood in the middle of all the activity, arguing and emphasizing their disagreement by pointing at piles and shouting.

Some of this cargo might have come from the merchant the *Wastrel* had brought in, but there was clearly too much here for a freighter that size. This looked like either one large cargo transport or maybe the combined spoils of several smaller ships.

Watching the scene uneasily, Terae said, "The Letaki didn't say which tunnel to take, just that it was down here."

Everyone in the loading area looked angry and suspicious, and as far as Han could see they were all armed. "We can't just wander down there like tourists," he said. "We need to find a map."

Sian asked, "You think they're using the old mine's detention center? That would be marked on a map."

"Maybe." A mine this big must have had some kind of facility to deal with the miners who stole or got drunk or did spice or got into fights about stealing and drinking and doing spice. "If it's big enough."

"I saw a small tunnel marked for engineering admin back there," Terae said. "Some of the lumas were still lit, so it might be worth a try. But to get to it, we're going to have to go back through that dark area where the castaways were."

"The dark area doesn't have anything to do with it," Han told her. "Those castaways will be all over this place. Come on."

CHAPTER SEVEN

AFTER SEARCHING TWO of the side corridors, Han, Sian, and Terae found a rock-carved chamber marked TECH SERVICES 112. It looked like it had been trashed in a drunken party, which probably meant there wasn't anything left here that was useful. They split up to search, and after a moment Sian found some general access terminals back against the far wall, tucked under a small rock outcropping.

One still had working power cells and Han managed to get it turned on, but the holoimage was too obscured by static to see. He had to pry open the console and clean a few contacts, but finally an old mining company's logo swam into focus. Han was guessing that anything important the system could access, like codes for the mining equipment or docking rings or storage, would be access-protected, but an internal map should be readily available.

After a little poking around in the admin screens and arguing with Terae about the most likely sections to try, they found it. The map blossomed above the vid plate, and the asteroid's interior glowed in green and red in the rotating image. Han squinted at it, trying to read the tiny print. The thing wouldn't enlarge.

The mine was a maze of odd-sized chambers and shafts, some straight and some in long spirals. Corridors were marked as traverses and haulage tunnels, many of the chambers had names instead of designations, and levels seemed to be called floors and were divided into upper, lower, and middle in some system Han couldn't easily decipher. Gravity was marked as fluctuating throughout, with lighter levels in the bigger shafts and spirals and many of the haulage tunnels. The middle of the place was a giant cavern, curving up through the whole center of the asteroid for hundreds of meters.

Terae held up her comlink to record it, and angled her head, trying to see the labels. "I think that's a brig, but it's way over on the other side."

"Yes, but look here." Sian pointed to an area not far from their current location. "That's all marked as living quarters, and it's in the right place, where the Letaki told you."

"I bet they converted it into a slave pen," Han said, ignoring Terae's wince at the blunt terminology. He traced the corridor layout around it and saw there was only one way in: the center tunnel that led from the loading area where the pirates had been fighting over their cargoes. Getting near that wasn't going to be easy.

But the map showed a very narrow tunnel running directly beneath the living quarters all the way to the center of the asteroid. It was crossed by quite a few other tunnels, including one traverse that they should be able to get to from here. There were no chambers off the tunnel, and it was weirdly straight, where everything else curved or spiraled through the rock. "Think that's a maintenance access?" Han said.

"It looks like one." Sian tried to adjust the size again, but the touch pad didn't respond. She leaned close and squinted. "It says WASTE DISPOSAL."

Han nodded to himself. "If we can get into it, then work our way back up to where we think the slave pen is—" He cut himself off sharply as a clanking sounded from outside the chamber.

"Get down," he whispered, hitting the main power on the console. The map dissolved as they crouched down to take cover behind the trashed equipment. Carefully lifting his head just enough, Han saw an old maintenance droid rattle slowly past the doorway. It had multiple arms and seemed to be trying unsuccessfully to clean the floor of the corridor. He waited, but nothing followed it. "Okay, we're clear."

"You really think those half-dead droids are reporting to the pirates?" Terae asked. She got to her feet, pointedly dusting off her pants. Han thought she was mostly mad that she had obeyed a command from him without thinking twice.

"Maybe," he told her. "I don't want to bet my life on it. You can run out and shoot at that one if you want. Just give us time to get out of here before you do it."

Terae glared at him, and Sian said, "The ones down in the loading area were sure reporting to the pirates." She reached the console first and tried to turn it back on. It just beeped weakly at her. "That's it for this console. Want to try another?"

What Han wanted was not to waste any more time.

He asked Terae, "Did you get a good copy of the map?" At her nod, he continued, "Then let's go."

After Viest finished her drink, she called the Aqualish and some more guards to take Leia and Metara down to the game arena. She said, "I'll join you shortly," and then added, "Oh, leave your weapons here. We don't let any of the players go armed. We wouldn't want any accidents."

Metara and Leia handed over their blasters, and grimly, Leia relinquished her hold-out pistol when the pirates' surprisingly state-of-the-art weapons scanner found it in the holster concealed just above her right boot.

The Aqualish and the other guards led them to a lift tube at the far side of the control center. The other pirates in the room watched them with a worrying combination of anticipation and unease. Leia found herself wondering just what allegiance they owed to Viest, if their loyalty was bought with threats or gifts or both.

When they were inside the lift tube, Leia asked, "What exactly is this game?"

"That's for Viest to tell you," the Aqualish said, but added, "Anybody else says anything about it, they end up playing it with you."

That wasn't encouraging. And judging from the uneasy way the other guards were reacting, it was true. Leia made her voice dry. "So is it really a game, or just an exciting way for Viest to execute people she doesn't care for?"

The Aqualish made a coughing noise that Leia realized was bitter laughter. "It's both. If she wants to take you on as personal crew, or if you ask to do business with her and she isn't sure about you, she makes you play. That part is true."

He didn't seem to approve. "You sound like you speak from experience," Leia said. "Bad experience."

One of the other guards shifted uneasily, as if even enforced association with people who were speaking about it was dangerous. The Aqualish looked down at her, his eyes going half lidded to conceal any emotion. "My captain played. Now I'm stuck here."

That was what Leia had thought it might be. Metara glanced at her, brow furrowed with concern.

They stopped at a level some distance below the control center and followed the Aqualish out onto a long gallery. It looked down into the bottom of the giant cavern that formed the center of the asteroid.

The huge space was cooler than the tunnels had been, and the air was even more damp; rivulets ran down the slabs of cut stone, leaving white and red mineral streaks. The whole place smelled of wet dirt, burned metal, and ozone. Leia blinked and found herself staring upward. The giant mining machinery hung overhead, just shadowy shapes in the dimness. There were diggers with drills as large as the *Gamble,* and extractors with scoops that could have carried the *Aegis.*

"Wait here," the Aqualish told them, and headed back toward the lift tube.

Above the gallery, linked to it by a set of curving metal stairs, was a smaller balcony, with couches and chairs arranged on it. It was empty at the moment, but Leia guessed it was where the spectators would

sit. A few guards stood around on the gallery, some
human and others of different species, all holding
blast rifles. The only other unarmed people in the
chamber were two pairs of pirates, standing at opposite ends of the gallery. They had to be the other
players.

Two of them were members of an amphibious species that Leia recognized as Ishori, from a world in
the Core. They were tall and slim, with green-gray
skin, long narrow skulls, no noses, and the marks of
gills on their cheeks and throats. Feathery fins ran
down their arms and legs. Both wore metal devices on
their hands, and Leia at first thought they were weapons, but then she realized they had only three fingers
on each hand; the devices were prosthetics, giving
them three more fingers to make it easier to use stan-
dardized equipment.

The other two were the tough-looking Twi'lek
woman Leia had seen in the docking ring and a somewhat grungy young human man. The Twi'lek had her
arms folded and was glaring angrily at the playing
field.

The amphibians didn't seem happy to be here, either, talking to each other in soft worried voices and
seeming agitated. So the Aqualish had been telling the
truth, Leia thought. Either the other players were
being punished, or they were new to the clearinghouse and were being forced to do this before they
could join Viest's crew or conduct business here. She
would bet they were all small-time operators, with
modest ships and little in the way of resources or status. She doubted Viest could force the captains of the

large powerful ships like the *Wastrel* to dance to her tune this way.

Metara touched Leia's arm to get her attention. "I think that must be their game arena."

Looking down, Leia realized that a few pieces of the seemingly random equipment were containment-field generators, kept in place by repulsor anchors. Once activated, they would probably form a sphere around the central area. Suspended inside it, also on repulsor anchors, were some sort of heavy mining devices, all shaped like big rings about three meters wide.

"I don't like the look of that," Leia said. There was something else floating inside the field area, something small; squinting, Leia saw that it was a sensor remote. She would bet that the object of the game was going to be to capture or destroy that remote, probably while it was shooting at them. But there had to be another complication. "Those rings—do you have any idea what they are?"

"For lifting something large, or processing ore . . ." Metara trailed off, and she and Leia exchanged a look. Leia wasn't sure what sort of processing the rings would do, but she was certain it wouldn't have a pleasant effect on a sentient body.

"The others might know," Leia said, and started over to the Twi'lek's team. But a human guard stepped in front of her, barring her way.

"No talking to the others."

It made sense to keep the players from speaking with one another beforehand. If Leia had had a chance to pay them off or bargain with them to throw the game, she would certainly have taken it. "Are they proving their mettle for Viest, too?" she asked.

His expression twisted with amusement. "She is." With his blast rifle still casually pointed in Leia's direction, he nodded toward the Twi'lek, then jerked his head toward the Ishori. "Those two got their ship and crew indentured by another captain, and they're trying to get the flightmaster to buy them out of it." He jerked the gun at her. "Get back to your place."

"Lovely," she muttered, and returned to Metara's side.

Leia waited until the nearest guards had started talking among themselves, then lowered her voice to say carefully, "Metara, I appreciate the thought, but you should not have volunteered for this."

Metara wore the calm, solemn expression of someone who had absolutely no idea she had made a terrible tactical error. "I'm sorry, I didn't mean for you to be included. I'll do my best to protect you, I swear it."

Leia decided to ignore that in the interest of keeping her carefully cultivated patience. "Did you notice that Viest is a Lorrdian? Have you ever heard of Lorrdian readers?"

Metara shook her head slightly, confused. "I know Lorrdians are supposed to be good at reading body language—"

"Some of them are more than good at it; some of them make a living at it. And they're excellent at distinguishing truth from lies." Leia wondered what Viest's history was, how she had ended up here. If Viest had been hired—or bought—to be some pirate leader's reader and had eventually managed to use her skills to rise to this position, she would be even more dangerous.

Metara took that in but didn't appear to entirely believe it. "She knew we were lying? Why didn't she have us killed immediately?"

"Because she didn't know what we were lying about, and she wants to find out before she kills us." Leia saw that Metara at least seemed to be taking her warning seriously. "She picked up on the fact that you wanted to protect me, so . . . you need to stop that." It wasn't a very effective or specific request, but Leia felt compelled to make it.

Her expression turning stubborn, Metara shook her head. "I can't let anything happen to you. It's my fault that you're here at all."

Leia agreed that it was Metara's fault, but there was no point in dwelling on it. "If we're going to salvage this situation, you have to let me take care of myself."

Metara drew breath for what was clearly going to be an argument. Leia fixed her with the steely expression that was usually effective on everyone but Han Solo, and Metara let the breath out. "I'll try, Your Hi—Leia."

The lift tube opened again and Viest stepped out, followed by about a dozen assorted pirates. Most of the others wandered up to the spectator area, but Viest strolled over to Leia and Metara. "The object is to defeat the remote," she explained. "It will be firing high-energy training pulses—not strong enough to wound, but they certainly hurt."

Leia felt some relief that the object was not to slaughter the opposing players. "And those rings?"

she asked. "I'm assuming they're some sort of ore processor. What are they for?"

Viest smiled. "They're called crushers. Just to add a little extra tension."

Oh, we're calling it tension, *are we?* "You really force new business associates to do this?" Leia asked. "Why?"

Viest's expression did something complicated and then went blank. It probably would have been crystal clear to another Lorrdian, but it was completely opaque to Leia. She did, however, think it had been a very long time since anyone had asked Viest to explain her actions. "As I said, we like to test their mettle."

Leia inclined her head in acknowledgment. So Viest did it for fun, then. Because she enjoyed seeing desperate people struggle. Leia had thought of Viest as ruthless, but now she wondered just how twisted the woman was. "So if we lose, we can still discuss an arrangement?"

Viest shrugged. "That will depend."

Leia prodded a little harder. "On whether we survive."

Viest abruptly decided to stop playing with her. "Exactly."

Leia met her gaze. "Then I look forward to discussing an arrangement with you when we win."

They found the maintenance tunnel or, as Han now thought of it, the dark, dank hole in the floor.

The traverse corridor they had followed here had bridged a couple of low-gravity shafts, and the tunnel entrance could almost be mistaken for another one. The access to it was just a ragged hole in the rock. They had figured out that a traverse was meant for people and droids to travel from one part of the mine to another, and that a haulage tunnel was meant for automated ore carts. The difference was that haulage tunnels had either a grid or sensors to guide the carts, rough uneven floors, and no lumas. Han thought that someone smart enough to set up camp here and sell handlights and glow rods would make a hell of a lot more credits than the average pirate.

Now he sat on his heels and flashed his light down into the hole. He could make out metal support panels fastened onto the rock, with vents beneath them. The tunnel was about three meters wide and looked like it was meant for droids to move refuse loads. He said, "I'll go. You two wait up here."

Terae frowned but didn't argue. Sian lifted a brow at him. "You sure?"

Han wanted somebody up here to take the word back if he got caught. "I'm just gonna take a look, see if we can actually use it to get near the slave pen. I don't need help for that." He dropped down into the tunnel.

He started back in the direction of the docking ring, toward where they thought the slave pen was located. After a short distance, the dim light that fell from the access hole started to fade. It was dead quiet, and the back of his neck prickled with unease.

Han caught movement low to the ground, just at the edge of the light's beam. He froze and flashed the light down. A small, square shape scuttled by. He snorted in relief, feeling his skin itch with the unused burst of adrenaline.

It was a little cleaning droid, limping along, scraping mold off the stone floor. It didn't show any interest in him, and small cleaners like that usually didn't have any higher reasoning functions. Han kept walking.

After a short distance it became apparent that there were dozens of cleaning droids, some of them creeping around slowly, barely functioning, but not much else. Playing his light over the tunnel roof, he could see an occasional sealed hatch, with no controls and no way to open them. He suspected they were meant for droids who would open them with coded signals from below, for waste collection. Then a draft of recycled air told him there was another hole somewhere.

After a moment of flashing his light around, he found a meter-square opening in the ceiling near the wall. It couldn't lead to the slave pen or a guard station; the space above it was silent and almost completely dark. But it did have a ladder below it, built into the tunnel wall, as if it was meant for an actual living being and not just hauler droids.

Han climbed the ladder and cautiously poked his head and his light out, but saw only another traverse corridor. Two dying lumas floating aimlessly around, providing only dim light. It didn't look any more inhabited than the other traverse corridor. They were probably lucky the place was so badly sealed off that it was impossible to depressurize the unused areas, or it would have been far more difficult to move through here. Han filed the access away for future reference if needed and dropped back down to continue up the tunnel.

Right at the point where he was beginning to think this idea was a bust, he saw a faint glow ahead.

As he drew closer, he saw that the light fell through a doorway in the side of the passage. It was about a head shorter than he was, and he had to duck to step through. The new corridor looked like another maintenance passage for mechanicals, with panels hanging off the walls and slots where components had been removed; a heavy smell of mold hung in the stale air. The light grew brighter as he continued, coming from an overhead source somewhere ahead.

He found it at the end: a half-meter-square grid at the top of a short shaft. The sides bore signs that something here had been removed, leaving behind gouges, clamps, and broken fastenings. He wasn't sure what the original purpose had been, but if he was right that the space above was living quarters, this shaft might have been another kind of waste-disposal arrangement. He could hear quiet voices.

He switched his light off and tucked it away in the satchel. Then he jumped, caught hold of a bar at the bottom of the shaft, and climbed the rough projections in the wall to just below the grid. From this angle he could see there was another grid above it, this one of fine mesh, and it had been inexpertly but solidly welded into place. The voices were a little louder, and he could hear people moving around.

Suddenly he found himself looking up at a human woman. She gasped and jerked back, then leaned forward to stare at him. Now he saw that she was actually Arkanian, not human: she had the distinctive white hair and eyes, and the claws on her hands. Her clothes were torn and stained, and she wasn't armed—and she hadn't shouted for help at the sight of him, so he was guessing she wasn't here voluntarily. Keeping his voice low, he said, "Hey, I'm looking for the prisoners' lockup. This it?"

The Arkanian spun around and whispered urgently, "There's someone down here!"

There were more gasps and quiet exclamations, and then suddenly a dozen other faces, human and other sentients, peered down at him. The strange thing was, he actually recognized one of the faces. Startled, he said, "Davit?"

"Solo!" Kearn-sa'Davit crouched down close to the grid. He was a Videllan, with gold-brown skin of a leathery texture, a high forehead curving back to a fringe of fluffy golden hair, a beard, and large, expressive eyes with high, tufted brows. "What are you doing here?"

"Yeah, I was about to ask *you* that," Han said. "You were on that merchant ship?" Davit was the Alliance contact who had arranged the meeting with the local merchant consortium to get the construction materials for Echo Base, though of course the merchants hadn't known what their cargoes were going to be used for. Han had had some suspicions of Davit, but the fact that he was currently locked up in a pirates' slave pen mitigated his instinctive distrust. "You were coming to meet us on the station?"

"Yes. You followed us here?"

Han adjusted his grip on the bars. "Sort of. Was the whole consortium aboard?"

Davit shook his head. "No, no. Only the Ceelon

Syndicate, and their crew. The others meant to come but changed their plans at the last moment, and took their own vessels, so they were not trapped. At least, I hope not."

This couldn't be a coincidence. "So somebody in the consortium sold you out to the pirates?"

"Of course. It was Janlan. He was aboard our ship, and he was not much pleased with our failure to sur-render immediately when the pirate attacked." Davit made a disgusted gesture. "Despite his shouts that we stop defending ourselves, the others didn't believe he was a traitor until we arrived here and he was con-ducted off for an audience with the pirate leader. He has not returned."

Han hadn't been privy to every detail of the Alli-ance's arrangement for the meeting with the consor-tium, and he really hoped those details hadn't included Leia's presence. "Davit, this is important. Is there any way Janlan knew who specifically was coming to meet with the consortium, any way he could find out?"

"You must not fear—they know we two are only brokers, facilitators of meetings, and that we know little of our employers' business, or who they were sending to seal the agreement." Davit kept his voice even, but Han got the message. None of the mer-chants knew Davit was Alliance, they just thought he was a hired middleman, and he was making certain any of them listening now thought Han was just a hired middleman, too. And none of them knew that Leia or General Willard had been on the ship they were going to the station to meet.

Imperials wouldn't have bought Davit's story, but

pirates and merchants might, at least long enough for them all to get out of here. "Good." Han met Davit's gaze, making sure the Videllan knew Han had gotten the message. "Any chance Janlan talked to the Imperials, too? That he knew where our ship was coming out of hyperspace to get your transmission?"

"No, Solo, Janlan did not know those coordinates. Only I knew them, and I sent the transmission myself. It is part of my service, as a facilitator, to make sure secrets such as that stay secret. If there was a difficulty, it did not originate from the consortium's end." He lifted his brows, but Han didn't explain why he had asked the question.

"As to whether he betrayed us to Imperials . . ." Davit considered it, stroking his beard. "I don't think so. I don't think Janlan would know whom to contact among the Imperials. There is no governor over this area, you know, and not much Imperial presence beyond the occasional patrol or customs ship. Janlan knew the other merchants meant to use the profit from our deal to purchase weapons to defend their ships against the pirates. I think he sold this information in return for promises to leave his trading ships be. He's an idiot if he thinks they will fulfill his bargain. They are more likely to dump him back in here and sell him with the rest of us, once they are certain he knows no more of use to them."

Okay, so there were two different leaks, Han thought. One in the Alliance's communications somewhere, who had told the Imperials where the *Gamble* would be coming out of hyperspace. The other was purely on the consortium side, Janlan selling out his partners for protection from the pirates. "That's good. It means the Imperials don't know we're here."

"That is good, I suppose. Relatively speaking." Davit frowned. "Are you rescuing us or escaping yourself?"

"Both." Han adjusted his hold on the grid, feeling around it for weak points. The bars were thick and strong. The mesh above prevented any chance of handing up weapons and small explosives to the prisoners, at least for the moment. Han could cut through both grids, if he brought a heavy-duty fusioncutter. That meant they would have a way to get the prisoners out, if Leia couldn't talk the pirates into handing the merchants over to the *Aegis*. And while Han had a lot of faith in Leia Organa's level of determination, he had the feeling that they were probably going to do this the hard way. "How many people are up there with you?"

"Thirty-two. Most are from our ship. We lost three on the way here, when they died from wounds received during the battle, and the pirates shot the captain and copilot of our ship when we arrived. There are a few others who have been here longer, who were captured on a passenger ship going to Commenor and were brought here to be sold." Davit added, "They have not put collars on us yet."

That was good news. Han figured the slaving guilds, not the pirates, probably handled that part. He hesitated over how much to tell Davit, and decided not to mention that someone was trying to negotiate for the merchant ship's release. "I don't know yet what's going to happen. Right now, we're stuck on this rock ourselves. We can't get out of dock and make it into hyperspace without getting caught in a tractor beam or blown to pieces."

"At least we have hope now." Davit spread his hands. "That still makes us all better off than what we were before. And Solo, make sure our employers know, whether we can be rescued or not, that I will keep my bond to them."

I won't betray the Alliance, was what Davit was saying. Han's hands were getting sore and he wasn't sure how much longer he could perch here. "Any time I should avoid visiting? Like when the guards come by?"

"Wait." Davit drew back and Han heard him speaking to the other prisoners, checking with the ones who had been here longer. He leaned back over the grid to say, "Their visits are not always regular, but they tend to come about every six to ten standard hours. They don't come inside; they dump the food packets down a small shaft, so there is no chance to jump them."

"Right. Look, it's complicated and I can't make promises, but I'm here with someone who feels responsible for your ship getting caught. If we can help you, we will."

"Ah. Then I wish you luck, and I hope I have the chance to thank your someone in person." Another voice murmured something, and Davit turned to listen. After a moment, he said, "You might have mentioned that earlier." He turned back to Han. "Solo, those who have been here longer say that periodically they hear and feel rumblings under this section of the floor, as if some mechanism passes beneath it. Take care when—if—you return."

"Thanks. See you soon, I hope."

Han dropped to the floor, took his light out again, and made his way back through the passage into the wider tunnel.

He was mostly thinking about logistics. Getting that many people out through this tunnel and to the *Aegis*'s bay would be tricky, but possible.

And after talking to Davit, Han was less and less happy with the idea of leaving him and the others behind in the slave pens. It reminded him too much of what Chewie had gone through. And there had been too many times since then when it could have been him or Chewie trapped and looking at a life of hard labor with a collar designed to kill them if they tried to escape, or a bad death if the slavers decided they were too dangerous to attract buyers. He would leave Davit and the merchants if he had to, to get Leia, Sian—and yes, even Kifar Itran—out of here alive, but he wouldn't like it. The fact that Davit had seemed so understanding about it didn't help, either.

Then Han felt a faint vibration in the stone underfoot. He stopped and listened. From far up the tunnel came a faint clank. *Just another maintenance droid,* he thought.

But suddenly all the little cleaning droids within reach of his light scuttled into the vents at the bottom of the rock walls, one last straggler limping belatedly after the others. *That's not good.*

Taking it as a sign he should get out of there a little faster, Han started to jog. He would take that second access he had found, the one with the ladder. It was much closer than the one where Sian and Terae waited.

Then the clanking turned into the low-frequency rumble of a large repulsor engine.

Han ran faster, but the sound grew louder and louder, echoing off the walls. He risked a look back, and his light framed a big round dark metal wall shooting toward him.

Han swore and almost stumbled. *Yeah, that's a problem.* The brief glimpse told him the thing took up the whole width of the corridor and there was no way he could outrun it. He shoved the light into his satchel to leave his hands free and thought, *You better get this right the first time, Solo.*

He spun around, had time to take a breath, then lunged forward and jumped as the metal wall rushed toward him. He grabbed for the top and caught the rim. Gritting his teeth, he scrabbled to keep his grip on metal that was slick with dust and moisture. A fall would be the end. A squashed, bloody, painful end.

Then his hands found a slot he could actually wrap his fingers around, and his boots found purchase on an uneven projection at the bottom. Breathing hard, his heart pounding almost loud enough to drown out the rumble of the engine, he had time to realize that the thing he was gripping was the front of an automated hauler—for sewage, if the smell of new and ancient decay was any indication. At least, he hoped the blasted thing was automated.

Han crouched down and craned his neck, trying to examine the front of the hauler to see if there was some way to take control of it, or at least an access panel. If there was, he would have to pry it off with his teeth, because it was hard enough to hold on with two hands, let alone one. But there was nothing he could spot.

He turned his head to look over his shoulder, just in time to watch the dimly lit access up into the second traverse fly past. He thought he heard Sian yell, but wasn't sure over the noise of the hauler. If she had seen him, at least they would know where he was—or at least where he had been a moment ago. Not that they would be able to do anything about it. The tunnel ahead was dark, and he had no idea where he was going.

Then suddenly the world rushed down into darkness, and Han's precarious grip on the hauler was his only anchor with reality. He stifled a yell and clung for all he was worth. Belatedly, he realized that there must have been an opening to a vertical tunnel and the hauler had dropped down it, was dropping down it, moving even faster than it had in the tunnel.

Yeah, Solo, this was not one of your better ideas, Han told himself, shaking with the effort of holding on. He just hoped he survived it.

CHAPTER EIGHT

LEIA WATCHED VIEST CLIMB the steps to the balcony spectators' area and join the other members of her entourage already seated there. As if that had been a signal, a technician approached Leia and Metara to hand them repulsor pads for their hands and feet, and stood by while they carefully checked to make sure each pad was working. Once they had, he nodded grimly and went to the next pair of players.

Metara glanced up at Viest, lounging on a couch on the balcony with her hangers-on. "Hopefully she'll keep her word when we win."

Leia wished it was that simple, and that she had any belief whatsoever that Viest would keep her word about anything. "The game is not going to be that easy to win. There has to be another factor."

"Another factor?" Metara frowned, and looked over the arena again. "You mean something to inter-fere with us while we're after the remote? Besides the other players?"

"Like more remotes, or something else," Leia said. "It's mainly the something else I'm worried about." There was nothing they could do about it now but be aware that the rules might change drastically at any moment. "I'll go for the remote; you try to keep the others off me. And please don't get pulverized."

Metara just looked worriedly at Leia. "Please don't take any chances."

Leia didn't reply, because this was yet another argument that she was bone-weary of having. She knew Metara didn't want to be the Alderaanian who got Princess Leia Organa killed, but Leia had been taking responsibility for herself for a long time.

The equipment below started to hum and crackle as the power increased. "Players get ready," the technician shouted.

Following the example of the others, Leia and Metara took off their boots and put on the pads, then spent a few moments getting used to the pressure controls for toes and fingers. Leia saw that the Ishori had to take off their prosthetics to get the pads to fit over their hands, and wondered if that would put them at a disadvantage. She didn't want anyone to be sucked into a crusher, but it would be nice if the lack of prosthetics made it difficult for them to manipulate the pads.

The technician waved the teams forward to the edge of the arena. Leia could feel the fringe of the gravity field, right at the point where it started to dissipate; it lifted her braided hair and made her steps lighter. She wondered how well regulated the gravity field was; if it varied throughout the space, that could affect the performance of the repulsor pads.

The technician explained the rules again, which were as Viest had said: knock the remote, which would be set to fire at them on maximum pain level, through one of

the crushers. It still sounded deceptively simple. Leia
didn't know enough about the Ishori to interpret anything from their expressions or demeanor, but the
Twi'lek looked far grimmer and her human companion
far more worried than the bare description of the game
seemed to warrant. *They know something, or suspect
something.* She wished again that they had been allowed
the chance to talk before the game started.

Then Viest stood, and the technician told them,
"Into the arena."

Leia, Metara, and the others stepped off into the
zero-g field, and Leia felt her stomach give a tiny lurch
at the abrupt transition from near-normal weight to
almost none. She curled her toes and the foot pads
responded; the repulsors pushed her into a gentle glide
into the arena. The propulsion was much faster and
more erratic here in the light-grav area than it had
been up on the rock shelf, and the pad on her left foot
was a bit slow to respond. One of the Ishori and the
human man seemed to be having a little trouble getting both foot pads to respond at the same time, but
the others looked to be getting the hang of it easily.

Along with everyone else, Leia used her hand pads
to stop once they were in the center of the arena. As
all the players hovered in place, the containment field
sprang into life with a sizzle in the damp air and a
strong smell of ozone. The faint glow of it formed a
sphere around the whole arena.

Leia saw Viest draw her blaster and experienced an
adrenaline spike of fear that this all might just have
been an insane buildup for a summary execution.
Then Viest fired toward the top of the chamber and
shouted, "Go!"

Leia swore at herself, and the others dived for the remote. Leia used her foot pads to circle the outside, Metara following her. One of the Ishori reached the remote first, grabbed it despite the volley of stinging blasts it released, and headed straight for the nearest crusher.

Leia swooped to intercept him, and his teammate dived for her. Metara knocked the teammate aside by turning her hand pads on him, and used the repulsors to propel him halfway across the arena. Then she kicked out with a foot, using the repulsor pad to deflect an assault from the male human on the Twi'lek's team. Leia grabbed the Ishori by the legs and swung him around. He lost his grip on the struggling remote and she released him and lunged for it.

She stretched to grab it and it shot her in the right shoulder. Leia had thought she would be able to ignore the sting and just grab the damn thing, but the impact was like being stabbed by a very thin, heated blade. She jerked back, her right arm went numb, and the remote whizzed away.

"Are you all right?" Metara shouted.

"Yes!" Leia snapped. Furious, blinking back tears of pain, she circled after the remote. She flexed her shoulder to get the feeling back. Apparently they had been serious about "maximum pain level." That might be the extra difficulty Viest had wanted to conceal until the last moment, but somehow Leia didn't think so.

Everyone had seen Metara's maneuver, and now they knew how to use the pads for offense and defense. The game became considerably more than just a wrestling match for the remote, with the players swooping around, sending one another spinning across the arena, and propelling the increasingly active remote out of reach. Leia almost managed to push it into a crusher three times, only to have it shoved out of its trajectory or to find herself knocked off course. Sweat was streaming down her back, plastering her hair to her forehead, and her body was covered with stinging bruises from the blasted remote. She was still wary, but so far no one had tried to shove another player into a crusher, and they all seemed to be working under an implied agreement not to try.

Without the threat of the crushers, and with the remote on a less violent setting, she could actually see how this could be an exciting game. For other people, not her.

Leia ducked under the Twi'lek's attempt to send her careening off and came up with a clear path to the remote. Metara flew past overhead to cover her. Leia shot toward the remote, ready to swing her foot pads up to push it into the nearest crusher.

She heard a *whump* as the containment field dissolved and re-formed. *Just a glitch,* she thought, distracted. A shadow fell over her, and she realized something large loomed directly overhead. Then Metara slammed into her and knocked them both away.

They spun together for an instant, and Leia ended up on top with a good view of the thing that had just dropped out of the darkness at the top of the cavern and into the arena. It was an enormous, barrel-shaped droid, at least three meters tall and maybe four meters wide, and it bristled with appendages, each with a drilling or cutting tool or claw at the end.

The other players had scattered. Metara gasped, "It's a mining droid."

The droid's head rotated, revealing a set of glass ocular devices for taking in visual data and a large round orifice for testing samples. The orifice opened, bared a set of blades for grinding and cutting, and emitted a high-pitched shriek of pure rage.

The Twi'lek woman hovered nearby, and Leia heard her spit an astonished curse. "It's an *insane* mining droid," Leia said.

A glance up at Viest, now standing at the edge of the arena to watch, told Leia that this was no accident. "I'll draw it off, you try to destroy the remote."

"But—" Metara began. Leia ignored her and shot away to the other side of the droid.

The hauler dropped into darkness for what felt like forever, long enough for Han to entertain some nightmarish scenarios, mostly about dropping suddenly into a vacuum. Then it made another abrupt turn that nearly threw him off and suddenly moved forward again. Han adjusted his grip and took a deep breath. *That was bad.* Shooting forward again wasn't exactly a picnic, but it was better than waiting for the hauler to jerk and scrape him off on the shaft wall. His fingers were going numb, his hands were starting to cramp from holding on so tightly, and sweat made his skin itch.

But after a few moments he realized the darkness wasn't nearly as impenetrable as it had been at first. He twisted to look over his shoulder. Ahead the tunnel brightened a little, a blue-gray light gradually appearing at the far end, as the hauler rapidly approached a round exit into a lighted chamber. *At least it isn't a blast furnace,* Han told himself. He hoped.

The hauler shot out of the tunnel into a big shadowy space, then slammed to a halt so abruptly that Han almost lost his grip and his legs were flung straight out. He strangled back a yell, but then his weight eased off his strained arms; the gravity was much lighter here. He swore in weary relief and pulled himself atop the hauler.

Flexing his sore hands, he looked around. He was in a huge cavern, mostly shadowed except for lumalight falling down from a source a couple of hundred meters above him. More haulers like the one he was on and some huge repulsor ore carts drifted aimlessly, though some were moored to projections in the walls.

The hauler creaked and jerked, and started to move again—downward. Han decided it was time to get off the tour. He braced his feet against the top, then pushed up and off. He had just enough momentum to reach a drifting ore cart; he grabbed onto the wide rim and clung to it. Watching the hauler vanish into shadow below, he took a moment to enjoy the sensation of not plunging into darkness. Then he looked around for his next perch.

The grappling hook in his satchel wasn't going to do him any good, since he couldn't throw it in low g. He could hook it onto something and play out the fibercord to give himself a safety line, though. But he had to have something to push off from as he moved around the chamber; without a source of propulsion he could get stuck down here, floating around with no way to reach the walls of the cavern, until the pirates found him or he starved to death. He still had a comlink in his pocket, but it was the one locked into the secure frequency for the *Gamble*. He could change the settings and try to get hold of the *Aegis* if he did get stuck. But he preferred not to get stuck.

He couldn't spot any likely place from here, so he climbed around the edge of the hauler, trying to get a better view of the nearer wall. *Hah, there we go.* Some distance along the wall, six flatbed lifters were moored to a metal dock standing out from the rock. Han mapped out his route, then he pushed off and made the long jump to a drifting hauler, scrambled across it and down the side, and then shoved off to drift just within reach of the last lifter.

The lifters were flat slabs of metal about a meter and a half wide and three meters long, with a low rail around the outside, a small repulsor propulsion system, and a limited control panel. They had probably been used to transport miners, droids, and small equipment around this giant space, or up and down the larger traverses. Judging by the coating of wet dust and muck on the metal, they hadn't been used in years.

First Han had to find one with a little power still left; then he had to pry up the panel and tinker with it to get it started. He had forgotten how big a pain working in low g was, especially when he had to hold his handlight in his mouth to keep it from drifting away.

Finally the lifter's control console lit up and the repulsors started to hum. Feeling vindicated, Han pulled himself back to the control panel and slid his boots under the safety clips that kept the lifter's driver from floating away.

All right, Solo, where to now? He looked around, getting his bearings. He needed another way out. He could go back up the tunnel, but he didn't want to run into another automated hauler and end up repeating this whole adventure. He decided to go up and try to find a passage back into the asteroid's corridors that would be closer to the level he had started on. Gripping the safety rail, he steered the lifter slowly upward, toward the brighter glow of light from the upper part of the cavern.

The Twi'lek woman had the same idea as Leia, and they shot toward the far side of the arena together, drawing the droid's attention. They dodged back and forth as the droid flailed at them. It should have worked, with one of the other players taking the opportunity to knock the remote through a crusher and end the game.

But the remote was clearly programmed to make things as difficult as possible. It darted around close to the droid's barrel-shaped body, swung around its drill-tipped limbs, and lured the other players into danger.

Leia watched hopefully as the remote wheeled away from Metara and one of the Ishori dived down almost within reach of it. At the moment she didn't care who won the game, as long as somebody did. Though, she reminded herself with grim resolve, they had no guarantee that Viest would stop the game as she had promised. When the remote was destroyed, the flight-master might change the rules again.

Then the droid swung its drilling arm and struck the Ishori across the back. He flew across the arena and bounced off the containment field with a fizzle of energy. He drifted, his body limp. The other Ishori cried out and shot over to him.

Leia set her jaw. This had to end before that happened to all the players. As the droid turned, she dived in close to circle it and followed the gleam of the remote. The droid roared and turned toward her, but then it swung away, distracted by someone around the other side.

Leia ducked and suddenly found the remote barely a meter away. She lunged for it, gritting her teeth as its searing blast grazed her right arm. At the last moment she flipped and used the pads on her feet to slam it toward the nearest crusher.

The Twi'lek yelled and swooped in to intercept her. But the droid's drilling arm flailed and slammed into the Twi'lek. One of the woman's foot pads flew off, sending her into a spin right toward the crusher's maw. Leia reacted by pure instinct and surged forward with her foot pads to grab the woman's leg. She twisted around and used her pads to yank the Twi'lek to a stop, barely a meter from the crusher. There was no doubt the crusher's deadly field was operating; the ozone it generated filled Leia's lungs. The droid loomed over them, reached for them with four sets of arms, all tipped with cutters or spinning drills. *Got to get close,* Leia thought, and propelled herself and the Twi'lek toward it.

They shot past its reaching arms and struck its

metal body. Leia had time to realize that her hurried theory had been correct. The way the droid was constructed, it couldn't bend its limbs back far enough to reach them with its pincers and drills and cutters when they were this close to it.

Confused, the droid shrieked and clawed for them as they scrambled away around the curve of its torso. Leia felt a glancing blow, and a line of pain opened up across her back. One of its claws had grazed her; she gasped but kept scrabbling. The droid's head rotated down to glare at them, and two arms slammed down around them like a cage.

The Twi'lek grabbed the base of one arm, but couldn't wrestle past it. Leia gripped the dented metal body behind her and lifted her feet to try to use the repulsors to force the arms open.

The droid jerked and emitted that high-pitched metallic scream. Under the ear-piercing noise, Leia heard a *thunk* and a grinding sound. She exchanged a startled glance with the Twi'lek, then looked wildly around. The arch of the containment field's dome wasn't far above the droid's head, which meant they must be close to the edge of the field . . . "It backed into the crusher!" Leia said aloud.

Another *thunk* vibrated through the droid's body, and the grinding became louder. Not only was the droid caught in the crusher, it was being pulled farther in. *Oh, no,* Leia thought.

The Twi'lek must have realized the same thing at the same moment, because moving as one, they both flung themselves at the droid's nearest arm, using all their strength to try to push past. The Twi'lek had lost both her foot pads and didn't have much leverage.

Leia didn't think they had a chance, but then she saw Metara, the Twi'lek's crewmate, and even the remaining Ishori closing in on them, all grabbing for the arms.

Then the droid wrenched itself out of the crusher, scattering the other players, and lurched sideways and then back. Dragging Leia and the Twi'lek with it, it spun into the containment field. The field sizzled and Leia braced herself against the metal, ready to fight her way free when the droid stopped moving. A flare of energy blinded her. She winced, and suddenly the droid jerked again and plunged down and away from the arena.

It had shorted out the containment field, Leia realized as the droid plunged downward into the dark of the cavern. *And where is it taking us?* The light failed as they dropped away from the arena. With all her strength, Leia shoved at the arms that were pinning them, the Twi'lek with her, but the droid just tightened its hold.

Blasterfire sounded somewhere nearby. Leia hoped that meant someone was firing at the droid and not at them or the other players, but it was too close to be coming from the arena. A loud metal bang rang out and the droid jerked and spun. *What the*—Leia had time to think. Then it happened again. And again.

A grinding noise inside the droid deepened in pitch until it made Leia's bones vibrate. Something rattled inside it, then wheezed. Its grip on them relaxed and the arms fell away. Still wary, Leia pushed herself off with her pads, and drew the Twi'lek with her.

The droid rolled, the last of its momentum carrying it away. As its head passed them, she saw it was partly slagged from several blaster bolt impacts, but it must have been the last hit that had finally taken it out. Its eyes sparked and went dark, and it drifted slowly away . . . giving Leia a clear view of what had struck it.

A flatbed repulsor lifter had rammed the droid. No, Leia corrected herself, staring downward in amazement. Han Solo had rammed the droid with a flatbed repulsor lifter.

The lifter hung just below them, the whole front end dented in with the force of the multiple impacts on the droid's metal carapace. Han was holding on to the railing with one hand to keep from drifting off; the other gripped the lifter's small control unit. He looked up at her and said, "Next time, I want to go somewhere else on vacation."

"Me, too," Leia agreed. She was torn between blank surprise, deep relief that she wasn't about to be ripped apart by a giant droid, and annoyance that Han wasn't where she had meant him to stay until she got back. This storm of conflicting emotion had happened to her before, always coinciding with Han's sudden appearances, so maybe she should just stop being surprised, at least. "And what are you doing here, by the way?"

"I'm scouting," Han said, eyeing the dead droid warily. "What are *you* doing here?"

"The pirates—" Leia realized there was no time to give even a brief summary. "It's a long story."

The Twi'lek had kept her gaze on the arena above and now hissed, "They're coming! Send your man away before they see him!"

"We're just friends," Leia snapped by habit. She hesitated, but Metara was still up there, and the *Aegis* was still trapped in dock. If she bolted off with Han, Viest would hunt them down through the mine, and she would have no doubt that Leia had something to hide. No, the Twi'lek was right, it was better to stay here and not let Viest know anything had happened except the accidental death of her pet killer droid. Leia pulled one of the repulsor pads off her feet and handed it down to Han. "There, get back to the ship! Or whatever you were doing."

At least Han trusted her enough not to argue. He took the pad and slid it onto his arm. "See you later." He propelled himself in a backward flip over the flat-bed lifter and vanished into the darkness of the lower part of the chamber.

Leia looked up and saw figures appear over the edge of the platform. To the Twi'lek, she said, "Tell them the droid fell onto the lifter."

The Twi'lek nodded. "I owe you a debt. My name is Anakaret and I pledge to pay it."

"I accept your debt. I'm Leia, and I'm with the *Aegis*."

Anakaret glanced at her. "If they let us live, I'll try to come speak to you."

The technician, the Aqualish, and several guards with repulsor pads came to survey the damage. While the technician propelled himself around the drifting droid carcass, angrily assessing its injuries, the Aqualish handed Anakaret a couple of new pads so she could steer herself back up to the ledge. He said to Leia, "Viest isn't going to like this. It took a lot of time to program that droid to be this crazy."

Leia didn't try to keep the acid out of her voice. "We tried to be careful, but I suppose it was just too old for this kind of thing." The technician glared at her over the droid's dented carapace, but the Aqualish didn't seem displeased.

As they lifted back up toward the arena, Leia saw Metara and Anakaret's teammate waiting on the ledge, their repulsor pads off. The Ishori who had been hit by the droid lay on the floor, unmoving; one side of his body was mottled with dark green bruises. His companion sat mournfully beside him. The human man ran to Anakaret as soon as she landed and threw himself into her arms. She patted his head reassuringly.

"Leia!" Metara rushed forward. "Leia, are you all right?"

Leia wasn't in the mood for Metara's concern. She nodded toward the Ishori. "Will he recover?"

Metara looked back, wincing. "He's dead."

So this idiotic game had claimed a life for Viest's amusement. "At least the droid is out of commission. I'm assuming Viest won't try to force the survivors to play a rematch."

"But you won," Metara said. Anakaret's human seconded her, pointing emphatically at one of the crushers while speaking in a language Leia didn't understand.

"I did?" Leia frowned, startled. "When?"

"Right before the droid grabbed you," Metara told her. "You knocked the remote toward the crusher with your foot pads and the field caught it and pulled it in."

"Oh." Leia knew she had knocked the remote

toward the crusher, but hadn't thought it had gone all
the way in. "So we won." All it had taken was one
death and her and Anakaret almost being torn to
pieces.

But she didn't have time to contemplate the victory.
From above them, Viest said, "Oh, I'm calling it a
forfeit."

The flightmaster stood on the steps to the balcony,
surveying the players with a tight smile. "You damaged the arena. Those containment fields aren't
cheap, and the generators are burned out."

"You can't be serious!" Metara blurted.

Her eyes narrowed, Viest said, "Oh, I'm serious."

Anakaret swore, and her crewman threw his remaining repulsor pad down. Leia set her jaw. She
knew it was useless to protest. Fortunately, there was
no way the cutthroat, pirate-backing woman she was
supposed to be would let it go, either. Not bothering
to hide her anger, she said, "Your droid damaged the
containment field after I destroyed the remote."

Viest moved deliberately down the steps, watching
her closely. Leia knew she was being read, and she
knew there was nothing the flightmaster was going to
see at the moment but a strong desire to blast her
head off. Viest said, "What, no protest that releasing
the droid into the arena was unfair? I'm surprised."

"I'm not," Leia said. "I knew something like that
would happen. But I didn't think you'd cheat the winner out of the prize, like a child tipping over a game
because she doesn't want to lose."

Viest went still for a moment. Then she bared her
teeth in something that wasn't a smile. "You need
time to cool down."

I need a lot of things at the moment, Leia thought, *and that isn't one of them.* "How about a rematch?" she said. "Just you and me. Have you got another droid?"

There was a startled and uneasy stir among the pirate spectators. Viest laughed. "You'd like that. No, you and Metara go back to her ship and wait. Maybe we'll talk about your offer again. When I feel like it. Oh, and don't try to leave. I'll broadcast a bounty on the *Aegis* and you'll be blown to pieces before you make it out of dock." Her smile was pointed. "Maybe I'll do that anyway."

The remaining Ishori muttered something in its own language. Anakaret's expression was so cynical that it rivaled Han at his worst. Leia wasn't surprised. At least now they had the threat out in the open. On the other hand, Metara was rigid with anger.

"Viest, this wasn't our deal. We had an agreement. You promised us—"

Viest turned and strode away to the lift tube, her entourage following. Furious, Metara started after her, but Leia caught her arm and pulled her back. "There's no point," she said. "She's right, we'll talk later." In one way she was glad Viest had tried to kill them and threatened the ship, that their situation here was now clear, that there was no reason to pin their hopes on further negotiation.

It meant Leia could stop playing nice with pirates and slavers, and start playing for real.

As Viest and her followers cleared out, the Aqualish arrived, with guard backup, to shepherd Leia and Metara back to the *Aegis*. "See, I told you," the Aqualish said.

"You did," Leia replied. "I should have listened to you."

Metara gave her an odd look, but the Aqualish just grunted and led them away.

Han hid, waiting until Leia, the Twi'lek, and the pirates had gone back to the upper part of the chamber. Then he followed, using the beamdrills, tunnel borers, and other equipment moored to the cavern wall for cover. He found a spot where he could see everyone gathered on the ledge and watch the confrontation, though he was too far away to hear what they were saying.

He wasn't sure what had happened up there, but the way the crushers were tethered in a big circle below what was obviously a spectators' gallery on the balcony gave him a few ideas, and the droid's attack clearly hadn't been an accident. Whatever it was, somebody hadn't survived it. An amphibian sentient lay limp on the ledge, another huddled over him.

It could have been an elaborately staged execution, but in that case he was pretty sure Leia and the Twi'lek would have taken the opportunity to bolt with him. And people didn't usually stand around after failed executions arguing about the process, which was what it looked like they were doing here.

He watched the conversation until everyone started to leave. People came out to help the amphibian carry his dead friend away, and Leia and Metara and the others walked to the end of the ledge and disappeared into a couple of lift tubes. There were still pirates milling about on the ledge; others zoomed around the arena on repulsor pads, powered down the crushers, and collected debris from the dead droid, most of which they just pushed off to the sides of the cavern with the rest of the abandoned equipment. After a while, Han reluctantly conceded that he wasn't going to have a chance to follow Leia. Better to get back to the *Aegis* and hope that was where she was being taken.

If she wasn't . . . He would just have to figure something out.

When Degoren brought his light corvette out of hyperspace at the rendezvous coordinates, the *Darsumae* had already arrived.

The *Darsumae* was the armed freighter he used as a decoy for capturing pirates and smugglers, and he intended to transfer his command there. The rebel ship *Gamble* was damaged and had undoubtedly taken refuge at a commercial port or station somewhere in this area of the sector. The light corvette, with its ostensible duty as a customs ship, couldn't approach a port without making every merchant ship in dock wary and panicking all the smugglers. The rebels would be warned and have time to flee. The *Darsumae* could approach as just another freighter, and would go unnoticed until it was time to spring the trap.

He stood up from his command chair and started down the length of the ship to the stern shuttle bay, his second in command, Sorvir, following him. Degoren waited until they were alone in a corridor before he said, "It's disturbing that we've had no further contact from the deep cover agent."

"Yes, sir." Sorvir sounded grim. "The rebels may have realized that there's a leak in their communications."

"If they haven't realized it, they're fools." Degoren wished they were fools. It was hard to see the big picture from a post in the Mid Rim, but from what he could tell, the rebels were becoming better organized, even as the Empire devoted more and more resources to pursuing them. "We can't sit around waiting on this agent's convenience. Any word from our local informants?" Degoren had independent agents at several of the local ports, though they were mostly used for tracking smugglers.

"Not yet, sir."

Degoren grimaced. "If they want to remain employed, and alive, they need to produce results." But he knew threats were no real incentive. "Contact them again. Let them know whoever finds evidence of the rebels will be well rewarded. Enough to pay all their debts and buy their way out of this miserable sector."

"Yes, sir." Sorvir added, reluctantly, "There's always the chance that the rebels were picked up by pirates."

Degoren swore under his breath. He had already considered that possibility and dreaded it. "If they have, then we'll be lucky if there's anything left of them to interrogate." It would be even worse if that scheming spider Viest got her hands on them.

CHAPTER NINE

THE *MILLENNIUM FALCON* REACHED Arnot Station in record time.

The station regulations automatically downloaded to the comm system when they docked hadn't mentioned anything about no weapons, so Luke wore his belt with holstered blaster and his lightsaber, and Chewbacca carried his bowcaster.

As the *Falcon*'s hatch slid open, the first thing to hit Luke was the smell. The air was filled with the scents of strange spices, stale air, ozone, and a dozen other things he couldn't identify. "I had better stay here and help Artoo guard the ship, Master Luke," C-3PO said. The protocol droid's tone managed to convey pretty clearly that he didn't want anything to do with a run-down trading station deep in pirate territory.

"No, Threepio, I need you to translate," Luke said patiently. He had had variations on this conversation almost everywhere he went with C-3PO; the droid was just nervous. "Artoo can guard the ship by himself."

In the corridor, R2-D2 beeped reassuringly, then turned to trundle back up to the cockpit.

Chewbacca groaned under his breath as he tapped in the code to close and lock the hatch. He found Threepio's translations of Shyriiwook inadequate, though Luke didn't think he had any trouble making himself understood. They went down the ramp to see a bipedal figure dressed in somewhat disheveled brown knits coming toward them, carrying a datapad.

Across a broad corridor from the landing slots was a double gallery of what looked like cargo brokers and repair bays and other businesses that catered to trading ships. Humans and beings of various other species, as well as a few droids, moved along the walkways and bridges, and Luke heard a babble of voices as well as competing music from several different sources. The station looked shabby and well used, busy and cheerful, and he saw no sign of anyone in an Imperial uniform.

Beside him, Chewbacca made a comment. C-3PO translated, "He says it looks fairly promising. I don't know why he thinks that. It seems rather dingy to me."

Chewbacca grumbled low in his throat and gave Luke a look that combined reproach and irritation. Luke sighed. "Threepio, remember, we talked about leaving out the editorial commentary."

The person with the datapad drew near. He was very tall and thin, with light blue skin, cadaverous features, and a halo of gray hair. His craggy features and hollow cheeks made him seem daunting, but he was smiling as he approached.

Cover story prepared, Luke began, "Hello. We're new to your station—"

"I'm the portmaster. Are you trading? The docking fees are waived if you are trading. What are you trading?"

Luke abandoned their cover story, since the portmaster was apparently too busy to be interested. "We're not trading right now, we don't have a cargo. We're meeting our friends here. They came in on a freighter called the *Gamble*? The ship was damaged—"

"Yes! Yes, I know it." The portmaster tapped his datapad, rapidly filling out a docking form. "They were attacked by pirates."

Luke nodded. "That's them." They must have given the portmaster the story about pirates to explain the damage to the ship. "They said they were hit by pirates before they arrived here," he improvised.

"Yes, we saw it."

"Saw it?" Luke stared, and Chewbacca woofed in surprise. "It happened *here*?"

"I think it happened twice. Their ship was damaged when they arrived in the system, but they were not the ones fired on by the pirates. That was the merchant vessel that was captured by the second pirate ship. These pirates get worse and worse! Soon we will have no shipping at all through these routes. Or the pirates will take this station." He looked up from the datapad and took in their baffled expressions. "You must hear the story from them yourselves. It was a terrible incident." He held out the 'pad. "Mark the chit for your docking fee, please."

"Uh, right." Luke let Chewie mark the 'pad, and asked, "Where are they?"

"Oh, your friends? They are in slot V334, down that way."

As the portmaster left, Luke stared at Chewbacca in consternation. "You think he was just confused about what happened?"

Chewbacca shook his head pessimistically and motioned for Luke to hurry.

They started down the docking ring, C-3PO hurrying to keep up and worrying aloud that they might be attacked by pirates at any moment. The station seemed to be cycling into its "night" shift: most of the businesses were shutting down, while the music and noise from the cantinas was growing louder. After a short walk and a brief consultation with a battered old holodirectory pedestal, they found the *Gamble*'s slot.

As they came within sight of the ship, Luke said, "Wow, they weren't kidding about the damage." The hull was blackened and dented with blast impacts, and the engine housing for the starboard sublights was slagged.

Chewie grunted agreement. C-3PO translated, "He says that perhaps the portmaster wasn't confused about a pirate attack."

As they approached, Luke saw engineer Sorel standing near the ramp with a couple of techs he also recognized, sorting through crates of newly delivered supplies. Sorel glanced up and spotted them, and his expression showed pure relief. "Am I glad to see you!" he said, stepping forward.

Luke wasn't surprised. Even from here, he could tell the engines were in bad shape. "We brought the *Falcon* and can take you all out of here if you can't make repairs. I guess it was too late for the Princess and General Willard to make their meeting?"

"No, well . . ." Sorel hesitated, as if he had bad news he was reluctant to share. "The Princess isn't back yet."

"Back from where?" Luke asked. "Is she meeting with someone on the station?"

"No, she isn't on the station."

"What?" Luke stared. "Where is she? Where's Han? Is he with her?" Chewbacca punctuated that with a loud inquiry of his own, which Luke didn't need C-3PO to translate.

"They went off with an Alderaanian pirate ship." At their expressions, Sorel added, "You'd better come in and see General Willard."

The *Gamble* still bore signs of the battle, though the hasty repairs were evident everywhere in dismantled panels and scorched consoles, and the crew looked tired. Everyone seemed very relieved to see Luke and Chewbacca, though they had clearly been expecting a contact from the fleet to arrive at some point.

Willard, waiting for them in a small ready room, didn't look well. His temple was badly bruised, and his eyes were sunken. He said, "You don't know how good it is to see you."

Luke managed to say fairly calmly, "General, Sorel said Han and the Princess went off with pirates?" He found it impossible to believe, but he couldn't imagine why the engineer would have said it if it weren't true.

The general nodded. "I need you to go after them. Sit down, and I'll explain."

Once they were seated, General Willard quickly

told them the story, while Luke did his best to keep quiet and Chewbacca kept shaking his head and groaning. When Willard was finished, Luke burst out, "But do we have any idea where they went?"

"That's what I asked the station officials." The general took a data card out of his pocket. "They gave me these coordinates. They believe the pirates have some kind of base in this system. They've heard rumors of it for years, but no one they know of has ever seen it." His expression was bleak. "It's the only lead we have."

Luke took the data card. "Will you be all right here while we look into it? Our mission was to get all of you out of here and back to the fleet." He wanted to start after Leia and Han immediately, but he wasn't sure about leaving the *Gamble*'s crew here. Especially when he and Chewie had no idea how long it would take to pick up the pirate's trail and how far it would take them.

Willard said, "This is more important. And now that we've gotten medical attention for the wounded and the supplies we need to repair the hyperdrive, we should be able to get out of here on our own power in a few more days."

Luke pushed to his feet. "We'll send a message as soon as we find them."

"To me, not to the fleet command," Willard reminded him. "Until we discover who leaked the information about this mission, I don't want any hint of this getting out."

Chewbacca had gotten to his feet and slung his bowcaster over his shoulder. He eyed General Willard and made a comment to Luke. C-3PO translated,

"Chewbacca asks if General Willard means to exclude General Madine from our communications?"

Chewbacca grumbled in annoyance, and Luke winced. He was fairly certain what Chewbacca had said had been a good deal more succinct and probably a little rude.

"If it's someone in our communications chain, they may have a way to break into Madine's secure frequency," Willard said. "Until I find out where Leia is, I don't want to take the chance."

"Right," Luke said. "We'll find them." He hoped he managed to sound confident, not desperate. What he felt was mostly desperate.

Luke and Chewbacca hurried down the docking ring back toward the *Falcon*. Most of the brokers and repair bays were quiet and dark, but the bars were roaring with activity. There were only a few other people out on the walkways, and the droids they saw were mostly maintenance bots. Luke kept an eye out for dock thieves, but mostly his thoughts were on what it would be like to lose Leia and Han.

His first few months in the Alliance, most of the people Luke had met had either dismissed him as a farmboy recruit or expected him to be an instant Jedi, as if all it required was ownership of a lightsaber. Han was one of the few people who accepted Luke for who he was, who didn't expect him to be anything else.

Not that it had been easy to get to that point, even after everything they had gone through together on the Death Star. But it had occurred to Luke that someone who frequented places like Mos Eisley couldn't afford the luxury of easy trust. Han's attitude had reminded Luke of a pet anooba that his friend Biggs Darklighter had had as a kid. It had been half wild and abused by a former owner, and it had taken months of kind treatment before it had stopped snapping at everyone, before it decided it was safe in the Darklighter household. Luke had never thought Han would take kindly to the analogy, though, so he had kept it to himself.

But Luke had felt an instant bond with Leia. He could talk to her about anything. About his guilt over abandoning the farm on Tatooine after all the years of work his aunt and uncle had put into it, all for nothing now, their time there wasted. His hopes and his doubts about the Force, about whether he would ever be able to get the training and knowledge he needed to really use it. She had confided in him, too, but he always felt there was a wealth of things she just couldn't say. It was still hard for her to talk about Alderaan, as if letting out all that pain would open a door she couldn't close.

It worried him that these Alderaanian pirates might have found a way to play on that.

When they were almost to the *Falcon*, passing an empty docking slip, he said as much. Chewbacca snorted and rumbled a comment. "He says the pirates don't know what they're up against," C-3PO translated. "He says that he would sooner fight a pack of nightcrawlers than Leia in a mood and Han there to help her. And I agree, Master Luke," the droid finished, and for once Chewbacca didn't protest the addendum.

Luke started to reply when a green-skinned male Duros stepped out from behind the half-closed blast door of an empty shopfront. Luke had always had trouble reading Duros; they had no noses, lipless mouths, and elongated red eyes, and he had never gotten to know any well enough to pick up on the nuances of their expressions. But this one's intentions were clear: he was pointing a blaster at them. "Keep your hands where I can see them, and come with me," the Duros said.

Luke lifted his hands. Nobody was on the business gallery across from the *Falcon*'s slip, though the distant blare of music and voices told him that there was a well-occupied drinking establishment nearby. "Just the one of you?" he asked as casually as he could.

Chewbacca grunted, and C-3PO translated anxiously, "He says there is another one in the shop, and another across the docking corridor there behind that pillar."

"I'm impressed," the Duros said, still calm. "Now move."

Luke figured that would be a very bad idea. "I don't think so."

"Move, or I'll kill the Wookiee," the Duros said. "I only need one of you."

"You should have tried this farther down the dock," Luke said. He had seen the stealthy mechanical movement in the dark beneath the *Falcon*. The Ax-108, the small antipersonnel blaster cannon, had dropped out of its concealed compartment in the *Falcon*'s hull and now pointed at them. R2-D2 had clearly seen the altercation. "Because our ship has you covered."

Chewie barked a laugh. The Duros studied Luke's face, then took a step back and looked toward the *Falcon*. The cannon fired once, the blast impact striking the floor plates a meter away from the man's feet. Chewie twitched the bowcaster off his shoulder and fired into the control plate next to the shop's blast door, shutting the door on whoever was inside. Luke drew his blaster, but a burst of fire from the lookout across the walkway sent him diving sideways. He hit the deck and rolled, pointing his blaster, but the Duros had ducked back and aimed his weapon straight at Luke.

Chewie had the Duros in his bowcaster's sights, and Luke was fairly sure the lookout was aiming at Chewie. From what he could hear, the reinforcement in the shop was blasting a way out through the back door. But the station alarm wailed, and yells and pounding footsteps sounded from the gallery. To add to that, C-3PO was running awkwardly down the walkway, shouting, "Help! We're being robbed! Help!"

Luke's heart was thumping, but he said evenly, "You wanted to do this quietly, and you wanted to live through it. I don't think those are options anymore."

The Duros flicked a look at Chewbacca. "Later, then."

He stepped back, then jogged away into the shadows under the gallery as a pack of station workers and security guards ran down the dock toward them, shouting. All of them were heavily armed. The pirates must keep everybody who frequented the station jumpy at best, and Luke bet the locals didn't take kindly to dock robbers and shipjackers, either.

As the mob arrived, Luke rolled to his feet and pointed after their attackers. "They went that way! And some of them broke into this shop, too. They had a huge blaster cannon, look what it did to the deck!" The Ax-108 had already safely retreated into the *Falcon*'s hull.

Most of the mob went off after the fleeing Duros, while the rest spread out to search the shops along the gallery for damage. A security guard stopped beside the blasted section of deck, speaking urgently on her comlink.

As Chewbacca joined him, Luke said, "Shipjackers? Maybe working with pirates? Or bounty hunters?" '

Chewbacca shrugged, but his grumble sounded dubious. Yeah, Luke wasn't so sure, either. This might be just a coincidence, but somehow he didn't think so. If these guys had been keeping an eye on the *Gamble* and had followed Luke and Chewie back here . . . They might very well be pirates, sent by whoever had captured Leia and Han. "Let's get back to the ship. I'll call General Willard and warn him that the pirates might be watching the *Gamble*."

To get back to the bay corridor, Han had to avoid another band of hunting castaways and almost stumbled on a camp of beings who seemed to live by foraging near the docking ring and who had clearly been here way, way too long. By the time he got through it all, he felt tired, grungy, and like he had been in contact with a lot of substances that were either toxic or disgusting or both. He didn't know what he wanted most, a shower or to get his vaccinations renewed.

When he reached the docking ring corridor, he used the grappling hook to get up to the droid track in the ceiling. It was quieter now—it seemed that the party around the dead-droid bar had died down—but he was still wary of anybody who might be out hunting drunks and stragglers.

He knew Sian and Terae must have already returned when he reached the ore-cart hatch into the bay; they had left the smaller droid hatch open for him. As he closed it behind him, he noted two *Aegis* crew members on guard at the bottom of the ship's ramp. They spotted him immediately and one stepped forward to check the position of the pirates outside the bay doors, then waved for Han to come ahead. Han crossed the overhead rigging and used the grappler and line to drop down to the top of the ship's hull. By the time he reached it, the topside hatch was opening for him.

He climbed down through the cylinder air lock to find Kelvan and Kifar Itran waiting. Kelvan said, "Terae and Sian got back a little while ago, and the Princess wants to see you." He turned to lead the way down the corridor.

Itran was staring aggressively at him for no discernible reason, so Han kept the relief off his face. If Leia had still been with the pirates . . . *But she isn't, so stop thinking about it*.

"Took you long enough," Itran practically snarled. "She was worried."

Just what Han needed right now. "I stopped to chat

with the glitbiters who live in the sewage plant down the cross corridor."

Han followed Kelvan to the ship's ready room, where Leia paced up and down, clearly more angry than worried. Metara was there, with Sian and Terae, and they looked worried enough for everybody. "I'm sorry," Sian said immediately. "We tried to go after you, and we got to the part of the tunnel where it turned and dropped straight down. Then we heard another one of those haulers coming and had to get out through the nearest hole in the roof. It took us a while to find our way back."

Terae didn't look or sound nearly as sorry. "We almost ran into another group of castaways."

Han ignored her. He told Sian, "Don't worry about it."

Leia rounded on Han and glared. "Have a nice stroll around the pirate den?"

"I've had better," Han told her, looking her over without being obvious that he was looking her over. The sleeve of her jacket was torn and there was a perfectly round bruise on her cheek, but other than that she looked all right. She sounded furious, but he knew that very little of it was actually aimed at him. She had been genuinely furious at him so many times it was easy to tell when he was the cause and when she was just furious in general. "What were you doing with that mining droid?"

Leia's jaw hardened. "Trying to establish diplomatic relations with the pirates. We failed. The so-called flightmaster is called Viest, and she's a Lorrdian reader. She knew immediately we were hiding something from her."

"Great." Han had dealt with Lorrdians before. "How much did she get off you?"

"She didn't identify me as Alliance, but she identified us as *something*." Leia glanced at Metara. "I'm not sure why she didn't just order us killed. My guess is that she still wants control over this ship and she knew the crew would resist any attempt to take it over. And that I annoyed her enough that she wants to find out why I'm really here, and what my real interest in Metara is."

Metara sounded bitter. "She promised to release the *Aegis* from our agreement and turn over the merchant crew to us if we won that stupid game. She was just toying with us."

Han met Leia's gaze and they shared a moment of silent ironic understanding. *Yes, Metara wants to be a pirate and have her cake, too.* Hopefully this would teach her that pirates didn't keep agreements unless they couldn't find a way to just kill you or sell you and take your stuff.

Whatever they did, they were going to have to move fast. Han asked Sian, "When you were in the tunnel, do you remember how long it took for that second hauler to come along?"

She nodded, not sure what he was getting at. "Approximately, sure." Her expression cleared. "You found the slave pen?"

"Yeah. We'd have to cut through a couple of grids with a fusioncutter before we could hand them up any weapons or get them out of there, but it's doable." He was going to have to tell Leia in private about the fact that Davit had been on the merchant ship and had given him intel that pretty much proved there was an Imperial informant somewhere in the Alliance's comm chain, but for now he just said, "I talked to one of our merchants."

Leia's brow was still furrowed. "You think we can get them out through this tunnel without alerting the guards on the slave pen?"

"We can break them out," Itran said confidently. "I volunteer to go down the tunnel."

"Yeah, you're a big hero, we get it," Han told him. To Leia he said, "Probably, if we time it right. There's too many to sneak them in here through the droid hatch in the ore-cart grid. We'll have to take out the guards on the bay doors."

Kelvan said to Metara, "But we still can't take off without getting shot to pieces. We've been watching the sensors, and there's just too many ships out there." He seemed torn between hope and despair. It wasn't clear whether he had ever been on board with the idea of joining the clearinghouse in the first place, but it was obvious that Terae's report on what she had seen here had convinced him it was a terrible idea.

Watching Metara, Han still wasn't so sure what she thought. The woman let her breath out and said, "We have to do something. Viest is never going to let us go, with or without the merchant crew." She looked at Han. "The prisoners were unharmed, then?"

"Three died on the way here," Han told her, "and the pirates shot the captain and copilot when they took them off the ship."

Metara looked stricken, Kelvan shocked, and Terae bit her lip and stared at the deck. Han found himself meeting Leia's gaze again. Her mouth was a thin, straight line, and she was pale with anger. Problem was, he thought she was angrier at herself than at Metara and the others. As if she could have prevented this.

Sian broke the tense moment. She had been watching the *Aegis* officers with increasing exasperation. Now she said, "What did you think was going to happen? They're *pirates*."

Terae glared at her but didn't respond.

Leia took a deep breath, restoring that icy calm that masked so much. "We need a diversion."

"Explosions are always good," Han said.

Sian added, "Just from what little we saw of this place, there're so many failing systems, bad power cells. If we set off something on the far side of the asteroid, it might take them a while to realize it was sabotage."

Kelvan leapt on that suggestion. "That could work. But we'd have to make it into hyperspace before they realized what we were trying to do."

Han sorted through various ideas. Instead of causing an explosion on the opposite side of the asteroid, they could blow up this bay, and hope the debris field obscured the ship's departure. He could rig the ID to broadcast another ship's specs to help confuse the issue just long enough for them to jump to lightspeed. It would work if he could figure out a way to blow the bay up without also blowing up the *Aegis*. A timed explosion would be hard to manage, since it would have to go off just as the *Aegis* was exiting the bay.

Terae wasn't nearly as eager as Kelvan. "If one of the ships in orbit reports our departure to Viest, she would still have time to order them to fire on us. And she told the captain she would put a bounty on us."

"She can't if she's dead," Leia said.

Everyone stared at her. Han knew moments like this were why he found Leia Organa so attractive, and tried not to show it. He said, "I'm good with that."

Terae's lip curled. "I didn't realize rebels were so cold-blooded."

Leia regarded her with cool contempt. "I've never considered a career of destroying civilian ships and selling their crews into slavery, so don't call *me* cold-blooded, Lieutenant."

A slow flush crept up Terae's pale skin. Before she could reply, Metara said, "Terae, that's enough," then turned to Leia. "You want to plant an explosive in that control center?"

Leia nodded. "I would like to, yes. It doesn't have to kill Viest, though I certainly wouldn't be sorry if it did. But if she thinks she's the target of an assassination attempt, she's not going to be worried about what ships are leaving dock without permission. I got the distinct impression that we aren't the only enemies she has here, so we may be fairly low on a long list of possible culprits."

Sian folded her arms, thinking it over. "These bays aren't exactly secure. An explosion in the mine interior could make some of the ships docked here cut loose and run. I sure would, if I were them."

Kelvan looked like he was running calculations in his head. "We have seismic charges on board. We could rig one with a timing device, maybe combine it with a fragmentation grenade that would set the charge off . . ."

Han wasn't surprised Kelvan was thinking along those lines. A seismic charge could be dumped out an air lock and left to float behind a ship until a pursuer collided with it and set it off. Cargo transports used them against pirates, and pirates used them against picket and security ships. "Where's the control center?" Han said. "Is it near that arena?"

Leia lifted a brow. "It's some distance above it, in the low-gravity area. I thought we could find a route there that came out in the dark section of the cavern, then lift the device up and attach it to the outside of the control center's structure."

Han nodded. "Nice, Your Worship."

"Thank you," Leia said drily, but he thought she appreciated the compliment.

A crew member stepped through the hatch. "Captain? There's a disturbance at the bay doors. Looks like someone might be out there."

Metara frowned. She glanced at Leia. "Hopefully this isn't a visit from Viest."

Metara followed the crew member out, Kelvan and Terae going with her.

"I doubt Viest would come to us," Leia said, starting after the others.

Han stopped her at the hatch. "I need to talk to you—alone."

Leia took in his expression. "Now?"

"Yeah."

"I can watch the door," Itran offered, "keep the *Aegis* crew out."

Leia glanced around, taking in the ready room and

obviously finding it wanting. Han wasn't keen on it, either. There was a hatch into another corridor at the other end of the room, and with most of the crew having nothing to do but wait, someone might walk past at any moment. Itran policing the place would just make any private conversation look all the more suspicious.

"There's a 'fresher across the corridor," Sian said. "It's big enough for two people, I think."

"Perfect," Leia said. "Thank you."

Han followed Leia across into the refresher. "Big enough for two people" was a bit of a stretch. But the way the appliances were built into the bulkhead left just enough room for both of them to stand. They were so close they were almost breathing each other's breath.

"If anybody saw us come in here, we can just say we wanted to be alone," Han said, lifting his eyebrows. But as soon as the words were out, he felt sweat prickle on the back of his neck and wished he hadn't articulated the thought. To say this wasn't the time or place for fooling around was a vast understatement. He didn't want to be the idiot who got Leia Organa killed because he was busy trying to make time with her while they should have been planning a way out of this mess.

"Right." Leia was not amused. She leaned back against the door, clearly trying to get as far away from him as possible. "What is it?"

"Kearn-sa'Davit was in the slave pen," he told her. "That merchant ship? Belonged to some members of the consortium that he called you here to meet with, to buy the supplies for Echo Base."

Leia gritted her teeth and swore under her breath. That was nothing Han hadn't seen her do before, but at the moment it seemed hugely alluring. Her braids were unraveling along one side of her head, the left one lying down along her neck in a very distracting way. He wedged himself between the tiny hand-cleaner unit and the bulkhead to put more space between them, and Leia pretended not to notice the awkward contortion.

"Then someone told Viest about our meeting." Leia reached over and tapped the air control, directing it to drop the temperature in the compartment. Han tapped it, too, lowering it another couple of degrees.

"Yeah, the consortium had its own traitor." He told her what Davit had said about Janlan, the traitor on the consortium side, and what he was and wasn't likely to know. The flow of cool air and the need to concentrate on getting all the necessary facts out succinctly made the situation a little more bearable. "But it doesn't sound like this Janlan told the Imperials, so that means you're right that there was someone on the Alliance end who told them where the *Gamble* was coming out of hyperspace for the transmission."

Leia considered that, then shook her head. "Yes, but this is still a problem. Viest might suspect Davit's ship was there to meet with the Alliance—"

Han doubted this Viest would be able to put it together. "Nobody in the consortium knew who they were meeting with. But Viest knows the merchants wanted to use the payment they were going to get from us to buy weapons. If she has informants on Arnot Station—and she probably does—they may be watching the *Gamble,* looking for a chance to take it. Though they were probably expecting something more impressive than a shot-up freighter."

"That's why General Willard and I brought a freighter, though the shot-up part was unintentional." Leia tapped her lip, considering. That just drew Han's attention to her lips, which made his neck feel hot again. "You think Viest won't suspect that I'm Alliance, because if her informants realize what the *Gamble* is, she'll believe all the Alliance representatives are still on the ship?"

"Basically, yeah." Han had to shift position, since the hand cleaner was in danger of permanently deforming his right hip.

Leia snapped, "Han, stop that!"

He stared at her. "What?"

Leia grimaced and rubbed her eyes. Her cheeks were flushed, making her bruise look worse. A trickle of sweat ran down her brow. "Nothing. Never mind. I just hope Viest doesn't send these hypothetical informants after the *Gamble.*"

"She'd have to send more than one ship to take anything on the station. It looked pretty well armed." That was another complication. Han just hoped the *Falcon* had arrived at the station by now. If it had, General Willard and the rest of the crew would have a fast way out if they had to abandon the damaged *Gamble.*

"True, and I wonder how many ships Viest personally controls. She obviously has complete authority over this place, but I got the impression she would have to pay or bargain with the other captains to get them to take on a mission for her. She isn't a military commander and this isn't a fleet; she can't just give orders. I think her power is limited to the ships that she has a personal investment in, like the *Aegis*." She added, "Did Davit seem likely to try to trade information about us for his freedom?"

Han shook his head. "He said he wouldn't. I believed him."

Leia winced and rubbed her forehead again, as if trying to massage away a headache. Han's hand twitched to rub her forehead for her, or her neck, or . . .

With an effort, he brought his mind back to the matter at hand. Anyway, he was pretty sure the next thing he had to say might cause Leia to rip his head off. But that had never stopped him before. "Here's another thing," he told her. "Viest sent Metara after Davit's ship. Metara didn't happen to mention that to you, did she?"

Leia eyed him, her expression impossible to read.

Han forged on. "Metara let us think she just had to snatch a cargo, any cargo, and take it back to Viest to seal their deal and start paying off what she owed. But Viest didn't care about the cargo—she wanted Davit and those other merchants dead or in her slave pen. That was the whole point." All that stuff about Metara always meaning to let the crew go was just so much mynock dung. It might have been Metara not wanting Leia, and maybe even her own crew, to know just how low she was planning to go, but Han didn't like it. If Metara had lied about that, there was no telling what else she had lied about, and they were depending on the *Aegis*'s crew to get off this blasted mine.

Leia's eyes narrowed, but all she said was, "Hmm. We'll see. I've been waiting for Metara to pull something. She's been far too cooperative. I know she doesn't want me killed or injured, and she does want to get out from under Viest's thumb, but I'm not sure what else she has in mind." She must have read his expression, because she lifted her brows. "You didn't think I trusted Metara, did you? An Alderaanian turned pirate—of course I don't trust her. But I've recruited a lot of people for the Alliance whose morals I've found wanting. All that matters is whether they mean to fight the Empire."

Suddenly Han felt like he had been pinned to the wall. Before he could stop himself, he asked, "And I'm one of them?"

Leia rolled her eyes in pure exasperation. "Not everything is about you, Han."

Han was formulating a reply to that when someone knocked on the door, and Sian's voice said, "Princess? There's someone here who wants to talk to you."

CHAPTER TEN

AS THEY SPILLED OUT of the refresher, Leia grimly reminded herself that she couldn't afford lapses like that. It was all right to be attracted to Han, but she couldn't be tempted, especially not in the middle of a mission, and being attracted at such close range, watching him shifting around in that confined space, made her think about warm skin and hard muscle . . . She *couldn't* be tempted, especially not in the middle of a mission.

Sometimes she felt like the Empire had killed part of her when they killed Alderaan, but moments like that made her remember she was still alive, still whole. It made her want to take all she could while she could, before the Empire killed her again. But there was never any time. Not when there were so many more important things to do.

Maybe that was why she had little difficulty in sympathizing with Metara, no matter how reprehensible she found the woman's choice to pursue piracy. They were both arrested in time, in that moment when their home had cracked and burned and turned to dust. But they were coping with it in very different ways.

Leia was relieved to hear that her visitor was Anakaret. The Twi'lek had come alone, talking her way past the guards at the bay doors by pointing out very reasonably that Viest had said the *Aegis* crew wasn't to leave the bay, but nothing had been said about them receiving visitors.

"They won't tell Viest," Anakaret said as Kelvan led her into the ready room. "They aren't so stupid; they know what she would do to them. And they don't like to obey her orders like good little clones, either, but they don't have much choice, unless they can get berths on a ship, and no one will give them any without Viest's say-so."

Anakaret took a seat on the couch built against the bulkhead and looked around expectantly. Leia was fairly certain she knew what the etiquette was in this situation and glanced at Metara. "Do we have a drink for our friend?"

Metara nodded to Terae, who looked startled but got up and went out, returning a moment later with a bottle of Corellian wine and some glasses. Leia hoped they had bought it at a port somewhere and not taken it off some unfortunate ship. At Metara's nod, Terae opened it and poured out glasses for Anakaret, Leia, and Metara.

Anakaret took a drink and nodded to the others. "These are your people?" she asked Leia.

Leia knew what she meant. She nodded to Han, Sian, and Kifar. "They're my people. The others are our allies, and prospective business partners." She took a small sip of wine, mindful that she couldn't

afford to lose her edge; she hadn't even done anything
for her bruises except take the mildest painkiller
the ship's medic had. The impacts from the remote
weren't so bad, but the place on her back where the
droid's claw had slapped her ached badly.

With a nod, Anakaret got right to the point. "You
know now Viest wants to kill you. Maybe she didn't
want to when you first arrived, but now she thinks
you've challenged her authority."

Leia was all too aware of that. "I shouldn't have
provoked her after the game."

Anakaret waved that away. "It was too late to talk
reason to her when she sent you down there to play.
When she has it in for you, she has it in for you, and
nothing you do can change it. Others warned me about
this, and I didn't listen. I didn't know about the droid,
either. I thought we would play, appease her, and then
I could do business here. But she didn't keep her bargain with you, who won her lousy game, so why should
I trust her now? That's why I'll be leaving as soon as my
crew readies our ship."

"So Viest will try to . . . what?" Metara asked.
"Summon us to her control center again so she can kill
us? Attack the ship while we're in dock?"

Anakaret shrugged. "She won't order anything directly, because it would anger too many of the other
captains. They don't like her in the first place. If they
see that she isn't dealing fairly with a ship that hasn't
made any trouble, then they'll have reason to turn
against her." She added, "But you'll have to watch
your backs. She has other ways of making things happen. The others here have told me rumors of ships

that dock here and then just disappear, never leave the mine, are never seen or heard from again."

Leia wasn't certain what to make of the rumors, but the rest fit with what she had expected. Viest would keep them trapped here in dock, hoping they would make a run for it so she could order the ships who owed her debts to destroy them. If they didn't make a run for it, she would call in a favor and have someone attack them. But Leia wanted to know more of Anakaret's motivation. "I know why Viest hates me. She thinks I'm lying to her about being able to buy this ship's debt from her, and she's angry that I even made the offer. Why does she hate you?"

Anakaret sighed and held out her glass for a refill. "She doesn't like my attitude. It's not the first time I've had this problem."

Han snorted. "I know how that goes." Leia lifted her brows. *He'd better not be talking about me,* she thought. But he said, "People who set up little kingdoms like this are touchy about anybody who looks like trouble."

Anakaret gave him an understanding nod. "I thought this place was a good idea for my ship, until I got here and saw the way things were. Besides, I don't like being told what to do."

Leia could see that. Han and Anakaret did both look like trouble, by anybody's definition. "I'm not keen on being told what to do, either," she said.

"Then this place isn't for people like us." Anakaret set her glass down. "I have a small ship; my crew is only six strong. I thought we could increase our business and make ourselves rich by working with this clearinghouse, but I didn't figure on these killing games and Viest being so capricious. We're smugglers, not pirates, and I don't owe Viest money like so many of the others. Since I didn't win her blasted game she doesn't care if I leave or not. What will you do?"

"We want to get this ship out of here and away from Viest." Leia hesitated, but Anakaret had seemed to hold a high opinion of debts and honor. "Viest confiscated a prize from this ship, a merchant freighter. We don't want the freighter itself back, but we want the crew. Viest will sell them as slaves, and we promised we would release them if they surrendered. We want to keep our promise." In light of what Han had discovered, she was keeping an even closer eye on Metara for her reaction. But Metara didn't betray anything. It was exasperating that Metara couldn't have kept her expression under this much control in Viest's presence.

Anakaret grimaced. "Viest won't give anything back, once she gets her hands on it. She doesn't care about other people's promises and honor." She regarded Leia. "As I said, I owe you a debt. I'll help you if I can. But if you ask me to help you free the captured crew, I can't. I can't do anything that would endanger my own crew. My promises to them come first."

"I understand." Leia hadn't expected Anakaret to join their escape effort; she had just been thinking of ways the Twi'lek might aid their plan without putting her own life on the line. The idea to distract the pirates with an explosion would be more effective if they could combine it with something that made all the pirate ships in orbit, and not just those in dock and close enough to detect the blast, think the asteroid was being attacked. Something from outside the asteroid, from farther out in the system.

And suddenly Leia thought she knew what that was. "When we arrived, the ship was given a local comm frequency for alerts and messages. Do all the ships in orbit monitor that frequency?"

Anakaret looked interested. "If they have any sense. It's where warnings would be broadcast, if the clearinghouse was attacked by raiders from a rival organization, or Imperials, or security ships, or any other threat." Watching Leia's face, she said, "You have an idea."

Leia nodded. "As you're leaving the system, could you send a transmission on that frequency, telling all the pirates that you've just detected Imperial ships coming out of hyperspace?" Everyone was watching Leia now, either baffled or intrigued.

Anakaret quirked her lips, clearly taken with the idea. "But why should they listen to me? Maybe I'm just an angry troublemaker."

Leia turned to Metara. "Do you still have the recording of the transmissions you intercepted that time, of Imperial ships entering a system?"

It took Metara a moment to realize what Leia meant, and then she was shocked. "Yes, but . . ." Her eyes narrowed in thought as the possibilities occurred to her. "The codes they used would have been changed since then . . ."

"The pirates won't know that," Leia said. "With some careful editing, it should be convincing." They could fake something up using the *Aegis*'s comm system, but starting with a genuine transmission would add that much more verisimilitude. Leia turned back to Anakaret. "We can give you a short audio recording that you can play over the frequency, as proof of what you've seen."

Anakaret smiled slowly. "I like this plan."

It took Leia and the *Aegis*'s comm tech less time to get the fake transmission ready than it did for Terae and her munitions team to alter the seismic charge. As the comm tech played the final version for Leia's approval, she said, "No disrespect, Your Highness, but this just seems . . . sacrilegious, to use the transmission that the Death Star made when it was coming within range of Alderaan."

They weren't trying to make Viest and the other pirates think a new Death Star was entering the system. The tech had carefully cut out any identifying ship's IDs and obscured the voices with static. What it did sound like was that something large, heavily armed, and brimming with Imperial might was entering a system with the specific purpose of destroying an already selected target. Viest might suspect it was a trick, especially with it being relayed by Anakaret's ship. If even one of the guards passed on the information that Anakaret had visited the *Aegis,* she would certainly suspect something. But Leia was betting many of the pirates in orbit wouldn't wait around to find out, and the flightmaster would hopefully be too busy dealing with the explosion to give any orders. If Viest wasn't dead or injured herself.

Leia had heard versions of this transmission and others, captured in bits and pieces by other Alderaanian survivors and by Alliance intelligence sources. She told herself it no longer affected her, and maybe that was true. She only said, "I don't think anything is so sacred that it can't be used to save lives." She added, "I just hope this works the way we think it will."

She took the slim data card with the edited transmission and carried it back to the ready room, where Anakaret waited with Metara. "Here it is."

Anakaret accepted the card and stood. Her smile was predatory. "My only regret is that I won't be around to watch them all scatter like startled rycrits."

Leia smiled back. "I wish we could take a vid of it for you, but I doubt we'll have time."

She walked Anakaret to the hatch with Metara following. They spent a few moments making sure their chronos were all reading approximately the same time. Leia just hoped they had planned on enough leeway in the schedule for everyone to get into position. She thought they had, but she knew how seldom even the most careful plans survived contact with reality. "Thank you for doing this, Anakaret."

"I might have done it even if I didn't owe you a favor," Anakaret said. She patted Leia on the cheek. "Take care of yourself, Leia."

"You, too," Leia said. She watched Anakaret walk down the ramp and across the bay, wanting to make certain she got out without any trouble from the guards. Anakaret sailed past them without a word, and Leia breathed out in relief. She turned to see Metara staring at her. "What?"

Metara shook her head slightly, as if she would rather not say, then admitted, "It surprises me. That you got along with her so well."

Leia was honestly baffled for a moment. "Why? Because she was working with pirates?" Leia certainly objected to Anakaret's career path, but she didn't know enough about the woman's past to judge her. Unlike Metara, Anakaret might not have had a choice.

Metara looked away, clearly uncomfortable. "Partly that. But she's not exactly the kind of person that Alderaanian royalty would normally . . . interact with."

"You'd be surprised," Leia said drily. She waited a moment, watching Metara, then said, "I know Viest sent you to capture that merchant ship's passengers. When you offered to release them at Arnot Station so I would come aboard the *Aegis,* did you have any intention of keeping your word?"

"Yes, I . . ." Metara hesitated, and then all the stiffness and resolve seemed to go out of her body at once, and she rubbed her temple wearily. "I don't know what I meant to do. All this time, since Alderaan, I haven't had one doubt that what I was doing was right. Right for me, right for my crew, the right thing to honor the memory of our dead. But . . . when I spoke to you, it was as if . . . I woke up from a dream. Since then, I haven't been sure about anything." She laughed a little bitterly. "This is the part where I should swear to you again that I won't do anything to harm or betray you or your people, but after that little speech, why should you believe me?"

"Because you're being honest with me." Leia knew this was not the moment to push. By admitting doubt, Metara had just made an enormous concession. What she needed now was time to think. And continuing to work with Leia wouldn't hurt, either. "We'll talk about it once we're all safe and away from here."

Metara took a deep breath and nodded. By the time they stepped back into the ready room, she was as perfectly composed as if nothing had happened.

The most difficult part of the plan was going to be getting the merchants out. Leia and Metara walked into the ready room where Han, Sian, Kelvan, Terae, and Kifar were doing the planning. They had an image of a map of the mine displayed above the holo-table, but they must have copied it from a faulty source because it was blurry and apparently couldn't be adjusted. Still, it was better than nothing. Kifar was saying, "Blasting them out would be quicker."

"Also stupid," Han told him. "The whole idea is to do this quiet-like, until we get to the bay doors, or did you miss the memo on that?"

Kifar bristled, but before tensions could rise even further Leia interrupted, "Quietly is exactly how we're going to do it. What's the plan?" She wasn't certain what problem Kifar had with Han, but it was more than tiresome, and if he let it interfere with the mission she would be happy to order him to wait in the *Aegis* instead of participating.

Kelvan answered, "We have to coordinate this with the movements of the refuse haulers Solo encountered, but we'll send someone in first to cut through the grids blocking the tunnel's access to the detention area. It's bringing the prisoners out and down the tunnel to the nearest exit where the timing gets tricky."

"Ideally, we could rig something up to stall the hauler or knock out its power source," Terae added, "but we're not sure what frequency it's operating on. Also, I'm worried that if something goes wrong with it, it will activate a maintenance system somewhere that will set off an alarm or summon a higher-level droid."

Leia nodded. "In any other part of the mine, it wouldn't be a problem, but someone might take notice of an alarm directly under the slave pen." She turned to Han. "Are you sure you can get all these people out through the corridors without anyone noticing?"

Han shrugged. "It's not going to be easy, but this place isn't run like an Imperial base, or even a commercial port. The only security we saw was right around the cargo receiving area and the slave pen. They guard what they think is valuable, and the rest they let go to hell."

Sian added, "We thought we'd divide up into smaller groups and take them out through different routes, so even if one of the bands of castaways sees us on the way, they'll assume we're a crew exploring for salvage or a new group of castaways."

Leia checked her chrono again, though she was well aware she had just looked at it while saying good-bye to Anakaret. *There's no time for nerves, Organa,* she reminded herself. They had a couple of hours until Anakaret had said her ship would be ready to depart. It was enough time to finish getting the seismic charge ready to move safely and also to get some food and a little sleep. She looked at Metara, to give the woman her due as captain of the *Aegis.* "Are you in agreement?"

Studying the map, Metara didn't hesitate. "Yes, I

think it's our best chance." She gave Leia a thoughtful look. "And our only real option."

"Good," Leia said. *I just hope you mean that.*

Han was too jumpy to grab any sleep, but he managed time to clean up and eat. Then, after checking that Terae and Sian had the handlights, grapplers, and weapons sorted out for the *Aegis* crew who would be coming with them, he went to pick out the other equipment they would need.

Sian was going with Leia's group, which Han was glad of because it gave the Princess at least one person to watch her back who wasn't under Metara's thumb. The downside was that, in addition to two other *Aegis* crew members, Terae was going with Han, and he was also saddled with Itran. It made sense to have Terae along, since she knew the way and had explored the maintenance tunnel a little, but Han would have preferred to do this without Itran, whom he didn't trust and who obviously didn't trust him. He would actually have preferred to do this alone but had to admit, as they had already discussed, that just wasn't practical.

Then Itran cornered Han in the *Aegis*'s engineering tool storage area as Han was collecting the fusioncutters and other equipment they would need. "You sure we should take Terae and the others? If they wanted to turn us over to the pirates, this would be a perfect opportunity."

Han wanted to punch him just from exasperation. Of course it would be a perfect opportunity, if Metara had decided she would rather be a pirate after all. They had no guarantee she wouldn't, and no guarantee that even if the plan went perfectly and they all got out of here, Metara would let them and the merchants go as promised. But there wasn't any other way off this rock except to cooperate. So Han just said, "Why, are you trying to get me alone? Sorry, I don't like you that way."

Itran's expression flickered from blankly startled to confused. Han relented, mostly because the confusion cast some doubt over just how quick on the uptake Itran was. "There's a chance they could turn on us, but if we have to split up, we need the others to help lead the prisoners out."

Itran's expression cleared, and he just said darkly, "I hope we don't regret it."

Han shook his head incredulously at Itran's retreating back. *No kidding.* He wished again that Chewie were here. Having a partner to do this with whom he trusted completely would be a relief, but it would be a bonus just to have someone along who got his sense of humor.

They got out through the ore-cart hatch carefully, one at a time, moving quietly down the droid track away from the bay doors and the bored guards. It went as well as possible, but Han's nerves were still on edge. The seismic charge was bulky and a little tricky to handle, but one of the *Aegis*'s techs had attached a couple of small repulsors to it so its weight was negligible.

Leia was going to place the charge with Metara, Sian, and two *Aegis* crew members. Metara had been wearing the conflicted expression of someone who wanted to argue but had somehow missed the opportunity, and Han suspected she had thought that Leia would stay at the ship with Kelvan and the rest of the crew, had probably expected it up until the last minute when Leia had followed her down the ramp. But Leia was so expert by now at circumventing the-Princess-shouldn't-risk-herself arguments that Han knew there was no point in him or anyone else objecting.

Also, Metara had no emotional attachment to Sian and no compelling reason to listen to her. If Metara tried to change her mind at the last moment, Leia could stop her; Sian on her own couldn't.

Once they were safely out of eye- and earshot of the bay doors, they parted ways while still on the droid track. Han and his happy band would go farther down the dock ring and then into the interior toward the maintenance tunnel. Leia and Metara's group were to head straight across the docking ring corridor into the first traverse, to make their way to the lower portion of the central cavern.

As the others were climbing down the fibercord from the ore track to the corridor floor, Han turned to Leia. She said briskly, "We'll get into position and wait for your signal."

"Yeah." Han never knew what to say in these moments. They were friends, nothing more—sometimes not even that—and they always had an audience. This time it seemed like a particularly attentive audience, at least on Itran and Terae's part. He settled for, "Good luck, Princess. Watch your back."

Leia's expression was slightly ironic. "Thanks, Han, I'll do that."

As usual, Han felt that she was expecting something from him that he didn't know how to give her. The only thing that made these moments less aggravating was that there were plenty of times when he was expecting something from her that she wasn't giving him—and he actually had no idea what it was. So he just led his group away, fairly certain she was rolling her eyes at his back.

They had decided to try to go for the access closer to the slave pen, the one Han had stuck his head up through on the way down the maintenance tunnel. He led the others along the original route he, Sian, and Terae had taken. The farther they went down the traverse, the darker it got, and their lights caught only the scattered parts of an old droid carcass and the gleam of dying power cells in the occasional looted wall console.

"You sure there's a cross corridor down here, Solo?" Itran asked.

It was Terae who answered impatiently, "The map showed both traverses connect to the same haulage tunnel. We're not idiots—we didn't just pick this route randomly."

Itran didn't argue, and Han decided he might have to stop disliking Terae quite so much if she could shut Itran down like that more often.

The traverse finally turned into an open bridge above the haulage tunnel they had been looking for. The haulage tunnel was darker than a black hole, without even the few dying lumas that still floated through the traverse. But the gravity was lighter in it, and they were able to drop down to the uneven floor without risking any broken legs or ankles.

Han's handlight showed that this passage was in far worse shape than the others. They had to climb past piles of crumbled rock debris and the occasional smashed ore cart. Han kept an eye out but didn't see any signs of castaways camping down here. A thick layer of muck, that oily combination of rock dust and recycled moisture from the ventilation system, lay over everything, and there were no footmarks or any other evidence that anybody had been through here in a long time.

They passed a shaft entrance, a big round opening in the floor, dark and dank and emitting an odor of rot; shortly thereafter they came to an overhead traverse access bridge entirely blocked by an ore cart that had apparently gone rogue and tried to wedge itself up through the opening. A couple of abandoned flatbed lifters lay crumpled in the debris below it. Ahead the haulage tunnel curved, and Han spotted a dim glow of light.

"That's it?" Terae whispered.

"Should be," Han said. So far the map had been right.

As they got closer, the faint light from above showed Han where the roof of the haulage tunnel opened up and the traverse they wanted bridged it. His handlight found a set of rough steps carved up the rock wall. They managed the climb easily, though Fera, the smaller *Aegis* crew member, slipped off once. Fortunately, the lighter gravity gave Itran plenty of time to reach down and catch her hand to pull her back up.

The traverse was only a little better lit than the haulage tunnel, with dying lumas scattered at wide intervals. Han's nerves began to jump from the quiet. There was still no sign of castaways, which was odd, but maybe they were careful about getting too near the slave pen. Probably for fear of ending up in it.

Ahead he saw two lumas hovering in a widened junction in a way that looked familiar, and figured they were close. He played his light over the floor until he found the square access to the maintenance tunnel.

"This is it," Han said. "Terae, you—"

There was a click about two meters to Han's right. He stepped sideways, spun, and drew his blaster just as a dark spheroid shape rose out of a pile of debris against the far wall. Han registered that it was a droid and felt a flush of relief. Then in the next heartbeat he realized that though the black metal carapace was just as dirty as everything else, it moved smoothly and its near-silent hum meant it was new, not a remnant from the old mine. *This could be trouble* . . .

Then the top segment rotated toward him, and a nozzle extended. Han snapped to the others, "Get down!" and dived sideways. The droid fired as he hit the ground, and he felt the heat of a near miss. He fired back in multiple bursts, trying to keep it focused on him so the others could return fire with better aim.

Blasts from behind him struck the droid and he heard Terae yell, "Security droid, fall back, fall back!"

The droid's shield flared as it deflected the bolts and moved inexorably forward. Han scrambled behind a too-small pile of metal debris as it fired again, but it aimed past him at the others. The pirates obviously had skipped the security droid's *challenge* and *detain* options and gone straight to *terminate intruders*. He threw a glance around to see who was in a better position. Itran was flattened back against the wall; catching his eye, Han mouthed the words, *You hit low, I'll hit high*. Itran nodded.

Han shoved to his feet and fired at the droid's rotating control module. Itran's bolts struck lower down in the power module. The droid's deflector shield flared, and Han had time to hope the pirates had been too cheap to get one of the higher-power models. Then the deflector overloaded with an eye-searing flash, and Han's next bolt hit the control module. The droid shuddered, slid sideways on its repulsors, and slammed into the wall with a metallic shriek. It collapsed in a heap.

Behind Han, Terae said, "Can we still go on? You think—"

"We've got to get out of here," Han told her. "There's gonna be more than one. It's signaled whoever put it here by now."

On cue, a searchlight flashed down the corridor as another dark shape moved into sight. Somewhere ahead, an alarm started to wail.

Nobody needed to discuss it anymore. They ran back down the traverse, dodging the piles of debris. This traverse had to lead to a secure storage area, one that had been added later by the pirates, that wasn't on the old map. There must be security droids at all the entrances to it, protecting the cargoes stored there. Earlier, Han sticking his head out of the access hadn't been enough to trip the droids, but he was lucky he hadn't tried to climb out and scout around.

Luck was relative, of course.

Han covered the others as they half climbed, half jumped down into the haulage tunnel. More lights and shapes moved at the end of the dim traverse, and from the way the new lights jerked around he was pretty certain most were carried by living beings, not droids. It had to be the crew whose cargo storage they had gotten too close to, alerted by a signal from the droid. Below, Itran called, "Solo, come on!" and Han scrambled down the rough steps.

Terae had already dimmed her handlight to the lowest setting, and the others had turned theirs off. Han did the same, and they moved as fast as they could down the haulage tunnel. Terae swept her light across the floor as they ran. It would have been better to cut all the lights, but there was too much debris in this tunnel, plus the open shaft somewhere ahead. Even with the lighter gravity in the shafts and tunnels, they didn't have time to stop and haul someone out.

Terae was the first to reach the traverse they had come down. She climbed the rough wall to reach it and popped her head over the edge. When she swore and let go to drop back down, Han figured it wasn't good news.

"They're coming down that way, too!" she whispered.

Han didn't need to look for himself. He heard shouts and boots pounding somewhere above, echoing off the rock.

They could keep going down the haulage tunnel, in the dark, and it might be blocked at any point. Han couldn't let them catch Terae, Fera, or Allian. If they were identified as *Aegis* crew, somebody might demand to see Leia and Metara, find them gone, and start a search.

"Take them and keep going," he told Terae. "I'll cover you."

She stared up at him. "But—"

"That's an order," Han snapped, and Metara had trained her so well it was almost that simple.

She jerked away, then remembered who he was and glared at him. "You're not my commanding officer!"

Looking up at the traverse, he said, "If you've got a better idea, I'd love to hear it."

Terae hesitated, but they were obviously running out of time. She turned away, gestured sharply at Fera and Allian, and they ran up the tunnel into darkness.

Han switched his handlight on and started back the way they had come, very conscious of the pirates and security droids coming at him from both ends of the tunnel.

Catching up to him, Itran asked, "You planning to get caught?"

"I'm planning to get their attention and then head for that shaft we passed." The only droid that had gotten close enough to count the intruders was a blasted mess, and Han bet nobody would take the time to check its memory storage, if there was anything still left of it. If they saw him running away, they wouldn't stop and search for anybody else. "Now get out of here!"

In the glow of his handlight, Han saw Itran shake his head, as stubborn as a rock. "I'm with you. It'll be more convincing with two of us."

Han set his jaw and didn't bother to argue. If the idiot wanted to play hero, fine.

Behind them, the pirates arrived at the bridge with wild flashes of handlights and shouts, pebbles clattering down the wall of the haulage tunnel as they reached the edge. Han switched his own light off and spun to fire up at them, a short burst of bolts that made certain the pursuit would focus on this end of the tunnel. The returned fire slagged the tunnel wall just half a meter short of his head, and Han ducked and ran.

The flash of the pirates' lights had temporarily ruined Han's night vision. He couldn't see Itran at all, but he could hear heavy footsteps crunch over the crushed rock on the tunnel floor. Han figured it was going to be a long scramble down the shaft, even with the lighter gravity.

He thought he heard an engine whine somewhere ahead, but it was hard to tell with the echoes in the tunnel. It might be another heavy-duty security droid; that would be about all they needed. He glanced back and saw jumping lights as the pirates pounded toward them. There were only five of them, which was a relief. It would be hard for five to spread out and search multiple passages. *Now we just have to get down to the multiple passages,* Han thought.

"It's here," Itran gasped, and Han almost fell headlong into the shaft.

Fortunately the gravity was even lighter in the shaft than it was in the haulage tunnel. Han slid down a near-vertical slope but caught a rocky projection on the wall and stopped his fall. Making enough noise for a reek in heat, Itran scrambled down after him.

They climbed down as fast as they could, trying to be quiet, but Han knew that as soon as the two groups of pursuers met in the haulage tunnel, they would realize this shaft was the only escape route. Then he heard pebbles and debris rattle somewhere above, and the echo of voices. Angry voices.

"Faster," he whispered to Itran. He looked down and saw that the darkness at the bottom of the shaft was more gray than black; the next haulage tunnel was maybe fifty meters below them. It was tempting to let go and drop, relying on the lighter gravity, but he couldn't see what was down there, and a broken ankle would mean a messy death at the hands of the pirates.

"Going as fast as I can," Itran muttered back.

Still climbing, still looking down, Han saw a shape in that darkness, something partially blocking the end of the shaft. Another rogue ore cart, maybe.

Then something creaked and groaned in the shaft above them. Han looked up into blinding light as someone aimed an arc light down at them.

"Drop!" he told Itran.

Itran looked down and grimaced, then pushed off from the wall. As Han launched himself, blasterfire filled the shaft, impacting the rock above and showering him with burning-hot rock fragments as the bolts shattered and heated the stone.

The problem with the light gravity was that the fall was too slow. The light flicked away, searched for them as they dropped out of its reach. Han heard a metallic thump and a scrabble as Itran hit the ore cart wedged across the shaft. Han resisted the urge to brace for the impact and made himself go limp instead. He hit feetfirst and his body folded up; the impact was bone jarring, but he didn't break anything. The metal surface was tilted, and Han half slid down toward where he could hear Itran ahead of him. Then the light hit him again, eye searing and disorienting. He looked up as something blocked the light just in time to see a big, flat shape plunge down toward them. *What in the . . .* he had time to think, and then he flung himself backward.

Whatever it was slammed into the ore cart and knocked Han into the air. He felt his shoulder bang into solid rock, and that was the last thing he knew.

In the near darkness, Leia carefully picked her way after Metara. A distant yell, sounding weirdly animal-like, sounded from one of the connecting tunnels. The crew member behind Leia stepped on the back of her boot and apologized in an embarrassed whisper. "It's all right," she whispered back.

The route from the docking ring to the center of the mine went through an unused maze of haulage tunnels; it was some very ugly terrain.

Judging by the refuse Leia had seen and the stench, it was clear many of the castaways were badly addicted to spice; where they were getting it from was another question. She wondered if Viest or other pirates used a supply of spice to control them, or traded it to them in exchange for work or favors or other services Leia preferred not to contemplate too closely.

Leia didn't want anyone to see the seismic charge and get the idea to turn them in for a reward from Viest. But five well-armed humans, whether you knew they were carrying an explosive or not, was a large enough party that the smaller groups they had heard or glimpsed in the shadows seemed to be deliberately avoiding them. It helped that there were few lumas down here, and that most of those had been moved into clusters around the castaways' camps.

As they drew near the opening to one of the large spiral chambers, Metara signaled for everyone to mute their comlinks and extinguish their lights. Leia tucked her light away and thumbed the switch on her comlink, then drew her blaster. Silently, they crept around the opening to the spiral. A dim glow shone from it, and she heard faint noises echoing up: a shuffle of movement, voices, a clank that might have been a droid or a piece of old mining equipment. The draft rising from it stank of unwashed bodies and spice.

No one relaxed until they were well past, almost to the dim light at the end of the tunnel that marked the cavern entrance. When Metara switched her light back on, Leia took the mute off her comlink. Terae's voice whispered immediately, "Captain, Captain Metara, please come in." Terae was breathing hard, agitated. Leia thought, *Oh, no . . .*

Frowning, Metara lifted her own comlink. "This is Metara. Report, Terae."

"We encountered a security droid," Terae said. "There must have been a secure cargo dump down there that wasn't on the map and we almost walked into it. Solo held them off so we could fall back—"

Leia broke in. "Where is he?"

"They caught him, and Itran. I think they must be taking them to the control area. Fera is trailing them, and I'm monitoring her on another frequency."

The other crew members shifted uneasily. Metara grimaced in dismay. Leia locked gazes with her.

"Do I continue with the mission?" Terae asked.

Leia knew that was a terrible idea. "If the pirates think this was an attempt to steal cargo, surely they'll increase the security on the slave pen."

"I agree," Metara told Terae. "Withdraw to a safe distance, but don't return to the ship. We may need you with us. Report to me as soon as you hear from Fera."

Leia waited until she signed off, then said, "We should keep going. If they do take them to Viest in the control center, we have a chance to get them back."

Metara eyed her. "One question. If it was two of my people, would you still say that?"

Leia understood what she meant; still, she couldn't help feeling offended. "Of course I would."

Metara must have believed her. "Then we'll go on. Though as to what this does to the rest of our plan . . ."

The only part of the plan that was still on track was the transmission from Anakaret, and the timing for that had just gone all to ruin. Her voice firm, Leia said, "We're winging it."

CHAPTER ELEVEN

WAKING UP PROVED to be an experience Han could have done without. The first thing he was aware of was that his arms and shoulders ached like fire, more painful than the heavy pounding in his head. Eventually he got his eyes open. His vision was too bleary to make out much detail, but his head was tipped backward and his wrists were locked into binders suspended from a repulsor by a power coupling. His boots just managed to touch the floor. *Yeah, not good.*

He felt like he had been run over by a large piece of mining equipment. *Oh, right, that's what happened.* He thought the pirates had taken one of the abandoned flatbed lifters in the haulage tunnel, one that must have still had just enough juice left in its power cells, and aimed it down the shaft at them.

He licked his lips and tasted blood. He thought he could move his head forward if he tried, though he wasn't certain it was worth it. Then he realized the noise he had thought was part of the ringing in his ears was actually someone nearby breathing heavily. He slowly lifted his head to look.

He was in a dome-shaped room, with a hatch at the far end, lit by a few drifting lumas. The remnants of old control panels were built into the walls, a few hanging open, the components inside looted long ago. A new sensor console with a large holographic plate had been installed, with exposed cables where it had been jury-rigged into the existing system. A large, round port on the far wall looked out into a dark space; squinting, he thought it was probably the asteroid's central cavern. From Leia's description and the map, this had to be part of the mine's control center. The furniture scattered around was almost sybaritic, a large richly upholstered couch and a few floatpads, none of them matching. It made a strange contrast with the all-business sensor console.

The rough breathing came from the only other living thing in the room that Han could see: Kifar Itran, who sat nearby, his wrists bound to the arms of his chair. He had darkening bruises on his cheeks and a discolored swelling around one eye. The pirates might have knocked him around, or maybe that was just from the crash with the ore cart—Han couldn't tell. Han groaned to himself. There was nothing worse than being taken prisoner with somebody who annoyed the hell out of you.

Itran looked toward the door, eyes narrowed and worried. His voice weak and rasping, Han managed to say, "Why aren't we dead?"

Itran jerked, startled, and stared up at him. "I don't know," he said.

That was an unsatisfactory answer. Han noted that Itran's clothes were disarranged, as if he had been thoroughly searched without much regard for

his privacy. Han looked down and saw he looked the
same way. Han had returned the secure comlink from
the *Gamble* to Leia, and the *Aegis* comlinks were old
Alderaanian planetary security force issue, designed
specifically with nothing to identify them, not the
ship they were assigned to or their manufacturer or
even their planet of origin. He hoped Terae had realized what had happened and been quick enough to
cut them out of the comm network before any pirate
smart enough to listen in had gotten hold of them.
The tools would look just as likely to be used to cut
open a secure door into cargo storage as to liberate a
slave pen. *So why didn't they blast us already?*

Choosing his words carefully, because somebody
might be listening to them even now, Han said to
Itran, "Did they ask you anything?" *Did you tell
them anything?* was what he really wanted to know.

Itran shook his head. "They thought we were trying to steal from some kind of cargo storage near that
traverse where the droid was posted."

"Right," Han said. If Itran was telling the truth,
then that meant they had been kept alive to be made
an example of, as what happened to stupid pirates
who tried to steal other pirates' cargoes. *They're
going to ask us what ship we came from. That could
be tricky.* The only other shipowner Han knew by
name here besides Metara was Anakaret. They could
say they had been kicked off her ship before she left.
It would work only if Viest hadn't met the rest of
Anakaret's small crew. And if Anakaret had already
taken her ship out of dock. "Itran," Han rasped, "do
you know how long we've been—"

The door slid open.

The first pirates to come in were clearly the muscle: a Gamorrean, a few big male humans, a couple of green-skinned Mirialans. The woman who strolled in after them was clearly the leader. This had to be Viest, the Lorrdian flightmaster. She smiled up at Han. "Good, he's awake." She lifted a hand in a come-along gesture.

Two more pirates dragged in another human, or near-human, male. He was tall and thin, with straight, dark hair and a faintly green tint to his pale skin that might be his normal color or something caused by fear or rough handling. He was dressed in what had been a very fine robe over pants and a jacket but was now disarrayed and stained. He staggered, looked around nervously, then saw Han and blanched in horror.

I don't look that bad, Han thought.

"Is that one of them, Janlan?" Viest asked.

Janlan, from the merchant consortium—the one who had told the pirates about the meeting on Arnot Station, Han realized.

Janlan shook his head. "I don't know. I never saw any of them. I told you, Davit made all the arrangements, and even he didn't know the names of the people we were going to meet."

Oh, great, Han thought. He winced, which made his head hurt worse. Obviously Viest had heard all about the meeting from Janlan, but what had made her suspect that Han and Itran had anything to do with it? *Well, there's one obvious answer to that.* Han looked down at Itran, trying to gauge his reaction. Itran's face was shocked and angry and worried; if he had talked, he was doing a good job of seeming

surprised. So maybe he hadn't talked, maybe Viest
had just questioned him and read the answers off his
face and body.

Viest shook her head, her expression suggesting she
felt sorrow rather than anger, as if Janlan were a
friend who had disappointed her terribly. Han already didn't like her, and that little show didn't im-
prove his opinion any.

"That's not how you presented this to us before,
Janlan. You said you had all this information for us
about how your merchant friends were selling off
their goods to get ships to blow this place to nothing.
You didn't tell us they were selling their goods to the
Rebel Alliance."

Han felt his insides freeze. The situation had just
gotten a lot worse. He looked at Itran, who was still
sitting there like he was a wounded hero, like he
hadn't opened his big mouth and spilled everything to
the pirates. *You piece of . . .*

"I didn't know!" Janlan sounded weary, as if he
knew a protest was useless, but still he went on, "I
told you all I know, and you have the consortium's
ship. You can ransom all those aboard. Their families, their trading partners, will pay for their release—"

It almost made Han feel sorry for Janlan. Almost.
Had he really thought the pirates would just ransom
his buddies? It was naïve at best. This whole mission
had been plagued by people like Metara and Janlan,
who seemed to think they could play both sides of the
moral divide, steal and betray and get people killed,
but still make it right. Like playing with a laser without getting burned. *There's a lesson there,* Han
thought. *I think it's "naïve people will get you killed."*

If loudmouthed idiots like Itran don't get you killed first.

"Ransom always sounds like a lot of work for not much return," Viest told Janlan. She pointed at Han again. "Tell me if he's one of the rebels, and if he is, tell me what he's doing here."

"I don't know!" Janlan shouted. "If he says he is, he must be one!"

Han rolled his eyes. "You know he's telling the truth—stop playing with him." He realized a moment later that that was his head injury talking, that he should have just kept his mouth shut.

Viest stared up at him, as startled as if one of the chairs had spoken. Then she lifted her brows. "So who are you, then? And why are you here?"

"You tell me. You're the one who had us dragged here." Han wondered if she would be able to read him, if he was giving anything away past "ow, everything hurts" and "probably going to die here in this room." He didn't see how she could be reading his body language in this position.

Viest grimaced in annoyance. "Oh, come on, do you really want to prolong this? Just tell me why you came to this asteroid."

Han noticed she wasn't asking how he had gotten here. Itran must have told her everything, maybe even about the *Aegis* and Leia. And from the looks of it, all the pirates had done was slap the guy around a little. It made Han want to pick up where they had left off.

Trying to ignore the sinking feeling of despair, Han wondered if Viest had ordered an attack on the *Aegis* yet, if Terae had been able to warn Leia. And what Leia was doing. Without some kind of cover for the

Aegis's departure, Leia and the others couldn't even cut and run. Still playing the game, though he didn't think it would do much good, he said, "I came here to make money; same reason as anybody else."

"That's certainly why Janlan here came to us," Viest said, eyeing the merchant almost fondly. He looked away, trembling. "He wanted to trade his friends for safety, but I don't make deals with traitors. I just let them think I do." She regarded Han again. "But I think you're here to see how many ships we have, how hard it would be to break up our little home."

There was no point in denying it, but Han wanted to hear just how much she knew. "I don't work for anybody but myself."

Viest nodded toward Itran. "What about your friend, here?"

This gave Han a reason to look at Itran. Itran glared defiantly up at him. Was he actually thinking that Han wouldn't be able to tell where Viest had gotten her information? *Idiot.* Han put some bored contempt into his voice. "He's just the hired help."

Viest regarded him thoughtfully. "Hmm. Then I suppose I'm done with Janlan."

She lifted a hand, and one of the pirates grabbed Janlan's shoulder and shoved him down on his knees. He struggled, shouting, "No, we had an agreement, you swore to me—"

Han winced, knowing what was coming next. Viest reached for her holster, and Han thought she would draw her blaster and blow the guy's head off. Instead, she drew a slim dagger out of a sheath beside the holster. It was too thin for a vibroblade, but she pressed something on the handle and Han felt a faint sonic hum that made the bones in his ears vibrate and his back teeth ache. It wasn't a knife—it was some kind of sonic probe. Maybe something meant for mining, for testing for mineral traces. Which meant it had to be able to pierce solid rock . . . She stepped forward as Janlan tried desperately to twist away. Her expression completely opaque, she gripped his hair and slid the probe into his shoulder. It passed through his clothing as if it were passing through air.

Janlan shuddered once, his expression confused, eyes wide, as if something was happening to his body and he had no way to process it.

Then he made a wet, choking sound, blood ran from his mouth, and his skull just collapsed.

Han flinched as the body fell into a heap, nothing left of the head but a steaming ruin. He wondered if this was what Viest had threatened Itran with, why the man had broken so easily—but Itran stared, eyes wide, as if this was a shock to him, too. *It was quicker than it could have been,* Han thought. He had expected her to draw the execution out much longer. But then, Viest had had plenty of time to torment Janlan, making him think she would keep her promise and let him go if he just twitched the right way for her. And now she had no one to play with besides Han and Itran.

Viest watched two of the pirates drag the body out. She glanced up at Han. "A ship just entered our system. Its ID says it's the *Millennium Falcon.*"

Oh, no, not now. Han tried to keep his reaction off his face, but he wasn't sure he was successful. And he wasn't sure it would matter one bit if he did. If she

knew enough to say this to him, then she at least
knew he was Han Solo, that the *Falcon* was his ship.
Stalling was about the only thing he could do at the
moment, so he said, "What's that to me?"

"Then you don't mind if I order it destroyed."

At the end of the tunnel, Leia saw a glow of bright
light. *Are we in the wrong place?* she thought, frustrated. If the map was right, the tunnel should open
into the asteroid's central cavern and there shouldn't
be any active light source nearby. She motioned for
Metara and the others to hang back, then stepped to
the edge of the tunnel to carefully look out.

She found herself staring down at a work area on a
large balcony extending from the wall of the cavern,
lit by arc lumas positioned on stands, with tools, large
power-cell chargers, and dismantled droids strewn
across it. It had obviously been a recent addition. It
was also occupied. Leia gritted her teeth, annoyed.
They should have come out farther down.

The technician from the arena stood there, staring
contemplatively at some project taking up most of the
platform's open space. He looked up, spotted Leia,
and his face lit with recognition. He fumbled for his
holstered weapon just as she stunned him.

He collapsed onto the tool bench and a second figure, a Gamorrean, popped up from where he had
been asleep behind one of the fabricating consoles.
Leia fired again, and the Gamorrean snorted in dismay and fell backward. Leia carefully scanned the
shadowy chamber for movement, but as far as she
could make out it was empty. The arena was some

distance below them, still lit by a few drifting lumas, but the spectator area was empty and the lift tubes were quiet. Above were the heavy shapes of the old drilling and digging vehicles. Any number of sentients could be hiding anywhere in the big chamber, but this part of it was silent and felt empty. Keeping her voice low, she said, "We're clear, as far as I can tell."

Metara gestured for two of her crew to move ahead and search the platform, and stepped out to the edge of the tunnel to cover them. Leia had noted that the work platform must have its own gravity generator, probably for the convenience of the technician. The two crew members had to push themselves across to it in the light gravity of the cavern, but once they neared the platform both sank down onto it.

As they searched, Leia took a moment to get her bearings. They had come out higher in the cavern than they had originally intended. Once Terae, Fera, and Allian had joined them, they had altered their route to enter the cavern closer to the control center. Squinting in the dark, trying to see past the giant shapes of the defunct mining machinery, Leia could make out the curving shape of the control center maybe two hundred meters above them. The transparent wall that looked out over the cavern was only a gray shape in the dimness, as if the lights behind it were dimmed. She wished Viest had shown them more of her domain; they had no idea what the layout of rooms in the control center was, or where Viest would be likely to take Han and Kifar. Fera had been able to follow them only to the bridge across to the main control area, and no farther.

The two crew members below signaled that the platform was clear, and Metara said, "What now?"

Leia had been asking herself just that question. "You take the seismic charge and attach it to the outside wall of the control center, just as we planned. I'll go around and try to find a way inside."

Metara shook her head. "I'll go with you. Terae and the others can attach the charge."

Sian lifted her brows and nodded toward the seismic charge floating patiently on its repulsor. "You want us to put the explosive into place while you go inside the thing we're planning to blow up?"

"Yes." Leia wet her lips. "When you put it that way, it does sound impractical," she admitted. "But I plan to be out of there with Han and Kifar before it goes off." She hoped.

"I should go with you. It's not going to take all of us to place the charge," Sian said. She was watching Metara carefully, as if she expected an objection. Leia was getting the distinct impression that Sian didn't think much of their Alderaanian allies' trustworthiness, and that Han and Kifar being captured on Terae's watch hadn't exactly helped any. She was clearly worried that Leia might be the next casualty unless Sian went with her. "If Solo and Kifar are hurt, you'll need help getting them out."

"And me," Terae said. Sian stared at her pointedly. Terae flushed self-consciously. "I was with them. It's my responsibility that they were caught."

At least Terae was acknowledging it. Leia wasn't sure how far she trusted Terae, but the woman did seem to have a strong sense of responsibility, though her loyalty to Metara obviously took precedence.

But Sian was right: Han and Kifar might need to be carried out. *If they're still alive,* Leia thought, and ignored the tight feeling in her stomach. Viest had taken them for a reason, and if she intended to kill them, she would surely make a spectacle of it. Leia had half expected to find them in the arena already. She checked the time on her comlink again and suppressed a curse. They were already off schedule, and the time was ticking down to when Anakaret was due to send her transmission. "All right, we'll leave four crew members to set the charge, and the rest of us will head for the control center."

Metara confirmed that order with a nod, then looked up at the control center. "We need a distraction," she said. "Something to get their attention, so we have time to search for the prisoners. I'd really like to be out of there before the charge goes off. It isn't powerful enough to destabilize this cavern, but we don't know what it's going to do to those interior passages."

Sian didn't look entirely happy about having Terae included in the rescue party, but she didn't make any objections. She pivoted, studying the upper part of the chamber. "You think any of those drillers have power left? If we turned one on, aimed it below the control center . . . Except how stable is that seismic charge? Would something like that set it off?"

"I adjusted the impact sensors when I installed our timing device," Terae said. "Just a rumble or a vibration won't do it—it would have to be a direct hit on the charge." She frowned up at the driller. "Though those things must make a pretty big rumble."

Leia didn't think it was practical. They didn't even

know if any of the drillers or core borers up there still had active power cells, or if their parts had been looted by scavengers. But as she looked back down at the platform for ideas, she realized just what project the technician had been working on. "Or . . . Terae, how are you at programming droids?"

Lying on its side in the repair area was the large mining droid that Viest had used in her game. Its control module segment was turned to face up, and its ocular devices stared emptily at nothing. Leia knew her feeling was completely irrational, but it still seemed to her that mad hatred emanated from those powered-down sensors. The technician had already removed the armored panels damaged by the crusher and dented by Han's lifter. One drilling arm had been taken off, but the exposed components looked newly installed, with jury-rigged cabling hanging out.

Terae followed her gaze, frowning. "I'm all right, but Allian is better at it."

Metara didn't seem any more thrilled than Leia was to be encountering the droid again. "The thing was clearly . . . I suppose you can't call it insane . . ."

"No, it was definitely insane," Leia said.

"Even if its programming functions are disturbed, I can still make it do what we want," Allian said. He sounded completely confident.

Metara glanced at him. "You'd better be right, Allian."

Allian seemed more encouraged by that than daunted. "I'm certain, Captain. Fera, come help me."

* * *

Leia, Metara, Sian, and Terae used the lift tube shafts to go upward toward the control center. Taking repulsors from the technician's work area, they moved through a dark vertical maintenance passage that paralleled the main shaft. Leia's handlight caught water dripping down the stained rock, and cool air that smelled strongly of damp rot flowed down from above; a major part of the ventilation system must be somewhere above them. She heard a faint rumble of machinery deep in the rock, and drops rained down on her, landing on her head and running into the back of her jacket.

They had left Allian working on the droid and Fera leading the other crew members around the side of the central cavern to place the seismic charge just below the control center. Leia knew they didn't have much time.

Above her, Metara slowed to a stop, and Leia drew even with her to see an access panel set into the rock. Metara felt around the edge until she located the release. She whispered, "From the position of the lift tube, this will open somewhere toward the center of the control area. It might open right into the middle of Viest's quarters, or into a group of guards."

Leia grimaced in frustration and flashed her light upward. She could tell the gravity was heavier here, close to normal, and their little repulsors were straining against it. Above them, the shaft narrowed and split into vents and small passages that must be for maintenance droids. She caught movement and jerked her blaster up, but it was a tiny cleaning droid, climbing around the outside of the passages, trying in vain to soak up the dripping water. No help there. "We have to risk it."

Terae and Sian arranged themselves on one side of the hatch, and Leia and Metara took the other. Metara whispered, "Go!"

Terae blasted the hatch release, and Sian used her repulsor to knock the panel open. Metara propelled herself through, and Leia dived after her.

They landed in an almost empty room, littered with a few piles of looted parts and some chairs and couches so old and battered they might have come from the original mining company. Someone had been sleeping on one, and he rolled off and hit the floor, making a garbled noise of surprise.

It was the Aqualish. He lifted his hands in surrender. "Don't shoot!"

There were two hatches at opposite ends of the room, one shut and one open to a gallery that looked down on the big shaft and the bridge that crossed it back toward the asteroid's docking ring. Leia switched off her repulsor, careful not to take her attention off the Aqualish. Metara motioned sharply for Terae to cover the open hatch to the bridge. Sian switched off her own repulsor and eased forward to hook the blaster out of the Aqualish's holster.

The Aqualish stared at them, and Leia expected him to ask what they were doing here. Instead he said, "I've no quarrel with you. Just stun me and go on with your business."

Metara started to lift her blaster.

"Wait," Leia said.

Metara frowned. "What?"

Leia stepped forward. "What's your name?"

The Aqualish's cheeks wrinkled, possibly a sign of bemusement. "Call me Andevid."

"Andevid, I'm Leia, and that's Captain Metara, and Terae and Sian."

Andevid nodded to the others. "So you always make introductions before you stun somebody? Sounds like an awkward custom."

"It would be," Leia agreed. The weak point of their new plan was the part where they burst in on Viest with no idea where she was holding Han and Kifar or how many guards were with her. They didn't have time to get into a hostage standoff, and if Andevid would cooperate, they might be able to get close enough to avoid one before Viest knew what had happened. "But instead of us stunning you, why don't you help us?"

Andevid tilted his head, studying her closely. He seemed intrigued. "Why should I?"

"Because Viest has two of our people, and we want them back," Leia explained. "Then we want to get away from this mine, and to do that, we have to make sure Viest isn't in any shape to stop us." She added, "And you've never sounded like somebody who had a lot to lose."

"Hmm." Andevid considered. "What do you want? I'm not going to get in a blaster standoff for you. I'd rather just sit here and get stunned."

Leia's and Metara's comlinks were on the same frequency, and Leia felt three faint but deliberate clicks from it in her jacket pocket. That was Fera's signal that the charge was in place and the timer running. Metara glanced at Leia to make certain she had gotten the signal, too, and Leia nodded. She said to Andevid, "Just take us in to Viest. Say we tried to get out of the bay past the guards and demanded to see her, so you brought us here."

Andevid frowned. "But what do I get out of it, except a nice slow death from Viest if it goes against you?"

"You get out of here, too," Metara said. "A ride to a planet with a good spaceport, where you can make your own way."

Andevid didn't react, didn't give anything away. It occurred to Leia that he had probably had a great deal of experience in concealing his emotions from Viest. He watched her a moment more, then snorted. "If you leave Viest alive, just make sure you kill me first."

Han thought fast, aided by the fact that Viest was absently tapping the mining probe against her thigh. Stalling had become an urgent priority. "All right, so the *Falcon*'s my ship," he said. "But why destroy a perfectly good freighter when we could make a deal?"

Viest seemed amused. "I know you're with the Rebel Alliance. You didn't come here to make a deal."

"Yeah, but I'm sure interested in making a deal now." His right shoulder cramped, and he didn't try to conceal his grimace of pain. "I work for the rebels, lady, but I'm not one of them."

She looked at Itran. "Is that true?"

Itran eyed Han narrowly. "That's what I've always thought. He's just a scrounger, there for whatever scraps he can pick up from the rebel ships."

Han was pretty sure that was what Itran actually thought, and not him trying to back Han's play. This would be easier if he had any clue how much Itran had told Viest already. Itran was acting all huffy and outraged, as if he hadn't said anything and Han was the one playing both sides. That made it twice as hard to even play *one* side.

Viest seemed intrigued. "So what sort of deal are we talking about?"

This was the part where Han was going to have to get creative. "I can give you intel on the new Alliance base. It'll be in this sector, close to Arnot Station."

Itran frowned, startled. Viest stepped closer, staring hard at Han. She tapped the probe against his chest, and every muscle in his body tensed. "And is that why the rebels were so anxious to help these scheming little merchants?"

"'Course it is. They don't have any other reason to come to this backwater."

Viest's brow furrowed. "You're lying."

Uh-oh, Han thought.

Then the door in the far wall slid open.

All the pirates twitched, startled, hands going to weapons, and Viest spun around. "What is this?"

Coming through the hatch was the big Aqualish, and following him were Leia and Metara. Han swore under his breath. They weren't armed, but clearly Viest hadn't expected to see them.

Viest stepped forward, her eyes narrowing. She slid the mining probe back into its sheath and let her hand rest on her blaster. Han saw Leia's gaze flick toward him and then over to Itran, but her expression stayed cool.

"Why did you bring them here?" Viest asked the Aqualish.

The Aqualish shrugged. "They shoved their way out of the docking bay, wanted to see you. So I told them it was on their heads."

Viest didn't like that answer. Clearly suspicious, she said, "Why didn't you use the comm and call me?"

That was a good question. Han looked at Leia again, but she didn't betray anything, not even a flicker of unease. Metara looked stiff, but then she usually did. Sullen and bored, the Aqualish said, "Didn't know I needed an appointment."

Viest ignored him, her gaze moving from Leia to Metara and back. "It's just as well," she said, and smiled. "I wanted to see you two. I've been chatting with one of your people." She glanced back at Han. "Oh, don't try pretending you don't know who he is. I know his name is Han Solo, and that he came here on your ship."

Metara's jaw tensed; even Han saw that tell, and Viest couldn't possibly have missed it. But either Leia wasn't surprised, or she was just too tough to show it. Han was betting on the latter. Still cool, Leia said to Viest, "Then you know we'd like him back. We can still be reasonable about this."

No, we really can't, Han thought, and tried to catch Leia's eye. He considered just yelling out that the *Falcon* was in orbit, but he had no idea what kind of game Leia was playing. Itran kept his mouth shut, too, just watching the confrontation. Too bad he hadn't kept his mouth shut earlier.

Viest strolled forward until she was within a pace

of Leia. "You talk as if you've got an unseen weapon aimed at my head."

"You're very perceptive." Leia considered her thoughtfully. Han hoped she wasn't bluffing. Her expression hardened just a trace. "So let him down."

"Oh, not quite yet." Viest's gaze moved over Leia's face, as if searching for something. "I always wanted to meet an Alderaanian Princess."

Han rolled his eyes and shook his head. He wanted to live long enough to kill Itran—that was all he was asking here. If they died in the next moment, he just hoped Leia knew he wasn't the one who had talked.

Metara's indrawn breath was clearly audible. The woman would make a terrible sabacc player. All Leia did was lift a brow and nod slightly, as if awarding Viest a point in the game they were playing. "When did you find out?"

Viest smiled, arch and sardonic and clearly enjoying the situation. She obviously wanted to make Leia show fear. But Leia had faced down Darth Vader; Han figured Viest didn't have a chance. "That I had such a famous guest? I just read it off you."

Leia let a trace of amusement cross her expression. "I don't think so. You're good, but you're not that good."

Metara stepped forward, closer to Viest, as if trying to stand between her and Leia. "Why do you care? Everyone here has a past. Why does it matter to you?"

Viest threw her an angry look. "I care because you lied to me. And because the rebels were hired to break up my business."

Metara's brow furrowed. "What?"

"She lied to you, too?" Viest laughed. "When I first

heard about an Alderaanian gunship stuck in a repair dock, I thought you'd be a good tool, but obviously I'm not the first to use you."

Leia cut in, telling Metara, "I came here to buy supplies from a merchant consortium. They wanted to raise money to defend their ships, but Viest knows that." She eyed the flightmaster. "We knew there was a traitor among the merchants, but you have information that could only have come from an Imperial source." She folded her arms. Han was pretty certain she had a blaster tucked inside her jacket, but the problem was Viest would probably guess that, too. "How many of the ships that dock here know you trade intel with the Empire? How many have you sold out to Imperial patrols and customs?"

Leia paused a beat, clearly waiting for all the avidly listening pirates to absorb that idea. Managing to sound somewhat disappointed in Viest, she added, "I never saw you as an Imperial lackey, but maybe I'm a poor judge of character."

Viest obviously didn't like the direction the conversation was going. "I don't give a damn about the Empire, and I certainly don't take orders from them." She tried to keep her expression controlled, but her gaze hardened, her anger so intense not even her Lorrdian training could hide it. "So you admit you're here to help some ignorant merchants ruin what took years to build."

"Their trade took years to build, too," Leia said. "And you know all about survival at any cost, don't you? You can understand why they have to fight you."

"Those soft, planetbound grubbers don't know

anything about survival." Viest stepped closer to
Leia. "I took this place from Ingan dire Stane, a Zy-
gerrian slaver, and it took years of crawling and beg-
ging and making myself his pet before he gave me
enough time and freedom to take over. He never
guessed what I was really after, not until the moment
I cut his throat. No one will take it from me, especially not some little Princess from a dead planet."

Furious, Metara shoved Viest back. Every pirate
tensed. Han looked at all those blasters aimed at them
and thought, *I hope you have a better plan than this,
Your Holiness.*

Leia lifted her hands. "Let's be calm. We came here
to talk—"

"No, you didn't." Viest stared, reading something
from Leia's expression that Han couldn't see. "You're
waiting for something." She stepped back and ordered the pirates, "Kill them—"

That was when something huge, metal, and angry
slammed into the port with a crash that made the
floor vibrate.

CHAPTER TWELVE

FINALLY, LEIA THOUGHT. *Did the blasted thing swing by Coruscant before it climbed up here?* The droid's ocular devices glared, somehow radiating savage fury despite the fact that they were only metal and lenses. Spidering cracks shot through the transparent port, and the droid's drilling arm punched through with a crash and an ear-piercing whine. The horrified pirates fired their blasters at it, which was absolutely the wrong thing to do.

As Viest reflexively drew her blaster, Leia lunged for her, twisted the blaster out of Viest's grip, and slammed a punch into the woman's face. Viest staggered and fell back. Leia hesitated, but Viest lay still. *Well, that wasn't very satisfying.*

Metara drew her own blaster from her jacket and fired at the confused pirates. Andevid scrambled away to take cover behind the holovid console. It was just as well; Leia had removed the power cell from his blaster.

The droid plunged through the room, bowled over the Gamorrean, and slammed two more pirates aside. Viest tried to get up and had to fling herself down again as the droid seized a float-lounge and threw it across the room. With Viest's blaster, Leia fired past the droid at the pirates who had taken cover behind the old consoles at the far end of the room. Seeing that they had enough to distract them, she ran for Han. She had to free him and Kifar; right now they were the best targets in the room, for both the droid *and* the pirates.

Behind her the droid tore through the chamber, flinging aside furniture, consoles, and anything else that got in its way. Allian was supposed to have programmed the droid to make straight for the exit to the room, but when the pirates shot at it its defensive routines must have taken over. Allian was also supposed to have disarmed those defenses, but clearly he hadn't been able to eliminate all of them. Leia ducked as a chair flew over her head and hoped they hadn't made a terrible mistake.

The door slid open and Sian and Terae barreled in and fired at a Mirialan and two humans, the last pirates on their feet. The droid roared and they scrambled for cover. Leia reached Han, but she couldn't see the control for the power coupling. "Where is it?" she demanded.

"Don't know," he told her. "Just shoot it!"

Leia was afraid that would either short out the field or kill him. "Are you sure?"

"Yes—" he began. Then: *"Get down!"*

Leia hit the floor just as something heavy flew past. She looked up as the Mirialan pirate slammed into the far wall, knocked across the room by the droid. Leia shoved to her feet and aimed carefully at the small power-coupling generator half a meter above Han's bound hands, then fired.

The field flared and vanished. Han hit the floor and collapsed. Leia squelched the urge to make sure he was all right and turned toward Kifar Itran. He was only a few meters away and had managed to knock his chair over to get out of the line of fire. His binders were locked to the metal arms; he struggled to break them but couldn't get free. Leia flung herself down again as the droid threw another console across the room. Apparently happy with the destruction it had wrought here, it roared again and dived out through the port.

Leia shoved to her feet. Viest and three other pirates sprawled on the floor; the others had either fled or been hurled elsewhere by the droid. Sian, Terae, and Andevid cautiously climbed out of the cover of the piles of shattered furniture. Metara stepped around the wreckage of the expensive holoconsole. She had her comlink out and was saying, "Fera, Fera, come in. The droid just went back out into the cavern. Are you clear?"

Leia reached Kifar and crouched beside his chair. "Are you all right?"

"Yes. Yes, Your Highness, I'm sorry—" Kifar began.

"Don't worry," Leia replied, more concerned with trying to free him so they could get away. Whatever he wanted to apologize for, it could wait; anyway, considering how much Viest had learned about her, she had a good idea of what it was. She realized she didn't have anything to cut the binders and Kifar was too twisted around to risk using the blaster. "Metara, do you have a—"

Kifar's eyes widened as he stared past her. "Princess!" he gasped.

Leia twisted around to see Viest roll to her feet, pointing something at her. It didn't look like a blaster. Han yelled an incoherent warning, and a hard shove to her shoulder knocked Leia aside.

Leia hit the floor just as something like a weird sonic pulse passed through her. It made no audible sound, but her bones vibrated from the deep bass of it. She lifted her head just as blaster bolts from two different directions hit Viest.

Viest collapsed. The bolts had struck her chest and stomach, leaving searing wounds that must have killed her instantly. Confused, Leia looked up at Metara, still standing over her. "What was that thing she—"

Fired at us, she meant to finish. But Metara swayed and her knees started to buckle. Alarmed, Leia sat up and caught her as she fell, took her whole weight and guided her to the floor as the woman went limp. She couldn't see any wound. There was no blood on Metara's gray shirt or jacket, no mark from any kind of projectile. She was still breathing, her eyes aware but wide in shock.

"Metara, can you hear me?" Leia demanded. "Where are you hurt?"

Han knelt at Metara's side, his wrists still in binders. Staring down at her, he said, "It was some kind of sonic mining probe. I didn't know she could use it from a distance." He met Leia's gaze. "This is about to get ugly."

Terae flung herself down beside them, calling out, "Captain!"

Han made room for her. The color had drained from Metara's face, and she still looked more surprised than in pain.

"You're going to be fine," Leia said automatically. Maybe she was just stunned. If they could get her to the ship—

Then Metara drew a breath, and blood bubbled at her lips. She gripped Leia's hand and said, her voice thick and strained, "Take care of them."

"You know I will," Leia whispered.

Metara's body convulsed once and started to collapse inward, as if she were being crushed by some force they couldn't see. Her eyes went blank; blood ran from her mouth and nose. Terae made a strangled, horrified noise in her throat.

Leia's stomach tried to turn and she swallowed hard. She sat back, released Metara's hand, and carefully folded the captain's limp arm across the ruin of her body. *Stupid waste.* All of it was a stupid waste. Metara, Viest, the pirates, this whole place. She shook her head and looked up. She didn't have time for the emotion, not now. "Somebody get Han and Kifar out of those binders. We have to get out of here."

Sian moved first, fumbling a small cutter out of her pocket and stepping over to Kifar. Terae stayed where she was, staring down at her captain, anguish on her face. Leia pushed to her feet. "Terae, we have to go. The seismic charge."

Terae's face was terrible to look at, drained and sick as if she had been shot as well. But she nodded, took Metara's comlink and her blaster, and got to her feet.

"The what?" Han asked, lifting his hands for Sian to cut the binders off. Kifar staggered to his feet, stretching his neck. "You still set the charge?"

"You're blowing the place up?" Andevid asked, startled.

Leia told Han, "Yes, but we should have plenty of time to—"

She heard Fera yell, "Captain! The charge—" over the comlink, just before the floor flew up and hit her.

Lying on her back, her ears ringing, tasting blood from a bitten lip, Leia had time to realize the metal floor plates had not actually risen up and slammed her in the back of the head. Her body had been knocked flat by the concussion of the blast.

She sat up in time to see the last sheet of transparent material in the port slide out and drift away in the cavern. The others were all groaning, trying to rise.

Sprawled nearby, Han inquired acidly, "You were saying, Your Worship?"

Leia shoved herself upright, saying through gritted teeth, "You know, you could be a little more supportive right now."

Terae struggled to sit up, then pulled her comlink out and said frantically, "Fera, report!"

A moment later Fera's shaken voice came over the com. "It went off early, Lieutenant—the droid set it off. We'd nearly made it back to the tunnel when we saw it climb down the wall from the control center. It was going back and forth along the wall there, just flailing around, and it must have gotten too close to the charge . . . Are you all right?"

Terae shook her head in mute denial. *No, we're not all right,* Leia thought bitterly, but Fera and the others didn't need to know about Metara just now.

"Get back to the ship, as fast as you can," Terae ordered. "We'll meet you there."

Leia said, "Right, let's get moving." They had just run out of time. Anakaret wouldn't have sent her transmission yet, so there would be no confusion among the ships in orbit or the other ships docked here. Somebody would be on their way to find out just what had exploded. And if Leia knew anything about pirates, everybody on the asteroid who had ever hoped to kill Viest and take over her part of the operation would be coming to find out if she was dead or injured. As Han got to his feet, she handed him Viest's blaster and drew her own from inside her jacket.

"Terae, you—" She was interrupted by a loud *crack* reverberating through the metal floor. The whole control center shuddered. Leia grabbed the side of the holotable to steady herself.

Sian staggered but stayed on her feet. "That sounded like—I hope we didn't just come loose from that bridge . . ."

Deep under the floor somewhere, metal shrieked and groaned. "I think that's exactly what happened." Leia started for the doorway.

Moving cautiously, Leia led the way out of what had been Viest's private quarters and into the main room of the control center. As they reached it, another screech of strained metal echoed through the chamber and the whole structure lurched sideways. Leia stumbled into Han and he caught her arm, swaying to keep his balance. Keeping his voice low, he said, "Hey, it wasn't me that talked."

"I know," she told him. She had never seriously considered the thought that he might have.

Han eyed her suspiciously, as if he doubted her word, but then said, "Give me your comlink—the *Falcon*'s here."

Startled, Leia handed the comlink over. "What?"

"Yeah, Viest told me about it; she knew it was my ship." He was eyeing Kifar, who had gotten a blaster from one of the dead pirates and was following Sian toward the doorway. It was clear whom Han suspected.

He adjusted the comlink's frequency and said, "Chewie, Chewie, come in." There was a long moment of static, and Leia had a moment of doubt. Viest might have been lying, or she might already have ordered one of her pet captains to fire on the *Falcon*. From Han's expression, she knew similar thoughts were going through his head. Then they heard a welcome and familiar Wookiee growl.

Leia let out her breath in relief. Chewbacca went on at length, probably with questions and a lot of comments about dumb Corellians who thought it was a good idea to run off to pirate ports. With difficulty, Han managed to interrupt. "Hey, hey, listen to me! Yeah, we're fine, but we're busy. Just stay where you are and don't do anything until I say so."

Han signed off before Chewbacca could protest, and Leia took back the comlink. Ahead of them, Sian had made it up the stairs, which now slanted to the right as the floor shifted. She took a look through the hatch and reported, "Princess, the bridge is torn out of the wall."

Leia dragged her focus back to the immediate problem and followed Sian up the steps. Cool, dank air flowed down from the shaft, now heavy with the smell of ozone and superheated metal. The entire control center had moved back toward the cavern, and the bridge that crossed from it to the main section of the asteroid had been torn from its moorings. One large piece still hung from the gallery of the control center, festooned with the moored lifters dragged down with it.

"We can still get across," Terae said. "One of those liftpallets—"

Sian stepped down to try to grab the mooring chain for the nearest one. Then Leia spotted movement in the waiting area across the shaft. Han snapped, "Get back!"

Sian retreated hastily, and they all ducked back through the doorway as a dozen or more pirates ran into the waiting area, shouting, exclaiming in alarm as they saw the broken bridge. Leia assumed they were the scavengers, here to see if Viest was dead, as she had predicted. Some of them undoubtedly hoped to finish the job if they found her only wounded. Once the word spread, more would be arriving from the ships in orbit.

"We can go out through the cavern and take one of the haulage tunnels," she said. The lift tubes were likely broken, too, but there were enough old repulsorsleds and lifters around that the pirates would have no trouble getting over here. They could also go around via the tunnels and come up through the low-gravity area of the cavern. "We have to move fast, before we're trapped here."

"They're going to be right behind us," Han said.

Leia crossed the room to the port and looked out into the cavern. Dust floated in the air, swirling in odd patterns due to the low gravity, with chunks and fragments of rock. Light from the control center glinted off metal shrapnel, possibly the remains of the unfortunate droid. She couldn't see the lights in the arena or the technician's work area below. "We can get out through the lift tube shaft—Blast!" Small lights suddenly appeared below, long, glowing shafts moving erratically but coming closer. They were hand-lights, carried on lifters or small repulsors. "They're already coming up that way."

"We could go straight through to the docking ring if we take the tunnel borer," Andevid suggested.

Leia turned to face him. "The what?"

"Piece of machinery left over from the old mine," he explained. "Viest used it to destroy ships in dock. They would be expecting an attack from the docking ring, or for some ship to fire on them from outside. But she and her crew would take it through the deep tunnels, then up through the bay and under the ship, and use the excavating lasers on it." He shrugged. "Never could open those docking bays again. Even these pirates aren't dumb enough to put their ships down in a docking bay with a big hole in the floor."

Leia thought of all the closed bay doors they had passed along the docking ring. Presumably pirates wouldn't want to put their ships down in a bay filled with wreckage and skeletal remains, either. "Show us where it is," she said.

Andevid turned away. "Out here. If it didn't get destroyed in that blast."

They followed him across the chamber to the passage that led to the lift tubes. "Viest had some imagination," Han commented.

"You don't know half of it," Andevid told him. He added to Leia, "That's what she was planning to do to your ship. Got it all powered up and ready."

Leia wasn't surprised. Terae swore under her breath and looked toward the chamber where Viest and Metara lay.

Andevid continued, "She was going to do it a couple of hours from now, once the ships that are in dock at the cargo port finished their trading and left. They're independents, not beholden to her, and she never wanted them to know too much about what she was doing. In case she decided to take them out someday."

All the lift tube control panels blinked with fault warnings, damaged when the control center shifted. Andevid took them past the tubes and down a curving stair, into a smaller control room lined with old dead consoles, with a large hatch opening toward the cavern. Two ports on either side showed something bulky blocking it. Andevid tapped the controls, and the hatch slid open. Leia and Han stepped over to take a look.

The tunnel borer was shaped like a long tube, about twice the size of a multiple-passenger escape pod. It had a cone-shaped disk on its nose to emit the cutting lasers. This part of the cavern was in deep shadow, and if anyone looked up from the arena or the other spaces below, the tunnel borer would just be another piece of derelict mining equipment. In the light from the ports, Leia could see that while the metal sides were stained with mineral streaks, the hatch keypad was clean and faint ready lights shone from it and from the cutting disk.

Han leaned out, braced himself with one hand on the side of the borer, and touched the keypad. The hatch slid open. Automatic lights blinked on, showing a narrow interior with a small cockpit and long bench seats along the walls.

"Can you run this thing?" Han asked Andevid.

"Never been in it," Andevid told him. "I know which tunnel they used to get it to the docking ring, though."

Sian had dropped back by the doorway to listen for pursuit. "I can hear them banging around somewhere above us," she said quietly. "Must be searching the place."

"Heavy machinery is the same all over," Kifar said. "Should be easy enough to figure out."

Han swung into the hatch and folded himself into the borer's tiny cockpit. "That depends on who built it."

Leia motioned for the others to follow him. Andevid and Terae stepped lightly across and Kifar followed, ducking and turning sideways to make it through the borer's narrow hatchway. Sian and Leia boarded last. Han had already gotten the life support started, so Leia sealed the hatch.

Sian activated a small console on the wall and tried to get the display to come up as Kifar and Andevid looked over her shoulders. "I think this is a mapping utility," she muttered. "Yes, here we go."

A small holoimage of the mine sprang to life in mid-air, a few centimeters from Leia's nose. She stepped back to get a better view. Even at first glance, it was far more complete than the map Han and Sian had managed to copy earlier: it showed the asteroid riddled with tunnels that followed the paths of what must have been veins of various ores. A few sections seemed to have been left untouched, but not many.

"The other map only showed the tunnels and traverses meant for the small transports and droids," Sian said. "This one has all the tunnels for the actual digging equipment. Solo, can you get this up in the cockpit?"

"Hold it . . . Yeah."

Leia stepped forward and looked over Han's shoulder. The controls were complicated and labeled with symbols she didn't recognize. "Can you drive this thing?" she asked, keeping her voice low. From this angle she could see blood matting the hair at Han's temple and recalled belatedly that he must have had some kind of head injury. She hoped he didn't have a concussion.

"Sure. Sort of. Maybe," Han murmured, more concerned with figuring out the operation of the controls. A smaller version of the map had appeared above the console. There was no viewport: this vehicle had been designed to travel through solid rock or the darkness of a completed tunnel. Leia felt the deck vibrate as the powerful engine rumbled to life. Then she grabbed a safety handle as the vehicle rolled away from the control center, maneuvering lightly on repulsors. A sensor view of the cavern that had appeared below the

map rolled with it, showing the walls and the other
moored mining machines in outline.

"Good, that works like it looked like it did," Han
said, not reassuringly. "Andevid, get up here and
show me that tunnel."

Leia stepped back to make room, and the Aqualish
squeezed past her to stab a clawed finger toward the
holoimage of the cavern. "There, down and under the
control center," he said.

"Right." Han didn't sound thrilled, and Leia could
see why. *Yes, right below the control center—which
is in the process of pulling free from the rock and
sliding down into the cavern.* It was doing it slowly,
because of the low gravity, but it was still doing it.

Han rolled the borer around again and dropped it
down until it was pointed toward the rock face below
the control center. "This looks like it," he said as the
holo displayed a blue-lined round opening among the
red streaks depicting the folds in the rock.

Loud bangs echoed through the compartment,
though the hull didn't vibrate. Leia thought it was
debris falling onto them, then remembered the low
gravity. "The pirates are firing on us." Unless they
had brought up something bigger than hand blasters,
she didn't think they had a chance of getting through
the hull, but if they were able to damage the engines . . .

"Can we shoot back?" Kifar asked.

Han said, "Yeah, let's open the hatch, and you can
stick your head out—"

Andevid snorted.

Leia set her jaw. "Han. Just drive."

"Yes, Your Worship." Han took the borer forward

into the tunnel. Leia winced away from the scraping sound as the hull vibrated. Swearing under his breath, Han corrected their course slightly and increased the power to the repulsors. "Gravity kicked back in—it threw us off a little."

They moved forward slowly, leaving the cavern behind. Leia started to breathe easier. There was no way anyone with any sense was going to follow them down here. They would all be trying to loot or seize control of Viest's headquarters.

The tunnel borer rumbled around a curve, and suddenly the display showed a solid wall of red.

"What happened?" Han demanded.

"Oh." Andevid stared at the holomap. "Maybe it wasn't this tunnel."

"Maybe?" Leia stared at him. The others watched in a combination of concern and incredulity.

"It's not like Viest took me for rides in this thing," Andevid said, studying the map. "Wait, wait, here it is. It was lower down, and to the right."

Han twisted around to give Andevid a dark look. Leia was pretty certain it matched the one on her face. Andevid said, "Sorry, but I'm sure this time."

"Can we back out?" Leia asked, thinking, *The pirates must be almost at the control center by now.*

"No, we'll do it this way," Han said, and hit a control on the panel. A high-powered hum traveled through the deck, and another holodisplay appeared.

Leia recognized the disk shapes. "The laser cutters? Are you—"

Crazy, she meant to finish, but Han pushed the control yoke down and the rumble turned into a roar.

Leia grabbed the safety handle and watched, fascinated, as the rock on the holodisplay dissolved.

"This is kind of fun," Andevid commented.

"You've got to get out more, buddy," Han told him.

"That's true," Andevid agreed.

Leia told herself the machine had been designed for this. The machine was also who-knew-how-old, probably poorly maintained, had been used as an impromptu means of destroying starships, and was being driven by Han Solo. She was in the process of developing claustrophobia when the last of the rock fell away and they came out into a tunnel. This one was barely bigger than the borer; it had probably been dug by it at some point.

Behind her, Leia heard Sian swear with relief. She glanced back to see Kifar holding on to a handle so tightly that his knuckles had gone dark orange, and Terae looked ill. Leia took out her comlink to call the *Aegis,* but all she got was static. She looked at Terae and Sian. "Can you get anything?"

Both checked, and both shook their heads. "This thing's hull must be heavily shielded," Terae said. "Signals just aren't getting through."

Leia looked around for anything that resembled a comm but couldn't find one. "Han, how close can you get us to the *Aegis*?"

Cool and vaguely preoccupied, as if he did this every day, Han steered the machine down the tunnel. "Check the map; look for a good route."

Leia traced the tunnels, finding the docking ring immediately. The borer's guidance system had marked all the old exploratory tunnels used to find ore veins

in the bulk of the asteroid, some distance below the
cavern. But the new tunnels toward the docking bays
were flagged with warning symbols. Clearly, Viest
had been overriding the machine's safety features to
make them. It was a good thing there were nearly a
hundred bays along the length of the docking ring,
since Viest had destroyed twenty of them over the
years. The closest one to the *Aegis* was six bays down,
at the end of the ring, where it split to head toward
the larger loading area that Han had said the pirates
used to store and trade cargoes.

Leia leaned closer suddenly. *And the slave pen.* She
pulled out her comlink and checked the time to Anakaret's transmission. She smiled. "I have an idea."

In the cockpit of the *Millennium Falcon*, in orbit
above the asteroid, Luke said, "Wait, ask him—"

Chewbacca flung his arms in the air in frustration
as Han signed off.

"Blast it! He didn't even say if Leia was with him!"
Luke exclaimed.

Luke tried to raise Han again but got no answer.
"Nothing," he told Chewie. Either the comlink was
turned off, or they were cut off by some kind of inter-
ference.

Chewie shook his head and rumbled something
that sounded unhappy.

From behind them, C-3PO translated, "He says
that Captain Solo said to wait. He was very rude.
Captain Solo, I mean, not Chewbacca. Not that time,
anyway."

Chewbacca scrubbed his forehead and moaned in frustration.

"Wait, fine," Luke muttered. At least they knew Han and Leia were here, and alive. Or at least that Han was alive. But surely Han would have sounded worse if things had gone so badly.

He tapped his fingers on the console and stopped when Chewie glanced at him in irritation. Luke didn't think he could wait anymore without losing his mind.

They had spent the trip here trying not to talk about how worried they were. Chewbacca had sat in the cockpit disassembling, cleaning, and reassembling his bowcaster over and over again, with nervous precision. With nothing else to do but watch him, Luke was now fully prepared for a life-or-death situation where he had to assemble a bowcaster blindfolded. All the questions like *what if they aren't here, what if we can't find them, what if we never see them again* had hung in the air between them.

Now at least those questions were answered. Before Han's call, Chewie had been going through the ships' IDs that had shown up in the comm system and trying to find the *Aegis,* while Luke searched the sensor data for any ship that matched its description. If that hadn't turned up anything, they had been planning to call the asteroid's controller and try to talk their way into a landing berth.

So far the *Falcon* hadn't drawn any unwanted attention, mostly because there were dozens of other small, battered freighters in the vicinity, and Luke thought they were doing a good job of blending in. They had had to identify themselves when they arrived, but the controller hadn't seemed interested.

Good thing Han and Chewie hadn't been out this way in a long while, he thought wryly.

Luke couldn't just sit here. "We could try finding the *Aegis* and contacting it."

Chewbacca gave him a look with lowered brows. Luke knew enough about Wookiee facial expressions to realize it meant *Is there something wrong with you?* He said, "Yeah, yeah, I know. It's probably not a good idea until we know what the situation is."

Then the comm system signaled a transmission coming in on the asteroid's all-ship frequency. Luke listened to the beginning and blew out his breath. "Chewie, listen to this."

Chewie stabbed a blunt-clawed finger at the board, gesturing for Luke to turn up the volume. They listened as a female voice repeated a warning of Imperial ships entering the system and then played a fragment of the transmission her ship had picked up.

Chewbacca growled in frustration. The sensors showed ships already accelerating out of their orbits, scattering like startled womp rats. Luke shook his head, bit his lip in thought.

"Wait, wait, there's something funny about this." At Chewie's interrogatory growl, he added, "I don't know . . . Hold on."

The system had automatically recorded the transmission, and Luke played it again as Chewie listened intently.

"It's chopped up a lot," Luke said. "That's odd. Like her ship didn't receive the whole message." He ran it through the comm system, trying to match it to a type of Imperial ship. The *Falcon*'s database had been augmented by the Alliance's, so if this was a known class of ship, it should be in there. In another moment, the system signaled a match. Luke checked the result and thought, *Huh?* He sent it to Chewie's display. "This doesn't make any sense."

Chewie growled and waved his hands. C-3PO said, "He says that it can't be the Death Star, as you might recall the memorable occasion when it blew up. I think he's right about that, Master Luke. He says it has to be some kind of strange error in the transmission itself."

Luke listened to it again. He noted that the source never called itself the Death Star; the call signals were all clearly Imperial, but he bet the *Falcon,* the only ship here that had actually been in comm contact with the real Death Star, would be the only one to recognize that particular identifier in the signal. "It's funny how it's real clear in the part where it identifies itself as Imperial, but all chopped up when it gives the position and system information. This has to be a fake." He turned to Chewie. "Who do we know who might think of using an old copy of a Death Star transmission for this?"

Chewie sat up straight, hooted with delight, and gave Luke a shove to the head. Luke was glad he knew that was a gesture of approval. He turned back to the console. This had to be a plan concocted by Leia or Han or both.

Luke just wished he knew what the plan was, and how well it was going.

CHAPTER THIRTEEN

LEIA STOOD BY THE HATCHWAY, blaster drawn, braced to hit the door release. The others gathered behind her, with Han still in the cockpit and Andevid working the map utility. Han asked her, "Ready?"

The borer was buried in solid rock some fifty or so meters below what Leia sincerely hoped was the guard station for the living quarters the pirates had converted into a slave pen.

"If this thing doesn't come apart," Kifar said worriedly.

At this point, Leia was more concerned about the asteroid coming apart than the tunnel borer, considering how riddled the rock was with tunnels and pockets that weren't on the map. She told Han, "Ready."

Han leaned on the controls and the hull shook as the borer leapt upward, the laser disk slicing through the rock. Warning lights blinked in the cockpit. Leia held on to the overhead handrail and exchanged a grim look with Sian. They had agreed the borer would need to move as fast as possible so no one in the chamber above realized it was coming, but it felt like

Han had apparently found a way to push the machine past its already generous safety limits.

Their comlinks still weren't picking up any signals, but if Anakaret had kept her promise, she had sent her transmission just a few moments earlier. The docking ring and the ships in orbit should have just gotten the message warning of an Imperial force moving into range of the asteroid.

Leia very much hoped that Anakaret had kept her promise.

The borer rumbled and shuddered, then the deck swayed and bucked underfoot and the borer stopped abruptly, angled upward. All the warning lights flashed and the engines made an ominous clunking noise. But Han said, "We're there. Go!"

Leia hit the hatch release and Kifar jumped out. *He could have looked first,* Leia thought, exasperated. But Kifar obviously thought he had something to prove. He fired twice, then yelled, "We're clear!"

Sian and Terae surged out after him. As Leia started to follow, Han scrambled out of the borer's cockpit behind her. "Sweetheart, this thing is dead," he told her. "One of the power cells went out when we broke through the shielding on this floor."

Leia hesitated. "But we won't need it to get out of here."

Han shrugged. "Probably not."

Leia groaned under her breath and jumped out of the hatch into a chamber that looked as if it had been hit by an ion cannon. Lumas clustered near the high ceiling, pushed there by the tunnel borer's shields. They shone down on a jumble of stone rubble and torn metal floor plates. The hatch that must have se-

cured a large archway lay in the next chamber, twisted
and mangled. Two armed pirates lay sprawled near
it, unconscious or dead. Leia lifted her comlink, already tuned to the asteroid's emergency frequency,
and heard a babble of voices in Basic and other languages. Some were warning comrades of an Imperial
attack, others demanding to know the heading the
Imperials were coming in on; all were panicked.
Good, Leia thought with relief. *Thank you, Anakaret.*

In the far wall was a security blast door, clearly
jury-rigged into a wider space that had to be the entrance to the slave pen. Leia half climbed, half stumbled across the ruined floor to the door. It had an
access panel to one side, with a pad to enter a code
lock; the manual emergency release was blocked by a
plate welded into place. As Andevid climbed warily
out of the borer, Leia gestured with her blaster toward
the door. "You don't have the code for this lock, do
you?"

He shook his head. "Only Mekerel, who was in
charge of guarding the slaves for Viest, had it." He
glanced back at the borer and did a double take.
There was blood splashed on the rubble below the
cutter disk, and what looked like fragments of leather
and metal. "Maybe that's him."

Leia wasn't concerned with Mekerel's fate. As a slaver, he had probably deserved a great deal worse. But
it meant the code was unavailable, and they would
just have to get in the hard way. "Terae, if you
would," Leia said.

Terae stepped forward and pulled a fusioncutter
out of her tool satchel. She switched it on, crouched

beside the door, and started to cut through the armor over the door's manual release. "Shouldn't take long."

"Good, because we don't have long." Leia looked toward the archway, where Han, Kifar, and Sian had taken up guard positions. She could hear confused yelling somewhere ahead, and the distant rumble of ships' engines. After a moment Han slipped out and vanished down the passage. Sian followed him.

They were checking the escape route, making sure it was clear. Once away from the borer, with nothing to show they weren't just another crew of pirates, they could all walk out of here. Theoretically.

"Got it," Terae said. The panel fell away and she pulled the manual release. The door started to slide upward.

Leia stepped back, in case the prisoners had to be persuaded that they were actually being rescued. Terae moved to the side, drawing her blaster.

But the door opened to a small secure guard booth, protected by the flicker of a containment field. Beyond it, Leia could see a large bare room, with metal walls and floor, filled with battered, weary people staring warily at her.

"Hello," she said, as Terae stepped into the guard booth to examine the control panel. "I'm Leia Durane. We're here to rescue you." She didn't get to do this kind of thing very often and she meant to enjoy it, even knowing they might all be killed trying to get off the asteroid.

There were gasps, and a gold-skinned Videllan man pushed forward, asking, "You are with Captain Solo?"

"Yes. Are you Kearn-sa'Davit? I believe Han Solo told you we might be coming by."

The Videllan turned to face the others and declared, "We are saved!"

Terae glanced at Leia and nodded, indicating that she could drop the containment field. Leia told the prisoners, "We're going to take you to a ship now, and then we'll make a run for Arnot Station. You have to stay together, stay quiet, and follow us, is that clear?"

Davit consulted the others with a look, then assured Leia, "We are prepared, Leia Durane."

Leia signaled to Terae to drop the containment field. "All right, let's go."

Han and Sian found a wide, arched hatch that opened into the loading dock. They had seen this area from the end of the docking ring corridor, but then it had been filled with bickering pirates. Han had been hoping to find it empty, with everybody sensibly scrambling to get back to their ships, but the blasterfire that echoed through it told him that this particular hope was in vain.

He reached the hatch first, put his back to the wall, and took a careful look around the edge of the seal. Sian took the opposite side.

Bodies, blasted droids, and broken pressure crates lay strewn across the big loading bay. Just above it, where the ramp curved up to the docking bays, there was a blaster battle raging. One group had taken cover behind an old ore cart and a broken cargo lifter and were firing up at a second group, which held the entrance to the docking ring. Han couldn't tell how many were up there; they were hiding behind piles of broken droids and consoles on both sides of the entrance. A third group, which seemed to be shooting at both the other groups, was stationed out along the gallery just below the row of docking bay entrances that overlooked the loading area, firing from the cover of a mound of crates and storage barrels. The cargo that had apparently sparked the battle—little lumps of varicolored metal, spilled out of a scattering of broken security crates—was strewn across the far end of the loading area.

"Oh, you have to be kidding," Sian muttered. "Why don't they just run?"

"Because if they had any sense, they wouldn't be pirates," Han told her. He felt for his comlink and realized it was back at Viest's control center. "You got a comlink?" She tossed him one and he tuned it to the *Aegis*'s frequency. "*Aegis*, come in, this is Solo."

"This is *Aegis*," Kelvan's relieved voice said. "Where are you? Fera and Allian and the others said they lost contact with Captain Metara, and we haven't been able to raise anyone on the comlink."

"Yeah, we had to take another way out, and we couldn't get a signal through." There was no time to update Kelvan on everything that had happened; anyway, there was no way Han was going to be the one to give him the bad news about his captain. "We're breaking the prisoners out now. What's the situation in the docking ring?"

"Not good. Some of the ships farther down have taken off, but we can hear fighting out in the corridor. More ships are leaving orbit every moment, so if you can get to us, we should be able to make it out of here."

That was a pretty big "if" at the moment. These pirates were grabbing anything that wasn't nailed down and shooting anything that moved. If they tried to make their way through the cargo area, Han thought the chances were good that they would get shot as potential rivals for the goods. "We need a distraction."

"Like what?" Sian asked worriedly.

They needed something to remind the pirates that they were supposed to be under Imperial attack. "Kelvan," Han said, "I'm going to get a ship to fire on the bays in the docking ring between the *Aegis* and the cargo area. Just stay where you are until we call you."

He cut off Kelvan's startled "What ship—" and tuned the comlink, searching for the *Falcon*'s frequency. "Chewie, come in, it's me."

The quick response was a relief, and the first thing Chewbacca tried to do was demand to know if Han and Leia were behind the fake Death Star transmission and just what was going on down there? Han managed to get a word in edgewise to tell him, "Listen to me, I need your help right now. We're stuck here and we need a distraction. This is what I need you to do—"

Leia led the way through a set of smaller chambers and passages that had been torn apart by years of pirate occupation. She had put Kifar and Terae behind the prisoners, to guard their retreat and to make sure the stragglers kept up. The merchants and crew who had been captured on the ship with Davit were in the best shape, able to help the wounded. The ones who had been imprisoned there longer were suspicious, desperate, and not entirely sure they were being rescued and not just being transferred to different captors. They were mostly human, except for a small group of Sullustans and Duros and an Arkanian woman. Leia couldn't keep an eye on all of them and could only hope that no one decided to pick up a weapon and use it on her or Kifar or Terae. Andevid followed by her side, which helped a little. Leia had no idea if he would actually risk his hide for any of them, but he did look tough, so at least that was something.

She reached the last chamber, where an arched hatchway opened into the loading area, and found Han and Sian. She winced at the sound of blasterfire and fighting; obviously the pirates hadn't panicked and fled en masse as they had hoped.

"Solo!" Davit greeted Han with relief. "It's good to see you again, and not through a metal mesh."

"Yeah, it's good to be seen," Han said, leaning to look around the edge of the hatchway.

"What was this idea of yours?" Leia asked Han. She had heard the brief comlink conversation with Kelvan at the *Aegis,* and the prospect of getting down the docking ring hadn't sounded promising.

"I called the *Falcon,*" Han said. "Chewie's going to—"

An explosion rattled the metal floor plates under Leia's feet and sent dust and mold raining down from the rocky ceiling. Leia leaned around Han to see the loading area. "What was that?" The three rival groups of pirates holding the entrance docking ring and the cargo area had stopped shooting to stare around. The freed prisoners whispered nervously, and Davit glanced worriedly over his shoulder, as if afraid they would bolt.

"That was Chewie." Han watched the scene in the loading area intently. "Let's hope these guys get the message."

Distant rumbles sounded from the outer corridors, muffled by the layers of rock overhead. "Chewie is strafing the asteroid," Leia said, not sure whether to be appalled or . . . "That might actually work," she finished reluctantly. With the explosion in the interior and Anakaret's fake transmission, the idea that it was time to flee might finally penetrate some thick pirate skulls.

The crew nearest the ring of docking bays above the loading area gave in first. Someone must have given an order, because they fell back with almost military precision, efficiently covering one another until they could dodge back into their docking bay. That released the other two crews from their stand-off, one bolting in a noisy mob to vanish down the curving corridor of the docking ring, the other scrambling to grab what they could of the metal fragments scattered across the loading area. As the docking bay doors shut behind the first crew, the third crew charged up the ramp and headed for the last open bay.

"That's it," Han said, and stepped cautiously out of the hatch. "Come on."

Leia clicked her comlink. "Terae, we're moving. Make sure they keep up."

"Yes, Cap—Your High—Leia," Terae replied.

Leia followed Han and Sian as both kept a wary eye out for pirate stragglers. Andevid, Davit, and the prisoners followed her. They crossed the large open space of the loading area, passing several bloody and blasted bodies of humans, a couple of Bith, and a Rodian. "We're going to go along the docking ring to our ship," Leia told Davit, mainly to distract the prisoners near him who were listening nervously. She hoped none of them had gotten a good enough view of the *Aegis* during the battle to recognize it in dock. She wanted to wait until they disembarked at Arnot Station to explain to them that the pirate ship rescuing them was the same pirate ship that had captured them in the first place. "It's not far. It's—"

A yell from Kifar interrupted her. "Security droids!"

Leia spun around. *Oh, no.* Dark, cylindrical shapes floated out of the hatchway barely twenty meters behind them. Multiple arms ended in gleaming blaster nozzles. They were the security droids that guarded the cargo storage. One of the embattled crews must have summoned them, and it had taken this long for the droids to get around the traverses and junctions collapsed by the tunnel borer. "Run!" she shouted to the prisoners. "Move, now, this way!"

Andevid bolted immediately for the ramp up and out of the loading area. His path showed the prisoners where to run, and they followed in an almost orderly group. Han turned to Leia. "Get them up to the docking ring. We'll cover you."

The first droid fired its blasters, and Kifar and Terae

returned fire. Their bolts slagged its metal carapace and it wheeled around sideways, but the other droids moved past it to shoot across the loading area. Leia shouted, "Kifar, Terae, fall back!"

Sian ducked behind a pile of cargo pressure crates and popped back up with a blast rifle dropped by one of the dead pirates. She steadied it atop the crate and opened fire. The Arkanian woman broke off from the mass of fleeing prisoners, grabbed a fallen pistol, and took cover beside Sian to pepper the droids with energy bolts.

As Kifar and Terae reached them and skidded around to dive behind the crates, Han gave Leia a push. "Just go! We'll catch up!"

Leia would have argued, but the next bolt slagged the rock barely a meter in front of them. She ran after the prisoners, throwing a worried glance back to see Han dive for cover and pop up again to return fire.

She caught up with the prisoners and kept going, dodging around them to get in front, since she had no idea where Andevid might lead them. There was no way Han and the others could make it all the way along the docking ring to the *Aegis* with those droids on their heels, but they might make it to the bays above the loading area. Leia pulled out her comlink. "Chewie, this is Leia, come in."

"Leia!" It was Luke's voice. Leia had a moment of heady relief, glad he was here as well as Chewbacca. "Are you all right? What—"

"Luke, listen." She threw a glance back. The droids were trying to advance on the cargo containers, their attention focused on the people shooting at them. "We need the *Falcon* to land and pick up Han and

some others. There are empty docking bays right
above their position. It's next to the spot Han had
you fire on."

"We're on it," Luke answered firmly. "We'll be
right there."

Han broke into the conversation. "Stop worrying
about us and get out of here, sweetheart!"

Leia could hear blasterfire and Sian cursing in the
background. She said, "Shut up and keep shooting
droids!"

She reached the top of the ramp just as Davit and
Andevid did. Davit had picked up a blaster. Past the
hatch, there was a wide bend in the ring corridor,
cutting off visibility ahead. It was a good spot for an
ambush.

"Wait," she snapped, and Andevid slid to a halt.
Davit flung out his arms to signal the others to stop.
Leia explained, "There might be some pirates left be-
hind in this corridor. I'll go first—"

A rumble shook the floor. Maybe fifty meters down
the curve of the corridor, dust and debris rained
down from the ceiling above the metal droid track.
"What—" Leia had time to say, then cracks opened
across the rock and chunks of stone crashed to the
floor. "Get back!" she yelled.

They scrambled back to the stone safety barrier at
the edge of the ramp, ducking down and huddling
against it. The rumble of falling and shifting stone
rattled Leia's teeth and echoed in her bones. A cloud
of dust and foul air rolled over them as the sound
faded.

Leia lifted her head. The prisoners coughed in the
dust; one of the wounded cried out in pain. Beside

her, Davit sat up and shook the dust out of his fluffy hair. "We're still breathing," he gasped. "That's good."

An optimist, Leia thought. She didn't know if they could get past the collapse. People were shouting on her comlink. One was Luke, and she heard him say, "Leia, we can't get through the containment fields on those bays." Chewie's yowl of frustration sounded in the background. "There's some kind of force-shield over them. I don't know: maybe it's a safety feature."

Or defensive feature. "That's very bad news, Luke," Leia said, thinking frantically. "Take the *Falcon* out of there and we'll call you—" *When I know what to do. Hopefully before we're all dead.* "We'll call you later."

Andevid, crouched close enough to listen, said, "Somebody activated the mine's defense system. Probably whoever took over the control center. Ships can get out, but nothing can get in."

Han's voice on her comlink demanded, "Are you all right? What happened?"

"This part of the docking ring collapsed." She had to stop to cough as a dust cloud rolled down the corridor. "Next time tell Chewie to strafe more carefully!"

"What now, Leia Durane?" Davit asked her, his face drawn and anxious. "There is another way around?"

"There has to be." Leia shoved to her feet and looked back at the loading area, hoping for inspiration. They were above the docking ring, with the automated ore-cart tracks running just below. She could see that the six large bays had open roofs to allow the carts to enter for loading. Five of those bays were now empty; one was still occupied, though from this angle she could only get a glimpse of the ship inside. "Andevid, what ship is in that bay?"

"It belongs to Ravin Thiss, one of Viest's captains. He probably went to the control center when the word came that she was killed."

"How many crew are likely to be in there?"

"Probably not many—maybe two or three," Andevid said. "He's small-time, only got a crew of twenty for boarding parties. If he was trying to take Viest's place, he would have needed most of them with him." He stared at her in admiration. "You want to take the ship?"

The possibility of twenty armed pirates didn't sound small-time to Leia. "No, but that's what we're going to do." She turned back to Davit. "Everyone with a weapon, follow me. The rest of you wait here." She gestured to the support pillar and the safety barrier the pirates had used to fire down on the loading area. "Take cover over there, and when you see the bay doors open, get inside as fast as you can."

Leia knew the bay doors were sealed and heavily shielded. If she blasted the lock, it would destroy the mechanism and they would have to try to crank them open manually. It would leave plenty of time for the people guarding the ship to realize what was going on. They were going to have to go in through the top.

She turned to the Aqualish. "Andevid, why are you still here? Is it because you think I'll shoot you if you try to leave?"

"Not really. I don't think you remember you captured me, most of the time." Andevid scratched his chin below his tusk. "I was going to run away, but my escape route keeps getting cut off."

"Where were you going to go?"

"I was going to try to steal a ship, but . . ." He shrugged. "Since you're doing that, too . . ."

"All right, I'd like to hire you, as a crewman, until we reach Arnot Station. I'll pay you five hundred credits."

"Done."

Leia handed him the power pack she had taken out of his blaster. "Right."

She holstered her blaster, took two running steps, and jumped down onto the ore-cart track. She landed in a crouch; the track trembled under her feet but didn't break. She started along it toward the bay, bracing herself as Andevid, Davit, and four other armed merchants landed behind her. She wished more of them had thought to grab weapons off dead pirates on their flight from the slave pen.

Her comlink beeped, and she answered it. "Yes?"

Kelvan said, "Don't try to approach our docking ring! Someone's trying to cut through the bay doors. They must be trying to take the ship—"

Leia opened a connection to both the *Falcon* and Han's comlink. "Kelvan, I want you to launch the *Aegis* and get away from the asteroid. There's another ship out there that's with us. ID *Millennium Falcon*. I want you to rendezvous with it and prepare to jump to lightspeed. Luke, did you copy that?"

Luke replied, "Yes, but Leia—"

Kelvan said, "But what—"

Han cut in, "Leia, what the hell are you doing?"

Leia snapped, "Luke, Kelvan, do as you're told.

We'll join you as soon as possible. Han, just give me a minute." Reaching the spot where the ore track extended over the thick bay wall, she motioned to Andevid and Davit and the others to hang back. She eased forward and took a cautious look over the edge. She could see the ship, a freighter about twice the size of the *Falcon* and in outwardly better condition. Its engines were steaming in the damp air. Good, it was hot and ready to go.

Which meant Thiss might be on his way back and ready to abandon the mine.

An armed Rodian was stationed by the ramp, and a human man stood near the bay doors. The human started to turn to survey the ore-cart track, and Leia ducked out of his line of sight. From this angle she could just see the top of the Rodian's head. She lowered her voice and said into the comlink, "Han, send someone up here to bang on the doors of this closed docking bay. I need the guard inside distracted."

Han swore incredulously, but she heard him say, "Itran, get up there!"

"Tell him to say he was sent by Ravin Thiss with a message," Leia added.

With a few whispers and gestures, she described the guards' positions to Andevid and Davit. A few moments later, Kifar ran up the ramp, waved to Leia from below, and stopped at the bay entrance. Leia nodded to him and he pounded on the door with his free hand, shouting, "Hey, open up, I've got a message from Thiss!"

Leia said, "Now!" and flung herself forward. She hit the track on her side and fired at the human guard near the doors. Andevid and Davit surged forward and fired at the Rodian near the ship's ramp. Leia hit her target in the shoulder and the chest, and the man went down. Andevid and Davit both missed, and Leia flattened herself to the filthy metal as the Rodian returned fire. She and Davit had their blasters on stun, but Andevid and the Rodian didn't and the bolts melted the track over Leia's head. She rolled over and crawled forward, trying for a better angle. Two meters farther and she could just catch a hint of green under the edge of the ramp where the Rodian had taken cover. She took a deep breath, lifted up on her elbow, and fired.

The Rodian stumbled backward, Davit hit him again, and the guard went down.

"Come on!" Leia shoved upright and ran along the track until she was above the ship's hull. The track was configured differently from the one in the *Aegis*'s bay, and it was only a three-meter drop. She holstered her blaster and swung down, then let go.

One of her ankles turned in as she landed and she let her weight go limp, hit the hard metal with her shoulder, and rolled. The landing still hurt, but she didn't break any bones. Cursing the ship for not having a topside hatch, she hobbled to the ramp and climbed down the support strut. The Rodian lay sprawled unconscious beside the ship's closed hatch. Leia stepped forward and hit the release. *Please, oh, please* . . . The hatch slid open and she let out the breath she was holding.

Andevid dropped to the ground near the ramp, with Davit and the other merchants awkwardly climbing down the struts after him. Leia stepped into the hatch, leaned against the safety sensor that would keep it open if someone tried to close it, and said, "Andevid, open the bay doors." The Aqualish might be somewhat trustworthy, but she wasn't letting him on this ship alone; he was still a pirate.

Andevid ran to obey. Leia opened the comlink again and said, "Han, we're leaving. Get everyone up here!"

Han didn't reply, but she heard his voice, thick with relief, as he told Sian and Terae and the Arkanian, "Come on, ladies, we're ditching this party."

Davit motioned for the merchants to precede him into the ship, telling them, "Search it quickly; make sure no one is inside," and took up a guard position with Leia. Leia felt momentarily grateful for Han's occasional good taste in acquaintances. The bay doors slid open for Andevid, and Kifar charged in.

A few tense moments later, he was followed by the first of the freed prisoners. "This way, hurry, into the ship!" Leia shouted.

The prisoners ran across the bay and up the ramp, some helping the limping wounded, two of the Sullustans carrying an unconscious comrade. On the comlink, Leia heard Han yelling, "Go, go!" and blasterfire. She said, "Davit, are you a pilot?"

"I am. You wish me to go to the cockpit and prepare for takeoff?"

"Yes, if you would."

Davit followed the last of the prisoners in, and Leia called out, "Andevid, Kifar, come on!"

Andevid came immediately, but Kifar hung back to take a look outside. He turned and started for the ship. "They're coming! The droids are chasing them!"

That was what Leia had thought might happen. As Kifar reached the ramp, Sian, Terae, and the Arkanian slammed through the bay doors at full speed. Leia had time for her heart to freeze before Han hit the side of the doorway, fired his blaster at whatever was chasing him, then slapped the control to seal the doors.

Leia stepped away from the safety sensor as the others ran through the hatch. Han pounded up the ramp and she stepped through with him, then hit the control to shut the hatch and raise the ramp. "You'd better get up to the cockpit," she told Han, "Davit will need some help."

Han, breathing hard, sweat sticking his shirt to his chest, paused to tell her, "You pulled this off just in time, Your Worship."

"You're welcome," Leia said, and holstered her blaster.

Degoren read the agent's comm transmission again. "'Will hold target here if possible,'" he quoted, incredulous. "Idiot. If the pirates kill her, we won't even have proof of her death."

"At least we know where Organa is," Sorvir said, though he couldn't keep the dubious tone out of his voice. "That's something."

"It's not enough." Degoren tapped the screen, making the gleaming letters vanish. "She's on Viest's clearinghouse. There's no telling what that scheming pirate will want in exchange for her."

They were on the bridge of the *Darsumae*, currently

heading for Arnot Station. Idlen Trehar, Degoren's agent on the station, had identified the rebel ship *Gamble,* docked under an altered ID, by the type of damage sustained in the attack. But Trehar hadn't been able to say for certain if Organa was actually aboard the *Gamble* or not.

Trehar had also reported that a small freighter had made contact with the *Gamble,* but station security had interfered with his attempt to capture and question the freighter's two crew members before the ship left. That was a setback, but not as much of a blow as the deep cover agent's belated report that Organa wasn't at Arnot Station but at the clearinghouse. Degoren hadn't worked with this agent before, and he hated dealing with personnel whose abilities he knew nothing about. Especially in a situation like this, with the outcome so vital to the Empire and to himself.

They had worked with Viest before, when she had offered them information on other pirate ships in exchange for pay and favors. Degoren hadn't trusted her then and he certainly didn't now that she apparently had Leia Organa in her clutches. Paid informants were always trouble, and Viest clearly had her own agenda.

"Do we go after Organa?" Sorvir asked. "If we try to take her in the middle of the clearinghouse, Viest will resist. We'll need more backup than just the corvette."

If they waited for assistance, this wouldn't be Degoren's mission anymore. But that wasn't the only consideration. "Charging into a pirate nest on the word of an agent we know nothing about, whose reports so far have always arrived just a little too late? Organa may already be dead."

Sorvir grimaced, acknowledging the point. Degoren added, "If the agent can't bring us Organa, we need to have something to show for our efforts. We'll continue to Arnot Station and seize the *Gamble*."

CHAPTER FOURTEEN

LEIA WAS RELIEVED to see that one part of their plan had worked perfectly: as the pirate ship powered out of the bay, the sensors showed that all but a few of the ships in orbit had vanished.

They rendezvoused with the *Millennium Falcon* and the *Aegis* in the far outskirts of the system, at a safe distance from the mine, and after a quick comm conversation all three ships went into hyperspace with coordinates for Arnot Station. Once they were safely under way, Han used the pirate ship's state-of-the-art hyperwave comm to call the *Falcon* again to give Chewbacca and Luke a quick rundown on everything that had happened. That done, Leia sat with Terae in the privacy of the small captain's cabin where there was an auxiliary comm station, while she called the *Aegis* to tell Kelvan and the rest of the crew about Metara.

It was not a pleasant conversation.

After Terae was done, Leia called Han in the cockpit and asked him to take the precaution of locking down the second comm set from the main station, so no one could use it without their knowledge. She

wasn't particularly suspicious of anyone, but even
Davit didn't know all the freed prisoners, and she
didn't want to take the chance that there was someone who might be unduly tempted to expose their location to the Empire or to anyone else who might be
interested. As she shut down the power on the station, she watched Terae. "Are you all right?"

Terae blinked and rubbed her face. "Yes, just . . .
Yes. Do you want me to tell Davit they can have this
cabin now?"

The ship was just barely big enough for all their
passengers, most of whom were sleeping wherever
they could find a chair or a bench or a quiet stretch of
deck. The wounded had been given priority access to
bunks, and Leia was letting Davit organize who got
what was left over. She said, "Yes, if you would."

Leia was glad they had ended up with Terae. For
one thing, the *Aegis* was unlikely to bolt without her,
and for another, Leia wanted Terae to spend a little
personal time with her ship's victims, and see close-up
the consequences of the *Aegis*'s actions.

They left the cabin, and Terae went to find Davit as
Leia headed for the cockpit. There was one more
comm transmission she needed to make.

She passed the hatch to the small galley where Andevid was investigating the food supply with some of
the Sullustans. She wasn't certain if any of the former
prisoners realized that Andevid was a pirate who had
defected. Leia was letting them assume he had always
been one of their group and had no intention of telling anyone otherwise.

In the corridor, she ran into Kifar, who asked her,

"You need me to keep an eye on that comm station, Your High—Leia?"

"No, it's not necessary. I had Han lock it down from the cockpit." He was clearly looking for a way to be helpful; Leia sympathized, but she still needed to deal with him. Later. "Get some sleep."

She stepped past him and went down the short passage into the ship's cockpit. It was similar to the *Falcon*'s but twice the size, and she could actually walk across it from the comp-console to the comm without hitting her head or climbing over a Wookiee. Han and Sian were at the main console, though there was nothing to do at the moment since the streaked stars of hyperspace filled the viewport. Sian was curled up in the copilot's chair, napping. Leia kept her voice quiet as she told Han, "I'm going to call General Willard and let him know we're alive. If you want to get some sleep, too, I can stand watch."

Han was leaning back in the roomy pilot's seat with his head propped on the broad headrest and his long legs stretched out. His whole demeanor suggested business as usual, except for the bruises and bloodstains. Leia tossed him the packet of concussion meds she had found in the medkit in the captain's cabin. He caught it and frowned at her. "Don't you ever sleep?"

"Of course I do." Leia took a seat at the comm station to send a hyperwave to the *Gamble,* which according to Luke was probably still docked at Arnot Station. "You've seen me sleep." It belatedly occurred to her that that was an opening for comments that she was too tired to field adequately at the moment.

But Han just snorted skeptically and dry-swallowed

a couple of the pills. Maybe he was feeling worse than he looked. As Leia worked on the unfamiliar comm system, he said, "What are you going to do about Itran?"

Leia sighed. "I'm going to give him a chance to talk to me, or his commanding officer, about what happened. If he doesn't . . ." The Alliance wasn't unused to personnel who were frightened or tortured into revealing information; the Empire's interrogation methods were highly effective, and it was a hazard that every command took into account. Leia knew all about those methods in intimate detail. But she was well aware that having experienced torture and the aftermath and effects of it, knowing what weak spots it had given her and how to handle them, didn't always let her know anything about how others would react. It was rare to get someone back alive after they had broken like that, and hard to tell what to do with them afterward. Some chose to leave the Alliance altogether; others had managed to go back into service. Kifar had conducted himself bravely during their escape, but Leia wasn't really certain how to evaluate him until she knew exactly what had happened with Viest. "I'm not sure yet. I think I'll worry about that when we get back to the fleet."

Han didn't argue or pursue the issue, beyond an editorial *hmmph* noise that didn't sound particularly pleased.

It took Leia a few moments to hit Arnot Station's comm relay, and then to hail the *Gamble*. When the comm board confirmed a connection, she sent her recognition code. The ship sent the correct response, and she said, "*Gamble,* this is Leia Organa. I need to speak to General Willard, please."

The voice that acknowledged her wasn't familiar, but then it wasn't as if she had had a chance to get to know every member of the crew. But the next voice wasn't familiar, either.

"Your Highness, this is Commander Degoren. I was sent by the Alliance High Command to assist General Willard, since he was injured. He's receiving medical treatment at the moment and can't come to the comm."

Degoren? Leia thought. She didn't recognize the name, and she was certain he wasn't one of the commanders assigned to the *Independence.* And the *Falcon* was the only ship that had been sent to assist the *Gamble,* at least according to Luke. *And General Willard was well enough to send the* Falcon *after us when it arrived.* "Commander, what ship are you assigned to?"

"I came aboard the *Visara,* a transport escort. I was told we were the closest ship. And we're all very relieved to know you're alive and well. General Willard was very worried."

Leia didn't like this. She remembered seeing the *Visara*'s name on a list of transport escort ships, but she knew nothing more about it. Her thoughts must have showed on her face, because Han sat up straight, watching her. Sian had woken and was squinting worriedly, still half asleep. Leia asked, "Are you taking the *Gamble* back to the fleet, is that your mission?"

"My mission is to accompany you to the site of the meeting with the traders, Your Highness. If you're still able to continue? You didn't say what your situation was."

Leia set her jaw to keep from swearing aloud. Han kept his swearing to a mutter. Sian sat bolt upright, staring in alarm. Leia made herself say, "I'm quite able to continue, Captain." Whoever this was, he hadn't been sent by the Alliance, and he hadn't spoken to General Willard. Or . . . "My situation is fine. What did General Willard tell you about the procedure for contacting the Alliance agent?"

"He said you would need to give us the decoded transmission with the coordinates, Your Highness."

"Of course," Leia said. Sian's brow was furrowed in confusion, and Han's expression was a study in ironic commentary. "I'll hand over the coordinates as soon as we arrive at the station."

There was a hesitation, clearly audible across all the empty space between the ship and Arnot Station. Then Degoren said smoothly, "Very well, Your Highness."

Leia signed off and tapped her fingers against the station chair's arm. There was a distinct sinking sensation in her middle. This was bad. Just how bad, she wasn't certain yet.

"You think Willard's alive?" Han asked.

Leia hoped he was. "I don't know. I wonder what they did to him before he let slip that little item of erroneous information." It had clearly been designed as a message to her, a warning.

"What erroneous information?" Sian asked. "The location of the meeting?"

"Yes. The location was Arnot Station," Leia told

her grimly. "General Willard and I are the only ones who know that."

Sian grimaced and sat back in her chair. "You think the Imperials . . . Obviously they have the *Gamble,* but do you think they've taken the whole station?"

"It's a possibility." Leia considered it. Would Degoren try to lure them in if there was something the size of an Imperial cruiser in the system? She shook her head. "I think it's unlikely. I think they want us to dock at Arnot Station and go to the *Gamble*. The trap will be set there."

"So we know this merchant Janlan told Viest that Davit's ship was going to Arnot Station," Han said, "and we know there's a leak somewhere in the Alliance's communications that told the Imperials where the *Gamble* was coming out of hyperspace to get the transmission. So who told the Imperials the *Gamble* was at Arnot Station and that at some point we—you—would be on the way back there? Because it's you they're after, sweetheart."

Leia was afraid he was right. Degoren, whoever he was, already had General Willard and the other Alliance personnel aboard the *Gamble*. The only reason to delay and set this trap was to capture her.

Thinking aloud, she said, "Someone at the clearinghouse contacted the Empire. It had to be Viest. She must have been an Imperial informant, or at least she knew an Imperial agent or officer fairly local to this space who would buy information from her. She told them I had a ship that docked at Arnot Station, and the Imperials took the chance that I'd go back there." Frustrated, Leia turned back to the comm. "We need to find out what the situation is on the station. If the

Imperials have seized control of it, if they've taken General Willard and the rest of the *Gamble*'s crew onto an Imperial ship . . ." If they had, it was over and they had no chance to get them back.

"We got that covered." Han slung himself out of his chair and crossed the cockpit in two long strides, heading for the hatch. "We've got Davit."

Leia stood beside the comm station, listening intently as Davit called his friend the portmaster of Arnot Station. Terae and Kifar both stood in the hatchway to listen, and a couple of the merchants, leaders of the consortium, had crowded into the compartment access behind them. Not that listening was doing most of them any good at the moment, since Davit was conducting his conversation in a language that wasn't Basic, but Leia forced herself to be patient.

Finally Davit signed off and turned to them to report, "The Imperials have not taken the station, or announced themselves in any way."

Behind her, Leia heard the merchants exclaim in relief. Davit continued, "The portmaster had no idea they were Imperials at all. Their ship docked only a few hours ago, an armed freighter with an ID that named it as the *Darsumae,* out of Sullust. It landed no cargo, which was somewhat suspicious to him, but the ship showed no other sign of being a pirate. He is not aware of any fighting or contretemps with the crew of the *Gamble,* but he checked for me and said that the *Gamble*'s bay doors are sealed now, as are the *Darsumae*'s."

It gave Leia a much better idea of what must have

happened. "Degoren must have talked his way aboard and taken General Willard hostage." She knew in her bones that if the general had had the chance he would have fought. He knew all too well what the captured crew would face, and he would have been desperate to keep them from being used as bait for Leia.

Sian seconded that with a grim nod. "With the captain and first officer dead, and the general taken prisoner, there wouldn't be anybody left to give orders except Jerell."

Han managed to confine his comment to, "Yeah, they wouldn't have had a chance."

Leia thought Jerell would see it as his duty to protect General Willard at any cost, including surrendering the ship to save him. Yes, she could see how this had played out. "Thank you, Davit. Your help has been invaluable."

"But what will we do now?" Davit asked, his high forehead furrowed in worry.

The first thing Leia wanted to do was get all these civilians they had just rescued out of this situation. "We need to talk to the *Aegis* and the *Falcon*. We need a plan." She already had the glimmers of one. But it all depended on what the *Aegis* was willing to do.

Leia signaled both the *Millennium Falcon* and the *Aegis* to drop out of hyperspace; they had to form a plan before they arrived at the station. In the darkness between stars they had a comm conference.

A quick call to the *Falcon* to talk to Luke confirmed Leia's suspicions, not that she particularly needed them confirmed. Luke told her, "No, General Willard was fine when I talked to him. He looked bad—you could tell he'd been slammed into a bulkhead or two—but that was it. And when we left the *Independence,* there was no plan to send a second ship. Madine was too worried about how the Empire got the information about the *Gamble* in the first place."

Then Leia opened the frequency to the *Aegis* and filled Kelvan in on what she believed had happened at Arnot Station.

Leia knew the worst thing she could do at this point was try to give Kelvan orders. He had just inherited command of the *Aegis,* a command that had depended so much on the whole crew's personal loyalty to Metara, and he and everyone aboard the ship were still in mourning. She had to give him options and hope he picked the one she needed. "Kelvan, I'm going to transfer to the *Falcon* and send the merchants back to Arnot Station on this ship, and then I'm going to try to free my captured crew. Obviously, I could use the help of you and the *Aegis,* but believe me, I understand if you don't want to take your crew into that situation. Whether you help us now or not, I want you to understand that the Alliance will always welcome the *Aegis* and everyone aboard it, if you choose to join, whenever you choose to join, as a crew or as individuals. I'll record a statement to that effect and send it over with Lieutenant Terae, as well as the locations of some message drop points where you can make contact with an Alliance agent. If I don't see you again, it was a privilege to meet you all, and to know Captain Metara. I just wish I had been able to know her better." She cut herself off there.

She wouldn't resort to a personal plea. If the *Aegis* didn't come freely, she didn't want it.

Kelvan's answer came back after only a moment, and his voice was unexpectedly decided. "We'll help you, Your Highness. Captain Metara would have never forgiven us for forgoing a chance at an Imperial target."

Leia lifted her brows and exchanged a look with Han, whose exasperated expression clearly conveyed what he thought of people who risked their ships for revenge. He tapped his finger significantly against his forehead. Leia narrowed her eyes at him and jerked her head toward Terae, who was looking down and fortunately hadn't seen the gesture.

She understood Kelvan's impulse. Viest and her pirates were beyond his reach, but the Imperials were available, and he didn't even have to manufacture a reason to attack them. His motive was so obviously revenge that she had to fight the urge to talk him out of it. "You're certain?"

"I'm certain, Your Highness."

Terae stepped forward, within range of the comm pickup. "It's the only thing we can do to honor Captain Metara's memory."

"You can honor Metara's memory by not risking your lives needlessly," Leia said drily.

"It's not needless," Terae said. "You need us. The crew of your ship needs us."

All right, she has me there, Leia thought. Kelvan added, "Captain Metara isn't here to see how we honor her. This is something we do for ourselves."

Leia couldn't argue with that one, either. Han's slight smirk and lifted brow indicated he rather en-

joyed seeing her stymied, even if he hadn't been the
one to do it.

"Very well," she said. "But we can't attack the Imperial ship at Arnot Station. The station itself is armed
against pirates and has picket ships. There's no reason the station authorities have to side with us at the
moment, and all Degoren would have to do was re-
veal that he was acting under Imperial authority, and
they would have to help him against us, whether they
wanted to or not. We need to lure the *Darsumae*
away from the station, make it come after us." The
inherent flaw in the plan was that Degoren might kill
the *Gamble*'s crew before he left the station. If he
hadn't killed them already. The only hope Leia had
was that he had been charged to capture and deliver
them to some higher authority for questioning, and
that he wouldn't execute them unless he had to. "Kelvan, do you know of any systems nearby with asteroid fields, something that could conceal us from their
sensors?"

Kelvan's voice was thoughtful. "No, but I think I
know of something even better. Terae, can you explain to the Princess about Rethel Point? I'll send you
the coordinates now."

The first step in the plan was to send the merchants
and freed prisoners on to Arnot Station. Three members of the ill-fated merchant ship's crew had survived, and Davit was a pilot, so Leia felt comfortable
handing over the ship to him. She, Han, Sian, Kifar,
and Terae would transfer to the *Millennium Falcon*

and follow the *Aegis* to the site they had picked for their trap.

The details of the plan had been carefully kept from all of the freed prisoners, so no one could betray them either accidentally or intentionally. Leia had let them believe that the *Falcon* and the *Aegis* would be fleeing the sector as soon as she and the others transferred off the pirate ship. She was fairly certain Davit might suspect otherwise, but she had faith in his discretion. Andevid also knew nothing of their plans, having been kept carefully out of the cockpit. Leia was sending him to Arnot Station with the merchants, as promised.

The two ships did not have compatible air locks, but the *Falcon* had an extendable pressure tunnel aboard. Chewbacca and Han were in the process of carefully maneuvering the two ships and extending the tunnel from the *Falcon*'s topside hatch to seal onto the pirate ship's larger portside hatch. Leia stayed in the cockpit long enough to hear Han's opinion that trying to make fine control adjustments in this ship was like driving a speeder bike while wearing pressure suit gloves. Then she went to wait in the ship's small galley, the only spot that didn't have anxious merchants gathered in it.

Sian found her there a few moments later, and from her expression she clearly wanted a word. From the way Sian had reacted, or tried not to react, while they had discussed the plan earlier, Leia was fairly sure she knew what the word was going to be about.

"Your Highness . . ."

"Go ahead." Leia smiled, to make it clear she really

did want Sian's honest opinion. "You don't like this plan, do you?"

"No, but it's not like we have a choice. It's either this, or leave everybody on the *Gamble* to the Empire." Sian hesitated. "I don't mean to question your judgment, but . . . Yeah, I guess I am questioning your judgment. Can we—can you really trust the *Aegis* crew? When we were all stuck on that rock and Viest turned against Metara so fast, we had a common goal. But now . . . we're handing them you, and an Imperial ship, and the crew of the *Gamble,* and the *Gamble* itself if we can get it back and it's not scrap by now, and the *Millennium Falcon,* which everyone knows is a hot smuggling ship. I just . . . They've been stealing and killing civilians for profit for two years now, even though they like to pretend the civilians are somehow not as dead when they're killed in righteous revenge for Alderaan." That one made Leia wince, and Sian saw it but forged on, "How do we know they won't turn on us?"

Leia let out her breath. "We don't. I don't know if I can trust them. I hope this plays out the way I think it will, but they have the upper hand, and I don't know that they won't take advantage of it at some point. All we can do is be careful, and watchful." It was nothing but the plain truth. Leia liked Kelvan, and even liked prickly Terae, but she had no real idea how they felt about her, and she had no idea what they would do in this situation. She was certain they wouldn't hand her or the others over to the Empire, but there were a lot of other possibilities for betrayal. And it was clear that their loyalty to Metara far outweighed any love they might still have for the princess of their lost home world.

Metara had been a fanatic, but she had also had a good amount of self-control, and would have put the welfare of her crew above anything. Kelvan and Terae and the others had been under her tight reins for two years; it was possible they really had no idea yet what they wanted to do.

Sian stared at her a moment. "See, this is the part where you yell at me and prove with, I don't know, brilliant logic or secret information, how of course we can trust them and I go away embarrassed but reassured."

Leia smiled wryly at her. "I wish."

Once the two ships were connected, Leia said good-bye to Davit and the other merchants. He told her, "I cannot thank you for rescuing us, for there is no thanks that would be adequate."

"It was partly my responsibility that you were in that situation to begin with," she told him, "and it was just lucky we found ourselves in a position to help you." Leia wouldn't forget the ship's murdered captain and copilot, and the others on board who had been killed or injured.

"Your responsibility because the pirates came from Alderaan? I could argue that with you, but I doubt I would convince you." He shook his head. "I am only sorry our conference will not continue. The consortium will be too fearful now. But . . ." He shrugged a little. "There are a few wealthy beings who will not be slaves because of your intervention, and I may be able to arrange something with them privately. The

death of that monster Viest was surely worth several
cargo loads of supplies."

"That would be very welcome," Leia told him. Especially at this point when all she wanted to do was
get out of this situation with all the surviving personnel she had brought into it. "You know how to contact Han."

"I do," he told her. "Good luck."

The pressure tunnel had been successfully attached
and both hatches were open, and Leia could hear
Luke up in the *Falcon,* talking to Chewie over the
ship's comm. "Yes, I'm keeping an eye on the seal.
Chewie, I know how to do it, okay?" There was insistent muttering in Wookiee in reply, and C-3PO's
worried, "Be careful, Master Luke!"

Kifar, Sian, and Terae had already started up the
tunnel to the *Falcon* when Leia and Han found Andevid sitting on a folded-down jumpseat in the ship's
common area. Leia handed him a small but heavy
box. He eyed her only a little suspiciously. "What's
this?"

Leia told him, "I can't go to the station as I planned,
so I don't have access to my own funds. But we found
this hidden in the captain's cabin. I think it will fulfill
the terms of our arrangement."

He opened the box, eyed the credcoins of various
planets crammed into it, and then closed it again.
"That'll do," he said. He hesitated. "You sure you
don't want to hire me permanently?"

Leia lifted a brow. "Do you want to join the Rebel
Alliance?"

Andevid recoiled in horror. "No!"

Han sighed. "Yeah, that's what I said. It didn't help. Run while you can."

Leia spared a moment to toss him a look, then told Andevid, "That's what I thought you'd say. Good luck, Andevid."

He peered after them. "Good luck, crazy human lady. It was fun destroying stuff with you."

As they headed toward the access ladder for the hatch, Leia asked Han, "Is that why you stick around? The thrill of destroying stuff with me?"

His sideways glance at her was hard to read. "One of the reasons."

Han had never heard of Rethel Point, but wasn't surprised by its existence. Smugglers were generally good at finding bolt-holes, and the locations tended to get passed around to the local operators.

It was only a short hyperspace jump from their current location, and an even shorter jump from Arnot Station, which made it ideal. On the way there, Terae explained that Rethel Point was a field emanating from a planet in a system that had only a numerical designation, no name. The rumor was that the Rethel had been the sentient race who had lived there at one time. But the ruins were so old, with so little evidence left behind by the builders, that the idea that their name had somehow survived, passed down among the pirates and smugglers who used their dead city, was hard to believe.

No one had ever investigated why, but at some point in the unremembered past, a smuggler's ship on the run from the authorities had discovered that something in the ruins generated a field that blocked sensors. Any kind of sensors, even the specialized military-grade system suites. The field spread across most of the planet, growing slightly weaker the farther it stretched from the ruins, finally ending just before reaching the orbital paths of the two small moons.

"You can send comm signals in and out," Terae said, "but sensors—any kind of sensors—don't show power signatures, life signs, or metallic substances. No one's ever figured out what does it, but there's been speculation it might be some sort of mineral. If you fly over the ruins, you can see places where there were old excavations, as if someone was digging to try to find jamming equipment, but the field's still there and no one knows why. It must be nearly impossible to search for whatever it is, since any kind of deep terrain sensors won't work there.

"But it's been used as a hiding place and a cargo transfer spot by smugglers and pirates for years. It has a breathable atmosphere, which just makes it all the more useful. We heard about it from Viest's people, when we first came to this sector."

"It sounds like a trap," Han said. That was the problem with bolt-holes that weren't kept private, and smugglers who arranged too many meetings in them and talked too much.

Terae frowned at him. It was the glare she usually reserved for him, but with an element of genuine curiosity added. "What do you mean?"

Han decided part of his problem with Terae was that she made him feel world-weary and old. "If pirates know smugglers use it for drops and meetings, then all they have to do is hang around and wait."

Terae clearly didn't like that, but reluctantly admitted, "I suppose that could happen."

Han snorted derisively.

Once they arrived, the *Aegis* went through the sensor disruption field to demonstrate. Han and the others on the *Falcon* watched it disappear from the sensors like a ghost fading into the afterlife. The planet itself showed up on the imaging screen, but any attempt to bring up closer images of the terrain or look for energy trails just made the pictures dissolve into static, as if the planet were moving out of range.

"See?" Terae said, bringing up a more detailed sensor view so they could watch the planet turn fuzzy. "And we can't pick up the *Aegis* at all."

"Wow," Sian commented softly, "this place lives up to its reputation."

Luke nodded. "Too bad no one can figure out how it works, or how to move it. We could sure use something like that."

Leia's mouth twisted in wry appreciation of the irony. "It would make a great site for a base, except for the fact that every pirate in the sector knows about it."

Han could see how useful it could be, but the apparent emptiness between the planet's surface and the two visible moons just gave him the creeps. The sensor blackout might mask anything, from orbital debris to an Imperial cruiser. "Yeah, I just hope nobody else got here first."

Chewbacca grumbled a comment about Han being

a pessimist that Han stopped listening to halfway through.

Leia leaned over the comm to call the *Aegis.* "Captain Kelvan, you're right, I think this will work."

The idea was to draw Degoren's ship, or whichever ship showed up, into the sensor disruption field so the *Aegis* could approach it for boarding without warning. This would hopefully prevent Degoren from using General Willard or any other *Gamble* crew members he might have aboard as hostages.

They decided to use the *Falcon* to carry a distress beacon down to the planet to lure Degoren's ship into position, while the *Aegis* waited in the shadow of the first small moon. That close to the field, the *Aegis*'s sensor capability would be somewhat erratic, but they would still be able to detect Degoren's ship entering the system. Han just hoped it didn't detect them.

Once Degoren's ship tried to contact the source of the distress signal, the *Falcon* could use its comm to help track the ship's position inside the field and tell the *Aegis* where to strike.

Han had intended to take the *Falcon* down to the planet himself, until Leia came into the cockpit to ask him to match locks with the *Aegis* so she, Sian, and Terae could go aboard.

"Why?" Han asked her, though he had a bad feeling he knew exactly why.

"We're going with the boarding party," Leia said as if it were obvious. "I need to be there to identify any prisoners from the *Gamble,* make certain that there isn't another attempt by Degoren to masquerade as Alliance personnel. Sian is going along as backup in case something happens to me."

"You've been shot at enough on this trip. Why don't you take a break?"

Leia's expression suggested that this was just nonsensical and she didn't have time for it. She put on her pretending-to-be-patient-with-you face and said, "This isn't the *Aegis*'s fight. They're doing this as a favor to me, to honor Metara's memory. I have to be there."

Han was angry, and he wasn't even sure why. He wanted to accuse Leia of acting like a martyr; he wanted to accuse the *Aegis*'s crew of expecting her to somehow fix their problems when she had enough of her own to deal with. "You think you have to be there, but you don't."

It wasn't exactly a persuasive speech, and Leia was clearly unimpressed. "I think I have to be there because I do."

"Fine," he said, "Chewie and I will come with you. You can get us killed, too. When we're all in a bloody pile, that'll teach the High Command a lesson."

Leia smiled, unperturbed. "I'm sure it will. And you'll have the satisfaction of being right, which I know is very important to you."

Chewbacca, who was apparently amusing himself by siding against Han and with Leia in every argument lately, made a growl of approval. Han wanted to argue, but everything that came to mind sounded lame and inadequate. He blamed his head wound. He said, "Hey, as long as you admit I'm right."

Leia made a decidedly un-Princess-like noise of derision. Then Han went to the ship's lounge to tell

Luke the new plan, and that someone needed to fly the *Falcon* down to the planet, and Han had nominated him. Unfortunately, Itran was there, too.

As Han finished explaining, Itran said, "I'll take it down. I've flown plenty of small freighters."

Han stared at him. Sometimes he wondered if Itran was really serious, or if he just had a sense of irony so deadpan it was indiscernible by normal humans. "Hah, no." Han turned to Luke. "Kid?"

Luke looked resigned. He had clearly intended to be in the boarding party, too, but knew there was no other option, at least as far as Han was concerned. "I'll do it."

"I'll go with you," Itran said.

Han tightened his jaw but didn't object. At least it would keep Itran out of the boarding party so he wouldn't accidentally shoot anybody or surrender.

"Glad to have you," Luke said. He sounded sincere. Han supposed that was because Luke barely knew Itran.

Luke waited until Itran had headed off before he clapped Han on the shoulder and said, "It'll be okay. He can't get into any trouble this way."

"He better not," Han said, making it a threat. Luke just grinned.

CHAPTER FIFTEEN

AS LUKE TOOK THE *FALCON* down, he watched the sensors slowly drop out, as if they were flying through a void, as if everything but the planet beneath them had slowly vanished. He found himself looking from the solid gray-brown landmass below to the blankness on the screens. After the earlier demonstration, he had expected the effect, but seeing it in action was somehow far creepier than he had thought it would be. "Weird, huh?" he commented to Kifar.

"Yeah," Kifar muttered back, most of his attention on the comm. "The terrain-following sensors are useless, too."

Leia had sent a garbled distress call to the *Gamble* on Arnot Station, then she, Han, Chewie, Sian, R2-D2, and Terae had all transferred to the *Aegis*, which had taken up its position near the closer moon. Luke was worried about them and would much rather have been there to worry in person. He suspected an indeterminate time's worth of desultory conversation with Kifar Itran in the *Falcon*'s cockpit wouldn't distract him much.

As the ship dropped down through the atmosphere,

they had a good view through the port. The ruins sat in the center of a gray, sandy plain, ringed by odd rock formations in twisted spirals. The wind that had formed them pushed and tugged at the *Falcon,* and Luke had to make careful corrections with the maneuvering jets. They crossed over a dry riverbed, lined by scrubby red vegetation, and then over the tumbled stone of the city. Outlines of curving streets wove circles through the shattered towers and plazas strewn with broken rock and choked with weeds. The environmental sensors, once they were in actual contact with the atmosphere, worked well enough to confirm Terae's statement that the air was breathable.

He spotted the place Terae had described, an enormous amphitheater with a curving, half-shell roof, still mostly intact, though cracks crawled across the surface. Luke banked around and brought the ship down toward the plaza in front of the theater's pillar-framed entrance. He had to pass between two tall columns to make it, and Kifar asked, "You sure you can get this bucket through there?"

The *Falcon* was light and responsive in a whole different way from an X-wing, but Luke was sure he could pull off the maneuver. He was also glad Han and Chewie weren't here to hear the slight. He just said, "No problem."

He brought the ship down onto the plaza, setting off a swirling dust storm. "I'll get the distress beacon ready," Kifar said, and headed out of the cockpit.

Since they would be taking off again in a short time, Luke set the boards on standby. The *Falcon* could go from cold start to ready to lift off within three minutes, but he wanted to be out of here a little faster than that. He tried to hail the *Aegis* on the comm to report that they were on the ground, and got a burst of static. He had to up the gain to punch through and get voice contact with the ship, though the confirmation came back clear enough. *That's weird.* There hadn't been any problem with the comms between the *Aegis* in the field and the *Falcon* outside it, and no problem calling in from the upper atmosphere. Luke filed it away as more Rethel Point strangeness. The distress beacon had a strong signal and should get through with no problem, so it shouldn't affect the plan. He climbed out of the pilot's seat and saw C-3PO peering in at him through the cockpit door. "Hey, you take care of the ship. I shouldn't be gone long."

C-3PO said, "Do be careful, Master Luke."

When Luke got to the hatch, Kifar was already waiting there, holding the distress beacon's canister. Taking in the fact that Luke had put on his weapons belt with his blaster and lightsaber, he said, a little self-consciously, "You coming along?"

"Yeah, we don't want to borrow trouble," Luke said, when what he actually meant was "no reason to be stupid." You didn't walk around on a strange, supposedly uninhabited planet alone, unless you didn't have a choice.

Kifar watched him a moment, eyes narrowed, then nodded and hit the control to cycle and release the hatch.

Luke didn't know Kifar well, having encountered him only a few times in the *Independence*'s ready rooms after Kifar had transferred there from the transport group. His impression from this, and from comments made by some of the other pilots and techs, was that Kifar had a big ego for a transport tender whose job was to avoid ship-to-ship conflict rather than fly right into turbolaser barrages. Luke guessed that, after Kifar had broken down and spilled Leia's identity to the pirate master, he probably felt he had something to prove. *Well, he does have something to prove.*

The hatch slid open and the air that wafted in was cool, bone-dry, and thin, as if they were on top of a mountain brushing the upper atmosphere instead of close to the equivalent of sea level.

Kifar started down the ramp. "Where do you want to put this thing? How about in that theater?"

Luke had figured they would just bury it in the sand somewhere. "The *Aegis* is supposed to hit them before they land."

Kifar didn't stop walking. "Sure, but if something goes wrong and they don't, the Imperials'll waste time looking for it."

"Yeah, good idea." Distracted, Luke hit the key combination that set the code lock on the *Falcon*'s hatch. The area looked and felt empty, but considering it was a hideout and drop spot for smugglers and pirates, he had no intention of being incautious. And he knew what Han would do if something happened to the *Falcon* because Luke didn't take obvious precautions.

Luke followed Kifar across the plaza, their boots crunching in the crystalline sand, the fitful breeze tugging at their clothes and hair. Luke kept one hand on his blaster and a wary eye on the empty windows of the ruined towers. He felt a nervous prickle at the back of his neck, as if something watched them.

The pillars supporting the theater's half shell were carved into spirals, the ridges barely still visible after the years of wind and sand. The back half of the big space was taken up with rows of carved stone benches stretching up toward the far wall, piled with sand drifts. The benches were oddly shaped, rounded in places, with carved holes in others, clearly meant to accommodate an anatomy that wasn't bipedal. If there had been a stage or anything else between the pillars, it was long gone.

As they walked into the shadow of the heavy curved stone roof, the uneasy prickle got worse. Luke realized suddenly that he had drawn his blaster. He holstered it again, glad Kifar was a few steps ahead and hadn't noticed. There was no reason to be jumpy. The place was hollow and empty, and felt like it. He didn't know what was wrong with him, that he could be simultaneously convinced that there was no life here, not even insects, and still feel a sense of dread, like something was stalking him. Maybe it was coming from the Imperial ship they planned to decoy. *Maybe it's already entered the system.* No, there hadn't been time.

It was one of those many times his erratic connection to the Force was more problematic than helpful.

Kifar headed for the end of the tier of seats and an archway that led into a dark passage. "This looks good."

Luke caught up with him and flashed his handlight into the opening to make sure it was empty of anything except sand drifts. Kifar set the beacon down and Luke drew breath to suggest they take it farther into the passage, but Kifar pushed the pad to activate it. Luke released his breath in annoyance. There was no point in bringing the thing in here if they left it where it could be easily found. Now they had to head back to the ship and bug out for the far side of the planet, with no time to find a better hiding spot. He wished he could have done this with Han or Chewie or Sian or anyone else, but he knew why Han didn't want Kifar in the boarding party. "Let's bury it," he said. "That might buy us some more time." He leaned down to scoop sand over it.

As soon as he took his hand off his blaster, the unease sharpened into a spike of alarm, and he actually turned toward Kifar in time to see the blaster pointed at him.

The blast knocked him backward and he had a moment's awareness of cold sand, then nothing.

Tension made Leia want to pace, but there was no room. The *Aegis* had detected a contact entering the star system just a short time earlier, and the boarding party had assembled in the hatch corridor. Leia, Han, Chewbacca, Sian, and R2-D2 were joined by a number of well-armed *Aegis* crew.

Kelvan had been keeping them apprised over the all-ship comm, and now he said, "We have a sensor image. It's a converted freighter, half again our size, ID is *Darsumae*. Four guns. Could have as many as thirty to forty crew."

Han grimaced. He said to Chewbacca, "Unless they've packed it with stormtroopers." Chewbacca combed fingers through his beard, an elaborate gesture of unconcern. Leia was plenty concerned; the *Aegis* crew seemed edgy but eager.

Then from the bridge, another voice reported, "Target has just launched a shuttle."

"Oh, no," Leia whispered, almost in chorus with Terae.

"The shuttle is heading into the sensor disruption zone," the bridge continued. They heard Kelvan tell the comm officer to warn the *Falcon*.

"Should we abort the mission?" Fera asked, looking from Leia to Terae.

Across the corridor, Han leaned forward to listen.

"No," Terae said. She flicked a glance at Leia and hesitated. "Are you—do you think we should?"

"Not if I can help it," Leia said. She lifted her comlink. "Kelvan, can we still initiate the boarding operation?" He was the captain: she had no authority over him, and she was desperately afraid he would change his mind. A converted freighter this large was sure to have space for prisoners, and it just increased her conviction that the crew of the *Gamble* was being held aboard.

There was a moment of hesitation; then Kelvan replied, "Agreed. We're going in." Addressing the pilot, he said, "Make their position, then take us into the sensor disruption field. We'll come at them from inside it. They'll have us on sensors as we come out, but we can still take them by surprise."

Leia hoped so. But it was a good plan, if not as good as their former one. Degoren was expecting a damaged ship grounded on the planet, not a well-armed pirate.

The deck thrummed as the engines engaged. Leia felt the gravity shift minutely under her feet as the compensators strained to keep up. Then she heard Kelvan give the order for weapons control to fire at will.

Listening to what she could hear of the battle from the bridge comm, Leia watched Han shift uneasily and knew he wanted to be up on the bridge or in a gun turret or anywhere but here; so did she. Return fire rocked the ship, then from the bridge she heard Kelvan order the tractor beam to engage.

Listening intently to the comm traffic from the bridge, Terae said, "It's good. We took them by surprise."

The whole ship vibrated, then there was banging and a clank that reverberated through the hull. Kelvan's voice came over the all-ship comm, "We're locked on! Go! Now!"

Terae hit the release, and as the hatch lifted Leia glimpsed the other ship's lock. Fera stepped in, slapped a small explosive against the controls for the opposite hatch, and stepped back. Terae closed their lock and nodded to her. Fera triggered the device.

The thump was barely audible through all the layers of metal. When Terae raised their hatch again, there was a smoking ruin in place of the other ship's control pad. Fera hit the manual release, and the lock cycled open. Terae tossed in a stun grenade, and the crew members nearest the lock ducked back.

This thump was much less muffled. Leia drew her blaster as the crew charged in. Leia followed Han and Chewbacca through the lock and heard the first spate of blasterfire.

The lock opened into a corridor that ran lengthwise down the side of the ship, and the *Aegis* crew hurried to take guard positions up and down it. Four human men lay collapsed on the deck. From the blasters they carried, they must have been dispatched to guard the lock.

With quick gestures, Terae sent five of her crew toward the stern and the engine compartment and signaled three to stay here and guard the lock itself. Leia sent Sian after the engineering group and R2-D2 rolled after her. The droid would help them get through any code-locked hatches.

Then she used her boot to roll one of the stunned men over onto his back. She didn't recognize him, and all were dressed as spacers, no uniforms. For an instant her stomach tightened in dread. *What if we're wrong?* If this was some terrible mistake and this ship had somehow intercepted their distress transmission and innocently responded . . . Then she crouched and pulled the man's comlink off his belt. It was standard Imperial issue. Han, leaning to look over her shoulder, muttered, "Good to know."

Terae had stopped, watching Leia. Leia lifted the comlink and showed her the Imperial seal stamped on it. Terae nodded sharply and motioned the rest of the crew forward toward the bridge. Han followed, Chewbacca with him, his big feet silent on the metal deck plates. Leia stood and went after them.

They passed open blast doors to empty crew and system compartments, and Terae sent two crew members off to temporarily disable the connections to the comm array. As they reached a cross corridor that curved toward the bridge area, blasterfire erupted suddenly. It slagged the opposite wall of the corridor and dropped one of the *Aegis* crew. Terae, Fera, and the two remaining crew crouched to return fire.

Han gestured to Chewbacca, an instruction that involved a lot of furious pointing, but Chewie evidently understood it. The Wookiee ducked back down the corridor and headed into the nearest cross passage. Then Leia's breath caught as Han ducked, rolled, and made it across the corridor to the far wall. Still in a crouch, he put his back against the wall and fired around the corner. Leia used the covering fire to crawl forward, and stretched to grab the injured crew member's jacket. It was Allian, she realized as she dragged him out of the firing zone. His shoulder and arm were badly burned, but he was still alive, sweat beading on his brown skin, eyes wide with shock. The air turned to ozone and smoke and she could hear shouts and blasterfire over her comlink now as the second group fought for control of engineering.

Fera whispered, "Solo!" and held up a small metal ball. Another stun grenade. Han nodded, set his blaster aside, and made a throw-it gesture. Fera tossed it to him. Terae lunged dangerously close to the kill zone to cover him, but ducked back as more blasterfire splashed off the bulkhead just above her head. Then the barrage cut off abruptly with the distinctive sound of bowcaster fire and a triumphant Wookiee howl.

Han armed the grenade, leaned around the corner, and tossed it down the corridor.

Leia scrambled back with the others. The grenade went off and the thump shook the deck plates.

Terae yelled, "Come on!" and surged into the corridor with the others behind her. Leia shoved to her feet and followed Han. Three groaning Imperials slumped in a heap near the blast door to the bridge. A curved blast shield lay nearby, the transparent surface still glowing from the blaster bolts it had deflected. Chewbacca stepped out of the doorway on the far end of the corridor and started toward them.

Terae motioned Fera forward to deal with the sealed blast door controls and stood with Han in the center of the corridor. She listened to her comlink a moment, then reported, "They had to cut through the blast door into the last engine bay, but the astromech droid was able to shut off any control access from the bridge and they're almost—"

Leia spotted movement down the corridor, where an open blast door gave way to another passage. She snapped, "Down!"

She fired just as the Imperial stepped out and lifted his blast rifle. Chewbacca, Fera, and the other two crew members dropped to the deck. Terae tried to turn and fire, but Han tackled her down and out of the way. The rifle's energy bolt came so close that the light of it whited out Leia's vision, but she squeezed off two more shots. She blinked away the dazzle in time to see the Imperial fall, the blast rifle clattering to the deck beside him.

Terae shoved upright, and snapped, "Merith, get down there and clear that junction!"

As the crew member hurried to comply, Terae said, a trace of shakiness in her voice, "Thank you, Your Highness."

"You're welcome," Leia said, and was glad her voice came out in the normal range.

Han rolled to his feet, frowning suspiciously at her. "You okay?"

"I'm fine," Leia told him. Her left cheek felt hot. As Han stepped over to take up a position beside the blast door to the bridge, she moved a short way back down the corridor to stand beside Chewbacca. She put a hand on the braids wrapping the left side of her head. They felt just on the edge of crackly, singed by the blast. Chewie sniffed, obviously detecting the burned-hair odor, then looked down at her and growled in concern.

"No, it's fine," Leia told him. Putting aside the image of herself lying in the corridor with her head blasted off, she lifted her blaster as Fera jimmied the door controls into the bridge.

The door slid open and Terae shouted, "You're pinned down, we have your ship—now surrender, or we'll use a concussion grenade! We don't need you alive."

When there was no answer, Terae said loudly, "Toss it in!"

Someone inside called out, "Don't! We surrender!" Han and the two other crew members slammed through the door.

Leia stepped in to see three Imperials dragged out of their station chairs, disarmed, and forced to lie down on the floor. As the *Aegis* crew covered them, Han dropped into the pilot's station and started bringing up schematics of the ship. Leia heard a triumphant yell over the comlink, and a moment later an *Aegis* crew member's voice, "Captain Kelvan, Lieutenant Terae, we've secured engineering!"

Leia stepped around the prisoners to look over

Han's shoulder. "We need to account for every member of the crew." *And find out what they did with General Willard and the others from the* Gamble. Her worst fear was that the Imperials had killed them back on Arnot Station. Her grip on the shoulder of the station chair tightened. She didn't want to start the interrogation until they had more information. Terae was slowly circling the prisoners, looking thoughtful and dangerous.

Han brought up a roster on the console's display and sent it to the *Aegis* comlink frequency so all the crew would receive it. "Yeah, they've got way more crew than a freighter like this needs. Imperial communication codes, too."

"Several of them must have gone off on the shuttle," Leia said. From Terae's comlink, she could hear reports coming in of sporadic fighting in the corridors and more surrenders.

Han continued, "And the cargo space has been converted to weapons and a tractor . . . Huh, this ship has a brig."

Leia could see that the security controls were active in that section, the red outlines showing sealed doors. "I'll check it out."

Chewbacca turned to follow her and Terae said, "Fera, go with them."

They made it down to the lower deck without much incident, Chewbacca flushing one lone Imperial out of a compartment so Leia could stun him. They reached the brig area, a secured junction with a containment field over the doorway and four sealed blast doors leading off it. Fera tried the control panel and grimaced. "It's code-locked. Should I burn it?"

Leia's heart pounded in hope. She lifted her comlink. "Han, can you open the security field to the brig
section from there?"

The field fizzled and the hum died away. Leia
stepped through to the first door, tapped the comm
pad, and said, "Is anyone in there?"

An incredulous voice answered, "What—Princess
Leia?"

Chewbacca stepped up beside her, lowing worriedly. Leia hit the release, and the door slid upward.
She found herself staring at a small, crowded compartment filled with ragged *Gamble* crew members,
their faces drawn with exhaustion, alight with startled hope.

"It's good to see you all again," Leia said. "Is
General Willard with you?"

A woman struggled to her feet. "He's here somewhere; we know they brought everyone."

Leia heard Fera reporting to Terae, saying, "We
have an unknown number of survivors and may need
medical assistance." She sounded as if she had re-
verted to her Alderaanian gunship crew training.

Leia stepped past her to hit the release on the next
blast door, and Chewbacca turned to do the two
against the far wall. As the third door went up, Leia
heard Jerell call out, "Princess Leia!"

Inside the little cell, General Willard was sitting up,
leaning back against the wall, battered but alive. She
stepped into the cell and crouched beside him, taking
his hand. "Are you all right?"

"I'm better now," he told her, smiling. He looked
up at Chewbacca, who leaned in the doorway. "I
knew you'd find her."

Chewbacca grumbled a triumphant acknowledgment. Leia asked, "What happened?"

The general grimaced. "They had the right codes, and we let them on board. They killed the two crewmen on guard duty and took me hostage. It was not our finest moment. But Ilen managed to purge the comps just before they broke into auxiliary control, so they weren't able to use any secure data in our systems."

Jerell shifted uncomfortably, his expression caught between guilt and humiliation. "It was my fault. I checked their codes and let them in. I thought they were from a transport crew, sent to evacuate us."

"We can go over it once we get back to the fleet," Leia said, though the two additional casualties on the *Gamble* made her stomach twist. "For now, let's get you out of here—"

Her comlink beeped urgently, and Han's voice said, "Princess, we got a problem. I tried to hail the *Falcon* and I'm not getting any response."

Luke became gradually aware that he was sitting up, slumped over in an acceleration seat, with sand all down the back of his shirt. His body felt heavy and numb, and his head ached, a tight pain right between his eyes. *I was stunned,* he thought, trying to remember how and why. Then things swam into focus and the numbness receded enough for him to realize he had binders locked around his wrists. He thought, *Luke, you idiot.*

He opened his eyes to see Kifar Itran seated across from him. They were on a ship, probably a small shuttle. Narrow ports farther forward showed the darkness of space, and Luke could just glimpse a cockpit through the open hatch. There was another human seated against the far wall, and eight more in jumpseats closer to the cockpit. They were all dressed in ordinary dark spacer clothes and there was nothing about them that said they were Imperial, except that their hair was cropped tightly and there was just something about them that was at odds with the spacer look.

Seated nearest Luke was a green Duros, casually holding a drawn blaster. A Duros whom Luke recognized. He groaned under his breath. It was the Duros who had tried to jump them at Arnot Station. He had been an Imperial agent, not a pirate.

"Your droid is stubborn," Kifar said. "It wouldn't let me back into the ship. Said you'd ordered it not to open the hatch to anyone but you."

Good work, C-3PO, Luke thought. At least the Imperials hadn't gotten the *Falcon.* "So you're an Imperial agent," he said. "The Princess thought you were just a coward who betrayed the mission the first time things got rough." Leia hadn't said anything of the kind, but there wasn't much Luke could do at the moment except provoke Kifar.

Kifar's expression tightened. "I did my job, and your Princess didn't suspect a thing. I didn't break; I made a deal with Viest. I told her she had a rebel Senator she could sell to the Empire, and in return she let me use her comm to call my commander and tell him the *Gamble* was on Arnot Station." He smiled. "Worked out pretty well, didn't it?"

"So far," Luke admitted. He could see that the big-ego part of Kifar's persona wasn't an act put on for the Alliance personnel's benefit. Kifar probably thought of himself as a hotshot agent, and here the Alliance had just shunted him off to transport duty all this time. "So you're the one who told the Imperials where the *Gamble* would come out of hyperspace to receive the transmission."

Kifar's expression wasn't quite a smirk, but it was definitely in the vicinity. "I just had time for a quick call to my commander, but it did the job."

That was good to know. At least the Alliance could trust their communication chain again. If Luke could ever get this information to anybody. "So what's the plan now?"

Kifar's face went hard, and he threw a tight glance at the Duros. The Duros laughed, a short, bitter exhalation, and said, "That's a good question."

Kifar sneered. "Shut it, Trehar. If you hadn't lost him and the Wookiee on the station—"

Trehar cut him off. "If I hadn't lost them, Degoren wouldn't have had to rely on you, and we wouldn't be in this mess."

Baffled, Luke looked from Trehar to Kifar. Then he got it. *Han was right, Kifar is a screwup.* "You never had a chance to warn them about the plan to take their ship with the *Aegis,* did you? Not till you stunned me. And then you couldn't use the *Falcon*'s comm, and my comlink didn't have the range to reach the ship, so you had to wait for the shuttle to land."

"I didn't have a chance," Kifar said. "If I'd taken control of the smugglers' ship on the way down to the planet, they would have known something was wrong when the distress beacon didn't go off, and they would have made a run for it."

It was Luke's turn to snort derisively. He knew Leia and Han and the others wouldn't have run, and if Kifar actually thought that it was likely, he was a lousy judge of character. *He's a lousy judge of a lot of things.* But if the distress beacon hadn't started broadcasting as planned, Leia would have gotten suspicious and might have sent one of the *Aegis*'s shuttles after them.

But his gratification in Kifar's lack of judgment faded as Trehar said, "You're lucky our backup is almost here."

"Backup?" Luke said.

Leia headed back to the bridge at a run, Chewbacca jogging behind her. "It might be the planet's damping field," she told him, "interfering with voice transmission."

Chewbacca's skeptical-sounding snort implied that this was highly unlikely.

Leia had to admit that she really didn't think so, either.

They reached the bridge, and she saw immediately from Han's expression that it was worse. Terae stood at his shoulder, and stepped away to tell Leia, "The shuttle is on its way back and we've received a hail from that Commander Degoren."

Leia's heart sank. *It didn't work—they're back too soon.* Degoren would have been able to get a sensor image of his ship as soon as he cleared the planet's field, and seen the *Aegis* locked on. He should have been running, and he wasn't. "Did he say anything about the *Falcon*?"

Terae shook her head. "Not yet. Solo's stalling him, trying to get him to talk, but it's not working. I've got Captain Kelvan patched in on the frequency, but no one's spoken to Degoren except Solo."

"Good." Leia went to Han's side. He had the headset on and was saying, "We were just cruising through the system and stumbled on it. If you didn't want somebody to take it, you shouldn't have left it lying around."

Leia picked up the other headset and held it to her ear. Chewbacca stepped up behind her, looming and breathing heavily, and leaned down to listen in. She recognized Degoren's voice immediately. He said, "Let me speak to your commander. You've made a tactical error, but we can still negotiate." His voice was smooth, and he sounded far too calm.

Leia muted the comm and asked Han, "Did he admit to being an Imperial agent?"

"No, he's playing for time," Han said, and she could tell his frustration was hiding deep worry. "I think he's got help on the way."

Chewbacca lowed anxiously and Terae turned to the sensor suite, expanding the field of view. Leia said, "Then we need to move fast." And she needed to find out if Degoren had discovered the *Falcon*.

She took the mute off and made her voice hard. "We've taken your ship, Commander Degoren. Surrender your shuttle immediately, or we'll blow you to pieces."

There was a slight pause. "You won't do that, Organa."

He's not surprised about this, Leia thought. *He's angry but not surprised.* That was a very bad sign. "I will, actually." She spoke to Terae, carefully not muting the comm frequency. "Are the concussion missiles ready to fire?"

"Yes, Your Highness." Terae gestured sharply and one of the crew members dropped into the weapons station chair, hesitated for a moment over the unfamiliar board, then started the charge sequence.

"We have two of your people aboard," Degoren said. "Kifar Itran and Luke Skywalker. But I'm perfectly willing to trade them for my ship. You can even take the other rebel prisoners on board; I won't protest."

Leia grimaced, Chewbacca made a faint noise of dismay, and Han swore under his breath. She thought, *Yes, that's what I was afraid of.* And Degoren was definitely stalling them. A prisoner transfer would take time, and that was what Degoren wanted. She made her voice hesitant. "Give us a moment to discuss it."

"Make it quick, I'm impatient," Degoren said.

Leia hit the mute on the comm. "He must have another ship en route. We can take that shuttle, but we need to move fast. Terae, we need the *Aegis*."

Terae hit the all-ship comm, speaking to all the crew still aboard. "We need to transfer command of this ship to the Alliance personnel. Get the rest of the Imperials to the brig and then get back to the *Aegis*. Transfer our casualties first. Move!"

Han leaned over to the comm to add, "Ilen, Barani, if you're still alive, get up here! Every *Gamble* crew member who can operate a station, find a station and operate it!"

Leia held up a hand for quiet and opened the frequency again. She said, "Very well, Degoren. I'll release your ship and crew in exchange for my people. Why don't you dock with your ship and we'll make the exchange."

Fera arrived, waving a comlink and making frantic motions at Leia. Leia muted the comm and Fera said, "I can transfer the connection here, to the *Aegis*'s comm system, and you can keep talking and he won't realize you aren't still on the bridge—"

"Do it." Leia opened the frequency again as Degoren was replying, "I don't think I'm quite that foolish, Organa. You'll have to come up with another arrangement."

Ilen and Barani appeared at the entrance to the bridge. Both looked bedraggled and exhausted. Ilen gasped, "Princess!"

Leia motioned for him to be quiet. Han shoved out of the pilot's station and signaled for them to take the stations. To Degoren, Leia said, "Perhaps we could both land on the planet."

Fera returned with the comlink and mouthed the word, "Ready."

Leia pointed urgently for her to go ahead. Any moment, Degoren was going to realize she was stalling, too.

Fera worked over the comm board for a moment, then plucked the headset off Leia's head, switched it off, and handed Leia the comlink. Leia heard Degoren, unconscious of the interruption, say, "That might be amenable. But how do I know it isn't a trick? There is some sort of sensor-blocking field in effect on the surface."

Han was already off the bridge, and Chewbacca stood in the doorway, shaking his bowcaster for Leia to hurry. "Let me discuss it with my crew," Leia said. "Perhaps we can find a way to reassure you." She muted the comlink and ran, with Terae and Fera and the other *Aegis* crew members on her heels.

She encountered General Willard and Jerell at the first junction, with engineer Sorel and the medic, Sarit. Han was there, explaining the situation briefly. The general nodded and said to Leia, "You're going on the *Aegis*?"

"Yes, and I want you to take this ship into hyperspace and head back to the fleet."

General Willard drew breath and Leia was certain he meant to argue with her. Conscious of their already small window of opportunity rapidly closing, she said, "Degoren has another ship en route and we have no idea what kind of firepower we're facing. I'm going to retrieve Luke and Kifar and then we'll be right behind you. You have to trust me to—"

The general held up a hand to stop the rush of words. "I trust you. Now go get our people so you can get out of here. If I have to come back for you, you'll never hear the end of it."

Leia hadn't been aware that she needed to hear something like that until he said it. She nodded sharply. "I'll see you on the *Independence*."

She and the others ran down the corridor. They passed other *Gamble* crew members, running or limping toward the bridge, to the weapons stations, or down toward engineering, and *Aegis* crew heading for the hatch connection. Everyone looked frantic and determined but not panicked. Leia felt she was panicking enough for everybody and wondered if all the others were just as good at hiding it as her. *Luke. You have to get him back.* If Degoren left the system with him, she would never be able to find him; he would be questioned, tortured. *I can't lose him.*

And it was her fault he had been captured. The more she thought about Degoren's appearance on the scene, what he had seemed to anticipate and what he hadn't, she suspected she had made a key and possibly devastating error in judgment.

Terae took a report on another comlink frequency and told Leia, "The Imperial crew is accounted for as best we can and secured in the brig. We think they have ten crew members in that shuttle, plus Degoren."

A crewman stood at the *Aegis*'s hatch with a data-pad, efficiently checking off the crew as they returned. Sian and R2-D2 waited beside him. Leia said, "You two, get to the bridge. The *Gamble*'s crew is going to need help up there."

R2 trundled off obediently, but Sian followed Leia through to the *Aegis*. Leia stopped her and said, "I meant you, too."

"I know," Sian said, "but I'm sticking with you." She jerked her head, indicating the *Aegis* and its failure so far to take advantage of the situation for profit. "You've been right so far."

Leia appreciated the vote of confidence, but she didn't think she deserved it. "I think I've been very wrong about one thing," she said, as she started after Terae.

Han glanced back at her. "You think Itran talked again."

"I'm worried he did more than that." She watched him as they hurried down the corridor. "You haven't said anything about the *Falcon* yet." There had been no sign of the ship on the sensors, and Leia hoped that meant the Imperials had left it down on the planet, undamaged.

Chewbacca made a worried noise in his throat, and Han said grimly, "If anything's happened to it, guess what you owe me?"

Leia didn't need to guess. "If anything's happened to it, you can have the *Darsumae*." *And if anything's happened to Luke, I'll have Degoren's head.*

CHAPTER SIXTEEN

WHEN THEY REACHED the junction that led to the bridge forward corridor, Leia held up a hand for quiet. She unmuted the comlink and said, "Commander Degoren, before we release your ship, we'd like some assurance that our people are still alive. Let me speak to Skywalker."

"You have no need to doubt my word. But I'll let you speak to Itran."

Right, Leia thought. "Give me a moment, please." She muted the comlink again and kept walking.

As the blast door to the bridge opened, Kelvan turned toward her. He was listening to a comm headset and told her, "The last of the crew is aboard and we've started to disengage the hatches. The *Darsumae* has been redesignated *Gamble Two,* and the pilot reports that they are configuring their jump and will enter hyperspace per your orders on our signal."

Terae reached the sensor station and said, "Shuttle is still holding position."

"Good." Leia lifted the comlink that connected her to Degoren, then hesitated. *How sure are you, Leia? This sure, at least.* She told Han, "Call General Willard on a secure frequency and tell him that if Kifar Itran shows up at the fleet without us, then he's probably an Imperial agent."

Han's expression went through several complicated changes, then he set his jaw. "Well, that explains a lot. He wanted the two of us to break open the slave pen, said he didn't trust the *Aegis*'s crew. But he must have thought he could get rid of me and find a comm system somewhere."

Sian stared in shock. "But he . . . The whole time he was . . . Oh, no. That's how they found the *Gamble* on Arnot Station."

Chewbacca drew his lips back in a grimace and made a comment that sounded remarkably accusing. Han glared at him. "It's not my fault. How was I supposed to know?"

Kelvan's brow furrowed and he clearly thought he had been left out of a rather important loop. He demanded, "When did you know?"

"Just now, actually," Leia said. "He must have been a deep-cover agent, intended to report on our movements and possibly sabotage our missions while the Empire prepared a trap for the Alliance fleet."

Terae clapped a hand to her head. "That lousy piece of—He didn't just tell Viest who you were, he made a deal with her."

"But after we rescued him, he couldn't get to a comm to tell Degoren that we planned this ambush." Leia eyed the sensors. The assistance that Degoren clearly expected might arrive at any moment.

Kelvan touched his headset as he listened to an internal report. He nodded to Leia. "The hatches are sealed, and we're ready to break off."

Leia pressed her lips together, then said, "We'll have to move fast, or he'll kill Luke."

Kelvan's smile was wry. "Believe me, it will be fast. We're good at this."

Terae added more grimly, "And we don't want to lose Itran. He made a deal with Viest, and got Captain Metara killed."

Leia wasn't certain there was a direct connection, but Itran certainly hadn't helped. She clicked on the comlink and said, "Commander Degoren, we're breaking off from your ship. We have your crew aboard, and we'll land on the planet to release them. Follow us down, or we'll space them and destroy your ship."

She cut the comm connection before Degoren could reply. "That's not going to hold him long. Let's go."

Kelvan signaled the pilot. Leia felt the deck sway underfoot as the *Aegis* powered away from the *Gamble II* so fast its gravity sensors couldn't compensate quickly enough.

Degoren wouldn't buy her distraction; he might believe she was confused and out of her depth, but he wasn't a fool. The *Aegis* dived toward the shuttle, which turned away immediately. Leia kept her eyes on the sensors as the newly named *Gamble II* began to accelerate in the opposite direction, readying itself for its hyperspace jump.

"Sir, we're almost in tractor beam range," the copilot said.

Kelvan touched his headset. "Tractor beam control, mark the target, ready—"

Fera, at the sensor station, said, "Sir, new contact exiting hyperspace!"

And we've run out of time, Leia thought. She stepped toward the sensor station as Fera enlarged the image of the incoming ship. It was an Imperial light corvette, likely the same one that had attacked the *Gamble.*

Fera said, "Sir, it's heading for *Gamble Two.*" The corvette's course curved toward the fleeing ship. Degoren must have managed to contact the corvette and inform it of his situation just as it hit realspace. *Or give orders,* Leia thought. *Degoren might be in charge of this whole operation.*

"Break off the shuttle, cover *Gamble Two*'s retreat." Kelvan glanced at Leia for her reaction, and she nodded sharply. Every nerve screamed at the idea of letting the shuttle go, but they had to protect the *Gamble II.*

Han watched the images from the sensor array fly across the displays. "That Degoren's one lucky Imp."

"And the corvette knows General Willard is aboard the *Gamble Two,*" Terae said, her voice tense.

She was right. Degoren would have informed them that he was holding the general prisoner aboard his ship. He might suspect that Willard had transferred to the *Aegis,* but with the *Gamble II* jumping to lightspeed, there was little doubt that the Alliance now controlled the ship.

The corvette fired turbolasers. But the *Aegis* cut across its field of fire and deflected the blasts on its own shields.

Leia looked at the sensors, just in time to see the *Gamble II* vanish. "*Gamble Two* is entering hyperspace," Fera reported. "Repeat, *Gamble Two* is away and clear."

Leia let out a pent breath. But the shuttle had taken advantage of the few moments to put distance between it and the *Aegis*. Now the corvette turned back toward it, shielding it from the *Aegis*'s weapons and tractor beam. Leia started to order Kelvan to pursue it, then stopped the words in her throat.

The light corvette was nearly twice the size of the gunship, though their weapons were equivalent, if the corvette hadn't been modified. The light corvettes were customs ships and had practically been designed to take on pirates.

She couldn't risk the *Aegis,* not for one life, not even if that life was Luke's. None of these people had signed on to the Alliance. She made herself say, "You'll have to break off."

Chewbacca made a faint noise, an aborted protest, and she could feel Sian staring at her. She thought Han would be the one to blow up, but instead he just said, quietly, "That may be a pirate-killer, but this isn't a modified freighter. The *Aegis* isn't as outgunned as you think."

"He's right." Kelvan faced her. "Your Highness, we can do this." There was nothing but complete conviction in his voice. "We couldn't help Alderaan— let us help you."

Leia wasn't sure what he was asking for, if it was absolution or atonement. She couldn't give him either, and attacking the Imperial ship didn't make tactical sense. "I'm not Alderaan."

"For us, you are. At least at this moment." Kelvan said again, "Let us help you."

Leia realized her hands were knotted into fists. She

couldn't leave Luke to the Empire. She just hoped she wasn't dooming all of them. "All right."

Kelvan nodded, and smiled gratefully. "You won't regret it."

I hope you don't regret it, Leia thought as Kelvan gave the orders and the *Aegis* accelerated in pursuit.

Chewbacca wuffed in relief. Han just stepped around her, heading for the sensor console. "I got an idea. That light corvette has external docking bays."

"We can't board it," Leia told him, frustrated. "It has at least a squad of eight stormtroopers aboard and more than fifty crew members."

"We can't board it if they know we're there," Han said. He leaned on the back of Fera's chair, studying the sensor displays. "Can you get them into the sensor field disruption?"

The *Aegis* drew into range of the corvette. The two ships seemed to dance as the corvette tried to protect the shuttle, but had to keep moving too fast for the shuttle to dock. Kelvan ordered, "Fire at will, keep their attention." To Han, he said, "Yes, but even with their sensors partly disabled, they could tell we were locking on and they'd hardly hold still for it."

"Or they would hold still, and blast through our lock before we could board them," Sian pointed out.

"Not if we use an escape pod," Han said.

Leia stared at him. "You're out of your mind. And that might just work."

Nobody liked the plan, but there was no time to argue about it.

Leia, Han, Chewbacca, and Sian raced for the *Ae-*

gis's shuttle bay where the *Gamble*'s escape pod still sat in the cradle, ready to be used. They were trailed by a protesting Terae, who couldn't seem to decide whether she wanted to talk them out of it or demand to go with them. Blast impacts made the deck shiver underfoot, though the shields still held. The *Aegis* darted back and forth to tease and lure the corvette farther into the sensor disruption area near the planet.

"You might need an engineer," Terae said desperately as Leia was about to climb into the pod. Han was already inside, starting its launch sequence, as Chewbacca adjusted the seat so he could fit into it.

"I appreciate the offer," Leia told her, "but with Han, Chewie, and Sian, I think we have it covered." Terae had handed Sian a satchel at the last moment, still packed with the small hatch-busting explosives and a few stun grenades left over from the boarding action against the *Darsumae*. Leia hesitated. "Terae, if I don't see you and Kelvan and the others again—"

"Don't say that!" Terae stopped, confused. "I just . . . After what happened to Captain Metara . . . I don't know what I mean."

Leia knew what Terae meant. After the traumatic death of her friend and mentor, after confronting the reality of the crew's life as pirates, Terae's world was spinning around her and some of her basic convictions had been shattered. Even after two years of hatred for the Alliance, of blaming it for Alderaan's destruction, Leia was still the only safe anchor in that world, and Terae didn't want her to leave, at least not yet. *You can't be responsible for every survivor of Alderaan,* Leia told herself. No one person could take that on and not go mad; it was worse than being the

Alliance's perfect shining symbol and figurehead. But walking away from Terae and the others tore at her. Maybe that was why she had been risking her neck so much lately. It was easier on her soul than the alternatives.

Sian helped shove Chewbacca into his seat and plopped down beside him, and Leia had no time left for negotiation or persuasion. She just said, "Think about what I've said to you. The offer is still open. If not, take care of each other."

Leia dropped into her seat and hit the sequence to seal the hatch and pressurize the pod. Terae hesitated for a moment, as if she might still protest, then turned and jogged for the blast doors, signaling the techs to follow her. Leia strapped in, and Han said into the comm, "We're ready when you are."

"We'll get you as close as we can," Kelvan's grim voice answered.

"Right." Han signed off but left the frequency open so they could hear the bridge. He gave Leia one of his typically hard-to-read looks. "You didn't have to come along, Your Worship."

"We've had this conversation before. My answer hasn't changed." This was Han's idea and she knew he was fine with the thought of risking himself on it, just not with risking anyone else. But Luke being in this mess was her responsibility.

Sian smiled tightly and Chewie grumbled low in his throat. Han had tried to order both of them to stay behind, too.

Besides customs enforcement and pirate hunting, the Imperial light corvettes had been designed for search-and-rescue after battles. They were equipped with exterior docking bays designed to handle multiple sizes of standard escape pods. Even in the sensor disruption area, the corvette would be able to detect something the size of the *Aegis* trying to lock onto it, but an escape pod would go unnoticed.

Hopefully.

Over the comm they could hear quiet voices from the bridge, tense but cool and determined. The *Aegis* fired at the corvette and its turbolasers fired back, the ship's hull vibrating at the impacts. Leia grimaced, imagining what would happen if the *Aegis* lost shielding. Then Kelvan's voice said, "We're coming in close. Get ready to launch on my mark."

The bay doors slid open and the pod's cradle tilted. Leia tensed, automatically checking the small console's sensor screen. They were deep in the sensor disruption area, so the screen displayed nothing but an error code, which was to be expected but still made her nerves jump.

Kelvan said, "Mark!"

As the pod dropped out of the cradle and spun out into space, the console's screen lit with a static image sent from the bridge: a diagram of the best estimate of the *Aegis*'s position relative to the corvette. That would be all Han had to navigate.

The stars wheeled outside as the pod tumbled away. Leia caught a confused view of the *Aegis*'s hull before a too-close blast impact dazzled her vision. She blinked hard to clear her eyes. Han bent over the console, and Chewbacca and Sian stretched forward to see. Leia leaned back as far as she could to get out of their way.

Han made a quick adjustment and the pod swiveled, came out of the tumble, and Leia felt the press of acceleration. Han stretched to look out the port. "I make it three degrees."

Sian bit her lip. "I think it's five."

Chewbacca barked an agreement.

"Let's split the difference and call it four," Han said. He hit the thrusters, and the pod shot forward.

Leia craned her neck to see. A metal wall rushed at them, a round docking port just off center. A blast somewhere above and forward blinded her for an instant, and she braced for an impact.

The pod jerked, threw them back in their seats. Then it slid forward with a screech of metal and slotted in to dock as if it had been built for this ship. Han let out a breath and said, "Automatic docking sequence. It activated when we got close enough."

"That's good flying, Solo," Sian said, a little breathless. "With nobody running a docking tractor beam for us, if we'd been too far off—"

"Get ready," Leia said. She already knew what would have happened if they'd been too far off. "We'll only have a few minutes before they realize we're here."

The last lock rotated into place, and the pod's hatch warning light went green. It slid open as Sian pressed the control, but the ship's inner hatch didn't open in response. That wasn't a surprise: battle conditions should require all the ship's outer hatches to lock from the inside. Leia lifted the satchel and handed Sian one of the small explosives designed for just this purpose. She slapped it into place, and they all huddled back as she triggered it.

It made a faint thump, the small charge sending an

energy bolt right through the hatch's lock controls. The hatch switched itself to manual, but the safeties kept it from sliding open. Chewbacca surged forward as Sian ducked back, gripped the hatch, and forced it to one side.

The Wookiee shoved through first, bowcaster ready, and Han, Sian, and Leia climbed out after him. The corridor was narrow and for the moment empty, lined on one side by outer hatches that led to more docking stations for pods and other small craft. "The shuttle should lock on at the main dock between the two stern modules," Han said. "We're about thirty meters forward from it."

Leia drew her blaster. "Let's go." Her skin prickled as they ran down the corridor. They passed a couple of closed blast doors, but both would connect to the heavily occupied forward section of the ship, where the crew would be running battle stations in weapons, engineering, and the bridge. They needed a way to the aft section and the docking station where the shuttle would be taken aboard.

Han reached the open blast door at the end and flattened himself against the wall. He took a quick look around the corner beyond the door, and Chewbacca leaned around him to see. Leia got enough of a view past them to see it was a junction, one corridor leading away toward starboard, the other heading into the port module.

Leia heard a whisper of sound behind her. She spun and lifted her blaster even before she identified it as the sound of a blast door opening.

Two dark-uniformed Imperial techs stepped out of it. Surprise froze them for an instant. One clawed for his blaster and Leia's first stun bolt hit him in the chest and dropped him. The other ducked back and hit the control to close the door. But Sian threw herself down onto the deck and fired under the closing door. Leia saw a body hit the deck just as the metal panel slid shut.

"Got him," Sian confirmed. "Should we—" Blaster-fire from behind them cut her words off, and Leia spun to see Han and Chewbacca returning fire at crew members running at them from the starboard corridor. Chewie took one last shot and pulled back as Han fired into the blast door's control mechanism, dropping and sealing the door.

That left them one option. Leia stepped to the side of the second sealed blast door, as Sian pushed to her feet and moved to cover her. Leia hit the control, and as it slid open, she ducked down into a firing position. The corridor beyond was empty for the moment. They would have to skirt the engineering section, but if they moved fast they might make it to the port module without the crew pinpointing their location. "This way." And it would help to give the crew something else to think about. "Sian, you have more of those explosive patches? Blow one of the escape pod hatches, please."

Chewie slipped past Leia and moved down the corridor to scout the way. Han waited with Leia, keeping a wary eye on the junction blast door. Someone on the other side was pounding on it and yelling for a fusioncutter. Sian moved a short distance down the corridor to attach the patch to the nearest escape pod hatch, then sprinted back toward Leia and Han at the blast door. Just as she she stepped through it, she triggered the explosive.

Han hit the release to seal the door and they pelted down the corridor as the decompression alarms sounded.

Luke watched Kifar start to sweat as the shuttle tried to match speed with the light corvette. The corvette was more worried about fighting off the *Aegis*, and the shuttle pilot was desperate to stay out of the line of fire and keep the corvette between it and the gunship. Luke was trying to decide if he would rather be blown up instantly or be an Imperial prisoner. On the whole, he was leaning toward the former.

The shuttle jerked and bucked; then he caught a glimpse of the hull of a ship through the forward ports. Trehar shifted and swore in Durese. "He almost took us right up the starboard engine."

Kifar grimaced. Luke's nerves itched. Much as being vaporized would probably be a preferable fate, the bad piloting made him twitchy.

The shuttle stopped vibrating, and Luke knew they must have finally been caught in a tractor beam. It pulled them in slowly toward a docking port between the corvette's two long stern modules. From what Luke could see, it wasn't a docking bay, just a large hatch structure designed to fit many different sizes of small craft. The shuttle was gradually drawn inside it and secured, and there was a loud *thunk* on the outside of the hull as the docking clamps locked on.

Luke heard the pilot doing final checks and talking to someone on the comm. An older man stepped out of the cockpit and came toward Luke. Kifar, Trehar, and the others unstrapped and stood, not quite at attention.

The man had dark hair, very pale skin, and hard square features. Like the others, he was dressed as a spacer, though his clothes looked more expensive. "The Princess didn't seem inclined to negotiate for your release," he said.

Luke was guessing this was Commander Degoren. He shrugged. "Why should she?" His instincts told him Leia and Han were up to something. He just didn't have a clue what that something would be.

Degoren smiled, a cold and skeptical expression. "Itran tells me that she's very attached to you. That you're a great confidant of hers, and perhaps something more . . ."

Luke thought, *Good old Kifar*. He made his smile bitterly amused. "Yeah, I just found out that Itran's not very reliable."

Kifar glared at him. Degoren's disgruntled sideways glance at Kifar suggested that he agreed with Luke. It wasn't a surprise; Kifar had failed to find an opportunity to warn Degoren that his ship was about to be boarded by Alderaanian pirates. That had to be a black mark on an Imperial agent's record.

And maybe Luke could convince Degoren that Kifar had done an even worse job than that.

"It doesn't matter," Degoren said. "Itran's told me who you are. You're the one who blew up the Death Star. And he's heard enough about your other exploits to know that we can have some very interesting conversations with you about rebel activities."

Luke gave Kifar a disgusted glance. "Is that what

you've told them?" He looked up at Degoren and made himself radiate earnest sincerity. Han had told him it was as effective as it was annoying. "The Death Star . . ." He shook his head helplessly. "That was just an accident. One of the older pilots talked me through it. Ever since then, I've been mostly working on X-wing maintenance. They haven't even sent me out on any other missions."

Degoren put on an expression of polite skepticism, but Luke thought he detected a trace of doubt. Kifar could have reacted in a lot of different ways, with amusement or exasperation, but instead he stiffened, his face darkening with anger. "You think this is going to work, Skywalker? You don't think we can break you?"

Luke let himself look scared and desperate. It wasn't hard; if he didn't pull something off and get out of here before the corvette jumped to lightspeed, he was in a lot of trouble. He said to Degoren, "Look, you've got me. I don't have any reason to lie to you." He glared at Kifar in angry reproach. "I know you're jealous about me and . . . and the Princess, I know how you feel about her, but you can't lie to them about me, they'll find out—"

Kifar snarled and swung at Luke. Luke ducked but still caught most of the blow on his left cheekbone. He awkwardly lifted his arms to block the next punch. Degoren snapped, "Enough."

Kifar reluctantly lowered his arm. His jaw worked and he said, "He's lying. He's in Red Squadron. And there's rumors that he was trained by a Jedi Knight." He turned to reach into the next seat compartment and held up Luke's lightsaber. "You saw he had this!"

Past the throbbing in his face, Luke gasped, baffled and incredulous. "You believe that? I bought it from a junk shop on Commenor."

Degoren pressed his lips together, aimed a death glare at Kifar, and said, "We'll settle this soon. Command has a cruiser en route. We wanted Organa, but if we can't get her, the pilot who destroyed the Death Star would be just enough of an acceptable substitute to keep us all alive. But you better hope he knows as much as you've said he does."

He turned away. The pilot had been waiting just outside the cockpit and now hit the opening sequence for the hatch. Trehar stepped forward and dragged Luke to his feet.

The shuttle's ramp lowered and Degoren stepped out, then the pilot and the other Imperials followed him. Kifar was next, and then Luke, then Trehar. As Kifar reached the hatch, a security alarm sounded out in the bay. And Luke thought, *Now.*

With his bound hands he shoved Kifar in the back. Kifar stumbled forward into the man in front of him and then whipped around, furious. In that moment, with all his strength, Luke jerked his head back at Trehar behind him, and slammed the back of his skull into the Duros's face.

Luke was pretty certain he felt a crack—hopefully Trehar's facial bone and not Luke's skull—but Kifar was already throwing a punch. Luke fell backward and it caught him a glancing blow. He went down on top of Trehar, grabbed the blaster out of his hand, and shot Kifar in the leg, the first available target.

Kifar dropped in front of the hatchway. Luke fired over him, out the hatchway, hitting the first man to try to lunge back inside and scattering the two men past him. Luke saw a stormtrooper helmet pop into view as he kept firing. Wedged between two injured but still moving bodies, another body half blocking the hatchway, his hands cuffed, Luke thought, *I don't think I'm getting out of this alive.* But it was better than ending up an Imperial prisoner.

That was when he heard the other shooting start.

They moved fast, and managed to bypass the passages to the engineering section that would surely be fully staffed with crew. So far the corvette conformed to the schematics Leia had seen, and it must have for Han, too, since he'd led the way unerringly so far.

Over the shipwide comm, a voice said, "Security to the main docking station."

"Is that for us?" Sian whispered.

"Maybe. Or Luke might be dragging his feet," Han said.

Ahead was another set of blast doors leading into a junction that should connect to the port docking module. Leia breathed, "It should be right up here."

Han and Chewbacca reached it first, and Han slid to an abrupt halt. Leia almost plowed into him. The junction was extended with a large slanted port looking down on the docking station. The far wall was open to space, the chamber protected and pressurized by containment fields, meant to accommodate ships of many shapes and sizes. Degoren's shuttle was in the center, locked into docking clamps, its ramp extended and hatch open. And a gun battle raged around the hatch, with someone inside the shuttle firing out and several men in spacers' garb and a couple of stormtroopers firing in, trying to angle for better positions.

Chewie hooted with delight and Leia exchanged a look with Han. Grimly, Han said, "Yeah, that's the kid in there."

Leia looked around for a way down into the docking station. To the right a blast door opened into a large lift platform that dropped the short distance to the lower floor. Leia said, "Sian—"

"Stun grenades?" Sian said, and pulled one out of her satchel.

That was the moment when the blast door behind them slid open. Leia spun with the others to see four surprised stormtroopers. Han and Chewbacca fired blaster and bowcaster as the first stormtrooper jerked his blaster up to fire. Sian whipped back her arm to throw the grenade. A blaster bolt struck her in the shoulder and she staggered and fell. The stun grenade spun across the floor and Leia lunged, grabbed it, pressed the trigger, and flung it through the blast door.

The concussion knocked her back, slammed her into the metal floor. Her ears ringing, she shoved herself up to see the four troopers strewn across the deck and down the corridor. Han staggered to the blast door, hit the release, and as it slid closed he stepped back and fired a bolt into the panel to slag the controls. "That wasn't a stun grenade, Your Worship!"

"I think that was a concussion grenade," Leia

agreed. She rolled to her feet and stumbled to Sian, who sat up, clutching her arm and grimacing in pain.

Guilty, Sian gasped, "I just pulled the first one out of the bag, I didn't look—"

"But it worked." Leia squinted at the burn in Sian's shoulder. The skin was blistered and raw around the open wound, the cloth of her jacket and shirt burned away. There was nothing they could do about it now. Leia dug in the satchel and held up a stun grenade. There were only three left. Chewbacca scooped it out of her hand and stepped to the blast door that looked down on the dock. Han grabbed another grenade and moved to his side. "Ready?" he said.

Leia pushed to her feet and saw that the Imperials below had scattered, some running toward a blast door in the lower part of the dock and others running for the lift tube. She said, "Chewie, throw long to port."

Han hit the door release and as it slid up he crouched and pitched his grenade. It landed among the men nearest the lift tube, who scattered back. As the door lifted out of the way, Chewbacca flung his grenade so hard and fast Leia couldn't see it, but she heard the muted crack as it hit the port wall of the bay. The Imperials must have thought these were concussion grenades, too, because the scramble to get away was violent. Han and Chewie ducked back, and the double thud of the muted explosions bounced off the viewport. Han straightened up, took a cautious look, and snapped, "Come on."

Leia grabbed Sian's uninjured arm and stood up with her. Han and Chewbacca dropped and climbed down the ladder next to the lift platform. They spread out, moved cautiously toward the shuttle past the unconscious or groaning bodies, watching the lower-level blast door in the far wall. With Chewbacca to cover him, Han shut it and shot the control panel. Helping Sian, Leia rode the lift platform down and staggered hurriedly toward the shuttle. The ship's security alarm wailed, louder in the docking station than it had been in the corridor. "Luke," she called out. "Is that you in there?"

"Leia?" Luke poked his head out, then stepped onto the ramp. His hands were in binders and he had a developing black eye but he was holding a blaster. "Good to see you guys!"

Dragging an Imperial out of the launch area, Han told him, "You better not have shot up the inside of that shuttle, junior, because that's our only way out of here."

"No, it's fine," Luke assured him. "Help me get rid of these guys in here. We've got to hurry—Degoren said there was a cruiser on the way."

Leia waited with Sian while Han hauled out an unconscious Duros and dumped him onto the deck. He told Leia, "Itran's in here, wounded. We're spacing him, right?"

Luke leaned out again. "You knew he was an Imperial agent?"

Leia said, "We figured it out, a little late. And no, Han, though it's a tempting thought." Sian slumped more heavily against her, slowly losing her grip on consciousness. Leia half helped, half hauled her forward, and Han caught Sian around the waist and carried her up into the shuttle.

Leia climbed in after him and saw Kifar Itran lying

on the floor toward the back of the shuttle. He was wounded in the leg, and Han and Luke must have found a couple of spare sets of binders because both his hands and feet were cuffed. Luke was struggling with a code-lock key, trying to get his binders off. Leia helped Han settle Sian into a seat and then strapped her in as Han headed for the cockpit.

Itran said, "Princess, it's a mistake—"

"Don't be an idiot," Leia told him. "You have until we reach the fleet to come up with a better story than that, and I recommend that you use the time wisely." She forgot Itran as Chewbacca climbed into the shuttle and she smelled burned fur. "Chewie, are you hurt?" she demanded.

He woofed a denial at her and hit the sequence to raise the ramp and seal the hatch. Then he dropped heavily into the first seat. There was blackened and singed fur all along his left arm, and the patches of skin she could now see looked raw and abraded. "You *are* hurt!"

Chewie shook his head vigorously.

Leia didn't have time to argue with him. She heard a muted clank against the hull as the docking clamps released and stepped forward through the cockpit hatch. Han's hands moved swiftly over the control board as the shuttle's systems came to life. He said, "They're gonna try to stop us. We need covering fire from the *Aegis*."

Leia dropped into the copilot's seat, strapped in, and brought up the comm board. "Chewie took a near miss but won't admit it."

"Yeah, but once we get out of here, he'll admit it

plenty. He just doesn't like sympathy while he's busy."

Leia didn't comment. The only thing more dubious than Han's catalog of Chewbacca's odd habits and behaviors was Chewie's catalog of Han's odd habits and behaviors. She hailed the *Aegis* and said, "We've taken Degoren's shuttle and we're about to leave the corvette in it. Be advised there is an Imperial cruiser en route." A crash out in the docking station interrupted her as the blast door Han had slagged blew open in a shower of sparks and smoke. Leia winced. "We need covering fire—"

The comm crackled and Kelvan's voice, desperate and urgent, said, "Your Highness, we have multiple comm ID contacts! We can't see them on the sensors yet—we're just at the edge of the sensor disruption zone—but at least a dozen ships must have come out of hyperspace!"

Han didn't glance away from the console but he grimaced. "Uh-oh."

"Imperial IDs?" Leia demanded.

Voices in the background gave conflicting reports, then Leia heard Terae swear. "It's the pirates!"

It can't be. Leia snapped, "Confirm that. These are ships from the clearinghouse?"

"They couldn't have followed us to this system. We didn't even know we were coming here," Han said, his jaw set in a grim line. "Unless somebody from the *Aegis* got to the comm and called them after we set our course here."

Leia shook her head. "No." Over the comm, she told Kelvan, "They must have put a tracer on the *Aegis* when Viest paid for your repairs. She wanted to

make sure you kept your end of her bargain. Whoever took over for her either suspects we killed her
and wants revenge, or just wants the *Aegis*."

There was a moment of shocked chagrin that Leia
could sense right through the comm. The corvette
couldn't see the pirate ships on its sensors from its
position in the sensor disruption cloud, but it had to
be picking up those ID contacts. The corvette's captain would think it was an elaborate trap, and they
might cut and run for hyperspace.

Stormtroopers, the rest of the squad that they had
met in the upper corridor, appeared out of the smoke.
Most had only blasters, but one had something bigger. Han said, "We can't wait, sweetheart."

"Kelvan, we're launching now," Leia said, ending
on a strangled gasp as Han fired the bow thrusters
and the sudden jolt shoved her forward in her seat.

The shuttle fell back through the containment field
and between the corvette's modules, down and away.
The starfield wheeled as Han brought the little ship
around. "I'm heading deeper into the sensor disruption field. If we can land and get to the *Falcon*, we'll
have a chance."

Leia didn't argue. The corvette wouldn't be able to
target them, and hopefully it would be too busy to
turn back and try to pick them up on visual. The
shuttle's sensors were showing nothing but error
codes and Leia doubted they could find the *Aegis*
without being hit, either by the corvette or the pirates.

Luke stepped into the cockpit hatch and said,
"How's it going?" He had managed to get the cuffs
off and retrieved his lightsaber.

"It's been better," Han said.

"How is Sian—" Leia started to ask, then the port dimmed and a too-near blast impact shuddered through the hull.

Han swore, sent the shuttle into an evasive flip that was better suited to a snubfighter, and made the metal hull groan. Leia got a confused view of the *Aegis* falling past their port. On the comm, Kelvan said calmly, "A pirate fired on you, Your Highness. We're engaging now."

"Thank you, Captain," Leia managed.

Han sent the shuttle hurtling away from the battle. "You're right, Your Worship, they got a tracer on the *Aegis*. That's the only way they found it and us so fast."

"She's breathing okay," Luke told Leia, answering her question. "But we need to get her some help fast. I couldn't find a medkit anywhere on board."

Leia could still hear the *Aegis*'s bridge. Someone reported that the corvette had engaged the other pirates, unintentionally teaming up with the *Aegis* and confusing the situation further. Listening, Luke said, "The Imperials must think the pirates are Alliance ships."

The shuttle fell toward the planet's gravity well, shuddering as it hit the upper atmosphere. They were close enough to make out the gray plains and the ridges that marked the ruined city. Luke leaned forward to type a course into the shuttle's nav screen. "This is where the *Falcon* is, if it's still there."

"*If?*" Han managed to get a world of appalled recrimination into that one word.

From the back, Chewbacca groaned.

"Hey, I was stunned," Luke protested. "I don't know what happened. But I code-locked the hatch, and See-Threepio was in there, so Itran couldn't get back inside."

"Why didn't he call the *Aegis*?" Leia asked, over some expressive cursing from Han that they didn't have time for.

Luke shook his head. "I was having trouble with the comm after I landed. I think the field is stronger on the surface; he probably couldn't get a signal through."

Following Luke's directions, Han brought the shuttle down over the empty stone city, past shattered towers and circular streets covered by sand drifts and vegetation. As the *Millennium Falcon* came into sight, still parked on the plaza where Luke had left it, there was a collective sigh of relief. Leia felt her heart unclench for Han and Chewie's sake, and for Sian. The *Falcon* had enough medical supplies on board to treat a blaster burn and stabilize her, at least until they could get her to the fleet.

Han landed the shuttle nearby and they hurriedly disembarked. Sian was conscious but in pain, and Luke carried her into the *Falcon* while Han ran ahead to start prepping the ship for a fast launch. The hatch slid open as he reached the ramp, revealing the gold droid. C-3PO said, "Oh, you're back! I was so worried! And I think Master Itran has been behaving very suspiciously."

Han shouldered past them and Leia said, "Thank you, See-Threepio. Please get the emergency medical station ready, we have wounded."

"At once, Your Highness. Oh, but where is Artoo?"

"He's fine. He's with General Willard, heading back to the fleet," Leia told him. Relieved, C-3PO hurried away as Chewbacca dragged Itran out of the shuttle. Once they were all safely inside the ship, Leia left Luke getting Sian settled on a bunk and went to the cockpit.

Han could get the *Falcon* ready to launch in three minutes, and this time she thought he did it in two. As the ship lifted out of the plaza, Leia dropped into the comm station. Chewbacca stepped into the cockpit and sank into his oversized copilot's chair.

She tried to hail the *Aegis* immediately but Luke was right, the signal was weak until they lifted into the upper atmosphere. As the *Aegis*'s comm station acknowledged her she could hear Kelvan giving orders in the background and Terae's urgent voice. "What's your situation?" she demanded.

The crewman monitoring the comm answered, "We're out of the sensor disruption area. The corvette's destroyed one ship and damaged two others. We've been engaged by three." His voice was young and he sounded tense, at the edge of fear. *It's bad*, Leia thought.

Finally, Kelvan's voice said, "Your Highness, are you safe?"

"Yes, we're on the *Falcon*." Leia hesitated, and thought, *You have to do this. They could be destroyed at any moment*. She didn't want to lose them. But she had to let them go. "Kelvan, get out of there. Take the *Aegis* into hyperspace."

There was a hesitation. "Princess, we can't leave you—"

"We're about to enter hyperspace ourselves. You

need to get out of here, and get rid of that tracer. If you—I gave Terae a list of message drop sites. If you change your mind about the Alliance, come to the first one on the list a month from now. I'll meet you."

"Your Highness, I can't promise you—I don't know what the others will want—I don't know what I want—" A blast that must have rocked the bridge interrupted him.

"Kelvan, please, go!" Leia said, and cut the connection.

The *Falcon* circled the planet and blasted into space.

As they shot away from the disruption field, contacts sprang up all over the sensors. But Han had chosen their escape route well, and none of the incoming pirate ships was close enough to reach them. The corvette was drawing most of the fire, and Leia saw the *Aegis* disable a persistent opponent with a pair of concussion missiles and then power away from the battle.

The coordinates for the nearest fleet rendezvous point were already programmed in, and Leia set the navicomputer to calculate the jump. Most of his attention on the console, Han said, "They'll be all right."

Leia shook her head. She hoped . . . She just hoped. The *Aegis*'s ID vanished from the contact screen as it disappeared into hyperspace. A few moments later, the *Falcon* followed it.

EPILOGUE

LEIA WAS ANXIOUS about the *Aegis,* though there were plenty of emergencies with the fleet to keep her occupied while she waited until it was time to go to the message drop point. Still, she found herself counting the days.

By the end of the month, Sian had recovered from her wound, Luke had been sent off on another mission, and Itran had been questioned extensively by Madine. One of the things that had kept Leia busy had been tracing Itran's progress through the Alliance, changing any codes or procedures or bolt-holes he might have had access to, checking heretofore unexplained mechanical failures and losses of supply sources that he might have engineered. Fortunately, Itran hadn't wanted to do anything that would have caused suspicion or drawn attention; he had been biding his time, waiting until he was transferred to the *Independence.*

Leia knew they had been lucky to uncover him when they did. He could have continued to lie low and collect information and perform small acts of sabotage until he learned the location of Echo Base.

But he had decided to risk it all with an attempt to hand Leia and General Willard over to Commander Degoren. Leia knew that was why Itran had volunteered to go with her to the *Aegis;* it must have been a spur-of-the-moment decision, caused by fear of losing one of his prizes. "He could have done much more damage to us, if he hadn't been so ambitious," Madine had told Leia at one point.

"Perhaps we should take that as a lesson," Leia had said. They had just come out of a meeting with Mon Mothma and several members of the High Command and Leia felt like she would have rather gone another round with Viest's mad mining droid. That she had dealt as much damage as she had taken wasn't much of a consolation.

"We should," Madine had admitted. "But we won't."

At least the whole episode of the clearinghouse hadn't been for nothing. Not long before the month was up, Han had taken the opportunity to find Kearn-sa'Davit at the trading port he was operating out of and get an update on the situation for the merchant consortium. With Viest out of the picture, things had gotten drastically better for shipping around Arnot Station and its trading partners. Davit wasn't certain, but he figured that many pirates had been frightened away from the clearinghouse permanently and wouldn't be coming back to the sector. The word through the black markets was that at least one, maybe two, of Viest's would-be successors had died at Rethel Point during the battle with the *Aegis* and the customs corvette.

But there hadn't been any noticeable gains for the

Alliance out of the situation, no new supply source for Echo Base, and that had been made clear to Leia. So she was glad for more than one reason to slip away from the fleet on the *Millennium Falcon,* with no one but Mon Mothma and Madine's knowledge, to spend the time in Han and Chewbacca's occasionally irascible but undemanding company. She had brought C-3PO with her, and had more than enough work to keep her occupied while they waited for the *Aegis* to arrive.

When they reached the message drop point, the *Aegis* wasn't there, but Leia wasn't too worried. Depending on where its travels had taken it, and what repairs it had needed, it might take a while for the gunship to make its way here.

"Here" was a small trading port on a world at the edge of the Inner Rim, a long way from the clearing-house and Arnot Station. The port was built out on raised platforms above a shallow freshwater sea, with docking pads, supply depots, cargo factors, ship-wrights, and the usual clusters of drink and food service establishments. Everything was accessed by bridges, with small fishing boats sailing beneath, and several causeways connected the structures to the small city spread out across the nearest archipelago. It wasn't a bad spot to bide some time, even with the humidity and the morning mists—though Chewie frequently ended up being the one to go out to get food, and he had made it clear that he didn't take requests and they would eat what he brought back and like it. Leia settled in to wait, and to read the reports she had collected on her datapad.

After the second day with no sign of the *Aegis,* she

was too anxious to relax. Waiting was becoming nerve racking rather than a pleasure.

The pointed absence of the *Aegis* was so painful to her that Chewbacca just watched her sympathetically, and even Han didn't mention the ship's failure to appear.

But finally, after four days, he said reluctantly, "If we stay here any longer, we're going to have to get jobs, or grow crops, or something."

"I know." Leia rubbed her eyes. They were sitting in the cockpit, where they had a good view of the other landing pads. The *Falcon*'s platform was a little higher than the others, and they could see the other ships, mostly freighters and small local transports, in between the stretches of water and the tall, green fern-reeds that grew between the pilings. "I just hoped they would change their minds."

It hadn't been just a hope—it had been almost a certainty. At the last, she had really thought Kelvan and even Terae had become open to the possibility of joining the Alliance. They had had every chance to betray Leia for profit, yet they hadn't done it. They had been honest with her, and trusted her. *They were honest with you, they wanted to help you, they trusted you. You, not the Alliance,* she thought. *And in the end, you failed them.* "I pushed too hard. I should have tried to set up another meeting just to talk. There was an implied commitment in coming here—that was a mistake."

Han swung the pilot's chair back and forth. "I don't know what else you were supposed to say. They knew the situation. They needed to make a decision."

Leia looked away, at the busy crews and droids

loading and unloading cargo. "And they must have made it."

"Hey," Han said softly. She turned back to look at him. "Let's give it one more day."

Leia got to her feet. She wanted to nurse her disappointment in private. "One more night," she said. She appreciated Han's generosity, but she knew there wasn't any point to remaining longer. "We can leave tomorrow morning."

Han nodded. "If that's what you want."

She woke at dawn the next morning to Han banging on her cabin door. Leia had already drawn her blaster, thinking the ship was being attacked, when she realized he was saying, "Get out here, sweetheart, there's something you need to see."

She threw her clothes on hastily, and ran up to the cockpit just in time to watch something very like an Alderaanian gunship landing on the next platform over.

Read on for an excerpt from

STAR WARS: EMPIRE AND REBELLION: HONOR AMONG THIEVES

BY
JAMES S. A. COREY

PUBLISHED BY CENTURY.

ONE

FROM THE IMPERIAL CORE to the out-flung stars of the Rim, the galaxy teemed with life. Planets, moons, asteroid bases, and space stations peopled with a thousand different species, all of them busy with the great ambitions of the powerful and also with the mundane problems of getting through their days, the ambitions of the Emperor all the way down to where to eat the next meal. Or whether there would be a next meal. Each city and town and station and ship had its own history and secrets, hopes and fears and half-articulated dreams.

But for every circle of light—every star, every planet, every beacon and outpost—there was vastly more darkness. The space between stars was and always would be unimaginably huge, and the mysteries that it hid would never be wholly discovered. One bad jump was all it took for a ship to be lost. Unless there was a way to reach out for help, to say, *Here I am. Come find me,* an escape pod or a ship or a fleet could vanish into the places between places that even light took a lifetime to reach.

And so a rendezvous point could be the size of a solar system, and the rebel fleet could still hide there like a flake in a snowstorm. Hundreds of ships from the cobbled-together, plasma-scorched cruisers and third-hand battleships to X- and Y-wings and everything in between. They flew through space together silently, drifting closer in or farther apart as the need arose. Repair droids crawled over the skins of the ships, welding back together the wounds of their last battles, sure in the knowledge that they were the needle in the Empire's haystack.

Their greatest danger wasn't the enemy but inaction. And the ways a certain kind of man coped with it.

"I wasn't cheating," Han Solo said as Chewbacca bent to pass through the door in the bulkhead. "I was playing better than they were."

The Wookiee growled.

"That's how I was playing better. It's not against the rules. Besides, what are they going to buy with their money out here?"

A dozen fighter pilots marching past in dirty orange-and-white uniforms saluted them. Han nodded to each one as he passed. They were an ugly bunch: middle-aged men who should have been back home on a planet somewhere spending too much time at the neighborhood bar and weedy boys still looking forward to their first wispy mustaches. Warriors for freedom, and terrible sabacc players.

Chewbacca let out a long, low groan.

"You wouldn't," Han said.

Chewbacca's blue eyes met his, and the Wookiee's silence was more eloquent than anything he might have said aloud.

"Fine," Han retorted. "But it's coming out of your cut. I don't know when you went soft on me."

"Han!"

Luke Skywalker came jogging down a side corridor, his helmet under his arm. Two droids followed him: the squat, cylindrical R2-D2 rolling along, chirping and squealing; the tall, golden C-3PO trotting along at the back, waving gold-chrome hands as if gesticulating in response to some unheard conversation. The kid's face was flushed and his hair was dark with sweat, but he was grinning like he'd just won something.

"Hey," Han said. "Just get back from maneuvers?"

"Yep. These guys are great. You should have seen the tight spin and recover they showed us. I could have stayed out there for hours, but Leia called me back in for some kind of emergency meeting."

"Her Worshipfulness called the meeting?" Han asked as they turned down the main access corridor together. The smell of welding torches and coolant hung in the air. Everything about the Rebel Alliance smelled like a repair bay. "I thought she was off to her big conference on Kiamurr."

"She was supposed to be. I guess she postponed leaving."

The little R2 droid squealed, and Han turned to it. "What's that, Artoo?"

C-3PO, catching up and giving a good impression of leaning forward to catch his breath even though he didn't have lungs, translated: "He's saying that she's postponed her departure twice. It's made a terrible shambles of the landing docks."

"Well, that's not good," Han said. "Anything that keeps her from sitting around a big table deciding the future of the galaxy . . . I mean, that's her favorite thing to do."

"You know that's not true!" Luke said, making room in the passageway for a bronze-colored droid that looked like it had barely crawled out of the trash heap. "I don't know why you don't like her more."

"I like her fine."

"You're always cutting her down, though. The Alliance needs good politicians and organizers."

"You can't have a government without a tax collector. Just because we'd both like it better if the Emperor wasn't in charge, it doesn't make me and her the same person."

Luke shook his head. The sweat was starting to dry, and his hair was getting some of its sandy color back.

"I think you two are more alike than you pretend."

Han laughed despite himself. "You're an optimist, kid."

When they reached the entrance to the command center, Luke sent the droids on, R2-D2 whistling and squeaking and C-3PO acting annoyed. The command center had taken a direct hit in the fighting at Yavin, and the reconstruction efforts still showed. New panels, blinding in their whiteness, covered most of one wall where the old ones had been shattered by the blast. Where the replacements ended, the old panels seemed even darker by contrast. The head-high displays marked the positions of the ships in the fleet and the fleet in the emptiness of the rendezvous point, the status of repair crews, the signals from the sensor arrays, and half a dozen other streams of information. None of the stations were manned. The data spooled out into the air, ignored.

Leia stood at the front of the room, the bright repair work and grimy original walls seeming to come together in her. Her dress was black with embroidery of gold and bronze, her hair a soft spill gathered at the nape of her neck in a style that made her seem both more mature and more powerful than the side buns she'd worn on the

Death Star. From what Han had heard around the fleet, losing Alderaan had made her older and harder. And as much as he hated to admit it, she wore the tragedy well.

The man she was talking to—Colonel Harcen—had his back to them, but his voice carried just fine. "With respect though, you have to see that not all allies are equal. Some of the factions that are going to be on Kiamurr, the Alliance would be better off without."

"I understand your concerns, Colonel," Leia said in a tone that didn't sound particularly understanding. "I think we can agree, though, that the Alliance isn't in a position to turn away whatever help we can get. The Battle of Yavin was a victory, but—"

Harcen raised a palm, interrupting her. He was an idiot, Han thought. "There are already some people who feel that we have become too lax in the sorts of people we're allowing into our ranks. In order to gain respect, we must be free of undesirable elements."

"I agree," Han said. Colonel Harcen jumped like a poked cat. "You've got to keep the scum out."

"Captain Solo," Harcen said. "I didn't see you there. I hope I gave no offense."

"No. Of course not," Han said, smiling insincerely. "I mean, you weren't talking about *me,* were you?"

"Everyone is very aware of the service you've done for the Alliance."

"Exactly. So there's no reason you'd have been talking about me."

Harcen flushed red and made a small, formal bow. "I was not talking about you, Captain Solo."

Han sat at one of the unmanned stations, stretching his arms out like he was in a cantina with a group of old friends. It might have been an illusion, but he thought he saw a flicker of a smile on Leia's lips.

"Then there's no offense taken," he said.

Harcen left, his shoulders back and his head held high. Chewbacca took a fraction of a second longer than strictly needed to step out of the man's way. Luke leaned against one of the displays, his weight warping the display enough that it sent little sprays of false color through the lines and curves.

When Harcen was gone, Leia sighed. "Thank you all for coming on short notice. I'm sorry I had to pull you off the training exercises, Luke."

"It's all right."

"I was in a sabacc game," Han said.

"I'm not sorry I pulled you out of that."

"I was winning."

Chewbacca chuffed and crossed his arms. Leia's expression softened a degree. "I was supposed to leave ten hours ago," she said, "and I can't stay much longer. We've had some unexpected developments, and I need to get you up to speed."

"What's going on?" Luke asked.

"We aren't going to be able to use the preliminary base in Targarth system," she said. "We've had positive identification of Imperial probes."

The silence lasted only a breath, but it carried a full load of disappointment.

"Not *again*," Luke said.

"Again." Leia crossed her arms. "We're looking at alternatives, but until we get something, construction and dry-dock plans are all being put on hold."

"Vader's really going all out to find you people," Han said. "What are your backup plans?"

"We're looking at Cerroban, Aestilan, and Hoth," Leia told him.

"That's the bottom of the barrel," Han said.

For a second, he thought she was going to fight, but

instead she only looked defeated. He knew as well as she did that the secret rebel base was going to be critical. Without a base, some kinds of repair, manufacturing, and training work just couldn't be done, and the Empire knew that, too. But Cerroban was a waterless, airless lump of stone hardly better than the rendezvous point, and one that was pounded by asteroids on a regular basis. Aestilan had air and water, but rock worms had made the planetary mantle so fragile that there were jokes about digging tunnels just by jumping up and down. And Hoth was an ice ball with an equatorial zone that only barely stayed warm enough to sustain human life, and that only when the sun was up.

Leia stepped to one of the displays, shifting the image with a flicker of her fingers. A map of the galaxy appeared, the immensity of a thousand million suns disguised by the fitting of it all onto the same screen.

"There is another possibility," she said. "The Seymarti system is near the major space lanes. There's some evidence that there was sentient life there at some point, but our probes don't show anything now. It may be the place we're looking for."

"That's a terrible idea," Han said. "You don't want to do that."

"Why not?" Luke asked.

"Ships get lost in Seymarti," Han said. "A lot of ships. They make the jump to hyperspace, and they don't come back out."

"What happens to them?"

"No one knows. Something that close to the lanes without an Imperial garrison on it can be mighty appealing to someone who needs a convenient place to not get found, but everyone I know still steers clear of that place. *Nobody* goes there."

Luke patted his helmet with one thoughtful hand.

"But if nobody goes there, how can a lot of ships get lost?"

Han scowled. "I'm just saying the place has a bad reputation."

"The science teams think there may be some kind of spatial anomaly that throws off sensor readings," Leia said. "If that's true, and we can find a way to navigate it ourselves, Seymarti may be our best hope for avoiding Imperial notice. As soon as Wedge Antilles is back from patrol, he's going to put together an escort force for the survey ships."

"I'd like to go with him," Luke said.

"We talked about that," Leia said. "Wedge thought it would be a good chance for you to get some practice. He's requested you as his second in command."

Luke's smile was so bright, Han could have read by it. "Absolutely," the kid said.

The communication panel beside Leia chimed. "Ma'am, we've kept the engines hot, but if we don't leave soon, we're going to have to recalibrate the jump. Do you want me to reschedule your meetings again?"

"No. I'll be right there," she said, and turned the connection off with an audible click.

Han leaned forward. "It's all right. I see how I fit in here," he said. "The weapons run from Minoth to Targarth is off. That's not a big deal. I'll just bring the guns here instead. Unless you want the *Falcon* to go along with the kid here."

"Actually, that's not why I wanted to talk with you," Leia said. "Something else happened. Two years ago, we placed an agent at the edge of Imperial space. The intelligence we've gotten since then has been some of the most valuable we've seen, but the reports stopped seven months ago. We assumed the worst. And then yesterday, we got a retrieval code. From the Saavin system. Cioran."

"That's not the *edge* of Imperial space," Han said. "That's the middle of it."

Chewbacca growled and moaned.

"It's not what I would have picked, either," Leia said. "There was no information with it. No context, no report. We don't know what happened between the last contact and now. We just got the signal that we should send a ship."

"Oh," Han said with a slowly widening grin. "No, it's all right. I get it. I absolutely understand. You've got this important guy trapped in enemy territory, and you need to get him out. Only with the Empire already swarming like a hive of Bacian blood hornets, you can't risk using anyone but the best. That about right?"

"I wouldn't put it that way, but it's in the neighborhood of right, yes," Leia said. "The risks are high. I won't order anyone to take the assignment. We can make it worth your time if you're willing to do it."

"You don't have to order us, does she, Chewie? All you have to do is ask, and we are on the job."

Leia's gaze softened a little. "Will you do this, then? For the Alliance?"

Han went on as if she hadn't spoken. "Just say 'please,' and we'll get the *Millennium Falcon* warmed up, skin out of here, grab your guy, and be back before you know it. Nothing to it."

Leia's expression went stony. "Please."

Han scratched his eyebrow. "Can I have a little time to think about it?"

The Wookiee made a low but rising howl and lifted his arms impatiently.

"Thank you, Chewie," Leia said. "There's also a real possibility that the whole operation was compromised and the retrieval code is bait in a trap. When you make your approach, you'll need to be very careful."

"Always am," Han said, and Luke coughed. "What?" Han demanded.

"You're always careful?"

"I'm always careful enough."

"Your first objective is to make the connection and complete the retrieval," Leia said. "If you can't do that, find out as much as you can about what happened and whether any of our people are in danger. But if you smell a trap, get out. If we've lost her, we've lost her. We don't want to sacrifice anyone else."

"Her?"

Leia touched the display controls again, and the image shifted. A green security warning flooded it, and she keyed in the override. A woman's face filled the screen. High cheekbones, dark eyes and hair, V-shaped chin, and a mouth that seemed on the verge of smiling. If Han had seen her in a city, he'd have looked twice, but not because she was suspicious. The data field beside the picture listed a life history too complex to take in at a glance. The name field read: Scarlet Hark.

"Don't get in over your head," Leia said.

Read on for an excerpt from

STAR WARS: MAUL: LOCKDOWN

BY
JOE SCHREIBER

PUBLISHED BY CENTURY.

HOT MESS

MAUL MOVED ACROSS THE PRISON MESS HALL like a predator recently released from its cage, passing sleekly through the mob, parting them with scarcely a glance. Some of the inmates took an uneasy step back to allow him to go by, while others simply froze in place. Heads swiveled to watch him pass. The continuous ambient drone of voices dropped to whispers and the whispers lapsed into watchful, estimating silence as he made his way among them.

He walked to the last table and sat down.

On the other side of the table, two inmates who had been in the middle of an argument—one a pallid, frightened-looking human with a four-day stubble, the other a Gotal who appeared to be missing an eye—stopped talking, picked up their trays, and made a hasty departure.

Maul sat motionless, observing everything around him without giving any indication that he was doing so. Although his peripheral vision still hadn't fully recovered from last night's attack, he saw enough to realize that he had become the current object of everyone's attention. Even the guards up on the catwalks overhead seemed to have gone on high alert, one hand on their blasters, the other resting on the small flat consoles that they wore on their belts. From both inmates and guards, Maul could smell a certain unmistakable commingling of fear, desperation, and the grinding monotony of paranoia that emerged when living things were penned up together in close quarters for indefinite spans of time.

It disgusted him.

Yet, for the time being at least, it was home.

He had stepped aboard this floating sewer less than twenty-four standard hours earlier, and in that time he'd come to understand all that he needed to know about the place. The rest of his time inside, he knew, would simply be a question of patience, of accomplishing his mission here without being discovered for what he truly was.

Neither of these things would be difficult for him.

They were simply the mandates of his assignment, and as such, beyond all question.

His arrival on Cog Hive Seven had come courtesy of the only transport of the day, a nameless prison barge with a stripped-down interior that reeked of high-carbon anthracite and unwashed flesh. The cargo hold was stocked with thirty-seven other inmates whose presence Maul barely registered after gauging none of them worth a moment of his time. They were a foul-smelling, nit-infested lot comprised of a dozen different species, some clearly deranged and muttering to themselves, others staring blankly through the vessel's only viewport as if something in the depthless black void might give perspective to their pointless and insubstantial lives.

Throughout it all, Maul had sat apart from his fellow inmates in absolute stillness. Some of them, apparently, couldn't wait to start fighting. As the trip wore on, boredom became restlessness and scuffles had broken out as sidelong glances, petty grievances erupted into acts of seemingly unprovoked violence. Several hours into the journey, an over-muscled ectomorph with bulging crab-stalk eyes had leapt up and lunged at a Rodian who'd somehow managed to smuggle a whip-band that he'd sharpened and apparently planned to use as a makeshift vibroblade. The fight hadn't lasted long, and only when the blade-bearer had accidentally bumped into him had Maul glanced up long enough to drive an elbow upward and shatter the Rodian's lower spine. The guards on-board hadn't even blinked as the Rodian pitched over sideways, wailing and paralyzed, to the deck where it lay whimpering for the duration of the trip, gazing up through moist and pleading eyes.

It was the only time during the entire trip that Maul had moved.

When they'd finally docked, a retinue of fatigued-looking corrections officers had met them in the hangar, herding them down the berthing port with static pikes and go-sticks, running the biometric scans as the new inmates had shambled forward, blinking into their new surroundings. Maul had seen more guards at this point in processing than anywhere else aboard the space station. At the end of the line, he stood motionless as a jumpy young CO whose ID badge read *Smight* swept a wand over him, scanning for infection and hidden weapons. There was no mistaking the tremor in the man's hand as he passed the wand in front of Maul's face.

"You know why you're here, maggot?" Smight had

asked, struggling to hide the quaver in his voice behind a pitiful note of bravado.

Maul had said nothing.

"Twenty-two standard hours a day," Smight told him, "you're free to roam the gallery and mess hall. Twice a day, when you hear the clarion call go off, you return to your cell for matching." The guard swallowed, the bump in his throat bulging up and down. "Any attempt to escape results in immediate termination. Failure to report back to your cell for matching will be treated as an escape attempt and will result in immediate termination. You got that?"

Maul had just stared back at him, waiting for the guard to finish his business and back away. As he'd walked away, he heard the young CO find enough courage to snarl out one final declaration.

"You'll die in here, maggot. They all do."

Medbay had come next, an hour's worth of decontamination and tox screens, neuro readouts and electroencephalograms administered by disinterested droids. After a long round of ultrasonic full-body scans, a refurbished GH-7 surgical unit had inserted a long syringe into Maul's chest, withdrawn it, only to plunge it back in again at a slightly different angle. A final scan had confirmed whatever the droid had done to him, and the CO at the far end of the concourse had waved him forward.

Afterward, two more officers armed with E-11 assault blasters had appeared and led him through a circuitous network of increasingly narrow concourses. The final walkway had led unceremoniously to his cell, a featureless, alloy-plated dome perhaps three meters in diameter. The carbon composite floor was the color of dirty

slate. A single air vent whirred overhead. Stepping inside, Maul had sat hunched on the single, narrow bench,
gazing at the only light source, an unremarkable panel
of blinking yellow lights on the opposite wall.

"This is where you'll come for lockdown and matching," one of the guards had told him. He was a grizzled
older man, a veteran whose ID badge identified him as
Voystock. "You hear the clarion, wherever you are, you
have five standard minutes to get back here for lockdown before you're terminated."

Maul looked at him coldly. "Terminated?"

"Yeah, I guess nobody told you." The guard nodded
down at the flat gray control unit strapped to his hip.
"We call this thing a dropbox. Wanna know why?"

Maul just gazed at him.

"Oh, you're a hard-case, right?" Voystock snorted.
"Yeah. They all start out that way. See, every inmate
who comes through medbay gets a subatomic electrostatic detonator implanted in the walls of his heart. *Both*
your hearts, since apparently you've got two of 'em.
What that means is, I type in your prison number here,
11240—" He ran his fingers over the dropbox's keypad.
"—those charges go off. And that's when you drop. Permanently."

Maul said nothing.

"But hey," Voystock said with a crooked grin, "a
tough guy like you shouldn't have any problems here."
He reached up and patted Maul's cheek. "Have yourself
a nice day, right?"

They left the hatch open behind them, but Maul had
stayed in his cell, crouched motionless, allowing his new
surroundings to creep in around him in the slow accre-
tion of physical detail.

There were words scratched on the walls, graffiti in a
dozen different languages, the usual cries of weakness—

pleas for help, forgiveness, recognition, a quick death. The bench was equipped with handgrips, their surface worn smooth by hundreds of palms, as if the inmates who'd occupied this cell before him had all needed something to hold onto. Maul had dismissed this detail as irrelevant.

Until the clarion had sounded.

Then he had sat up, snapped into total alertness, as the panel of yellow lights in front of him stopped blinking and turned solid red. The signal keened for five minutes. From outside, Maul had heard voices along with the frantic scuffle and clang of footsteps on floorboards as inmates had hurried back to their cells. As the alarms cut off, he heard the sounds of cells around him sealing shut.

The walls had started shaking. Complicated scraping noises came from somewhere deep inside the prison's infrastructure itself, gnashing together in complicated arrangements of pneumatics. Reconfiguration. Maul looked down. The floor beneath him had already begun to bow downward into a bowl shape as the dome became a perfect sphere.

And the cell had begun to turn.

Only then had the well-worn handgrips on the bench made sense. He'd taken hold of them for support, hanging on as his cell rotated completely upside down and backward again, then barrel-rolled sideways like a flight simulator with a broken oscillation throttle. Throughout it all, the metallic clacking and clanging continued, as the various plates of his cell reshaped themselves around him.

When the rotation stopped, a recessed hatchway had hissed open into what appeared to be another empty cell, thick with shadow and little else. At first Maul had simply stood gazing into it. Then he'd taken a step inside. By the time he'd picked up the presence of another life-form behind him—the warrior with mismatched arms and the amphistaff—the first blow had already come.

And now.

Sitting in the midst of the mess hall, feeling the eyes of the other prisoners upon him, sensing the slow accumulation of tension gathering around him like an electrically charged flow of ionized particles, Maul realized that the inmates of Cog Hive Seven, both individually and collectively, were already planning his demise.

Let them. It will only make your task easier.

From everything he'd gleaned so far, the prison was an open sewer, its circular layout fostering an illusory sense of false-bottomed freedom among the incarcerated. In actuality, the prisoners' ability to roam unimpeded between fights only heightened the steadily percolating sense of animosity among them, the willingness to rip one another to pieces at the slightest provocation.

Maul allowed his thoughts to cycle back to the electrostatic detonators that the droid had implanted in the chambers of both his hearts, tiny seeds of death that the population of Cog Hive Seven carried around with them every day. In the end, for all of these pathetic creatures, freedom was nothing but the promise of oblivion. No matter what they'd done to land themselves here—whatever they were running from or dreamed of or hoped to achieve—those detonators, mere microns in diameter, represented the totality of their lives, and the ease with which they could be taken away.

You are to locate Iram Radique, Sidious had told him, back on Coruscant, during their final moments together.

And then, perhaps sensing the physical reaction that Maul himself had not quite been able to suppress, the Sith Lord had added, *It will not be as easy as it sounds.*

According to Sidious, Radique was a highly reclusive arms dealer, legendary throughout the galaxy, a ghost whose base of operations was located somewhere within the Cog Hive Seven, although no one, even Sidious himself, could confirm this fact.

Radique's true identity was a closely guarded secret. As an alleged inmate in the prison, he operated exclusively behind a constantly shifting palimpsest of middlemen and fronts, guards and inmates and corrupt officials both inside and outside its shifting walls. Those who served him, directly or indirectly, might not know who they were working for, or if they did, they could never have identified his face.

You will not leave Cog Hive Seven, Sidious told him, *until you have identified Radique and met with him face to face to facilitate the business at hand. Is that understood?*

It was. Maul looked around the mess hall again at the hundreds of inmates who were now staring at him openly. At the next table, two human prisoners—they appeared to be father and son—were sitting close together as if for mutual protection. The older one, a powerfully built, scarred veteran of a thousand battles, was holding a piece of string with knots tied along carefully measured intervals, while the younger one looked on in mute fascination.

Three tables down, a group of inmates hunched over their trays, groping with utensils. When one of them lifted his head, Maul realized that the man's eyes were missing—as if they'd been gouged out of his skull. Had that happened in one of the matches? The man's hand found his fork, and he began, tentatively, to scoop food into his mouth.

Across the room, another inmate, a Twi'lek, was glaring directly at Maul. Beside him, a Weequay with a sunbaked face like a desert cliff and a half dozen topknot braids stood expressionless. Watchful. Any of them could have been Radique, Maul thought, or none of them.

Maul scanned the rest of the mess hall, absorbing all of it in a single sweeping glance. There were a hundred alliances here, he sensed, gangs and crews and whole webs of social order whose complexity would require his close attention if he was going to find his way among them to complete the mission for which he'd been dispatched. And time was not something that he had in unlimited quantities.

It was time to get to work.

Picking up his tray, he dumped the remains of his meal in the nearest waste bin, and cut diagonally across the mess hall. There were groups of inmates clustered around the exit. He turned left, following the wall to a hatchway in the corner, from which the smell of cheap prison food came wafting out, mixed with the stench of cleaning solution.

Exactly what he was looking for.

He slipped inside.